Todd Burke doesn't mince words...

"You're easy on the eyes. But I'm not in the market for a love affair. It's the challenge of getting your ranch out of hock that appeals to me—not seducing you."

"I'm impressed that you know me so well already," Jane returned, "and your modesty is refreshing! You feel that I'm so overcome with panting passion for you that I have to be warned off. I never realized I was that dangerous." She wiggled her eyebrows at him. "Since you're *sooo* attractive, Mr. Burke, aren't you afraid to be alone in the car with me? I might leap at you!"

"You're twisting my words."

"You're everything I've ever wanted in a man. You're handsome and intelligent and sexy. Shall we have sex right now or wait until you stop the car?"

He braked again to avoid going into the ditch. "Miss Parker!"

...and neither does Jeb Coltrain!

"Cold as ice, aren't you?" Coltrain drawled mockingly. "You'd freeze any normal man to death. Is that why you never married, Doctor?"

It was the most personal thing he'd ever said to her. And one of the most insulting. "Think what you like," Louise replied.

"You might be surprised at what I think..." Coltrain mused.

Then he looked down at the hand he'd just touched her with and laughed deep in his throat. "Frostbitten," he pronounced. "A man would need a blowtorch to loosen you up, wouldn't he?" he added with a meaningful blue stare.

"*You'd* need a grenade launcher," Louise retorted. And, happy to see him stiffen, she walked away without a backward glance.

Furious, she told herself she really shouldn't care what Jebediah Coltrain thought of her.

But she did care. Far too much. And that...

That was the whole problem.

DIANA PALMER

LONG, TALL TEXANS
BURKE & COLTRAIN

HQN™

ISBN 0-373-77087-1

LONG, TALL TEXANS: BURKE & COLTRAIN

Copyright © 2005 by Harlequin Books S.A.

The publisher acknowledges the copyright holder of the individual works as follows:

THAT BURKE MAN
Copyright © 1995 by Diana Palmer

COLTRAIN'S PROPOSAL
Copyright © 1995 by Diana Palmer

This edition published by arrangement with Harlequin Books S.A.

® and TM are trademarks of the publisher. Trademarks indicated with ® are registered in the United States Patent and Trademark Office, the Canadian Trade Marks Office and in other countries.

www.HQNBooks.com

Printed in U.S.A.

CONTENTS

THAT BURKE MAN

Dear Doctor Lou,

I am glad you got married to Dr. Coltrain and I hope you will be very happy. But don't ever let him take out your stitches, because he doesn't do it like you do He doesn't give candy to little kids he works on, either, and he gives real bad shots! But I guess you must like him, so I hope he doesn't ever have to give you a shot

Your friend,

Patrick

P.S.—Can I come over sometime and play with your Lionel trains?

Chapter One

Todd Burke sank lower in the rickety chair at the steel rail of the rodeo arena, glowering around him from under the brim of his Stetson. He crossed one powerful blue-jeaned leg over the other and surveyed his dusty, cream-colored boots. He'd worn his dress ones for the occasion, but he'd forgotten how messy things got around livestock. It had been a long time since he'd worked on his father's ranch, and several months since Cherry's last rodeo.

The girl had a good seat for riding, but she had no self-confidence. His ex-wife didn't approve of Cherry's sudden passion for barrel racing. But he did. Cherry was all he had to show for eight years of marriage that had ended six years ago in a messy divorce. He had custody of Cherry because Marie and her new husband were too occupied with business to raise a child. Cherry was fourteen now, and a handful at times. Todd had his own worries, with a huge computer company to run and no free time. He should make more time for Cherry, but he couldn't turn over the reins of his company to subordinates. He was president and it was his job to run things.

But he was bored. The challenges were all behind him. He'd made his millions and now he was stagnating for lack of something to occupy his quick, analytical mind. He was taking a few weeks off, reluctantly, to get a new perspective on life and business during Cherry's school holidays. But he was tired of it already.

He hated sitting here while he waited for Cherry's turn to race. He and Cherry had moved to Victoria, Texas, just recently, where his new head offices were located. Jacobsville, the little town they were now in, attending the rodeo, was a nice, short drive from Victoria, and Cherry had pleaded to come, because a barrel-racing rodeo champion she idolized was supposed to accept an award of some sort here tonight. Cherry's entry in the competition had been perfunctory and resigned, because she didn't ride well before an audience and she knew it.

Her name was called and he sat up, watching his daughter lean over her horse's neck as she raced out into the arena, her pigtail flying from under her wide-brimmed hat. She looked like him, with gray eyes and fair hair. She was going to be tall, too, and she was a good rider. But when she took the first turn she hesitated and the horse slowed almost to a crawl. The announcer made a sympathetic sound, and then she did it again on the next turn.

Todd watched her ride out of the arena as her part in the competition was finished. He had a heavy heart. She'd been so hopeful, but as always, she was going to finish last.

"What a shame," came a quiet, feminine voice from down the aisle. "She just freezes on the turns, did you see? She'll never be any good as a competitor, I'm afraid. No nerve."

A male voice made a commiserating comment.

Todd, infuriated by the superiority in that female voice, waited for its owner to come into view with anger building inside him. When she did, it was a surprise.

The tall beautiful blonde who'd said those things about Cherry Burke was just complimenting herself on her steady progress. For the first time in months, Jane Parker was managing without her wheelchair or her cane. Moreover, her usual betraying limp hadn't made an appearance. Of course, she was fresh because she'd rested all day, and she hadn't strained her back. She'd been very careful not to, so that she could get through the opening ceremonies of the annual Jacobsville Rodeo and wait until its end when she was going to accept a plaque on behalf of her father. Tim had raged at her for agreeing to ride today, but it hadn't done any good. After all, she was her father's daughter. Her pride wouldn't let her ride out into the arena in a buckboard.

She stopped along the way to watch the youth competition in barrel racing. That had been her event, and she'd won trophies for it in this and other rodeos around Texas since grammar school. One particular girl caught her eye, and she commented critically on the ride—a poor one—to one of the seasoned riders leaning on the iron arena rail beside her. It was a pity that the girl hadn't finished in the money, but not surprising.

The girl was afraid of the turns and it showed in the way she choked up on the reins and hindered the horse. Jane commented on it to the cowboy. The girl must be new to rodeo, Jane thought, because her name wasn't one she knew. Here in south Texas, where she'd lived all her life, Jane knew everyone on the rodeo circuit.

She smiled at the cowboy and moved on, shaking her head. She wasn't really watching where she was going. She was trying to straighten the fringe on her rhinestone-studded white fringe jacket—which matched her long riding skirt and boots—when a big, booted foot shot across the narrow space between the trailers and slammed into the bottom metal rail of the rodeo arena, effectively freezing the elegant glittery blonde in her tracks.

Shocked, she looked down into steely gray eyes in a lean face framed by thick, fair hair.

The cowboy sitting on the trailer hitch was braiding several pieces of rawhide in his strong fingers. They didn't still, even when he spoke.

"I heard what you just said to that cowboy about Cherry Burke's ride," he said coldly. "Who the hell do you think you are to criticize a cowgirl in Cherry's class?"

She lifted both eyebrows. He wasn't a regular on the Texas circuit, either. She and her father had circled it for years. "I beg your pardon?"

"What are you, anyway, a model?" he chided. "You look like one of those blond dress-up fashion dolls in that outfit," he added as his eyes punctuated the contempt of his voice. "Are you shacking up with one of the riders or are you part of the entertainment?"

She hadn't expected a verbal attack from a total stranger. She stared at him, too surprised to react.

"Are questions of more than one syllable too hard for you?" he persisted.

That got through the surprise. Her blue eyes glittered at him. "Funny, I'd have said they're the only kind you're capable of asking," she said in her soft, cultured voice. She looked at his leg, still blocking her path. "Move it or I'll break it, cowboy."

"A cream puff like you?" he scoffed.

"That's where you're wrong. I'm no cream puff." In his position on the hitch, he was precariously balanced. She reached over, grimacing because the movement hurt her back, caught his ankle and jerked it up. He went over backward with a harsh curse.

She dusted off her hands and kept walking, aware of a wide grin from two cowboys she passed on her way to the gate.

Tim Harley, her middle-aged ranch foreman, was waiting for her by the gate with Bracket, her palomino gelding. He held the horse for her, grimacing as he watched her slow, painful ascension into the saddle.

"You shouldn't try this," he said. "It's too soon!"

"Dad would have done it," she countered. "Jacobsville was his hometown, and it's mine. I couldn't refuse the invitation to accept the plaque for Dad. Today's rodeo is dedicated to him."

"You could have accepted the plaque on foot or in a buckboard," he muttered.

She glared down at him. "Listen, I wasn't always a cripple...!"

"Oh, for God's sake!"

The sound of the band tuning up got her attention. She soothed her nervous horse, aware of angry footsteps coming along the aisle between the trailers and the arena. Fortunately, before the fair-haired cowboy got close, the other riders joined her at the gate and arranged themselves in a flanking pattern.

The youth competition marked the end of the evening's entertainment. The money for top prizes had been announced and awarded. The band began to play "The Yellow Rose of Texas." The gate opened. Jane coaxed Bracket into his elegant trot and bit down on her lower lip to contain the agony of the horse's motion. He was smooth and gaited, but even so, the jarring was painful.

She didn't know if she'd make it around that arena, but she was going to try. With a wan smile, she forced herself to look happy, to take off her white Stetson and wave to the cheering crowd. Most of these people had known her father, and a good many of them knew her. She'd been a legend in barrel racing before her forced retirement at the age of twenty-four. Her father often said that she was heaven on a horse. She tried not to think about her last sight of him. She wanted to remember him as he had been, in the time before…

"Isn't she as pretty as a picture?" Bob Harris was saying from the press booth. "Miss Jane Parker, ladies and gentlemen, two-time world's champion barrel-racer and best all around in last year's women's division. As you know, she's retired from the ring now, but she's still one magnificent sight on a horse!"

She drank in the cheers and managed not to fall off or cry out in pain when she got to the reviewing stand. It had been touch and go.

Bob Harris came out into the arena with a plaque

and handed it up to her. "Don't try to get down," he said flatly, holding a hand over the microphone.

"Folks," he continued loudly, "as you know, Oren Parker was killed earlier this year in a car crash. He was best all-around four years running in this rodeo, and world's champion roper twice. I know you'll all join with me in our condolences as I dedicate this rodeo to his memory and present Jane with this plaque in honor of her father's matchless career as a top hand and a great rodeo cowboy. Miss Jane Parker, ladies and gentlemen!"

There were cheers and more applause. Jane waved the plaque and as Bob held the microphone up, she quickly thanked everyone for their kindness and for the plaque honoring her father. Then before she fell off the horse, she thanked Bob again and rode out of the arena.

She couldn't get down. That was the first real surprise of the evening. The second was to find that same angry, fair-haired cowboy standing there waiting for her to come out of the ring.

He caught her bridle and held her horse in place while he glared up at her. "Well, you sure as hell don't look the part," he said mockingly. "You ride like a raw beginner, as stiff as a board in the saddle. How did a rider as bad as you ever even get to the finals? Did you do it on *Daddy's* name?"

If she'd been hurting a little less, she was certain that she'd have put her boot right in his mouth. Sadly she was in too much pain to react.

"No spirit either, huh?" he persisted.

"Hold on, Jane, I'm coming!" came a gruff voice from behind her. "Damned fool stunt," Tim growled as he came up beside her, his gray hair and unruly beard making him look even more wizened than normal. "Can't get off, can you? Okay, Tim's here. You just come down at your own pace." He took the plaque from her.

"Does she always have to be lifted off a horse?" the stranger drawled. "I thought rodeo stars could mount and dismount all by themselves."

He didn't have a Texas accent. In fact, he didn't have much of an accent at all. She wondered where he was from.

Tim glared at him. "You won't last long on this circuit with that mouth," he told the man. "And especially not using it on Jane."

He turned back to her, holding his arms up. "Come on, pumpkin," he coaxed, in the same tone he'd used when she was only six, instead of twenty-five as she was now. "Come on. It's all right, I won't let you fall."

The new cowboy was watching with a scowl. It suddenly had occurred to him that her face was a pasty white and she was gritting her teeth as she tried to ease down. The wizened little cowboy was already straining. He was tiny, and she wasn't big, but she was tall and certainly no lightweight.

He moved forward. "Let me," he said, moving in front of Tim.

"Don't let her fall," Tim said quickly. "That back brace won't save her if you do."

"Back brace…" It certainly explained a lot. He felt it when he took her gently by the waist, the ribbing hard under his fingers. She was sweating now with the effort, and tears escaped her eyes. She closed them, shivering.

"I can't," she whispered, in agony.

"Put your arms around my neck," he said with authority. "I'll take your weight. You can slide along and I'll catch you when you've got the other foot out of the stirrup. Take it easy. Whenever you're ready."

She knew that she couldn't stay on the animal forever, but it was tempting. She managed a wan smile at Tim's worried figure. "Don't natter, Tim," she whispered hoarsely. "I've got this far. I'll get the rest of the way." She took a deep breath, set her teeth together and pulled.

The pain was excruciating. She felt it in every cell of her body before the cowboy had her carefully in his arms, clear of the ground, but she didn't whimper. Not once. She lay there against his broad chest, shuddering with pain.

"Where do you want her?" he asked the older man.

Tim hesitated, but he knew the girl couldn't walk and he sure as hell couldn't carry her. "This way," he said after a minute, and led the tall man to a motor home several hundred yards down the line.

It was a nice little trailer, with a large sitting area. There was a sofa along one side and next to it, a wheelchair. When the cowboy saw the wheelchair, his face contorted.

"I told you," Tim was raging at her. "I told you not to do it! God knows how much you've set yourself back!"

"No...not there!" Jane protested sharply when he started to put her down in the wheelchair. "For God's sake, not there!"

"It's the best place for you, you silly woman!" Tim snapped.

"On the sofa, please," she whispered, fighting back a sharp moan as he lowered her gently to the cushions.

"I'll get your pain capsules and something to drink," Tim said, moving into the small kitchen.

"Thank you," Jane told the tall cowboy. It was a grudging thank-you, because he'd said some harsh things and she was angry.

"No need," he replied quietly. "You might have stopped me before I made a complete fool of myself. I suppose you've forgotten more about racing than Cherry will ever learn. Cherry's my daughter," he added.

That explained a lot. She grimaced as she shifted. "I'm sorry you took the criticism the wrong way, but I won't apologize for it," she said stiffly. "She's got the talent, but she's afraid of the turns. Someone needs to help her…get better control of her fears and her horse."

"I can ride, but that's about it. I don't know enough about rodeo to do her any good," he said flatly, "even though we're as crazy about rodeo in Wyoming as you Texans are."

"You're from Wyoming?" she asked, curious.

"Yes. We moved to Texas a few weeks ago, so that…" He stopped, strangely reluctant to tell her it was because he'd moved his company headquarters there to deal with an expanded market in Texas. "So that we could be closer to Cherry's mother," he amended. In fact, that hadn't influenced his decision to move to Victoria. Marie was no one's idea of a mother, and she'd been overly critical of Cherry for some time. It was a coincidence that Marie and her husband moved to Victoria from Houston about the same time Todd had moved his company headquarters there. Or so Marie said. "She and her second husband live in Victoria."

She let her eyes slide over his lean, hard face. "Does her mother ride? Couldn't she help her?"

His eyes seemed to darken. "Her mother hates horses. She didn't want Cherry in rodeo at all, but I put my foot down. Rodeo is the most important thing in Cherry's life."

"Then she should be allowed to do it," she agreed, and she was thinking how sad it was that he and his wife were divorced. His poor little girl. She knew what it was like to grow up without a mother. Her mother had died of pneumonia when she was barely in school.

She glanced back at the man. He'd said they were from Wyoming. That explained the lack of a Texas accent. She lay back, and the pain bit into her slender body like teeth. Hot tears wet her eyes as she struggled with the anguish it caused her just to move.

Tim came back and handed her two capsules and a cola. She swallowed the medicine and sipped the cold liquid, savoring the nip of it against her tongue. If only the pain would stop.

"That's sweet," she said with a sigh.

The tall man stood looking down at her with a frown. "Are you all right?"

"Sure," she said. "I'm just dandy. Thanks for your help."

She wasn't forthcoming, and he had no right to expect it. He nodded and moved out of the trailer.

Tim came after him. "Thanks for your help, stranger," he said. "I'd never have got her here by myself."

They shook hands. "My pleasure." He paused. "What happened to her?" he added abruptly.

"Her daddy wrecked the car," he said simply. "He was killed instantly, but Jane was pinned in there with him for three hours or more. They thought she'd broken her back," he concluded.

There was a harsh intake of breath.

"Oh, it was a herniated disk instead. It's painful and slow to heal, and she'll most always have some pain with it. But they can work miracles these days. She couldn't walk right away, though, and we weren't sure if she'd be paralyzed. But she got up out of that bed and started working on herself. Stayed in physical therapy until even the doctors grinned. Never knew a girl like her," he mused. "This thing has taken some of the fight out of her, of course, but she's no quitter. Her dad would have been proud. Sad about her career, though. She'll never ride in competition again."

"What in hell was she doing on that horse this morning?"

"Showing everybody that nothing short of death will ever keep her down," Tim said simply. "Never did catch your name, stranger."

"Burke. Todd Burke."

"I'm Tim Harley. I'm proud to meet you."

"Same here." He hesitated for just a minute before he turned and went back along the aisles. He felt odd. He'd never felt so odd in his life before. Perhaps, he thought, it was that he wasn't used to proud women. She'd surprised him with the extent of her grit and stubbornness. She wasn't a quitter, in spite of impossible circumstances. He didn't doubt that she'd ride again, either, even if she didn't get back into competition. God, she was game! He was sorry he'd managed to get off on the wrong foot with her. He'd been irritated by the remarks she'd made about his daughter. Now he realized that she was trying to help, and he'd taken it the wrong way.

He was sensitive about Cherry. His daughter had taken more vicious criticism from her own mother than she was ever likely to get from a stranger. He'd overreacted. Now he was left with a case of badly bruised pride and a wounded ego. He smiled a little bitterly at his own embarrassment. He deserved it, being so cruel to a woman in that condition. It had been a long time since he'd made a mistake of such magnitude.

He wandered back down the lane to join his daughter, who was excitedly talking to one of the rodeo clowns.

"Dad, did you see her, that blond lady who accepted the plaque?" she asked when he was within earshot. "That was Jane Parker herself!"

"I saw her." He glanced at the young cowboy, who flushed and grinned at Cherry, and then quickly made himself scarce.

"I wish you wouldn't do that," Cherry said on a sigh. "Honestly, Dad, I'm fourteen!"

"And I'm an old bear. I know." He threw an affectionate arm around her. "You did fine, partner. I'm proud of you."

"Thanks! Where did you disappear to?"

"I helped your idol into her motor home," he said.

"My idol…Miss Parker?"

"The very same. She's got a bad back, that's why she doesn't ride anymore. She's game, though."

"She's the best barrel racer I ever saw," Cherry said. "I have a video of last year's rodeo and she's on it. The reason I begged to come to this rodeo was so that I could meet her, but she isn't riding this time. Gosh, I was disappointed when they said she'd retired. I didn't know she had a bad back."

"Neither did I," he murmured. He put an arm around her and hugged her close. She was precious to him, but he tended to busy himself too deeply in his work, especially in the years since her mother had walked out on them. "We haven't had much time together, have we? I'll make it up to you while we're on vacation."

"How about right now?" She grinned at him. "You could introduce me to Miss Parker."

He cleared his throat. How was he going to tell her that her idol thought he was about as low as a snake?

"She's so pretty," Cherry added without waiting for his answer. "Mother's pretty, too, but not like that." She grimaced. "Mother doesn't want me to come up next week, did she tell you?"

"Yes." He didn't add that they'd argued about it. Marie didn't spend any more time with Cherry than she had to. She'd walked out on the two of them for another man six years ago, declaring that Cherry was just too much for her to handle. It had devastated the young girl and left Todd Burke in the odd position of having to forego board meetings of his corporation to take care of his daughter. He hadn't minded, though. He was proud of the girl, and he'd encouraged her in everything she wanted to do, including rodeo. Marie had a fit over that. She didn't approve of her daughter riding rodeo, but Todd had put his foot down.

"What does she see in him?" Cherry asked, her gray eyes flashing and her blond pigtail swinging as she threw up her hands in a temper. "He's so picky about everything, especially his clothes. He doesn't like pets and he doesn't like children."

"He's brilliant. He has a national bestseller. It's number one on the *New York Times* list. It's been there for weeks," Todd replied.

"You're smart, too. And you're rich," she argued.

"Yes, but I'm not in his class. I'm a self-made man. I don't have a Harvard degree."

"Neither does he," Cherry said with a giggle. "He hasn't graduated. I heard Mama say so—not so that he could hear her, though."

He chuckled. "Never you mind. If she's happy, that's fine."

"Don't you love her anymore?" she asked.

His arm contracted. "Not the way I should to be married to her," he said honestly. "Marriage takes two people working to make each other happy. Your mother got tired of the long hours I had to spend at work."

"She got tired of me, too."

"She loves you, in her way," he replied. "Don't ever doubt that. But she and I found less in common the longer we lived together. Eventually we didn't have enough to sustain a marriage."

"You need someone to look after you," she told him.

"I'll get married one day, you know, and then where will you be?"

He chuckled. "Alone."

"Sure," she agreed, "except for those women you never bring home."

He cleared his throat. "Cherry…"

"Never mind, I'm not stupid." She looked around at the dwindling crowd. "But you need someone to come home to, besides me. You work late at the office and go on business trips all over the place, and you're never home. So I can't go home, either. I want to go to school in Victoria in the fall. I hate boarding school."

"You never told me that," he said, surprised.

"I didn't want to," she admitted reluctantly. "But it's just awful lately. I'm glad I'm out for the summer." She looked up at him with gray eyes so similar to his own. "I'm glad you took this vacation. We can do some things together, just you and me."

"I've been thinking about it for a long time," he confessed. "I'm looking forward to having a few weeks off," he lied convincingly, and wondered how he was going to survive the lack of anything challenging to do.

She grinned. "Good! You can help me work on those turns in barrel racing. I don't guess you noticed, but I'm having a real hard time with them."

He recalled what Jane Parker had said about Cherry, and he allowed himself to wonder if it might not do both women good to spend a little time talking together.

"You know," he mused aloud, "I think I may have some ideas about that."

"Really? What are they?"

"Wait and see." He led her toward their car. "Let's get something to eat. I don't know about you, but I'm starved!"

"Me, too. How about Chinese?"

"My favorite."

He put her into the old Ford he'd borrowed while his Ferrari was being serviced, and drove her back into Jacobsville.

They had lunch at the single Chinese restaurant that was nestled among half a dozen barbecue, steak and fast-food restaurants. When they finished, they went back out to the arena to watch the rest of the afternoon's competition. Cherry was only in one other event. She did poorly again, though, trying to go around the barrels. When she rode out of the arena, she was in tears.

"Now, now." Todd comforted her. "Rome wasn't built in a day."

"They didn't have barrel racing in Rome!" she wailed.

"Probably not, but the sentiment is the same." He hugged her gently. "Perk up, now. This is only the first rodeo in a whole string of them. You'll get better."

"It's a waste of time," she said, wiping her tears. "I might as well quit right now."

"Nobody ever got anywhere by quitting after one loss," he chided. "Where would I be if I'd given up when my first computer program didn't sell?"

"Not where you are today, that's for sure," she admitted. "Nobody does software like you do, Dad. That newest word processor is just radical! Everyone at school loves it. It makes term papers so easy!"

"I'm glad to hear that all those late hours we put into developing it were worth the effort," he said. He grinned at her. "We're working on a new accounting package right now."

"Oh, accounting," she muttered. "Who wants any boring old stuff like that?"

"Plenty of small businesses," he said on a chuckle. "And thank your lucky stars or we'd be in the hole."

Cherry was looking around while he spoke. Her face lit up and her eyes began to sparkle. "It's Miss Parker!" The smile faded. "Oh, my…"

He turned and the somber expression on his daughter's face was mirrored in his own. Jane was in the wheelchair, wearing jeans and a beige T-shirt and sneakers, looking fragile and depressed as Tim pushed her toward the motor home with the horse trailer hitched behind it.

Unless he missed his guess, they were about to leave. He couldn't let her get away, not before he had a chance to ask her about working with Cherry. It had occurred to him that they might kill two birds with one stone— give Miss Parker a new interest, and Cherry some badly needed help.

Chapter Two

"Miss Parker!" Todd called.

She glanced in his direction, aware that he and a young girl with fair hair in a pigtail were moving toward her. The wheelchair made her feel vulnerable and she bit down hard on her lip. She was in a bad temper because she didn't want that rude, unpleasant man to see her this way.

"Yes?" she asked through her teeth.

"This is my daughter, Cherry," he said, pulling the young girl forward. "She wanted to meet you."

Regardless, apparently, of whether Jane wanted the meeting or not. "How do you do," she said through numb lips.

"What happened to you?" Cherry spluttered.

Jane's face contorted.

"She was in a wreck," her father said shortly, "and it was rude of you to ask."

Cherry flushed. "I'm sorry, really I am." She went to the wheelchair, totally uninhibited, and squatted beside it. "I've watched all the videos you were on. You were just the best in the world," she said enthusiastically. "I couldn't get to the rodeos, but I had Dad buy me the videos from people who taped the events. I'm having a lot of trouble on the turns. Dad can ride, but he's just hopeless on rodeo, aren't you, Dad?" She put a gentle hand over Jane's arm. "Will you be able to ride again?"

"Cherry!" Todd raged.

"It's all right," Jane said quietly. She looked into the girl's clear, gray eyes, seeing no pity there, only honest concern and curiosity. The rigidity in her began to subside. She smiled. "No," she said honestly. "I don't think I'll be able to ride again. Not in competition, at least."

"I wish I could help you," Cherry said. "I'm going to be a surgeon when I grow up. I make straight A's in science and math, and Dad's already said I could go to Johns Hopkins when I'm old enough. That's the best school of medicine anywhere!"

"A surgeon," Jane echoed, surprised. She smiled. "I've never known anyone who wanted to be a surgeon before."

Cherry beamed. "Now you do. I wish you didn't have to leave so soon," she said wistfully. "I was going to pick your brain for ways to get over this fear of turns. Silly, isn't it, when the sight of blood doesn't bother me at all."

Jane was aware of an emptiness in herself as she stared into the young face. It was like seeing herself at that age. She lowered her eyes. "Yes, well, I'm sorry, but it's been a long day and I'm in a good deal of pain. And we're interviewing today."

"Interviewing?" Cherry asked with open curiosity.

"For a business manager," Jane said sadly, glancing at Tim, who winced. "Tim can't manage the books. He's willing to keep on as foreman, but we're losing money hand over fist since Dad's death because neither one of us can handle the books."

"Gosh, my dad would be perfect for that," Cherry said innocently. "He's a wizard with money. He keeps the books for his compu—"

"For the small computer company I work for in Victoria," Todd said quickly, with a speaking glance that his intelligent daughter interpreted immediately. She shut up, grinning.

Tim stepped forward. "Can you balance books?"

"Sure."

Tim looked at Jane. "There's the foreman's cabin empty, since Meg and I are living in the house with you," he remarked. "They could live there. And you could help the girl with her turns. It would give you something to do besides brooding around the house all day."

"Tim!" Jane burst out angrily. She glanced apprehensively at Todd Burke, who was watching her with unconcealed amusement. "I'm sure he has a job already."

"I do. Keeping books for my…the computer company," he lied. "But it doesn't take up all my time. In fact, I think I'd enjoy doing something different for a while." He pursed his lips. "If you're interested, that is," he added with practiced indifference.

Jane's eyes fell to her lap.

"I'd love to learn how to win at barrel racing," Cherry said with a sigh. "I guess I'll have to give it up, though. I mean, I'm so bad that it's a waste of Dad's money to keep paying my entrance fees and all."

Jane glowered at her. She glowered at him, too,

standing there like a movie cowboy with his firm lips pursed and his steely gray eyes twinkling with amusement. Laughing at her.

"She won't hire you," Tim said with a glare at her. "She's too proud to admit that you're just what she needs. She'd rather let the ranch go under while she sits on the porch and feels sorry for herself."

"Damn you!" She spat the words at Tim.

He chuckled. "See them eyes?" he asked Todd. "Like wet sapphires. She may look like a fashion doll, but she's all fur and claws when things get next to her, and she's no quitter."

Todd was looking at her with evident appreciation. He grinned. "Two week trial?" he asked. "While we see how well we all get along? I can't do you much damage in that short a time, and I might do you a lot of good. I have a way with balance sheets."

"We couldn't be much worse off," Tim reminded his boss.

Jane was silently weighing pros and cons. He had a daughter, so he had to be settled and fairly dependable, if Cherry was any indication. If she hired anyone else, she'd have no idea if she was giving succor to a thief or even a murderer. This man looked trustworthy and his daughter apparently adored him.

"We could try, I suppose," she said finally. "If you're willing. But the ranch isn't successful enough that I can offer you much of a salary." She named a figure. "You'll get meals and board free, but I'll understand if that isn't enough—"

"If I can keep on doing my present job, in the

evenings, we'll manage," Todd said without daring to look at his daughter. If he did, he knew he'd give the show away.

"Your boss won't mind?" Jane asked.

He cleared his throat. "He's very understanding. After all, I'm a single parent."

She nodded, convinced. "All right, then. Would you like to follow us out to the ranch, if you're through for the day?"

"We're through, all right," Cherry said on a sigh. "I'm dejected, demoralized and thoroughly depressed."

"Don't be silly," Jane said gently, and with a smile. "You've got an excellent seat, and you're good with horses. You just need to get over that irrational fear that you're going to go down on the turns."

"How did you know?" Cherry gasped.

"Because I was exactly the same when I started out. Stop worrying. I'll work with you. When we're through, you'll be taking home trophies."

"Really?"

Jane chuckled. "Really. Let's go, Tim."

He wheeled her to the cab of the motor home and opened the door. "I guess bringing this thing ten miles looks odd," Tim murmured to Todd, "but we had to have a place where Jane could rest. We've carried this old thing to many a rodeo over the years. She takes a little coaxing sometimes, but she always goes."

"Like Bracket," Jane mused, glancing back to the trailer where her palomino gelding rode.

"Like Bracket," Tim agreed. He reached down. "Let's get you inside, now, Jane."

Before he could lift her, Todd moved forward. "Here," he volunteered. "I'll do the honors."

Tim grinned, his relief all too obvious. Jane wasn't heavy, but Tim was feeling his age a bit.

Todd lifted Jane gently out of the wheelchair and into the cab of the big vehicle, positioning her on the seat with a minimum of discomfort. She eased her arms from around his neck a little self-consciously and smiled. "Thanks."

He shrugged powerful shoulders and smiled back. "No problem. Where does the chair go, Tim?"

He folded it and the older man climbed up into the motor home and stowed it away. He got behind the wheel and paused long enough to give directions to Todd about where in Jacobsville the ranch was located before he and Jane waved goodbye and drove away.

"Dad!" Cherry laughed. "Are we really going to do it? What will she say when she finds out?"

"We'll worry about that when the time comes. The ranch budget sounds like a challenge, and you could use some pointers with your riding," he added. "I think it may work out very well."

"But what about your company?" Cherry asked.

"I've got good people working for me and I'm on holiday." He ruffled her hair. "We'll think of it as summer vacation," he assured her. "It will give us some time together."

"I'd like that," she said solemnly. "After all, in four years I'll be in school, and you probably won't get to see me twice a year. I'll have to study very hard."

"You're smart. You'll do fine."

"Yes, I will," she assured him with a grin. "And you can have all your medical care free."

"I can hardly wait."

"Don't be sarcastic," she chided. "And you have to be nice to Miss Parker, too."

"She doesn't like me very much."

"You don't like her, either, do you?" she asked curiously.

He stuck his hands into his pockets and frowned. "She's all right."

"If you don't like her, why are you going to help her?"

He couldn't answer that. He didn't know why. She was a woman in a wheelchair, who looked as if in her heyday she'd been nothing more than a fashion doll on a horse. But she was crippled and in bad financial circumstances, and all alone, apparently. He felt sorry for her. Funny, that, because since his failed marriage, he didn't like women very much except when he had an overwhelming desire for someone female in his arms. Loving and leaving wouldn't be possible with Jane Parker. So why was he going out of his way to help her? He didn't know.

"Maybe I feel sorry for her," he told Cherry finally.

"Yes, so do I, but we mustn't let her know it," she said firmly. "She's very proud, did you notice?"

He nodded. "Proud and hot tempered."

"What familiar traits."

He glowered at her, but she just grinned.

At the luxurious house Todd had bought in Victoria, they packed up what gear they'd need for a few days, explained their forthcoming absence to their puzzled housekeeper, Rosa, promised to be back soon and drove in the borrowed Ford down to Jacobsville to the Parker ranch.

It wasn't much to look at from the road. There was a rickety gray wood and barbed-wire fence that had been mended just enough to hold in the mixed-breed steers in the pasture. The barn was still standing, but barely. The dirt road that led past a windmill to the house had potholes with water standing in them from the last rain. It had no gravel on it, and it looked as if it hadn't been graded in years. The yard was bare except for a few rosebushes and a handful of flowers around the long porch of the white clapboard house. It was two stories high, and needed painting. One of the steps had broken through and hadn't been replaced. There was a rickety ramp, presumably constructed hastily for the wheelchair, on the end of the porch. There was the motor home and horse trailer in the yard, next to a building that might be used as a garage by an optimist. A small cabin was nestled in high grass that needed cutting; the foreman's cabin, Todd thought, hoping that it was more than one room. Nearby was a bigger structure, a small one-story house. It was in better condition and it had rocking chairs on the porch. The bunkhouse?

"Welcome!" Tim called, coming out to meet them.

They got out and Todd shook hands with him. "Thanks. If you'll tell me where to put our stuff...?" He was looking toward the cabin.

"Oh, that's where old man Hughes lives." Tim chuckled. "He helps me look after the livestock. He can't do a lot, but he's worked here since he was a boy. We can't pension him off until he's sixty-five, two more years yet." He turned. "Here's where you and the girl will bunk down." He led them toward the small house and Todd heaved a sigh of relief.

"It needs some work, like everything else, but maybe you can manage. You can have meals with us in the house. There are three other hands who mend fences and look after the tanks and the machinery, do the planting and so forth. They're mostly part-time these days, but we hire on extra men when we need them, seasonally, you know."

The house wasn't bad. It had three big bedrooms and a small living room. There was a kitchen, too, but it didn't look used. There was a coffeepot and a small stove and refrigerator.

"I could learn to cook," Cherry began.

"No, you couldn't," Todd said shortly. "Time enough for that later."

"My wife Meg'll teach you if you want to learn," Tim said, volunteering his wife with a grin. "She likes young people. Never had any kids of our own, so she takes up with other people's. When you've settled, come on over to the house. We'll have sandwiches and something to drink."

"How's Miss Parker?" Cherry asked.

Tim grimaced. "Lying down. She's not well. I've called the doctor." He shook his head. "I told her not to get on that horse, but she wouldn't listen to me. Never could do anything with her, even when she was a youngster. It took her papa to hold her back, but he's gone now."

"She had no business on that horse," Todd said, pointedly.

"That was a bad attack of pride," Tim told him. "Some newspaperman wrote a column about the rodeo and mentioned that poor Jane Parker would probably come out to accept the plaque for her father in a wheelchair, because she was crippled now."

Todd's face hardened. "Which paper was it in?"

"That little weekly they publish in Jacobsville," he said with a grimace. "She took it to heart. I told her it was probably that Sikes kid who just started doing sports. He's fresh out of journalism school and fancies himself winning a Pulitzer for covering barrel racing. Huh!" he scoffed.

Todd mentally stored the name for future reference. "Will the doctor come out?"

"Sure!" the wizened little man assured him. "His dad was Jane's godfather. They're great friends. He has an assistant now, though—a female doctor named Lou. She might come instead." He chuckled. "They don't see eye to eye on anything. Amazing how they manage a practice between them."

"The doctor isn't married?"

He shook his head. "He was sweet on Jane, but after the accident, she cut him dead if he so much as smiled at her. That was just before Lou went into practice with him. Jane doesn't want to get involved, she says."

"She won't always be in that chair," Todd murmured as they walked toward the house.

"No. But she'll always have pain when she overdoes things, and she won't ride well enough for competition again."

"That's what she told Cherry."

Tim gave him a wary glance. "You won't hurt her?" he asked bluntly.

Todd smiled. "She's very attractive, and I like her spirit, but I've had a bad marriage and I don't want to risk another failure. I don't get serious about women anymore. And I'm not coldhearted enough to play around with Jane."

Tim sighed. "Thanks. I needed to hear that. She's more vulnerable than she realizes right now. I'm not related to her, but in a lot of ways, I'm the only family she's got—well, Meg and me."

"She's a lucky woman," Todd replied.

He shrugged. "Not so lucky, or she wouldn't be in that chair, would she?"

They walked up onto the porch, avoiding the broken step. "Meant to fix that, but I never get time," Tim murmured. "Now that you're here to tear your hair out over the books, maybe I'll be able to get a few odds and ends done."

"I can help, if you need me," he volunteered. "I do woodwork for a hobby."

"Do you!" Tim's face brightened. "There's a woodworking shop in the back of the barn. We built it years ago for her dad. He made all the furniture in the house. She'll like having it in use again."

"Are you sure?" he asked doubtfully.

"You can always ask her."

They walked into the living room. Jane was lying on the sofa, putting up a brave front even though her face was stark white with the effort. Cherry was curled up in an armchair beside the sofa, her cheek on her folded arms, listening raptly to her idol.

"Doctor should be here soon," Tim told Jane. He paused to pat her gently on the shoulder. "Hang on, kid."

She smiled at him, and laid her hand briefly over the one on her shoulder. "Thanks, Tim. What would I do without you?"

"Let's agree never to find out," he returned dryly.

"Okay." She glanced toward Todd Burke. The expression on his lean face made her angry. "I'm not a cripple," she said belligerently.

He knelt by the sofa and pushed back a strand of her hair. It was wet, not with sweat, but with tears she'd shed involuntarily as the pain bit into her. He felt more protective about her than he could understand.

"Don't you have something to take?"

"Yes," she said, shaken by his concern. "But it isn't working."

He tucked the strand of hair behind her small, pretty ear and smiled. "Guess why?"

She made a face. "I wouldn't have tried to ride out into the arena if it hadn't been for that damned reporter," she said gruffly. "He called me a cripple!"

"Cherry and I will rush right in to town and beat the stuffing out of him for you."

That brought a pained smile to her face. "Cover him in ink and wrap him up in his newspaper and hang him from a printing press."

"They don't have printing presses anymore," Cherry said knowledgeably. "Everything's cold type now...offset printing."

Jane's blue eyes widened. "My, my, you are a well-spring of information!" she said, impressed.

Cherry grinned smugly. "One of my new teachers used to work for a newspaper. Now he teaches English."

"She knows everything," Todd said with a resigned air. "Just ask her."

"Not *everything*, Dad." She chuckled. "I don't know how to do barrel-racing turns."

"I hear a car," Tim said, glancing out the window. "It's him."

Todd frowned at the way Jane's eyes fell when he looked into them. Did she have mixed feelings about the doctor and was trying to hide it? Maybe Tim had been wrong and Jane had been sweet on the doctor, not the other way around.

Todd got to his feet as a tall man with red hair came into the room, carrying a black bag. He was dressed in a nice gray Western-cut suit with a white shirt and a black string tie. Boots, too. He removed a pearl gray Stetson from his head, and tossed it onto the counter. Pale blue eyes swept the room, lingering on Todd Burke, who stared back, unsmiling.

"This is Dr. Jebediah Coltrain," Tim introduced the tall, slim man. "When he was younger, everybody used to call him Copper."

"They don't anymore. Not without a head start," the doctor said. He didn't smile, either.

"This is Todd Burke and his daughter Cherry," Tim said, introducing them. "Todd's going to take over the book work for us."

Coltrain didn't say much. He gave Todd a piercing

stare that all but impaled him before he nodded curtly, without offering a hand in greeting. He was less reserved with Cherry, if that faint upturn of his thin lips was actually a smile.

"Well, what fool thing have you done this time?" Coltrain asked Jane irritably. "Gone riding, I guess?"

She glared at him through waves of pain. "I wasn't going to let them push me out into that arena in a wheelchair," she said furiously. "Not after what that weasel of a sports reporter wrote about me!"

He made a sound deep in his throat that could have meant anything. He set about examining her with steely hands that looked menacing until they touched and probed with a tenderness that set Todd's teeth on edge.

"Muscle strain," Coltrain pronounced at last. "You'll need a few days in bed on muscle relaxers. Did you rent that traction rig I told you to get?"

"Yes, we did, under protest," Tim said with a chuckle.

"Well, get started, then."

He lifted her as if she were a feather and carried her off to her bedroom. Todd, incensed out of all reason, followed them with an audible tread.

Coltrain glanced over his shoulder at the other man with a faintly mocking smile. He didn't need a road map to find a marked trail, and he knew jealousy when he saw it.

He put Jane down gently on the double bed with its carved posts with the traction apparatus poised over it.

"Need to make a pit stop before I hook you up?" Coltrain asked her without a trace of embarrassment.

"No, I'm fine," she said through clenched teeth. "Go ahead."

He adjusted the brace that lifted her right leg, putting a pleasant pressure on the damaged hip that even surgery hadn't put completely back to rights. "This won't work any miracles, but it will help," Coltrain told her. "You put too much stock in articles written by idiots."

"He didn't write it about you!"

He lifted an eyebrow. "He wouldn't dare," he said simply.

She knew that. It irritated her. She closed her eyes. "It hurts."

"I can do something for that." Coltrain reached in his bag and drew out a small bottle and a syringe. He handed a package to Todd. "Open that and swab the top of the bottle with it."

He had the sort of voice that expects obedience. Todd, who never took orders, actually did it with only a lopsided grin. He liked the doctor, against his will.

Coltrain upended the bottle when Todd had finished, inserted the needle into the bottle and then drew up the correct amount of painkiller.

He handed Todd another package containing an alcohol-soaked gauze. "Swab her arm, here."

He indicated a vein in her right arm and Todd looked at him.

"It's not addictive," the doctor said gently. "I know what I'm doing."

Todd made a rough murmur and complied. It embarrassed him to show concern for a woman he barely knew. Coltrain's knowing look made it worse.

He swabbed her arm and Coltrain shot the needle in, efficiently and with a minimum of pain.

"Thanks, Copper," Jane told him quietly.

He shrugged. "What are friends for?" He took a few sample packages out of the bag and gave them to Todd. "Two every six hours for severe pain. They're stronger than the others I gave you," he told Jane. "You can push this to five hours if you can't bear it, but no sooner." Coltrain fastened his bag and gave Jane a reassuring smile. "Stay put. I'll check on you tomorrow."

"Okay." Her eyes were already closing.

"I'll sit with you until you go to sleep," Cherry volunteered, and Jane smiled her agreement.

Coltrain jerked his head toward the living room. Tim and Todd followed. He closed the bedroom door behind them.

"I want her X-rayed," he told them without preamble. "I think it's muscular, but I'm not going to stake my life on it. The last thing she needed was to get on a horse."

"I tried to stop her," Tim told him.

"I realize that. I'm not blaming you. She's a handful." He eyed Todd openly. "Can you keep her off horses?"

Todd smiled slowly. "Watch me."

"That's what I thought. She isn't safe to be let out alone these days, always trying to prove herself." He grabbed his Stetson and started toward the door. "She's in too much pain to be moved today. I'll send an ambulance for her in the morning and make all the necessary arrangements at Jacobsville Memorial. She won't like it," he added wryly.

"But she'll do it," Todd replied easily.

For the first time, Coltrain chuckled. "I'd like to be a fly on the wall tomorrow when that ambulance gets here."

The telephone rang and Tim answered it. He grimaced, holding it out to Coltrain.

The other man picked it up with a rough sigh. "Coltrain," he said as if he knew who was calling.

His face grew harder by the second. "Yes. No. I don't give a damn, it's my practice and that's how I do things. If you don't like it, get out. Damn the contract!" He glanced at the wide-eyed faces near him and shifted his posture. "We'll talk about this when I get back. Yes, you do that." He put the receiver down with a savagely controlled jerk of his lean hand. His eyes glittered like blue water on a snake's back. "Call me if you need me."

After he was gone, and was driving away in a cloud of dust, Tim whistled through his teeth. "It won't last."

"What won't?" Todd replied.

"Him and Lou," he said, shaking his head. "They'll kill each other one day, him with his old-fashioned way of practicing and her with all this newfangled technology."

Todd found himself vaguely relieved that the doctor had someone besides Jane to occupy his mind. He wasn't sure why, but he didn't like the tenderness Coltrain had shown Jane.

Chapter Three

Jane was restless all through the night. When Cherry went to bed, Todd sat with Jane. Tim had handed over the books earlier, so he took the heavy ledger with him. He looked through it while Jane slept, his reading glasses perched on his straight nose and a scowl between his eyes as he saw the inefficiency and waste there on the paper.

The ranch had almost gone under, all right, and there was no need. In addition to the beef cattle, Jane had four thoroughbred stallions, two of whom had won ribbons in competition, and on the racetrack before her father's death. She wasn't even putting them at stud, which could certainly have added to the coffers. The equipment she was using was obsolete. No maintenance had been done recently, either, and that would have made a handsome tax deduction. From what he'd seen, there was plenty of room for improvement in the equipment shed, the outbuildings, the barn and even the house itself. The ranch had great potential, but it wasn't being efficiently used.

He scowled, faintly aware of a tingling sensation, as if he were being watched. He lifted his head and looked into curious blue eyes.

"I didn't know you wore glasses," Jane said drowsily.

"I'm farsighted," he said with a chuckle. "It's irritating when people think I'm over forty because of these." He touched the glasses.

She studied his lean, hard face quietly. "How old are you?"

"Thirty-five," he said. "You?"

She grinned. "Twenty-five. A mere child, compared to you."

He lifted an eyebrow. "You must be feeling better."

"A little." She took a slow breath. "I hate being helpless."

"You won't always be," he reminded her. "One day, you won't have to worry about traction and pills. Try to think of this as a temporary setback."

"I'll bet you've never been helpless in your whole life."

"I had pneumonia once," he recalled. His face hardened with memory. He'd been violently ill, because he hadn't realized how serious his chest cold had become until his fever shot up and he couldn't walk for pain and lack of breath. The doctor had reluctantly allowed him to stay at home during treatment, with the proviso that he had to be carefully watched. But Marie had left him alone to go to a cocktail party with his best friend, smiling as she swept out the door. After all, it was just a little cough and he'd be fine, she'd said carelessly. Besides, this party was important to her. She was going to meet several society matrons who were potential clients for her new interior-design business. She couldn't pass that up. It wasn't as if pneumonia was even serious, she'd laughed lightly on her way out the door.

"Come back," Jane said softly.

His head jerked as he realized his thoughts had drifted away. "Sorry."

"What happened?" she persisted.

He shrugged. "Nothing much. I had pneumonia and my wife left me at home to go to a cocktail party."

"And?" she persisted.

"You're as stubborn as a bulldog, aren't you?" he asked irritably. "You're prying."

"Of course I am," she said easily. "Tell me."

"She went on to an all-night club after the cocktail party and didn't come home until late the next morning. She'd put my antibiotics away and hadn't told me where, and I was too sick to get up and look for them. By the time she got home, I was delirious with fever. She had to get an ambulance and rush me to the hospital. I very nearly died. That was the year Cherry was born."

"Why, the witch!" Jane said bluntly. "And you stayed with her?"

"Cherry was on the way," he said starkly. "I knew that if we got divorced, she wouldn't have the baby. I wanted Cherry," he said stiffly.

He said it as if it embarrassed him, and that made her smile. "I've noticed that you take fatherhood seriously."

"I always wanted kids," he said. "I was an only child. It's a lonely life for a kid on a big ranch. I wanted more than one, but…" He shrugged. "I'm glad I've got Cherry."

"Her mother didn't want her?"

He glowered. "Marie likes her when she's having guests, so that she can show the world what a sweet, devoted mother she is. It wins her brownie points in her business affairs. She's an interior designer and most of her work comes from very wealthy, very conservative, Texans. You know, the sort who like settled family men and women on the job?"

"Does Cherry know?"

"It's hard to miss, and Cherry's bright. Marie and I get along, most of the time, but I won't let her dictate Cherry's life for her." He intercepted a curious glance. "Rodeo," he said, answering the unspoken question. "Marie disapproves."

"But Cherry still rides."

He nodded. "I have custody," he said pointedly.

"And Cherry adores you," she agreed. She smiled, still drowsy from the pain medication. "I feel as if I'm flying. I don't know what Copper gave me, but it's very potent."

"Coltrain strikes me as something of a hell-raiser," he said.

"He was, and still is. I like him very much."

One gray eye narrowed. "Like?"

"Like." She was fighting sleep. Her slender hands smoothed over the light sheet that covered her. "I wanted to care about him, at first, but I couldn't feel like that with him. I think I'm cold, you see," she murmured sleepily. "I don't…feel those things…that women are supposed to feel…with men…"

Her voice drifted away and she was asleep.

Todd sat watching her with a faint frown, puzzled by that odd statement. She was a beauty. Surely there had been men over the years who attracted her, and at least one lover; perhaps Coltrain, for whom she hadn't felt anything. The thought was uncomfortable.

After a minute, he forced himself to concentrate more on the figures in the ledger and less on the lovely, sleeping woman in the bed. Jane's sex life was none of his business.

The ambulance came promptly at ten o'clock the next morning, and Jane's blue eyes snapped and sparkled when Todd told her that Coltrain had insisted on an X ray.

"I won't go!" she raged. "Do you hear me? I won't go to the hospital…!"

"He only wants you X-rayed to be sure that you haven't broken anything," Todd said. He was alone in the bedroom with Jane. Tim had prudently found something to do several miles away from the house, and Meg had gone shopping, taking Cherry with her. Only now did Todd realize why.

"I haven't broken anything!" she said hotly. She'd already had the traction apparatus removed so that she could go to the bathroom. Now she was sitting on the side of the bed in her pale blue cotton pajamas, her blond hair disheveled around her shoulders while she glared at the men who brought in the trolley.

"I won't go!" she continued.

The ambulance attendants looked doubtful.

Jane waved a hand at them. "Take that thing away!"

"Stay right where you are," Todd said quietly. He moved toward Jane. "Coltrain said you go. So you go."

She verbally lashed out at him, furious that she was being coerced into doing this. "I tell you, I won't…!"

He ignored her words and simply picked her up, cradling her gently against his broad chest as he turned toward the stretcher. She felt her breasts flatten against that warm strength and something incredible happened to her senses. She gasped audibly at the sensations that rippled through her slender body at the unfamiliar contact. Until now, the only man who'd ever seen her so scantily clad had been Coltrain, in a professional capacity only. And now here she was in arms that made a weakling of her, that made her whole body tingle and tremble with odd, empty longings.

All too soon, Todd put her on the stretcher and the ambulance attendants covered her with a white sheet. They were quick and professional, towing her right out toward the ambulance, which had backed up to the porch and was waiting for her.

"I'll follow you in the car," Todd told her. The way she was watching him made him uneasy. He couldn't help feeling her violent reaction to his touch. It had been in her whole body, even as it lay in her eyes right now, surprised and vulnerable eyes that made him very uncomfortable. "What, no more harsh words? No more fury?" he taunted, hoping to stop those soft eyes from eating his face.

Her teeth clenched, as much from physical discomfort as temper. "You're fired!" she yelled at him.

"Oh, you can't fire me," he assured her.

"Why can't I?"

"Because you'll lose the ranch if you do," he said, meeting her angry eyes levelly. "I can save it."

She wavered. "How?"

"We'll discuss that. After you're X-rayed," he added. He moved back and the ambulance attendant closed the double doors on Jane and her confused expression.

"I told you I was all right!" Jane raged at Coltrain when he'd read the X rays and assured her that nothing was broken, chipped or fractured.

"I didn't say you were all right," he returned, his hands deep in the pockets of his white lab coat. He looked very professional with the stethoscope draped loosely around his neck. "I said you hadn't broken anything. You were lucky," he added irritably. "My God, woman, do you want to break your back? Do you want to spend the rest of your life lying in bed, unable to move!"

She bit her lower lip hard. "No," she said gruffly.

"Then stop trying to prove yourself," he said shortly. "The only opinion that ever matters is your own! Damn the reporter. If he's too stupid to report the truth, he'll dig his own grave one day. If he hasn't already," he added.

"What do you mean?"

"I mean that the local rodeo association has banned him from the arena," he told her.

Her eyebrows shot up. "But rodeo is the biggest local sport going, especially this time of year!"

"I know." He smiled smugly. "I sit on the board of directors."

"You did it," she said.

"I had a lot of help," he replied. "It was a unanimous decision. I wish you could have seen Craig Fox's face when he was told he couldn't send his new reporter to cover any more rodeos." He fingered his tie. "As a matter of fact, the hardware store and the auto parts place pulled their ads this week. Their owners have sons who compete in the rodeo."

She whistled through her teeth. "Oh, boy."

"I understand that the reporter is making a public apology, in print, in this week's edition," he added. "You, uh, might take a look on the editorial page when your copy comes." He patted her shoulder absently. "He eats crow very well."

She laughed, her bad temper gone. "You devil!"

"You're my friend," he said with a smile—something rare in that taciturn face.

"And you're mine." She reached out and held his lean hand. "Thanks, Copper."

He nodded.

Todd Burke, coming into the treatment room with Dr. Lou Blakely, stopped and glared at the tableau they made. The lovely blond woman beside him didn't give away anything in her expression, but her eyelids flickered.

"When you're through here, I'd like to speak to you, Dr. Coltrain," Lou said quietly. "I had Ned Rogers come in for some lab work. It isn't good, I'm afraid. I let him go home, but we'll have to have him back to give him the results."

He let go of Jane's hand, reluctantly it seemed to Todd, and turned to his partner. "Was it so urgent that you couldn't tell me after I'd done my rounds here?" he asked shortly. "Who's minding the office?"

Her cheeks flushed. "I've just finished doing my own rounds," she said, furious that he thought she was chas-

ing him here. "And it *is* noon," she said pointedly. "I'm
on my lunch hour. Betty's had her lunch. She's minding the phone."

"Noon?" He checked his watch. "So it is." He turned
toward Jane and started to speak.

"I'll drive Jane back home, if she's through here,"
Todd interjected, joining them. "I have some questions
about the book work. I can't do anything more until
they're answered."

Lou studied the newcomer curiously and with a nice
smile. "I'm Dr. Louise Blakely," she said, holding a hand
out to be shaken. "Dr. Coltrain's partner."

"Assistant," Coltrain said carelessly, and with a
pointed glare. There was no interest in his eyes, no curiosity, nothing except a faint glitter of hostility.

"Todd Burke," Todd introduced himself, and smiled.
"Nice to meet you, Dr. Blakely."

Lou glanced at Coltrain. "The contract I signed says
that we're partners, Dr. Coltrain," she persisted. "For
a year."

He didn't reply. His pale eyes went back to Jane
and he smiled. "I'll be around if you need me. Take it
easy, okay?"

Jane smiled back. "Okay."

He patted her shoulder reassuringly and started for
the door. "All right," he told Lou curtly. "Let's have a
look at Mr. Rogers's test results."

Todd watched them go before he helped Jane into
the wheelchair the nurse had brought into the room.
She was wheeled out to the exit and Todd loaded her
into his Ford. They were underway before he spoke.

"Are you jealous of Lou?" he asked abruptly, because he'd seen the way she watched Coltrain and Lou Blakely.

"Because of Copper? No," she said easily. "I was wondering about Lou. She's…I don't know…fragile around him. It's odd, because she's such a strong, independent woman most of the time."

"Maybe she's sweet on him," he suggested.

"For her sake, I hope not," she replied. "Copper is a confirmed bachelor. His work is his whole life, and he likes women but only in numbers."

Todd smiled faintly.

She glanced at him with twinkling eyes. "I see that you understand the way he feels. That's the way you are, too, isn't it?"

He nodded. "A man who's been burned doesn't go around looking for fires," he said pointedly. He braked for a traffic light and then pulled out into the road that led out of Jacobsville toward the Parker ranch.

She stared out at the summer landscape as they left town, smiling at the beauty of flowers and crops in the field. "I can understand why you might feel that way," she said absently.

"I'm glad," he replied curtly, "because there was a look in your eyes that worried me when I lifted you onto the stretcher back at the house."

Her eyebrows raised. "You're blunt," she said.

"Yes, I am. I've found that it's easier to be honest than to prevaricate." His hands tightened on the steering wheel. "You're easy on the eyes and I think I'll enjoy working for you. But I'm not in the market for a love affair. It's the challenge of getting your ranch out of hock that appeals to me—not seducing you."

She didn't react visibly. She folded her arms over her breasts lazily and leaned back against the seat. It didn't show that she felt cold and empty and wounded inside. "I see."

"And now you're offended," he said with a cutting edge to his voice, "and you'll pout for the rest of the day."

She laughed. "I'm impressed that you know me so well already, Mr. Burke," she returned. "And your modesty is refreshing!"

His brows collided. He hadn't expected that mocking reply. "I beg your pardon?"

"You feel that I'm so overcome with panting passion for you that I have to be warned off. I never realized I was that dangerous. And in a wheelchair, too." She wiggled her eyebrows at him. "Since you're *sooooo* attractive, Mr. Burke, aren't you afraid to be alone in the car with me? I might leap on you!"

He was disconcerted. He glanced at her and the car swerved. He muttered under his breath as he righted it in his lane.

Jane began to enjoy herself. He didn't seem the sort of man who was easily rattled. She'd managed that quite nicely. She couldn't wait to do it again. Two could play at his game.

"You're making me sound conceited," he began.

"Really? Well, you do seem to think that no normal woman can resist you."

He sighed angrily. "You're twisting my words."

"I do find you attractive," she said. "You're everything I've ever wanted in a man. I think you're handsome and intelligent and sexy. Shall we just have sex right now or wait until you stop the car?"

The car swerved again and he braked to avoid going into the ditch. "Miss Parker!"

She was enjoying herself. For the first time since the wreck, she could laugh. She had to fight to get herself under control at all.

"Oh, I'm sorry," she said when she got a glimpse at his hard features. "Really, I am."

He pulled onto the ranch road, his teeth clenched. She made him out to be an utter fool, and he didn't like it. He wasn't used to women who were that good at verbal repartee. Marie was sarcastic and biting at times, but she was never condescending. Jane Parker was another kettle of fish. He had to remember that her body was fragile, even if her ego wasn't.

"I haven't laughed like that in months," she said, calmer when he pulled up at the front door. "I do apologize, but it felt good to laugh."

He cut off the ignition and turned in the seat to face her. His eyes glittered, as they had at their first meeting. He was trying to control emotions he'd never felt to such an extent.

"I don't like being the butt of anyone's joke," he said curtly. "We'll get along very well if you remember that."

Her eyes iced over. "We'll get along better if you remember that I don't like men who talk to me as if I were a giddy adolescent on a hero-worshiping tangent."

His jaw clenched. "Miss Parker, I'm no boy. And I do know how a woman reacts—"

"No doubt you do, with your wide experience of them." She cut him off. "I've been alone for some time now," she added, "and I'm not used to being touched. So before you read too much into my reactions, you might consider that any man would have produced the same reaction."

He didn't like that. His expression went from surprise to cold courtesy. "I'll get you into the house."

"No, you won't," she said pleasantly. The look in her eyes wasn't pleasant at all. "Please ask Tim to bring the wheelchair. I find that I prefer it to you."

His face registered the insult. He knew already how she hated the stigma of the chair. But he didn't react. He should have kept his mouth shut.

"I'll get it," he said.

He left her in the car and went into the house, fuming. Tim came out of the kitchen where he'd been talking to Meg.

"How is she?" he asked at once.

"Out of humor, but physically undamaged," Todd said. He grimaced. "I made her mad."

"That's a step in the right direction," the older man said, smiling. "She needs shaking up. Pity she doesn't like Copper," he added on a sigh. "He'd be perfect for her."

"Because he's a doctor?" Todd asked impatiently.

"Because they grew up together and he knows ranching," came the reply. "He'd never have let the place get in this mess." He eyed Todd narrowly. "Do you think you can get us out of the financial tangle I landed us in?"

Todd reached for the wheelchair. "I think so," he said. "It's not as bad as you think. Mainly it's a matter of improving the operation and utilizing some resources. It will take time, though," he added as he pushed the chair toward the porch. "Don't expect instant answers."

"I don't," Tim assured him. "Why can't you just carry her inside?" he asked as an afterthought.

"Never mind." Todd bit off the words.

Tim's eyes twinkled. He followed the younger man out to the car and watched the byplay as Todd eased Jane into the chair and pushed her up onto the porch. She was stifling hot words, and he was controlling a temper that almost slipped its bonds. Tim took a longer look and liked what he saw. She wasn't brooding anymore, that was obvious. If anything, she was seething.

"Will you call Cherry and tell her I'm putting lunch on the table, Todd?" Meg called from the kitchen.

"Sure."

He put the car away and went to find his daughter, who was riding in the fenced arena, going around the barrels very slowly.

"Hi, Dad," she called, waving her hand.

"How's it going?" he yelled.

"Fine! I'm working slowly, like Jane told me to. How is she?"

"She's all right," he replied. "Meg's got lunch ready. Put your horse up and come on in."

"Okay, Dad!"

He stuck his hands into the pockets of his slacks and went back to the house. Meg had coffee and sandwiches on the long dining-room table, where Jane and Tim were sitting. He washed up and then they waited for Cherry, who came to join them a few minutes later.

"You'll need some food before you start on those books again." Tim chuckled, watching Todd raid the sandwich platter before he passed it along to his daughter. She helped herself, talking animatedly to Meg and Tim.

"I love to see a man with a healthy appetite," Jane murmured, to needle him. She was sitting next to him and nibbling delicately on her own sandwich.

Todd glared at her. She finished her sandwich and leaned toward him, sniffing.

"Umm," she murmured huskily, so that only he could hear while Tim and Meg were talking. "What *is* that cologne you're wearing? It's very sexy."

He didn't reply, reaching for his coffee cup instead with an expression as hard as steel.

"Jane, Todd said that he thinks he can get us operating in the black," Tim said to Jane.

"Really?" Jane smiled at him. "Can we afford it?"

He sipped his coffee and put a sandwich on his plate. "It's going to require some belt tightening, if that's what you mean," he said, refusing to rise to the bait. He looked directly at her. "And you're going to have to borrow enough to make some improvements."

She let out a long breath. "I was afraid you'd say that. I don't think we can borrow any more."

"Yes, you can," he said, without telling her why he was sure of it. His name would convince any banker to let her have the loan, if he was willing to stand behind it. And he was. He dealt in amounts that would make her mind boggle. The amount she needed to get the ranch on its feet was paltry indeed compared to his annual budget. His backing would give her a good start, and it was an investment that would pay dividends one day. Not that he expected to capitalize on it. He'd be in the guise of a guardian angel, not a working partner.

She gnawed her lower lip, all signs of humor gone. "What would we have to do?"

He outlined the changes he had in mind, including the improvements to buildings, putting the stallions out to stud, building a breeding herd, leasing out unused land and applying for land development funds through government agencies.

Jane caught her breath mentally at the picture he painted of what could become a successful ranch, with horses for its foundation instead of cattle. It had been her father's dream to make the ranch self-supporting. Jane had tried, but she had no real knowledge of finance. All she knew was horses.

"Besides these changes," Todd added, "you have a name with commercial potential. It's a hell of a shame not to capitalize on it. Have you considered endorsing a line of Western clothing? Other rodeo stars have gone into such licensing. Why not you?"

"I...couldn't do that," she said hesitantly.

"Why?"

"I'm not going to be photographed in a wheelchair!"

"You wouldn't have to be," he said curtly. "The wheelchair is only temporary. Didn't the doctor tell you so?"

She rubbed her temples. She was on the way to a king-size headache. Todd Burke headache number one, she thought whimsically, and had to bite back a grin.

"I can't think that anyone would be interested in a line of clothing advertised by a has-been."

"You aren't a has-been," Cherry said quietly. "You're a legend. My gosh, at the riding school I went to they had posters of you all over the place!"

She knew the poster had been made, but she didn't realize that anybody had actually paid money for one. She looked blankly at Cherry.

"You've forgotten, haven't you?" Tim asked. "I told you that they had to reprint the posters because of the demand. But it was right after the wreck. I guess you weren't listening."

"No," she agreed. "I was in shock." She looked at Todd. "If there's a chance that we can make the ranch into a paying operation, I want to take it. If I lose, okay. But I'm not going under without a fight. Do whatever you like about the loan and the financing, and then just point me in the right direction. I'll do whatever you want me to."

"All right," Todd said. "We'll give it a shot."

Chapter Four

Todd insisted on going to the Jacobsville bank alone when he went to apply for the loan. It wouldn't do for Jane to find out how he was going to manage financing for his improvement program.

The bank manager was sworn to silence and he had received Todd's written backing for the loan. A few phone calls and it was all arranged. He had the necessary amount credited to Jane's account and then he set about replacing old equipment and hiring contractors to make improvements to existing buildings on the ranch.

When Jane saw the first bill, she almost called for a shot of whiskey.

"I can't afford this," she gasped.

"Yes, you can," Todd assured her. He sat across from her at the desk in the study. "You certainly can't afford to let things go further downhill. In the long run, maintenance is much less expensive than replacing everything you own."

She groaned. "But the electric fence…!"

"Less expensive than replacing a wood and barbed wire one, and less damaging to livestock," he said. "I've also contacted the Soil Conservation Service about assistance with a pond for water impoundment."

"A tank," she said absently. "We call them tanks here in Texas."

He raised an eyebrow but he made no further comment. "Another thing," he added, "I've arranged for some roof repairs on the house. You've got pots and pans all over the place to catch the water from leaks. If you don't fix the roof, you'll have to replace it. The wood will eventually rot."

"How will I pay for it all?" she asked the ceiling.

"I'm glad you asked," he said with a smile. He leaned back, propping one big booted foot against the lower rung of a nearby chair. In the pose, he looked lean and fit and very masculine. Jane had to control a sigh, and hide the surge of attraction she felt.

"Well?" she prompted.

"I'm advertising two of the stallions for stud purposes," he said. "They're champions with well-known bloodlines and they'll command a high price. I'm also going to purchase two or three good brood mares. We're going to breed them to other champions. Their offspring will add to our own blood stock, and the ones we don't add to the stud, we'll sell."

"We'll need a better barn," she began.

"We're going to build one," he said. "I've already hired a contractor."

"You take my breath away," she said, leaning back. "But all this will take time, and the ranch is on the edge of bankruptcy as it is," she added worriedly.

"That's where you come in," he said quietly. "I've approached a clothing manufacturer in Houston. They're interested in having you promote a line of women's Western wear, primarily leisure wear, such as jeans."

"Do they know…?"

He nodded. "They won't photograph you in a wheel-chair." He told her the sum they were offering and she flushed.

"You're kidding!" she bellowed.

He shook his head. "Not at all. You'll want to see the manufacturer, of course. I wouldn't expect you to endorse clothing you haven't seen."

She was excited at the prospect of having her name on a line of clothes, but she was afraid to become over-enthusiastic. No deal was final until contracts were signed. And there might be a reason to keep her from signing. "I won't endorse something cheap or sloppy," she agreed.

"I'm fairly sure that this is a reputable clothier," he told her, "and not a fly-by-night enterprise. We'll see. They'd like to come down and talk to you next Friday."

She smiled. "Okay."

He watched her with interest. Her face was animated, her blue eyes twinkling. She looked like a different woman. Her hair was in its usual long braid, held in place with a rubber band, a few wisps of it escaping down into her face. She brushed it away impatiently and his eyes fell reluctantly to the soft thrust of her breasts against the knit fabric of her blue pullover shirt.

"Stop that," she said at once, lifting her chin. "If I can't ogle you, you can't ogle me."

His eyebrows arched. "I don't remember saying you couldn't ogle me."

"Yes, you did. Quite emphatically. This is a business relationship now. Let's keep it that way."

He chuckled softly, then pursed his lips. "Are you sure you want to?" he asked with a honeyed drawl.

She was already out of her league, and she knew it, but she wasn't going to let *him* gain the upper hand. She simply smiled. "Yes, I'm sure," she told him. "Now what time next Friday do these people want to see me?"

By the next Thursday morning, all the arrangements were finalized for the meeting with the clothing manufacturers and the public relations people. The improvements on the house were underway, and noise had become a part of everyday life.

Jane escaped to the corral with Cherry after breakfast to get away from the carpenters. Todd was holed up in the study with the telephone, and the door was firmly closed. Jane wondered how he could hear above the chaos.

"Noise, noise," she groaned, holding her head. "I'm going to shoot those men just to get the hammers stopped!"

"It will be better to get the leaks stopped," Cherry told her with a cheeky grin.

"Ha!"

Cherry finished saddling the nice little quarter horse mare her father had bought her. "I named her Feather. Isn't she pretty?" she asked.

"She's very pretty, and she can do those turns blindfolded," Jane assured her. "You have to trust her, Cherry. You have to sit loose in the saddle and not pull on the reins. If you can do that, she'll make those turns as tight as a drum."

Cherry slumped a little. "I can't," she said miserably. She sat down on a bale of hay beside Jane, holding the reins in one hand while Feather nibbled at the hay. "I do try, Jane, but when she goes so fast around those turns…"

"You're afraid you'll fall off," Jane finished for her.

"Well, there's that, too," Cherry said. She picked at a piece of straw and snapped it between her fingers. "But it's the horse I'm most afraid for. My first time on the barrel-racing circuit, a rider went down and so did the horse. The fall broke the horse's leg." She threw away the straw. "They were going to put her down, but I begged and begged, and Dad bought her for me. She lives with a relative back in Wyoming, and she's doing fine, but I've had a hard time racing ever since that day."

Todd hadn't told Jane that. She slid an affectionate arm around the girl and hugged her warmly.

"That's very rare, you know," she said gently. "People in rodeo, people who ride, love their horses. Nobody ever uses an animal in a way that will harm it—not if they want to stay in rodeo. Cherry, I've been riding for twenty years, since I was five, and I've never had a horse go down under me when I was barrel racing. Never. I've fallen off," she added humorously. "And once I had a rib broken when a horse kicked as I fell. But when I was racing, there wasn't a single mishap."

"Really?" Cherry asked, brightening.

"Really. Riding skill is largely a matter of having a well-trained horse and then not trying to exert too much control over the horse. Haven't you watched riders put quarter horses through their paces?"

"Sure. They're wonderful to watch. All a good rider has to do is just sit and the horse does all the work of cutting a steer out of a herd."

"That's right. The horse knows his job, and does it. Where the problem begins is when the rider thinks he knows more than the horse and tries to take control."

Cherry's gray eyes widened. "Oh. Oh!"

Jane grinned. "You're getting the picture, aren't you?"

"Wow! Am I ever!"

"Now let that sink in while you're putting Feather through her paces," she suggested. "And don't rush. Just go slow and easy."

"Slow and easy," Cherry echoed.

"What is this, a conference?" Todd asked from the doorway.

"Cowgirl talk." His daughter chuckled. "Hi, Dad! Want to come and watch me?"

"Sure, in just a minute. I have to talk to the boss."

"I always thought *you* were the boss," she murmured as she went past, sharing a private joke with him.

He chuckled. "So did I," he agreed.

"See you later, Jane!" Cherry called. She led Feather out into the sunlight and climbed aboard with ease.

"She looks happy," Todd remarked.

He was looking very Western in his jeans and boots and blue patterned shirt with the gray Stetson pulled low over his eyes. He had a rodeo rider's physique, square shouldered and lean hipped, with long, powerful legs. Jane tried not to notice and failed miserably. It was a good thing there was so much shadow in the barn.

"We were talking about barrel racing. She told me about the injured horse you bought for her, back in Wyoming. That was kind of you."

"Kind." He shrugged. "I didn't stand a chance once she started crying. Tears wear me down."

"I'll have to remember that."

He cocked an eyebrow. "*Cherry's* tears," he said emphatically. "I'm immune to any others."

She snapped her fingers. "Darn the luck!"

His pale eyes swept over her slender body. She hadn't come down here in the wheelchair. She had her crutches instead. "That's dangerous," he said pointedly. "You could take a bad fall trying to maneuver through the gravel."

"No pain, no gain," she told him. "I can manage or I wouldn't have tried. I don't enjoy spending weeks in bed."

He decided that it might be best to ignore the remark. "I've been talking to Cherry's mother. She does want her this weekend after all," he said. "She's going to take Cherry shopping, so I'll drive her up about ten tomorrow morning. With any luck, I'll be back before those clothing representatives arrive. But in any case you need to have your attorney read the contract before you sign it."

"I know that," she said.

"Good."

She got up from the bale slowly and held on to her crutches, easing them under her arms. It was hard going, balancing on them, but she was doing better at it every day.

"Do Cherry and her mother get along?" she asked as they left the barn and went toward the corral where Cherry was practicing.

"Yes, most of the time. Cherry doesn't like her stepfather."

"I don't imagine she does. Many children of divorced parents live with a hope that their real parents will get together again, or so I've heard."

"Cherry knows better. She hated the way it was before the divorce. Too many arguments can make home life hell for a young girl."

"I suppose so."

"Didn't your parents ever argue?" he asked her.

"I don't know. My mother died when I was barely old enough to start school. My dad raised me. Well, my dad and Tim and Meg," Jane amended.

"It must have hit you hard to lose him."

She nodded. "At least I still had Tim and Meg. That made it easier. In an odd way, the injury helped, too. It gave me a challenge, kept me going. If I'd had time to sit and brood, I think I might have gone crazy. I miss him so."

Her voice was husky with feeling. He glanced down at her with mingled emotions. "I lost my mother nine years ago," he said. "My dad followed her two years later. I remember how it felt. We were a close-knit family."

"I'm sorry."

His broad shoulders rose and fell. "People die. It's the way of things."

"That doesn't make it easy."

"No."

They stopped at the corral fence. Cherry was leaning over Feather's neck, talking softly to her. She glanced at Todd and Jane, grinned and suddenly urged Feather into a gallop.

As they watched, she bent low over Feather's mane, her hands not clinging to the reins, closed her eyes and let nature take its course. Feather took the first barrel so low that she seemed to slither around it, easily regaining her balance and heading for the barrel at the other end of the corral at the same feverish pace. She circled that one with the same ease, and kept going until an elated Cherry whooped loudly and gently reined her in on the side of the corral where the surprised, delighted adults were standing.

"Did you see?" Cherry burst out, red-faced and laughing so hard that tears ran down her dusty cheeks. "Oh, did you see! I did it!"

"I saw," Jane said with a smile. "Cherry, you're just great!"

"You're the great one," the girl said shyly. "After all, you told me how to do it. I won't be afraid anymore. Feather knows just what to do. All I have to do is let her."

"That's right. Slow and easy. You're doing fine now."

"I am, aren't I?" Cherry asked.

"You're a champ," Todd said as he found his voice, his eyes sparkling with pleasure. "I'm proud of you."

"Thanks, Dad!" She laughed again, and gave Feather her head.

"Don't overdo!" he yelled after her.

"No way!" came floating back over the sound of hoofbeats.

"So much for slow and easy," Jane murmured, watching the young girl.

Todd had a booted foot propped on the lowest fence rail. He glanced down at Jane with hooded eyes, unsmiling. She looked frail, but her slender body had a nice curve to it, and her breasts were firm and pert under that open-neck knit shirt. Her hair was loose around her shoulders for a change, faintly wavy and very pretty. Like Jane herself.

"Slow and easy," he said half under his breath, thinking of another exercise, one that made his heart begin to race.

Jane heard the deep note in his voice and looked up. Her eyes were trapped in the gray glitter under his hat brim. His lean hand came up to her face, cupping her cheek in its warmth while his thumb slowly traced the line of her upper lip until he made it tremble.

She couldn't get a breath of air into her starving lungs. She swallowed, and her lips parted helplessly while she struggled to find a teasing remark to break the tension.

Todd's own lips opened as he watched hers. His thumb slid down to the edge of her white teeth and caressed it lazily. Her mouth was as soft as a petal, warm, full.

Then suddenly, somehow, she was closer to him. She could see the pulse in his neck throbbing, feel the heat off his body. That cologne he wore was in her nostrils as the wind picked up and blew at his back.

He hadn't moved. His body was open and she was at an angle to that propped leg, so that they were standing in an intimacy that was respectable and tantalizing at the same time. She could almost feel the hard pressure of his legs against hers, the threat of his body so close to hers. Her heart was beating madly in her throat. Her eyes fell to his hard mouth, where it parted, and for an endless space of seconds, she saw it in her mind's eye, pressed ruthlessly, demandingly, against her own.

His breath was warm and unsteady. She could taste the coffee on it. He breathed and she felt his breath against her parted lips where his thumb was exploring. She felt it, felt him, felt the hunger that had been a stranger all her life until now.

She moved closer, as if he willed her to, moved jerkily on her crutches until she was standing right in the fork of his body and she could feel him just barely touching her—his long legs, his chest, his flat stomach, his hips—barely, barely touching, teasing, intimidating.

She made a husky, whimpering little sound in her throat and suddenly pressed herself to him.

Tim whistled loudly, Feather snorted, the roar of a car's engine all exploded into the tension and Jane actually moaned.

She jerked away from Todd so fast that she fell against the fence. His arm shot out to spare her the impact of a fall, righting her and the crutches, all without looking directly into her eyes. He was as shaken as she seemed to be, and angry that she'd gotten to him at all.

"Damn you." He bit off the words furiously.

She hit his broad chest with a flat hand. "You started that!" she accused hotly. "Damn you, too!"

"Todd! That building contractor's coming up the driveway!" Tim called before he went back to meet the man.

"I told you," Todd continued, ignoring the interruption, "that I'm not in the mood for an affair!"

"I'm the one on crutches," she snapped back. "It isn't as if I threw myself at you!"

"Isn't it? I didn't come to you!"

"Todd!" Tim called again.

He released Jane from his furious glare long enough to look toward Tim. "I'll be right there!"

Tim made a thumbs-up gesture and greeted the newcomer.

Todd looked back at Jane, who was pale but not backing down an inch. Her chin was thrust out and she was looking at him with eyes as angry as his own.

"You know what you do to a man with those bedroom eyes," he accused curtly. "You've probably had more lovers than I have."

"And just think, I didn't have to pay them!"

His breath inverted and he seemed to grow taller and more threatening in the space of a few seconds. "You...!" he began in a thunderous undertone.

She pulled herself up as tall as she could with the crutches and her hand slipped, grabbing at the cross-piece for support. She managed it, barely.

The pathetic little movement brought Todd back to his senses. Disabled she might be, but she had spirit. She wouldn't back down, or give up, no matter how formidable the opposition. He was furious, but even through his anger he felt admiration for her spunk.

"When you get back on your feet properly," he said deeply, "we'll have this out."

"What's the matter, big man, afraid to try your

boxing gloves on a woman with crutches?" she taunted.

He chuckled despite his bad temper. "Not when the woman's got a switchblade in her tongue," he retorted. "Hellcat!"

"Pig!"

His eyebrows lifted. "Who, me?"

"Oink, oink!"

He searched her flushed face, her tousled hair, her wide angry blue eyes for a long moment, aware of faint regret. He wasn't going to let himself be seduced into another dead-end relationship. But, oh, he was tempted. This woman wasn't like anyone he'd ever known.

"And don't drool over me," she snapped.

"Optimist," he countered lazily.

She made a rough sound under her breath and turned unsteadily on her crutches. "I want to be there when you talk to the contractor. It's my ranch he'll be working on."

"I planned for you to meet him," he assured her. "That's why he's here."

"You might have given me a little advance notice," she said angrily.

"That's why I came down to the barn in the first place," he told her. "We got sidetracked."

"*You* got sidetracked," she accused with a harsh glare. "You started it."

"I had help," he returned. He stared her down. "How many men did it take to perfect that simpering, hungry look of yours?"

She glared and turned away. She didn't answer him, hobbling along on her crutches as fast as she could.

"If I could balance on one leg, I'd crack one of these crutches over your head," she said icily.

"You must have given the good doctor fits," he mused. "He still drools over you."

"He's a good man," she said shortly. "And he knows me."

"I don't doubt it," he drawled meaningfully.

She flushed. The going was rough on that gravel. She blew a strand of hair out of her face as she soldiered on.

The contractor was leaning against the hood of a nice green Mercedes, waiting for them. He was lean and elegant looking, darkly tanned, with black eyes in a swarthy face topped by straight, long black hair in a ponytail.

"This is Sloan Hayes," Todd introduced them. The Native American builder shook hands with Jane and then with Tim.

"We haven't met, but I've certainly heard of you," Jane said with a polite smile. Most people had. He was very famous and she was surprised that Todd knew him. "This is a small job…"

"We're glad to get it," Hayes replied suavely. "It's been slow lately," he hedged. "Your, uh, manager here has gone over the plans with me, but he wanted you to see them before we finalize the work. I brought the blueprints along so that you could inspect them."

"That's very nice of you," Jane said with a smile.

He cocked an eyebrow and smiled back. "I should have mentioned that I've been a rodeo fan all my life. I've seen you ride." He shook his head. "Hell of a shame about the accident. I'm sorry."

She was surprised, but not offended, by his openness. "I'm sorry, too, but life has these pitfalls. We have to adapt."

"Any idea what you'll substitute for rodeo in your life?" he continued.

She smiled. "How about raising champion horses?"

He chuckled. "Sounds like a winner. That's one of my own hobbies." His eyes narrowed appreciatively on her slender body.

Todd's face went stiff. "The plans?" he prompted.

Sloan gave him a deep look. "I'll get them."

"We can look them over in the study," Jane said. "Tim, will you have Meg get some coffee and cake and bring it on a tray when she's ready?"

"Sure thing!" Tim said, grinning.

Jane smiled at Todd as they waited for Sloan Hayes to get his blueprints. "He's very nice," she said with a deliberate sweetness. "I think this project is going to be a lot of fun."

"Just don't get too wound up in the project director," he cautioned. "He isn't marriage material, but he likes women...."

"Is *that* why you hired him? Thanks!" she said under her breath and smiled broadly when Sloan joined them on the porch.

"Here, let me help you with those crutches," the builder offered as they went into the house.

"Why, how very kind of you!" Jane said enthusiastically.

Todd followed them inside, the gnashing of his teeth all but audible. Complications were breaking out all over. First the redheaded doctor, now the builder. Well, he wasn't joining any queues and he didn't want her in the first place. Having settled that in the privacy of his own mind, he forced himself to concentrate on the business at hand.

They went over the blueprints. Jane had several questions, but all in all, she was very satisfied with what the builder had drawn up.

"Do we need so much space in the barn?" she asked finally, when they were drinking coffee and eating slices of Meg's wonderful lemon pound cake.

"You do if you're serious about turning this place into a stud ranch," Sloan said quietly. "You have to have immaculate facilities for the livestock. That sort of thing doesn't go unnoticed by customers. There will be a certain amount of socializing necessary, also. And you'll have to do some renovation to the house to make it fit in with the overall look of the ranch."

She bit her lower lip and glanced at Todd worriedly.

"You can do it," he said simply. "The money's there. It's all arranged."

"I didn't think that far ahead," she said, troubled.

"You'll have to," Sloan said. "This change is going to foster others. It's a commitment."

She stared down into her lap. She wasn't sure she wanted such a change.

"We'll talk about it later," Todd said. "Meanwhile, sleep on it before you decide. Sloan's got a few other jobs to finish first."

"That's right," the builder said with a nice smile.

"You don't have to jump into anything. Weigh the consequences. Then decide what you want to do."

"I will. Thank you for being patient," she said gently.

He smiled at her. "Oh, I'm known for my patience," he said, tongue-in-cheek. "Ask Todd."

Todd lifted an eyebrow. "I won't lie for you."

"I would for you," the other man said with hidden intent. "In fact, I have." Which was true, because Sloan had put up a warehouse for Todd's computer company, and now he was keeping mum about Todd's real background.

"Have some more coffee and shut up," Todd murmured with a grin.

"Point taken. Now about these outbuildings," he told Jane. "This is what I'd suggest…"

By the time he left, Jane had a picture of what the ranch would look like once it had been transformed. The cost was enormous, but the profit could be enormous as well.

Now, it all rested on her ability to sell her name for that endorsement, so that she could afford the improvements. But she wasn't going to say yes unless she felt she was doing the right thing. And she wouldn't know that until she met the manufacturer. She was going to reserve judgment until the next day, when they conferred.

Chapter Five

Jane barely slept that night, wondering what would come of her meeting with the clothier and the company's public relations representative. It didn't help that Todd left early the next morning with Cherry for Victoria.

"I'll be back before they get here," he assured Jane. "Stop brooding."

"I'll try. It's a big decision. I just hope that they'll ask me to endorse a line I can feel comfortable putting my name on." She hugged Cherry, and the girl returned the embrace with genuine fondness. In a short time, they'd become close. "Have a good time with your mother, and have fun shopping."

"Sure. You take care of yourself. No dancing," she teased, nodding toward the crutches.

Jane laughed softly. "Okay."

"I'll see you Monday."

Jane nodded, and waved them off. Todd looked glad to go. Perhaps, like her, he needed some breathing space. She wondered if he planned to spend the weekend at the ranch or go off on his own. Probably, she thought bitterly, he had plenty of women just waiting for the chance to go out with him. As good-looking as he was, she didn't doubt his attraction for the opposite sex. In a way, she was glad that she was exempt from his attentions. The very brief glimpse she'd had of his ardor the day before at the corral made her knees weak in retrospect. He wasn't the sort of man to play games with inexperienced women. He didn't know that she was inexperienced, either, and she had no intention of giving herself away.

She went back inside, glad of the time she was getting to distance herself from Todd's disturbing presence. She went over the books, amazed at what he'd accomplished in so short a time. He really was a wizard with figures. How, she wondered, could a man with such superb business sense spend his life working for someone else? He could have made a fortune by putting his analytical mind to work in his own interests. Perhaps he had no ambition, she decided finally.

She might have changed her mind if she could have seen him later that morning, sitting behind the desk in the president's office at Burke-Hathaway Business Systems. He'd long since bought out the Hathaway who was the old head of the company, but he left the name. It was known in south Texas, as Burke wasn't, and that made it good for business.

He made several pressing telephone calls, dictated letters and made arrangements to have leftover business sent down by fax. He'd installed a machine in the study, and he told his secretary that he'd telephone her with instructions as to when he wanted business documents sent. It wouldn't do for Jane to be in the study when he was working. He felt a twinge of guilt at keeping this from her, but after all, he *had* told her that he would be keeping his job and working for her on the side. In effect, he was.

That might bother him one day, but there was no reason for her to know the truth about his private life. She was just a temporarily disabled woman whom he felt sorry for. On a whim he'd decided to help her. It was a diversion, a challenge. Life had gone sour for him lately, with his business prospering and orders coming in faster than he could fill them. He'd been stagnating with nothing to challenge his quick mind. He had good people, subordinates, who did all the really interesting work—inventing new software, balancing books, marketing. All he did was public relations work, making contacts, conducting high-level meetings, signing contracts and talking to bankers and stockholders. The thing that had made the company fun in the first place was the risk. He'd left any real risk behind when the company became one of the Fortune 500. These days, he was the chief executive officer and president of Burke-Hathaway.

He was a figurehead.

But not on the Parker ranch. No, sir. There, he was necessary. He was the one thing standing between Jane and bankruptcy, and it made him feel good to know that he could make such a difference in her life. There was the challenge he needed to put the color back into his life. And it was helping Cherry, too. She and Jane were already friends. The girl hadn't had much fun in her life, but she really loved rodeo and Jane was the perfect person to help her learn the ropes. In fact, it had helped Jane already. She was less broody and more determined than ever to get her broken body back into some semblance of normalcy. All around, to sign on as Jane's business manager was one of the better decisions of Todd's life.

Then if it was such a great move, why, he asked himself as he signed letters on the mahogany desk, did he feel so morose and out of humor? He and Jane should have been friends, but they weren't. Jane fought him at every turn, and all at once, yesterday, he'd precipitated a physical awareness in her that he regretted. She was vulnerable now, and he should have known better than to start something he couldn't finish.

She was so lovely, he thought angrily. Under different circumstances, he'd have made a dead set at her. But although she was old enough to have had lovers, he wondered about that side of her life. The doctor was interested in her, but there was no hint of real intimacy between the two of them. Old lovers would show it. They couldn't help but show it.

"Mr. Burke, you have to initial this contract as well," his secretary reminded him gently, pointing to two circles in the margin.

"Sorry." He initialed all three copies in the appropriate places and pushed them toward her. "Anything else pressing?"

"No, sir, not until next week."

He got up from the desk. "I'll be in and out," he said. "Mostly out. But I've left a number where I can be reached in case of an emergency." His steely gray eyes met hers. "Notice that I said *emergency*."

"Yes, sir." Miss Emory was in her early fifties and unflappable. She smiled. "Are you in disguise, sir?"

He chuckled. "In a manner of speaking, yes, so take care."

"Yes, sir."

"I'll check with you periodically. If anything urgent crops up, fax me. You don't need to explain anything, just state that I need to phone you. Sign your first name, not your last, to the fax. That way if anyone sees it, they'll just think I'm getting messages from a girlfriend."

Miss Emory chuckled. "Yes, sir."

He stacked the paperwork on the edge of the desk and left Miss Emory to deal with it. He had a feeling that she was going to earn more than her regular check for the next few weeks. He hoped he wasn't going to regret the decision that had taken him to Jacobsville.

The executive vice president from SlimTogs leisure wear was a young woman named Micki Lane. She had a nice smile and a firm handshake. Jane liked her at once. Her companion, however, was another sort altogether. Rick Wardell was a high-powered promoter with a fixed smile and determination in every line of his body. He verbally pushed Micki to one side and began to outline what would be expected of Jane if the company decided to use her.

Micki started to protest, but she was no match for Rick's verbal onslaught. Jane, however, was.

She held up a firm hand when the man was in full

spate. "Wait a minute," she said pleasantly. "I haven't said that I want or need to do this endorsement. Furthermore, I'm not endorsing anything that I haven't seen."

"But we're very well-known," Rick said, sounding less confident than before.

"Of course you're well-known to most people," Jane replied. "But not to me," she said emphatically. "I'm rodeo from the boots up. I come from a long line of rodeo people. That means that if I endorse a product, a lot of fans will buy it. I want to be sure that I'm putting my name on something that's attractive, fairly priced and durable."

Rick's face tautened. "Listen, honey, you don't seem to understand that we're doing you a favor—" he began angrily.

"Nobody calls me *honey* unless I say they can," Jane interrupted. "I'm no wallpaper girl." Jane's blue eyes were flashing like lightning, and the man's mouth closed abruptly as he realized that he'd overstepped the mark and the situation was deteriorating rapidly.

Before Jane could say anything more, the borrowed car Todd was driving pulled up behind Rick's flashy little red sports car. He got out and joined the small group, taking in the situation with one long look.

"Burke! Glad you're here. I don't think Miss Parker understands what a favor we'd be doing her to put her name on this new line," Rick began, smiling as if he were certain that another man would surely side with him. "Maybe you can talk some sense into her."

"Surely the 'favor' extends in both directions?" Todd interrupted suavely. "Or hasn't your sales manager told you that several boutiques are queueing up already to place orders for any merchandise endorsed by Jane Parker?"

Rick laughed nervously. "Well, certainly, but…" He laughed again. "Perhaps we could start over?"

Micki was standing near Jane, looking irritated.

"Ms. Lane, isn't it?" Todd asked, and moved forward to shake hands with her. His eyes narrowed. "Excuse me, but I thought you were sent here to negotiate with Miss Parker?" He glanced pointedly toward Rick Wardell as he spoke.

"I was," Micki replied. "Mr. Wardell is in charge of sales and promotion."

Jane smiled at Rick. It wasn't a nice smile. She hadn't liked his condescending tone. "In order to have something to promote, I have to sign a contract. Frankly I don't think there's a chance in hell that it's going to happen. But it was nice of you to come out, Mr. Wardell. You, too, Miss Lane."

Micki stepped in front of Rick. "I'd like to show you our new line of jeans," she said quietly, "along with some of the new T-shirts we've adapted to imitate rodeo styling—with fringe and sequins and beads. They're machine-washable and guaranteed not to shrink or fade. I think you might like them."

Jane was impressed. She smiled. "Well…"

Micki glanced toward a very defensive-looking Rick, and the buried steel in her makeup began to show itself in her cool smile. "Mr. Wardell wanted to come along so that he could meet you. Now that he has, I'm sure that he won't mind leaving the contractual discussion in my hands. Will you, Mr. Wardell?" she added pointedly.

He smiled uncertainly, then cleared his throat. "As you say, that might be best." He grinned, showing all his teeth. "Nice to have met you, Miss Parker, and I hope we'll be doing business. Burke." He nodded, still grinning, and turned to stride quickly back toward his sports car.

"If I sign anything, it had better have a clause that that man isn't to come within shooting range of me," Jane said bluntly, glaring after him. "I hate being talked down to!"

"Rick has his drawbacks, but he could sell ice to Eskimos. We're slowly drawing him into the twentieth century," Micki said with a grin. "I'll have a few words with the division boss about it when I get back. Meanwhile, couldn't I show you these samples, now that I'm here?"

"Well…I guess so," Jane agreed.

Micki smiled and went to get the case from her own car, a neat little tan sedan.

"It seems as though I arrived in the nick of time," Todd said quietly.

Jane looked up at him, still defensive. "Just in time to save that man's life, for a fact. The condescending, stuck-up son of a—"

"He's a super salesman," he said pointedly. "He's a master at sucking up to people when he feels he has to."

"He'll think he's found lemon heaven if he tries it on me!"

Todd chuckled. He liked the way she looked when she was animated. "You've got a temper."

"No kidding!"

"Calm down," he advised. "I won't try to force you to sign with them, but it would be to your advantage. The money for these repairs has to come from somewhere. This would almost pay for it. And if the line is as good as Micki says it is, you won't have a reason to refuse."

"I can give you a good one, and it drives a red sports car!"

"You won't even have to talk to him again. I promise."

She eased up a little. "Well, if you promise."

"That's the spirit."

Micki came back, the sun shining on her sleek black hair. She was a pretty woman, slight and sedate looking, with dark eyes and an olive complexion. She smiled, and her eyes sparkled.

"Can we sit down?" she asked. "I've been on my feet all day and I'm tired."

Probably, Jane thought sagely, because the woman could see that Jane was tiring as she leaned heavily on the crutches. Business sense and diplomacy were a nice mixture, and Jane knew even before she saw and approved of the clothing samples that she was going to sign that contract.

She gave the contract to her attorney to look over, but she sent Micki off with her assurances that she would do the endorsement. Micki was relieved and elated when she shook hands with both of them and left. Todd watched her out the door, his lips pursed thoughtfully.

"She isn't married," Jane remarked, aware of a faint twinge of jealousy that she was going to smother at once. "And she's very pretty."

He turned, his hands deep in the pockets of his tan slacks. Muscles rippled in his long arms, emphasized by the clinging knit of his yellow sports shirt. "So she is," he agreed. "But she's off limits."

"Why?"

"I don't seduce business contacts," he said frankly. "It's bad for my image."

Her eyebrows lifted. "I didn't know accountants worried about things like that."

Business executives did. But he couldn't say it. He'd almost made a serious blunder. He laughed off his own remark. "I might work for her one day," he explained. "It's better if I don't get involved with potential bosses."

"Or current ones?" She was fishing and grinning. "Thank God!"

He glowered at her. "There's no need to look so relieved."

"Sorry. It slipped out. Erase it from your memory." She leaned back on the sofa and stifled a yawn. "It's been a long day. I'm sleepy."

"Why don't you stretch out there and take a nap?" he asked. "I've got some figures to catch up and Meg and Tim have gone grocery shopping. You've got nothing to do, have you?"

"Not right now, anyway." She stretched back onto the cushions, stifling a grimace. She was sore from the walking she'd done for the past two days on the crutches. "I suppose I'm a little less fit than I thought," she said with a self-conscious smile. She tucked a pillow under her head. "The crutches are hard going." Her eyes closed. "But I hate the wheelchair."

"Go to sleep," he said gruffly. He stood there watching her, his eyes narrow on her pale face in its frame of long, silky blond hair. She did look like a fashion doll, all the way up and down, from her pretty face to her slender, curvaceous body and long, elegant legs. He liked the way she looked. But he couldn't afford to pay too much attention to it. This was a very temporary job, and soon he was going to be back in the fast lane. He had to be objective and remote.

He turned and went into the study, closing the door gently. He had enough paperwork of his own to occupy him until supper, much less the additional burden of Jane's. It was a shame that things in his company had become complicated at just the wrong time. But he'd manage. The challenge was refreshing. He couldn't remember when he'd enjoyed himself so much.

In the weeks that followed, a bond developed between Jane and Cherry. They were all but inseparable, especially out at the corral where Cherry worked on perfecting her technique on horseback. She was better. She had self-confidence and the turns weren't making her hesitate. She gave Feather her head and watched the little mare incredulously as she sailed through her paces.

Jane was proud of her pupil, and that showed, too. She spent less time brooding about her slow progress and began to show marked improvement as her therapy sessions became fewer and farther between.

Todd, on the other hand, was finding his job harder by the day. The paperwork and the building work were easy, but being close to Jane all the time was wearing him down. An accidental touch of their fingers sent his heart racing. A look that lingered too long made him tingle down to his toes. He found himself watching her for no reason at all, except that he liked to look at her. And his vulnerability made him bad-tempered. He was spending a lot of time with Micki Lane, going over the contracts with the attorneys before Jane signed them. She was pretty and interested in him, and he needed a diversion. So without counting the cost, he called her up and invited her to a dance.

The dance at the Jacobsville Civic Center was one of the monthly events that passed for socializing in Jacobsville. Jane had gone to them frequently before her accident, often with Copper Coltrain. But she'd given up dancing because of her injury. When Cherry mentioned casually that her dad was taking that pretty leisure wear executive to it, Jane was unprepared for the surge of jealousy she felt. She liked Micki, but it was hard to think of her with Todd. At least, she thought miserably, she'd have Cherry for company.

Only it didn't work out that way. Cherry accepted a last-minute invitation to spend the weekend with her mother and caught an early bus to Victoria. Then Tim and Meg announced that they'd be gone, too. Jane felt miserable and tried desperately not to show it. It seemed that everyone was going to desert her.

* * *

Todd thought that Jane seemed pale when he was ready to leave to pick Micki up that evening. He paused with the car keys jingling in his pocket. "You don't mind being here alone?" he asked. He looked very attractive in tan slacks, cream-colored boots and a patterned Western shirt and black string tie.

"Of course not," Jane said proudly. "I'm used to being by myself when Tim and Meg go to visit their daughter. They go at least one Saturday a month and they don't get in until late," she added.

He looked concerned. He didn't like having her on her own so far from any neighbors.

"This isn't a big city," she said, exasperated. "For heaven's sake, nobody's going to break in and kill me! I've got a shotgun over there behind the door, and I know how to use it!"

"If you have time to load it," he muttered. "Do you know where the shells are?"

She made a face. "I can find them if I have to."

He threw up his hands. "Oh, that's very reassuring! I hope any potential intruders are polite enough to wait while you do that!"

"I'm almost twenty-six years old!" she raged at him. "I can take care of myself without any tall, blond nursemaids! You just go on and mind your own business. I'm looking forward to a quiet evening with a good book!"

"I can see how that will benefit you," he said sarcastically. He picked up the book on the table beside the end of the sofa where she was lounging in jeans and a loose green shirt. "A source book on the battle of the Alamo. How enlightening."

"I like to read history," she said.

"Romance novels might do you more good," he returned. "A little vicarious pleasure would be better than nothing, surely."

Her blue eyes flashed. "If I want romance, I know where to go looking for it!"

"I'm flattered," he said, deliberately provocative.

"Not *you*," she said angrily. "Never you! That's wishful thinking on your part. You're not that attractive to me!"

"Really?" He bent toward her. She averted her face, but he reached behind her head with a steely hand and turned her face up to his. She had one quick glimpse of flint-hard gray eyes before his hard mouth came down on hers.

She reached up instinctively to push at him, but his teeth were nibbling her shocked, set lips apart. He tasted of mint and smelled of sexy cologne. The clean scents seduced her as much as the sharp, teasing movements of his mouth.

Her fingers clenched on his shirtfront in token protest. She made a sound, but his free hand came to her throat and he began to smooth it in gentle caresses. She felt her breath catch as the lazy pressure of his mouth touched something hidden and secret, deep inside her body. She felt like a coiled spring that was suddenly loosened. Her quick intake of breath was echoed by the faint groan that pushed past his hard mouth into her parting lips.

He caught her grasping fingers and spread them against the front of his soft shirt, moving them sensually from side to side over the hard, warm muscles. His breathing quickened, as did hers, and his hand moved to press her mouth closer into the demanding contact with his.

Her faint whimper excited him. He gave in to the red-hot waves of pleasure, hardly aware that he'd moved until he felt her body under his as he eased down on the sofa with her.

She felt the cushions at her back, his lean strength touching her from shoulders to thigh, his arms around her, his mouth touching and lifting, seducing, demanding in a silence so fraught with emotion that she could hear the sound of her own heartbeat.

His hands were under her blouse, against the skin of her back, exploring her as if she belonged to him. One long leg was insinuating itself between both of hers, gently so as not to jar her, seductively slow.

She managed to get a fraction of an inch between her mouth and his, and she struggled for breath and presence of mind.

"No..." she whispered jerkily.

His left hand tangled in her long hair while the right one roughly unsnapped the pearly studs of his shirt. He was wearing nothing underneath the fabric, and without hesitation, he gently pushed her face against thick hair and clean, cologne-scented bare skin, coaxing her mouth to touch him just below his collarbone.

She hadn't experienced that sort of intimacy. She fought it, trying to remember that he was on his way to another woman.

He shifted, so that her lips were touching the hard, tight thrust of a male nipple. His hand, behind her head, guided her, insisted, without a single word.

She was curious and attracted, so she did what he wanted her to do. She wasn't prepared for the ripple of muscle under her mouth or the soft, tortured moan that sounded above her head.

She hesitated, but his hand contracted in her hair and he moaned again, shifting. She gave in, suckling him, tasting him in a heated interlude that made her lower body seem to swell with new sensations.

Both his hands were in her hair now, guiding her mouth around the fascinating territory of his chest. It expanded violently as she kissed him, and he groaned even as he laughed at the delight her touch gave him.

He moved to lie on his back, his mouth swollen, his eyes glittering with emotion, his chest bare and throbbing when she finally lifted her head to look down at him.

He smiled with a kind of secret fever, stretching so that the shirt fell away. He arched, holding her eyes.

She pressed both hands to the wall of his broad chest, testing the wiry silkiness of the hair that covered him, watching him watch her while she touched him exploringly.

His hands pressed down over hers, holding them where his heart beat roughly, quickly, at his rib cage.

"You don't even know what to do," he said half angrily. "Do you need an instruction manual?"

She blinked, feeling sanity come back with a rush. Her hands jerked back and she gasped. She moved away from him and sat up, grimacing as the movement caught her painfully. She could only imagine how she must look with her hair disheveled and her mouth swollen and her face flushed. Her eyes were like saucers.

He stared at her as if, for a moment, he didn't even recognize her. In fact, she hardly resembled the pale, composed woman he saw every day. He remembered her stinging comment and bending to kiss her in anger. Then the whole situation had gotten out of hand. How could he have forgotten himself so completely?

With a muffled curse, he got to his feet and fastened his shirt, straining to breathe normally. Of all the harebrained, stupid things he'd ever done…!

Jane was feeling equally addled. After that last sarcastic remark he'd made, he was going to be lucky if she ever spoke to him again! She picked up her book and opened it in her lap, refusing to even look at him. She was embarrassed, nervous and defensive because she'd been so vulnerable.

He finished snapping his shirt and tucked it back into his slacks. His hands were faintly unsteady, which made him furious. She got to him without even trying. He seemed to have no control whatsoever once he touched her. That had never happened with Marie, even in the early days of their romance. And she just sat there, so cool that butter wouldn't melt in her mouth, looking unaffected when he could barely breathe. That alone made him furious.

"Nothing to say?" he asked, glancing at her with steely gray eyes. "Would you like to repeat that bit about not finding me attractive?" he mocked.

She wouldn't look up. Her face reddened a little

more, but otherwise, no expression showed in it. She didn't say a word.

He moved to the door. "I'll lock this behind me."

She nodded, but he wasn't looking.

He went out without another comment. His heart was still racing and he wasn't sure that his knees wouldn't buckle on the way to his car. Whatever Jane did to him, he hated it. He only wished he knew how to handle it. He had nothing to give her. It wasn't fair to lead her on when he felt that way. If she could be led on, that is. She'd been responsive enough until the last, when she'd seemed shocked and outraged. But she hadn't said a word. Not a word. He wondered what was going on in her mind.

He cursed as he fumbled the key into the ignition of his car and started it. Well, it didn't really matter what she thought, because that wasn't going to happen again. He'd have a good time with Micki and forget that Jane even existed.

Chapter Six

Only it didn't quite work out that way. Micki was a delightful companion, but when Todd held her while they were dancing, he felt nothing beyond a comfortable pleasure. The wild excitement that Jane engendered just by looking at him with her big blue eyes was totally missing.

"It was nice of you to invite me," Micki said with a smile. "But won't Jane mind?"

He scowled. "Jane is my employer," he said stiffly.

"Oh. Sorry. It was just that the way she looked…"

He pounced on that at once. "The way she looked…?" he prompted, and tried not to appear as interested as he was in her answer.

She laughed apologetically. "I thought she was in love with you," she explained.

His face was shot through with color. He stopped dancing. "That's absurd," he said slowly.

"Not really. You've obviously been kind to her," Micki continued, "and she was badly hurt in the wreck, wasn't she? I suppose it's inevitable that a woman will feel something for a man who helps her when she's in trouble. Mr. Kemble, her attorney, said that you've literally pulled her out of bankruptcy in a few short weeks and helped her get the ranch back on its feet."

He looked troubled. "Perhaps. The ranch had plenty of potential. It just needed a few modifications."

"Which you've accomplished. Jane is lovely, isn't she? Our advertising people are ecstatic about building a television campaign around her because she's so photogenic."

"She's easy enough on the eyes," he said noncommittally.

"And surprisingly modest about it. I've known of her for years, of course, since I grew up in Jacobsville. I'd heard that Dr. Coltrain gave up when you came to the Parker place. He's been going around with Jane for a long time. He's not a man I'd find easy to think of romantically, not with his temper, but Jane was fiery enough to stand up to him. Everyone thought they'd make a match of it eventually."

His face tautened. "Did they? Well, he only comes out to the place once in a while to check on her."

Micki hid a smile. "Oh, I see."

His broad shoulders shifted. "I'm certain that she could have gotten married long before this if she'd wanted to."

"I don't know. Most men seem to think a woman as lovely as Jane has more admirers than she can sort out, and a lot of pretty women don't even get asked out because of that perception. Actually I don't remember Jane dating anyone seriously. Except Dr. Coltrain, of course."

He was getting tired of hearing about Coltrain. "At her age, she's bound to have had a serious love affair."

"Do you think so?" Micki asked with studied carelessness. "If she has, it's been very discreet. Her reputation is impeccable."

He swung her around to the music. "What do you think of the band?" he asked with a pleasant smile.

She chuckled to herself. "It's nice, isn't it? I do enjoy a good two-step."

Todd was out of sorts by the time he drove Micki home, leaving her at the door with a chaste kiss before he sped back toward the ranch. It had been a pleasant evening, but he hadn't been able to get Jane's hungry kisses out of his mind. Then there was Micki's careless comment that she thought Jane was in love with him. That had set his mind spinning so that he took Micki back long before he normally would have.

When he drove away from her apartment house, it was barely eleven o'clock, and he was damned if he was going home that early. He stopped by a small bar out in the country and had a couple of beers before he drove the rest of the way out. By then it was almost one, and a more respectable hour for a man who'd enjoyed himself to be getting in.

He'd planned to go straight to the little house where he and Cherry were staying, but the lights were still on in the ranch house and he didn't see Tim's car out by the garage.

Frowning, and a little concerned, he went up to the front door and tried it. It was unlocked. Really worried now, he opened it and went in, closing it with a quiet snap and then working his way cautiously past the empty living room and study, down to the bedrooms.

There was light under only one door. He opened it and Jane gaped at him. She was sitting up in bed reading, wearing a low-cut blue satin gown with spaghetti straps. Her hair was loose around her shoulders and the firm, silky slopes of her breasts were bare almost to the nipples in her relaxed pose.

Lamplight became her, he thought helplessly. She was the most beautiful woman he'd ever seen. His whole body clenched at the thought of what lay under that silky fabric.

"Why the hell is the front door unlocked?" he asked shortly.

"It isn't," she faltered. "I locked it and left the lights on in case Meg needed to come in…"

"It wasn't locked. I walked right in. And they haven't come back. Did you check the answering machine?"

She frowned. "No. I took a couple of aspirin because my back was hurting, and then I lay down," she began.

He averted his eyes from her body. "I'll check for any messages." He went out, grateful for something besides the sight of her to occupy his mind. He went to the telephone in the living room and pressed the Play button on the answering machine. Sure enough, Tim had phoned to say that he and Meg would be spending the night with their daughter so that they could go to church with her the next morning. A distant relative was visiting and they wanted to get reacquainted.

He listened dimly as the machine reset itself and beeped. His heart was beating furiously in his chest. Two beers didn't usually affect him, but he hadn't eaten in a while and his head was reeling with the sight of

Jane in that gown and what Micki had said about Jane being in love with him. What if he went into her bedroom and slid that silky gown off her breasts? Would she welcome him? If she loved him…

He muttered a curse and ran a hand through his damp hair. He should get out, right now, before he did something really stupid.

He got as far as the front door. He couldn't force himself to go through it. After a brief struggle with his conscience, he gave in to the pulsating need that was making him ache from head to toe. She could always say no, he told himself. But he knew that she wouldn't. Couldn't. He put on the locks, turned out the outside light and then the living room and study lights.

Jane had put down her book. When he walked back into her bedroom, she was sitting just where he'd left her, looking more vulnerable than ever.

"Did they…call?" she asked, her voice as choked as her body. She, too, was remembering the heated lovemaking of earlier in the evening and hungry for more of it. From the look on his hard face, so was he. She loved him so much that all thoughts of self-preservation had gone right out of her head in the hours since he'd left for his date. She had no pride left. Loneliness and love had eaten it away.

"They won't be home until morning," he said stiffly.

She looked at him with wide, helpless eyes, a little frightened and a little hungry. Everything she felt lay open to his searching eyes.

With a smile that was part self-contempt and part helpless need, he slowly closed and locked the bedroom door. He held her eyes while his hand went to snap off the main switch that controlled the bedside lamps.

The room went dark. She sat, breathing unsteadily, waiting. She saw the outline of him, big and threatening, as he came around the bed and slowly sat down beside her. Then she felt his lean, strong hands, warm on her arms as he slid the straps down and let the gown drop to her waist.

She felt herself shiver. Her breath caught. She felt the air on her body and the need for him was suddenly the most important thing in her life. She arched back with a faint moan, imploring, coaxing.

"I should be shot," he breathed. And then his warm mouth was on her soft, bare breasts, his hands gentle on her body as he eased her down on the bed.

She'd never known a man, but her responses were so acutely hungry that Todd didn't realize it at first. Her headlong acceptance of his deep kisses, of the caresses that grew more intimate as he eased her out of the gown and the faint briefs under it, made him too reckless to notice her shy hands on his chest.

She smelled of flowers and her body was the sweetest kind of warm silk under his mouth. He smoothed his lips over her from head to toe, enjoying her in a silence that trembled with sensation and sensuality.

When he was near the end of his patience, he divested himself of his clothing and drew her gently against the length of him. She caught her breath and tried to pull away, but his mouth on hers stilled the feeble protest.

"Are you using something?" he asked feverishly against her mouth.

"Wh…what?" she managed shakily.

"Are you on the Pill?" he persisted.

"N-no."

He groaned and reached down for his billfold. Thank God he was prepared. He'd never felt the blind need she kindled in his tall, fit body.

His question had almost brought Jane back to sanity as she realized the enormity of what she was doing, but his mouth found hers again, gently, while he did what was necessary. And the tender, passionate kisses and caresses weakened her so that all she felt was an aching emptiness that cried out to be filled.

"I'll be careful, baby," he whispered as he drew her to him, on his side, so that he wouldn't jar or injure her back. His long leg slid between hers and his hands positioned her gently so that he could ease into intimacy with her. "Easy, now."

Her nails bit into his shoulders. She wanted him, but it stung. She buried her mouth against his collarbone and whimpered, but even then she didn't fight.

He wasn't so far gone that he didn't realize what was wrong. He stilled, breathing roughly, his hands like steel clamps on her slender hips. "Jane…?" he whispered, shocked.

She was struggling to breathe. She moaned.

His powerful body shivered with the effort to hold back, even for a space of seconds. "God, baby, I didn't know…!" He groaned harshly. "I have to! Forgive me, I can't stop! I can't!"

He surged against her, blind with a need as old as time, as unstoppable as an avalanche.

There was a fierce flash of pain. She cried out. He heard her in the back of his mind, and hated himself for what was happening, but he was totally at the mercy of the white-hot need in his loins. Tormented seconds later, the painful tension in his body snapped and blinding, furious pleasure lifted him to heights he'd never known in his life. Then, he fell again to cold reality and felt the guilt and anguish of the trembling body containing his.

He kissed away the tears, his hands as gentle now as they had been demanding only minutes before. "Forgive me," he whispered piteously. "Oh, Lord, I'm sorry! It was too late by the time I realized."

She lay her cheek against his cool, damp chest and closed her wet eyes. It had been painful and uncomfortable, and now her back was hurting again.

"You're twenty-five years old," he groaned, smoothing her hair. "What were you doing, saving it for marriage?"

"That isn't funny." She choked.

He drew in a sharp breath. "I suppose you were. You're so damned traditional."

She bit her lower lip. "Will you leave, please?"

He kissed her closed eyes. "No. Not until I give you what I had."

"I won't let you do that again!" she said hotly, hitting at him. "It hurt!"

His lips brushed against hers. He drew her hand to his mouth and kissed it, too. "The first time usually does, or so I'm told," he said gently. "But I can give you tenderness now."

"I don't want…!"

His mouth covered hers softly, slowly. He coaxed it

to open to the lazy thrust of his tongue. His hands slid over her tense body, soothing her even as they began to incite her to passion. She didn't understand how it could happen. He'd hurt her. But she was moving closer to him. Her arms were lifting to enclose him. Her breasts were swelling under his hands and then his mouth, and she felt a tension building inside her that made her legs start to tremble.

He was gentle. He lay on his back and smoothed her body completely over him, deftly joining their bodies while he whispered soft, tender commands at her ear. His steely hands on her hips pulled and pushed and shifted her, so that she felt the fullness of him inside her building into an ache that blinded her with its promise.

She sobbed helplessly, clinging to him. "Oh…no," she whispered breathlessly as she felt her senses begin to climb some unbelievable peak.

"Don't fight it," he whispered at her temple. His voice was soft, but his breathing was quick and sharp, like the tug of his hard fingers and the thrust of his hips.

She whimpered as the pleasure caught her unaware and she stiffened on his body.

"Yes, that's it," he whispered feverishly. "That's it! Give in to me. Give in, Jane, give in! Let it happen!"

She heard her voice rising in sharp little cries as he increased the rhythm. Then, all at once, she went over an edge she hadn't expected, into realms of hot, black pleasure that took control of her body away from her brain and made her oblivious to everything except the hard heat of him filling her.

She pushed down as hard as she could and shuddered

endlessly, frozen in pleasure, deaf and blind to the joyous laughter of the man holding her. Only when she was completely satisfied did he allow himself the exquisite pleasure of release.

He smoothed her long, damp hair over her spine and lay dreaming of the ecstasy he'd shared with her for a long time, until her faint weeping ceased and she lay still, trembling a little, on his spent body.

Her breasts were as soft as down. He shifted a little, so that he could feel them rubbing against his chest. His hands slid down to her hips, where they were still joined, and he pressed her closer into him.

She gasped. The touch of him was unbearably pleasurable, even now.

He mistook the gasp. "It's all right," he said gently. "You were protected, both times. I don't take that sort of risk, ever."

She was too embarrassed to know what to say. Her fingers clenched against him and she lay still, uncertain and hesitant in the aftermath.

He stretched stiffly and laughed. "But it was a near thing, I'll tell you that," he confessed. "Is your back all right?"

She bit her lip. "Yes."

He eased her onto her side and pulled away. Her teeth went deeper into her lip as reality fell on her like a cold brick.

He felt on the floor for her gown and briefs and laid them on her breasts. He bent and kissed her tenderly. "You'd better get your things back on," he whispered. "It's chilly."

She fumbled into them, listening to the rustle of fabric as he dressed by the side of the bed. She felt tears sting her eyes and hated herself for the one lapse of a lifetime. She hadn't even had the presence of mind to protect herself. Thank God he'd thought of it. And now there was the future to think of. How could she ever face him again, after this? He'd know how she felt about him. But whatever he felt was well concealed. He hadn't said a word while he was making love to her, except for soft commands and endearments. But there hadn't been one confession of love.

While she was worrying, he tucked her under the sheet and pushed her hair away from her face. "Sleep well," he said, trying not to betray how awkward he felt. Her cheek was wet. Did she hate him? Was she sorry? She'd tried to stop him, but he couldn't stop. Did she understand? Then, afterward, he'd wanted to make amends in the only way possible. He knew he'd given her pleasure, but would it be enough to make up for what he'd taken?

She turned her face away with a faint sigh and he left her. There would be time enough in the morning for talking, for explanations and apologies.

Jane was stiff and sore when she woke up. She opened her eyes and blinked from the brightness, and then she remembered. She sat up in bed, flushing with memories that made her feel hot all over.

She moved the top sheet away and grimaced at the betraying faint stains on the bottom one. She got out of bed and stripped away the sheet, throwing it on the floor, and her gown and briefs along with it. She went into the bathroom and showered herself from head to toe before she dressed in jeans and a round-neck yellow T-shirt and sneakers. Then she bundled up the laundry and put it into the washing machine, starting the load before Meg came in.

"Hey, that's my job," Meg complained gaily when she got home and found the drier running and another load of clothes going through the spin cycle in the washer.

"I didn't have anything to do," Jane said with a poker face and a smile. "Everyone's gone for the weekend except Todd. He was late getting in last night. He took Micki Lane to a dance."

"She's pretty," Meg said, frowning. "I thought maybe you liked him."

She shrugged. "He's very nice. I think he's a great accountant."

Nice. Meg sighed mentally at her dashed dreams of a romance between the two of them, and shooed her charge out of the kitchen while she saw to lunch.

But when Meg put it on the table, Todd still hadn't come to the house. Jane had been dreading it since dawn, uncertain of how she was going to face him. She was ashamed and embarrassed and a little afraid of having him taunt her with her helplessness.

"Where's Todd?" Meg asked when she had the salad and bread on the table.

"I don't know. I haven't seen him today," Jane said.

"It isn't like him to miss lunch." She went to the window and looked out. "His car's gone."

"Maybe he had a date with Micki today," Jane ventured, not looking up.

"Wouldn't he have said?"

Jane smiled. "He doesn't have to report to us."

"I guess not. Well, I'll call Tim and we'll eat."

It was a brief, pleasant lunch. Meg talked about their daughter and the distant cousin who'd come to visit. And if Jane was unusually silent, it went unremarked if not unnoticed.

Just before dark, Todd drove up with Cherry. Obviously, Jane thought, he'd gone up to Victoria to get her even though she'd said she was going to take the bus. Perhaps he was as uncomfortable as Jane now, only wanting to forget what had happened and needful of putting some space between them.

She was sitting on the sofa watching the news when they came in.

"How was your weekend?" Jane asked Cherry.

"Not very pleasant," Cherry said, without saying why. She smiled at Jane. "You look pale. Are you okay?"

She had to fight not to look at Todd. "I'm fine. I've had a lazy day."

"I need to check some figures. I'll take the books back over to the house with me, if you don't mind," he said, addressing Jane for the first time, his tone formal and remote.

"Of course," she said to his chin and even smiled. "Have you both eaten?"

"We had supper on the way," Todd said shortly. He went to get the books and came back with them tucked under one arm. "Say good-night, Cherry."

"Good night," the girl said obediently, aware of a new tension between the two adults in her life. She was too sensitive to mention it, though. And anyway, her dad had been quiet and unapproachable. Probably, she thought sadly, there had been another argument. It saddened her that her father and her new friend couldn't get along.

Jane called good-night and went back to her television program. She hadn't looked directly at Todd, or he at her. She wondered if things would ever be the same again.

The builders worked diligently at the repairs and finished right on schedule. Inspecting the new barn, Jane was amazed at their progress. It was a good job, too, not a slipshod effort.

The next step was to buy brood mares. Jane and Cherry went with Todd to an auction at a well-known horse ranch outside Corpus Christi. Todd and Jane looked at the catalog, not at each other, and Cherry enthused over each horse as it was led into the rink.

Jane had an excellent eye for horseflesh. Before her father's death, even he had deferred to her on buying trips. Todd quickly realized her ability, and he followed her father's example. They bought three good brood mares and a colt with excellent bloodlines. Todd arranged for them to be transported to the ranch and rejoined Cherry and Jane.

"Can we stop and get an ice cream on the way back?" Cherry asked, wiping away sweat. "It's awfully hot!"

"If Jane isn't too tired," he said stiffly.

"I'm fine," she said carelessly, putting an affectionate arm around Cherry. She was walking without her crutches now, although not as quickly as before. Two or three times, she'd had to fight the impulse to get on her horse and ride like the wind. Perhaps that was a realizable dream, but not just yet.

"Then we'll stop down the road a bit," Todd replied.

There was a small ice cream shop in a stand of mesquite trees, just off the main road. Although it was a bit isolated, there were plenty of cars surrounding it, and the small picnic area was full.

"We can sit under the trees," Cherry said. "Jane and I will grab the seats while you get the ice cream, Dad. I want a chocolate shake."

His head turned and he looked at Jane. "What would you like?" he asked politely.

"I'll have the same, thanks," she said, avoiding his eyes. She turned and walked away with Cherry.

Todd watched her hungrily. He'd handled the whole situation badly, and now he didn't know what to do. His conscience had tortured him over the past few days. He didn't sleep at night for it. He hadn't exactly forced her to do something she didn't want to, but she'd wanted him to stop and he couldn't. He'd taken away her right to give her chastity to a man she married. She might have loved him once, but he no longer thought she cared at all. She wouldn't look at him. If he came into a room, she found an excuse to leave it. She was subdued and withdrawn except when Cherry was around. And it was his fault. If only he hadn't touched her in the first place.

The man asked him again for his order and he snapped back to the present long enough to give it. He took the paper tray of milkshakes when the man came back and paid for them.

Minutes later, the three of them were sitting under the tree with the breeze playing in Jane's hair, sipping the cold, refreshing shakes.

"Don't you love chocolate?" Cherry said enthusiastically.

Jane smiled at her. "Yes, but it doesn't love me. Sometimes it gives me migraines."

"Why the hell didn't you say so?" Todd demanded angrily.

She glanced at him, startled by the venom in his tone. "I love chocolate."

"Which is no reason to deliberately bring on a headache."

She glared back at him. "I'll eat what I like. You're not my keeper!"

"Uh, what do you think of the colt, Jane?" Cherry interrupted quickly.

"What?" She was staring into Todd's furious eyes and he was staring back. The anger slowly began to fade, to be replaced by something equally violent, simmering, smoldering hot.

Cherry hid a smile. "I'll get some more napkins," she said.

Neither of them seemed to notice her leaving. Jane's face was getting redder by the second, and Todd's eyes narrowed until they were gray slits, full of heat and possession.

His hand reached out and caught hers hungrily. "Shall we stop pretending that nothing happened?" he asked roughly.

Chapter Seven

Jane felt his fingers contracting, intimately interlacing themselves with her own. She couldn't quite breathe normally, and her eyes were giving her feelings away.

"We've been dancing around it for days," he said huskily. He held her eyes searchingly. "I still want you," he added heavily. "More than ever."

She tore her gaze from his and looked down at their hands. "It shouldn't have happened."

"I know," he said surprisingly. "But it did. I've never had it that good, Jane. I think you and I could have a very satisfying relationship."

She looked up, but that wasn't love in his eyes. It was hunger, certainly. But it was an empty hunger. "You mean, we could have an affair," she said quietly.

He nodded, dashing her faint hopes of something more. "I've tried marriage," he said bitterly. "I don't believe in it anymore. But you can't deny that we go up like fireworks when we're together. There won't be any consequences, any repercussions."

"What about Cherry?" she asked stiffly.

"Cherry's fourteen," he replied. "She knows that I'm no monk. She doesn't expect fairy-tale endings."

Her sad eyes searched his. "Doesn't she? I'm afraid that I do." She withdrew her hands from his.

His eyebrows arched. "You aren't serious, surely? You don't expect to marry a man and stay married for life, do you?" he added with a mocking laugh.

"Yes, I do, despite what…what happened the other night," she replied, her chin lifted proudly. "I'll be honest with him about it. But I do believe in love and I think people can stay together if they have common interests and they're willing to work at it."

He sat up straight, his mouth tightened into a thin line. "You don't think Marie and I worked at it?" he asked in a dangerously soft voice.

"It takes two people, committed…"

"Committed is the right word," he said on a harsh laugh. "People who get married should be committed!"

She saw then that his mind was closed on the subject, and all her hopes fell away. She smiled sadly. "I'm sorry. I don't have a bad marriage behind me, and I still believe in fairy tales. I don't want to have an affair with you, Todd."

His eyes glittered narrowly. "You loved what I did to you."

She shrugged, although it took her last bit of courage, and she smiled. "Sure I did. It was wonderful. Thanks."

He looked positively outraged. His high cheekbones flushed angrily and he opened his mouth to speak as Cherry came back with a handful of napkins.

"Here you go," she said, putting them down. "Isn't it nice here in the shade?"

Todd bit off what he was going to say. He finished his milkshake and got up. "We'd better get back," he said curtly. "I've got a lot of paperwork to catch up."

"But, Dad…" Cherry protested. She grimaced at the look he shot her. "Okay, okay, sorry!" She finished her milkshake with a wistful smile at Jane, and they all went back to the car.

The next few days were strained. Jane watched Cherry work with Feather and she conferred with Micki Lane about the plans for the advertising campaign.

"We'll need some publicity shots," Micki told her. "When can you come up to Victoria to do them?"

Jane picked a day and Micki offered to come and get her. "No, thanks," Jane said, "I'll have one of the hands run me up." She couldn't bear to see Micki with Todd.

"Oh. Well, okay," Micki said sadly. "How's Todd? I haven't heard from him lately."

"He's fine. Working hard, of course," she added matter-of-factly. "They're just finished putting up our new barn and he's been working closely with the contractor."

"I see," Micki said. She sounded happier. "I guess it takes up a lot of time, hmm?"

"A lot." More than he gave any other project, she thought, and probably it was just an excuse to keep out of Jane's way. Even Cherry was complaining about the fervor with which her father had approached the barn building and repairs.

"Then I'll see you Friday, yes?" Micki asked.

"Friday at nine," Jane agreed.

She didn't mention her trip to Todd or Cherry. She could ask Tim to drive her up, she was sure.

Meanwhile, she had to go to Dr. Coltrain for her checkup. He tested her reflexes, listened to her heart and lungs, checked her blood pressure and asked a dozen questions before he pronounced her blooming.

"Except for those bags under your eyes," he added, his piercing blue eyes on her drawn face. "Burke getting you down?"

She glared at him. "Todd Burke is none of your business."

He grinned at her. "I'm not blind, even if you are."

"What do you mean?"

"Oh, you'll find out one day." He leaned back in his chair and swiveled around. "Don't take it too fast, but I think you could start walking more."

"How about riding?"

He hesitated. "Slowly," he said. "For brief periods, and not on any of your usual mounts. That palomino gelding is gentle enough, I suppose. But don't overdo it."

"Bracket is gentle," she assured him. "He'd never toss me."

"Any horse will toss you under the right circumstances, and you know it."

She'd forgotten that he practically grew up on horseback. He rode as well as she did—better. He'd done some rodeo to help put himself through medical school.

"I'll be careful," she promised him.

"What's this I hear about you selling clothes?" he asked suddenly.

She grinned. "Meg told your mother, didn't she?" she

asked. "I thought she would. I'm going to endorse a line of women's Western wear. It's very well made and I'll be on television and in magazines promoting it. In fact," she added, "I'm going up to Victoria on Friday to do the publicity photos for the magazines."

"How are you going to get there?"

"I thought I'd ask Tim…"

"Ask me," he said with a slash of a grin. "I'm driving up to confer on a leukemia case at the hospital there. The patient is one of mine who moved away. You can ride with me."

"I may be there all day," she warned.

He shrugged. "I'll find something to keep me busy."

She smiled broadly. "Then I'd love to. Thanks."

"I'll pick you up at the ranch about eight-thirty. We can stop for coffee on the way."

"Okay. I'll look forward to it."

"How did you get here?"

"Meg dropped me off on her way to the grocery store. She'll be waiting in the parking lot. She only had a few things to get."

"Why didn't Burke bring you?" he asked.

She flushed. "Because I didn't ask him to!"

He pursed his lips. "I see."

She stood up. "No, you don't. Thanks for the ride. I'll see you in the morning."

"Jane."

She paused at the doorway, turning to meet his level gaze. "Do you need to ask me anything?"

She went scarlet, because she knew exactly what he meant. "No," she whispered huskily, "I do not!"

"Okay. No need to color up," he said gently, and smiled with affection. "But I'm here if you need me, and I'm not judgmental."

She drew in a slow breath. "Oh, Copper, I know that," she said miserably. "I wish…" she said huskily.

"No, you don't," he mused, smiling. "I had a case on you a few years ago, but our time passed. A blind man could see how you feel about Burke. Just be careful, will you? You're as green as spring grass, and that man knows his way around women."

"I'll be careful," she replied. "It's good to have a friend like you."

"That works both ways," he said.

There was a perfunctory knock on the door and Lou Blakely looked in. "Excuse me," she said with a glance at Jane, "Mr. Harris won't talk to me about his hemor-rhoids. Could you…?"

"I'll be with you in a minute," he said shortly.

She closed the door quickly.

"You're very rude to her, aren't you?" Jane remarked quietly. "She's a sweet woman. It hurts her when you snap, haven't you noticed?"

"Oh, yes," he said, and for a minute he didn't look like the man she knew. "I've noticed."

She let it drop, saying goodbye and pausing only to pay the receptionist before she went out to find Meg. Copper had been the kindest of boys when they were young, even though he was five years her senior. But he was different with Lou. He seemed to dislike her. Odd that he'd accepted her into his practice if he found her so irritating.

Meg drove Jane back to the ranch. She found Cherry waiting on the porch for her, beaming.

"I did it!" she told Jane excitedly. "I beat my old time! I wasn't even afraid! Oh, Jane, I've done it, I've overcome the fear! I can hardly wait for the next rodeo."

"I'm happy for you," Jane said with soft affection. "You're a great little rider. You're going to go far."

"I'll settle for being half as good as you," she said with worshiping eyes.

Jane laughed. "That won't be hard these days."

"Don't be silly. You'll always be Jane Parker. You've made your mark in rodeo already. You're famous! And you're going to be even more famous when you make those commercials."

"Well, we'll see. I'm not counting my chickens before they hatch!"

The photo session was the main topic of conversation at supper.

"I'll run you up to Victoria in the morning," Tim volunteered. "Or Todd might, if he can spare the time from that barn," he added, teasing the younger man, who was taciturn over his chicken and mashed potatoes and beans.

Todd looked up at Jane without any emotion. "If she wants me to, I don't mind," he said.

"Thank you both, but I have a ride," Jane said. She smiled. "Copper's got to go up there on a case, so he said I could go with him."

Todd didn't say a word, but the hand holding his fork stiffened. "The good doctor gets around, doesn't he?" he asked.

"Yes, he does. He's quite well-known in these parts. He graduated in the top ten percent of his class," she added. "He's very intelligent."

Todd, who'd never had the advantage of a college education, was touchy about it. He'd made millions and he was well-known in business circles, but there were still times when he felt uncomfortable around more educated businessmen.

"Dad's smart, too," Cherry said, as if she sensed her father's discomfort. "Even if he isn't a doctor, he's made lots of—"

"Cherry," her father said, cutting off the rest of her sentence.

"He's made lots of friends," Cherry amended, grinning cheekily at her parent. "And he's very handsome."

Jane wouldn't have touched that line with a pole. She finished her chicken and reached for her glass of milk.

"The chicken was great, Meg," she commented.

"It's nice to see everyone hungry again," Meg muttered. "I get tired of cooking for myself and Tim and Cherry."

"I guess the pain takes away your appetite sometimes, doesn't it, Jane?" Cherry asked innocently.

"Sometimes," she agreed, and couldn't look at Todd.

He tilted his coffee cup and drained it. "I'd better get back on the books."

"A couple of faxes came in for you today," Meg remarked. "One's from someone named Julia," she added with a twinkle in her eyes.

"Who's Julia?" Cherry asked, then her eyebrows lifted. "Oh. *Julia!*"

Her father's glance silenced her.

"I guess she's missing you, huh?" Cherry asked, grinning secretively.

"I don't doubt it," Todd agreed, thinking of the thousand and one daily headaches that Julia Emory was intercepting on his behalf while he lazed around in Jacobsville working for Jane. He put down his napkin. "I'd better get in touch with her. I'll, uh, reverse the charges," he assured Jane. "I wouldn't want to impose on my position here."

Jane only nodded. So he had other women. It shouldn't have come as a surprise. He was very handsome and fit, and she knew now why any woman would find him irresistible in bed. She flushed at her intimate memories of him and covered it by taking a large swallow of milk.

When Todd was gone, the conversation became more spontaneous and relaxed, but the room seemed empty.

"Did you ever think about marrying Dr. Coltrain?" Cherry asked Jane when Tim left and Meg started clearing away the supper things.

"Well, yes, I did, once," Jane confessed. "He's very attractive and we have a lot in common. But I never felt, well, the sort of attraction I'd need to feel to marry a man."

"You didn't want him in bed, in other words," Cherry said matter-of-factly.

"Cherry!"

"I don't live in a glass bottle," the young girl said. "I hear things at school and Dad's amazingly open about what I can watch on television. But I don't want to jump into any sort of intimacy at my age," she added, sounding very mature. "It's dangerous, you know. Besides, I have this romantic idea that it would be lovely to wait for marriage. Jane, did you know that some boys even feel that way?" she added with a giggle. "There's Mark, who goes to school with me, and he's very conservative. He says he'd rather wait and only do it with the girl he marries, so that they don't ever have to worry about STDs."

"About what?"

"Sexually transmitted diseases," she said. "Honestly, Jane, don't you watch television?"

Jane cleared her throat. "Well, obviously I haven't been watching the right programs, have I?"

"I'll have to educate you," the girl said firmly. "Didn't your parents tell you anything?"

"Sure, but since I never liked a boy enough…" She hesitated, thinking about how it had been with Todd, and her face colored.

"Oh, I see. Not even Dr. Coltrain?" she asked.

Jane shook her head.

"That's really sad."

"I'll find someone, one of these days," Jane assured her, and looked up, right into Todd's quiet, interested eyes.

"Hi, Dad! I've been explaining sex to Jane." She shook her head as she got up. "Boy, and I thought I was backward! See you later, Jane, I'm going to saddle up Feather!"

She ran out the door, leaving Todd alone with Jane, because Meg was in the kitchen rattling dishes as she loaded the dishwasher.

"Do you need a fourteen-year-old to explain sex to you?" he asked quietly. "I thought you learned all you needed to know from me."

She bit her lower lip. "Don't."

He moved closer, a sheaf of papers in one lean hand, and stood beside her chair. "Why deny us both the kind of pleasure we shared?" he asked. "You want me. I want you. What's wrong with it?"

She looked up into his eyes. "I want more than a physical relationship," she said.

He reached down and touched her cheek lightly. "Are you certain?" he said softly.

She grimaced and tried to look away, but he caught her chin and held her flushed face up to his eyes.

"So beautiful," he murmured. "And so naive. You want the moon, Jane. I can't give it to you. But I can give you pleasure so stark that you bite me and cry out with it."

She put her fingers against his hard mouth. "You mustn't!" she whispered frantically, looking toward the kitchen.

He caught her wrist and pulled her gently up out of the chair and against him, so that they were touching all the way up and down. "Meg wouldn't be embarrassed if she saw us kissing. No one would, except you." His hand tightened, steely around her fingers as he used his grip to force her even closer. Something untamed touched his face, glittered in his eyes as he looked down at her. His mouth hovered just above her lips. "You can deny it all you like, but when I hold out my arms, you'll walk into them. If I offer you my mouth, you'll take it.

You're a puppet on a string, baby," he whispered seductively, letting the word arouse explosive memories in her mind.

She meant to protest. She wanted to. It was just that his hard mouth was so close. She could feel its warmth, taste the minty scent of it on her parted lips. Of course she wanted to deny what he was saying. What *was* he saying?

He bent a fraction of an inch closer. "It's all right," he whispered, moving his hips lazily against her, so that she trembled with kindling fevers. "Take what you want," he challenged.

She was sure that she hated him. The arrogant swine...

But all she wanted to do was kiss him, and it was a shame to waste the opportunity. It was so easy to reach up to him, to pull his hard mouth onto hers and feel its warm, slow pressure. It was so sweet to press her slender body into his and feel his swift, unashamed arousal.

He wasn't even holding her. His free hand was in her hair, savoring its silky length while she kissed him hungrily, passionately. He tasted of coffee and he smelled of spicy cologne. He was clean and hard and warm and she loved the feel of his powerful body against hers. Her legs began to tremble from the contact and she wondered if they were going to support her for much longer.

It was a moot point. Her nearness was as potent to him as his was to her. Seconds later, he put the papers on the table and wrapped her up in his arms, so that not a breath separated them. His mouth opened, taking hers with it, and his tongue pushed deep inside her mouth in a slow, aching parody of what his body had done to hers that long night together.

She moaned with the onslaught of the pleasure, trembling in his arms as the kiss went on and on.

His hands slid up and down her sides until they eased between and his thumbs worked lazy circles around her taut breasts. He remembered the taste of them in his mouth, the warm envelope of her body encircling him in the darkness. One hand went to her hips and gathered her against him roughly, and she cried out at the stab of discomfort in her hip.

The sound shocked him into lifting his head. His eyes were blank with aroused ardor, but all at once they focused on her drawn face.

"Did I hurt your back?" he asked huskily.

"A little," she whispered.

"I'm sorry." He brushed the hair away from her face. "I'm sorry, baby. I wouldn't hurt you for all the world, don't you know that?"

"You did…" she blurted.

His eyes glittered. "Yes. God, yes!" He actually shivered. "I didn't know until I'd torn you, there…" His eyes closed and he shivered again with the memory. "I thought I might die of the pleasure, and the shame, because you asked me to stop and I couldn't." His mouth smoothed softly over hers. "You don't know what it's like, do you, to want someone past reason, past honor? I wanted you like that. I would have killed to have you, in those few blind seconds that robbed me of reason. I was ashamed, Jane," he breathed into her mouth, "but I was too excited to pull away. I'm sorry."

She closed her eyes, drinking in the feel of him. "It's all right. Afterward—" she hesitated, and her body clenched at the memory of afterward "—I...I think I understood."

His mouth was hot on her eyelids, her cheeks, her chin. "I thought you were never going to stop convulsing," he whispered. "I remember laughing with the pure joy of it, knowing that I'd given you so much pleasure."

"So that was why...!"

"Yes." His hands framed her face and he looked deep into her eyes. "Come to bed with me tonight. I'll give you that pleasure again, and again. I'll make love to you until you fall asleep in my arms."

She wanted to. Her eyes told him that she wanted to. But despite the pleasure she remembered, she also remembered his easy rejection of her when his passion was spent. He'd left her as soon as he was finished, with no tenderness, no explanations, no apologies. He wanted her now, desperately. But when he was satisfied, it would be the same as it had been before, because he only wanted her. He didn't love her. He was offering her an empty heart.

She closed her eyes against the terrible temptation he offered. That way lay self-destruction, no matter how much temporary relief he gave her.

"No," she said finally. "No, Todd. It isn't enough."

He scowled. She was trembling against him. Her mouth was swollen and still hungry for his, her arms still held him.

"You don't mean that," he accused gently.

She opened her eyes and looked up at him. "Yes, I

do," she said quietly. She pulled away from him, slowly, and stepped back. "You're handsome and sexy, and I love kissing you. But it's a dead end."

"You want promises," he said shortly.

"Oh, no," she corrected. "Promises are just words. I want years of togetherness and children." Her face softened as she thought of a little girl like Cherry, or perhaps a baby boy. "Lots of children."

His face went rigid. "I have a child."

She searched his eyes. "Yes, I know. She's a wonderful girl. But I want one of my own, and a husband to go with them."

He was seething with unsatisfied passion and anger. "Wouldn't it be a great world if we all got exactly what we wanted?"

"It certainly would." She moved away from him, concentrating on each breath. She held on to the back of her chair. "And maybe I never will. But my dreams are sweet," she added, lifting her eyes. "Much sweeter than a few weeks of lust that end with you walking right out of my life."

His face went even harder. "Lust?"

"Without love, that's all sex is."

"You little hypocrite," he accused flatly, and reached for her. He was kissing her blindly, ardently, when the door opened and a shocked Cherry stopped dead in the doorway.

Chapter Eight

Todd lifted his head, freezing in place, while Jane gently pushed away from him, red-faced.

"Sorry," Cherry murmured, and then grinned. "I was looking for Meg. Don't let me interrupt anything."

She darted past them into the kitchen and closed the door pointedly.

"I'm sorry," Todd said curtly, pushing his hair off his forehead. "That was a stupid thing to do."

Jane didn't know what stupid thing he meant, so she didn't reply. She moved away from him and sat down, her back aching from the unfamiliar exercise. He hesitated for a few seconds, but he couldn't think of a single defense for his uncharacteristic behavior.

"Excuse me," he said, picking up the papers from the table. "I'd better get to work."

He left her sitting there, and he didn't look back on the way out. Cherry came in a few minutes later, and grimaced when she saw that Jane was alone.

"I didn't mean to burst in," Cherry told her. "I didn't expect… Gosh, I never saw Dad kiss anyone like that! Not even my mother, when I was little!"

Jane flushed. "It was just a…mistake," she faltered.

"Some mistake. Wow!" She chuckled. Her whole face lit up. "Do you like him?"

"Don't start building dreams on me and your father," Jane said somberly. "There's no future in it. He doesn't want marriage and I don't want anything else," she added flatly.

Cherry's face fell. "Oh."

"You're still my friend, Cherry," she said with a smile. "Okay?"

Cherry's mouth curled down but after a minute she smiled back. "Okay."

Jane went up to Victoria with Copper and spent most of the day posing in various articles of SlimTogs for the photographer. He was nice, and very helpful, and considerate of Jane's back problem. It was worse today because of Todd's ardor the night before, but Jane wasn't about to mention that to anybody. It was only a twinge, anyway.

"That should wrap it up," Micki said a few minutes later, after she'd talked to the photographer. "Jack said that he got some great shots. We'll make our selection for the layout and then we'll be in touch with you. There may be a couple of promotional appearances, by the way, at a rodeo and maybe for the opening of one of our new stores. We'll let you know."

"It was fun," Jane said. "I enjoyed it. And I really do like the clothes."

"We like you," Micki said with a nice smile. "You're a good sport. Uh, Todd didn't come up with you, did he?"

She shook her head. "He's still up to his neck with projects on the ranch. My own men answer to him, now, not to me. I'm going to have a hard time getting control back when he leaves."

"Is he leaving?"

"Not anytime soon, I don't think," Jane replied. She hated Micki's probing questions, but she couldn't afford to say so and reveal her own feelings for the man.

"He's very attractive," Micki said, her smile wistful and a little sad. "I guess he's got plenty of girlfriends."

"I don't doubt it," Jane replied. "They even fax him letters," she said absently.

Micki chuckled. "Well, that lets me out of the running, I suppose. You're not sweet on him yourself, are you?" she added curiously.

"I'd have to get in line," Jane said. "And I'd be a long way back."

"Just our luck, isn't it? A dreamy man like that doesn't come along every day, but there's always a woman in possession, I guess." She shook her head. "I think I'm destined to be an old maid."

"Marriage isn't everything," Jane said. "You might become the head of your corporation."

"Anything's possible. But I have a secret, sinful hunger for dirty dishes and ironing a man's shirts and having babies. Shameful, isn't it? Don't tell anyone."

"You closet housewife, you!"

Micki chuckled. "I love what I do, and I make a lot of money. I can't complain. It's just that once in a while I don't want to live alone."

"Who does?" Jane asked. "But sometimes we don't have a choice."

"So they say. I'll be in touch soon, okay? Have a nice trip home."

"Thanks."

Jane went downstairs and phoned the hospital. Copper drove over to pick her up. But instead of heading home, he took her to Victoria's nicest restaurant for supper.

"But I'm not dressed properly," she protested, gesturing toward her chambray blouse and matching long skirt.

"Neither am I." He was wearing a sport jacket and a knit shirt with his slacks. "They can stare if they like. Can't they?"

She laughed. "All right, then. I'd be delighted to have dinner with you, if you don't mind the casual clothes."

"I never minded."

He took her inside the swanky restaurant, where he ordered her meal—lobster and steak and salad, topped off with an ice-cream-covered brownie.

"I'll have sweet dreams about that dessert for years," she murmured on the way home.

"So will I."

She turned her head toward him. He was single-minded when he drove. Probably he was like that when he operated, too. He specialized in diseases of the lung, and he was a surgeon of some note. He occasionally was called in to operate in the big city hospitals. But in recent years, he stayed close to home. He was mysterious in many ways. An enigma.

"Do you want children?" she asked suddenly.

He chuckled. "Sure. Are you offering?"

She flushed. "Don't be silly."

He glanced at her. "Say the word. I'm willing if you are. I like kids and I wouldn't balk at marriage. We've got more in common than a lot of people."

"Yes, we have. But there's just one thing missing."

He smiled ruefully. "And I know what it is."

"Two out of three isn't bad."

"No," he agreed. "But I couldn't live with a woman who suffered me in bed, Jane. That would be impossible."

"I know." She reached across the seat and slid her hand into his where it rested on the gearshift. "I'm sorry. I wish I felt that way."

His fingers contracted. "You do. But with Burke, not me."

She didn't deny it. She leaned her head against the headrest. "He wants to have a blazing affair and then go back to Victoria."

"What do you want?"

"Marriage. Children. Forever after."

"He might want those things, too, after he got used to you."

"He might get tired of me."

"Life doesn't come with guarantees," he said gently. He glanced at her drawn, unhappy face. "You have a history of migraine. I wouldn't dare prescribe birth control pills for you, because of that. But there are other tried-and-true methods."

"Copper!"

He held on to her hand. "Grow up. We don't always get the brass ring. That doesn't mean we can't get some pleasure out of the ride. At least you'd have some sweet memories."

"I'm surprised at you," she said.

He glanced at her. "No, you're not. And I'm not surprised or disappointed in you for being human. Sex is a natural, beautiful part of life. It's very rare that two people love each other enough to experience its heights. Burke may not want to marry you, honey, but he loves you."

"What!"

"I think you know it, too, deep down. He's pretty readable to another man. He was jealous of me the first time he saw me."

"That could be sexual jealousy."

"It could have been. But it wasn't. He's too protective of you." He patted her hand gently. "He had a bad marriage, didn't he, and he's probably afraid to take another chance. But if he cares enough, eventually he'll give in. Isn't it worth fighting for?"

"Fighting for." She grimaced. "I can't. I just can't. That…belongs in marriage."

"I couldn't agree more. It does. But, then, from my point of view, marriage is just a matter of time. He loves you. You love him. And he strikes me as a pretty conventional fellow. He has a daughter to think of, too."

"He says he'll never marry again."

"The president said he wouldn't raise taxes."

She looked at him and burst out laughing. "Don't compromise your principles," he advised. "But you can keep him interested without tearing your clothes off for him."

"I suppose so."

"Now, tell me about this ad promotion."

She did, glad to talk about some subject less complicated than Todd Burke.

When they got home it was well after dark and Todd was in the house with Meg, pacing the floor.

He went out to meet Jane as she came up the steps, having thanked Copper and waved goodbye.

"Where have you been?" he demanded.

She lifted both eyebrows. "Having lobster and steak."

"And then?" he challenged angrily.

"And then," she whispered, leaning close, "we got into the back seat and made love so violently that all four tires went flat!"

He stared at her long and hard and then suddenly laughed. "Damn you!"

She went close to him, putting both hands against his shirtfront. "I couldn't make love with anyone except you," she said, living up to her new resolve to tell him nothing but the truth, always. "I love you."

His heart ran away. She was the very picture of femininity, and the sight of her long hair made him ache to feel it against his bare chest, as he had the night they loved each other. He gathered up a handful of it and drew it to his cheek.

"I love you, too," he said unexpectedly. His breath sighed out at her temple while she stood still against him, unbelieving. "I loved you the night I took you." He kissed her eyelids closed. "People can't satisfy each other that completely unless they love, didn't you know?"

"No," she whispered, stunned by the revelation.

His mouth moved gently down to her soft lips and

traced them. "Won't you change your mind?" he asked huskily.

Her hands clenched on his shirtfront. "Copper won't give me the Pill because I have a history of migraines," she said bluntly.

His body froze in position. "You talked to that cowboy doctor about the Pill?"

"No, he talked to me about it! He knows that I love you."

He didn't know how to take it. For a moment, anger overshadowed what she was saying. And then, all at once, understanding pushed its way into his mind.

He moved back, frowning. "You can't take the Pill?"

"That's right. So the risk of a child would always be there. I couldn't...do anything about it, if I got pregnant," she added firmly. "And since I feel so strongly about it, I don't want to take any more chances with you. I didn't...that is, nothing happened last time."

"I took precautions," he said stiffly.

"Yes, I know. But accidents happen."

His hands stilled on her shoulders. He was quiet, thoughtful. A child with Jane would be a disaster. He couldn't walk away from a child. He could picture a little girl with long blond hair and big blue eyes in a taffeta dress. He could take her to birthday parties, as he'd taken Cherry when she was little. Or there might be a little boy, whom he and Jane could teach to ride. A son.

"You're very quiet," she remarked.

"Yes."

"I'm sorry," she said, lifting her eyes to his. "But it's

better not to start things we can't finish. And I'd be the last person in the world who'd want to trap you."

He searched her sad eyes. His fingers touched her lower lip, testing its softness. "Marie didn't want to make a baby with me," he said roughly. "We were both drunk and I knew she was on the Pill. But she'd forgotten to take it a few times. That's the only reason Cherry was conceived."

"For heaven's sake!"

"Are you shocked?" he asked lazily. "Jane, she didn't want a child. Some people don't."

"Yes, I know, but now she loves Cherry."

"So do I. With all my heart. And the day she was born, when they put her into my arms, I cried like a boy. It was unbelievable to have a child of my own."

The awe and wonder of the experience touched his eyes just briefly, before he banished it. He looked down at Jane and his hands cradled her hips. "Even if I were…willing—which I'm not," he added curtly, "you won't be able to carry a child, not for a long time." He grimaced. "And as you say, the risk would always be there, if you couldn't take the Pill. But you were willing to take any risk with me that night," he reminded her.

"Yes, but it didn't happen," she said curtly. "Nothing happened afterward!"

Her tone startled him. She sounded disappointed.

He didn't speak for a minute. His eyes searched her downcast face. "Jane…you wanted to get pregnant, didn't you?"

She bit her lower lip almost through and pulled away from him. "What I wanted is nobody's business except my own, and it's a good thing that you aren't forced into doing something you'd hate."

"Maybe so. But…"

She laughed. "Don't look so somber. Everything's all right. You'll go back to your job in Victoria and I'll make a fortune selling clothes with my name on them. We'll both do fine."

"Will you marry Coltrain?" he asked bluntly.

"I don't love him," she said sadly. "If I did, I'd marry him in a minute."

"Marriages have succeeded on less."

"And ended on more."

He couldn't debate that. He touched her lips with his. "I won't stop wanting you. If you change your mind, you only have to say so."

"I can't. I can't, Todd." She moved away and left him standing there. He wanted her, that was obvious, but he'd hate her if anything happened. He'd marry her, certainly, if there was a child. But it would be a hateful relationship. She didn't want him that way.

The next Friday, Todd drove Cherry up to Victoria to spend another weekend with her mother. He stayed in town, too, to get some of his own impending paperwork out of the way and to keep his mind off Jane. The hunger he felt for her was becoming a real problem.

Cherry waved goodbye to him from her mother's elegant front porch. The house Marie shared with William, her second husband, was a startling white restored Victorian, with gingerbread woodwork and a gazebo on a spotless manicured lawn. It had all the warmth of a photograph, but it suited a woman who was trying to build an interior design business in south Texas.

"Your father seemed very out of sorts," Marie remarked as she and Cherry went inside.

"I think it's because of Jane," the girl replied with a grin. "I caught them kissing, and I mean kissing!" she added, shaking her hand with appropriate facial expressions.

Marie made a curt movement. "Todd has said repeatedly that he doesn't want to marry again," she said.

"Never say never," Cherry murmured and grinned. "Jane's been helping me with my turns. She says I'm just the picture of elegance on horseback. I wish I could be more like her," she said, without realizing how dreamy she sounded. "She's so beautiful, and everyone knows who she is in rodeo. She's going to endorse some women's Western wear. They'll have her on TV and in magazines… Gosh, it's so exciting!"

Marie wasn't jealous of Todd anymore. Their marriage was history. But she was jealous of her only daughter, who now seemed to be transferring all her loyalties to a disabled rodeo star with a reputation that was already fading. She didn't like it one bit.

"I thought we might go shopping again tomorrow," Marie ventured.

Cherry started to speak and ended in a sigh. "All right."

"You should love pretty clothes, at your age," Marie said, clinging desperately to the only real common desire they still shared, a love of clothes.

"I do, I guess," Cherry said. "Rodeo clothes, at least. But I'd love some new books on horses and medicine."

"Books! What a waste of time!"

Cherry's eyebrows arched. "Mother, I'm going to be a surgeon."

Marie patted her shoulder gently. "Darling, you're very young. You'll change your mind."

"That isn't what Jane says, when I tell her about wanting to practice medicine," Cherry said sharply.

Marie glared at her. "And that's quite enough about Jane," she said sarcastically. "I'm your mother. You don't talk back to me."

Cherry's mouth pulled down. "Yes, ma'am."

Marie smoothed over her perfect coiffure. "Let's have tea. I've had a very hectic morning."

Doing what, arranging the flowers? Cherry thought irritably, but she only smiled and didn't say another word. Compared to Jane, who was always doing something or reading about ranching or genetics, Marie was very dull stuff indeed. Her life seemed to be composed of clothes and society, and she had no interests past them.

Her father, like Jane, had an active mind and he fed it constantly with books and educational television. Cherry remembered her parents being together very rarely during her childhood, because Marie didn't like horses or riding, or reading, or computers. Cherry and her father shared those interests and that had formed an early bond between them. Now Jane, also, shared the same interests. Cherry wondered if her father ever noticed. He seemed very attracted to Jane physically, but he paid little attention to her leisure pursuits. She'd have to get them together long enough to push them into really talking.

Remembering the pleasure in Jane's face when she'd said she was going to Victoria with Dr. Coltrain brought Cherry up short. The doctor would be formidable competition for her father. She'd have to see if she couldn't do something to help. The more she thought about having Jane for a stepmother, the happier she became.

Marie and William had an engagement Saturday night, so she decided to run Cherry back to the ranch early that afternoon. She phoned Todd at the office to tell him that she'd drop the girl off, but he was involved in a business meeting so Miss Emory took the message and promised to relay it.

Marie smiled to herself as she and Cherry got into her silver Mercedes. Somehow she was going to throw a spanner into Todd's spokes and prevent her daughter from becoming lost to the competition. She already had a good idea of how to do it, too.

"Does Jane know that your father is rich?" she asked Cherry.

"Heavens, no," Cherry said, defending her idol. "She doesn't even know that he owns a computer company. All Dad has told her is that he keeps the books for a company in Victoria."

"My, my. Why the subterfuge?"

"Well, Dad felt sorry for Jane," she said without thinking that she might be betraying her father to her mother. "She hurt her back in a wreck and she could barely walk. The ranch was in trouble. She didn't have anyone who could manage money to help her. So on an impulse, Dad offered to take over the manager's job.

You wouldn't believe what he's done for her. He's improved the property, bought livestock, got her into a licensing venture with that clothing manufacturer—all in a few weeks. I heard him say that the ranch is going to start paying back the investment any day now."

"Where did she get the money to do all that? Has she got money of her own?" Marie asked with studied carelessness.

"Oh, no, she was flat broke, Dad said. He went to the bank and stood good for a loan to make the improvements. She doesn't know."

Ammunition, Marie was thinking. "Tell me about Jane," Marie coaxed.

It didn't take much to get Cherry talking about the woman she worshiped. In the drive to Jacobsville, she told Marie everything she knew. By the time they reached the Parker ranch, Marie had enough to put the skids under the former rodeo queen and get back her daughter's loyalty.

"I do wish you'd consider spending the rest of the summer with me," Marie said as they pulled up at the front door. "We could go to Nassau or down to Jamaica. Even to Martinique."

"I'd love to, but I have to practice for the rodeo in August," Cherry explained. "I really need to work on my turns."

"Oh…horses!" Marie muttered. "Such a filthy hobby."

"They're very clean, actually. There's Jane!"

Marie got out of the car and studied the woman approaching them. Jane was wearing jeans and a pink

T-shirt. Her blond hair was in a braid down her back and she wasn't wearing any makeup, but that didn't lessen her beauty. If anything, it enhanced it. She was slender and elegant to look at, and she had grace of carriage despite her injury. She was twice as pretty as Marie. The other woman, at least ten years Jane's senior, had no difficulty understanding Todd's interest and Cherry's devotion to the woman. Marie hated her on sight.

"Jane, this is my mother. Mom, this is Jane," Cherry introduced them, beaming.

"I've heard so much about you," Marie said with reserved friendliness. "How nice to meet you at last, Miss Parker."

"Call me Jane, please," the other woman said kindly. She slid a welcoming arm around Cherry, who smiled up at her with the kind of affection she used to show her mother. It made Marie go cold inside. "I've missed you," she told Cherry.

"I've missed you, too," Cherry said warmly.

"Would you like tea, Mrs...."

"Oh, call me Marie. Yes, I'd love a cup," Marie said formally.

Jane grimaced. "I meant a glass of iced tea, actually."

"That would be fine."

"Come in, then."

Jane led the way into the spacious living room. Marie's keen eye could see dozens of ways to improve it and make it elegant, but she bit down on her comments. She wanted to worm her way into Jane's confidence and criticizing the decor wasn't going to accomplish that.

"Could you ask Meg to fix some tea and cookies on a tray?" Jane asked Cherry.

"Sure! I'll be right back!"

She was gone and Marie accepted Jane's offer of a seat on the wide, comfortably upholstered sofa.

"Well, you're not at all what I expected," Marie began with a kind smile. "When my husband—excuse me, my *ex*-husband," she amended sweetly, "told me that he'd taken a little job down in Jacobsville to help a poor crippled woman, I had someone older in mind!"

Chapter Nine

At first Jane thought that she might have misheard the other woman. But when she leaned forward and looked into Marie's cold eyes, she knew that she hadn't.

"I'm not crippled," Jane said proudly. "Temporarily slowed down, but not permanently disabled."

"Oh. I'm sorry. I must have misunderstood. It doesn't matter. Whatever your problem is, Todd felt sorry for you. He's a sucker for a hard-luck story. Amazing, isn't it," she added, watching Jane as she played her trump card, "that a multimillionaire, the head of an international corporation, would sacrifice his vacation to get an insignificant little horse ranch out of the red."

Jane didn't move, didn't breathe, didn't flinch. She stared at the older woman blankly. "I beg your pardon?"

Marie's pencil-thin brows rose. "You didn't know?" She laughed pleasantly. "Well, how incredible! He's been featured in God knows how many business magazines. Although, I don't suppose you read that sort of thing, do you?" she added, allowing her eyes to pause meaningfully on the latest issue of a magazine on horsemanship.

"I don't read business magazines, no," Jane said. She touched her throat lightly, as if she felt choked.

"Todd must have found it all so amusing, pretending to be a simple accountant," Marie said, leaning back on the sofa elegantly. "I mean, what a comedown for him! Living like this—" she waved a careless arm "—and driving that pitiful old sedan he borrowed. Honestly, he had to have the chauffeur drive the Ferrari and the Rolls twice a week just to keep them from getting carbon on the valves."

Rolls. Ferrari. Multimillionaire. Jane felt as if she were strangling. "But he keeps the books," she argued, trying desperately to come to grips with what she was being told.

"He's a wizard with figures, all right," Marie said. "He's an utter genius at math, and without a college education, too. He has a gift, they say."

"But, why?" she groaned. "Why didn't he tell me the truth?"

"I suppose he was afraid that you might fall in love with his bank account," Marie said with a calculating glance. "So many women have, and you were a poverty case. Not only that, a crippled poverty case. You might have thought he was the end of the rainbow."

Jane's face went rigid. She got to her feet slowly. "I make my own way," she said coldly. "I don't need any handouts, or anybody's pity."

"Well, of course you don't," Marie said. "I'm sure Todd would have told you the truth, eventually."

Jane's hands clenched by her side. She was white.

The sound of running footsteps distracted Marie.

"Meg says she'll bring the— Jane! What is it?" Cherry asked as she entered the room, concerned. "You look like you've seen a ghost!"

"Yes, you are very pale," Marie said. She glanced worriedly at her daughter. She hadn't counted the cost until now. Cherry was looking at her with eyes that grew steadily colder.

"What did you say, Mother?" she asked her parent.

Marie got up and clasped her hands in front of her. "I only told her the truth," she said defensively. "She'd have found out anyway."

"About Dad?" Cherry persisted. When Marie nodded, Cherry's face contorted. She looked at Jane and felt the older woman's pain and shock all the way to her feet.

Marie was feeling less confident by the second. Cherry's eyes were hostile and so were Jane's. "I should go, I suppose," Marie began.

"That might be a very good idea, Mother," Cherry said icily. "Before Dad comes home."

Another complication Marie hadn't considered. She gnawed her lower lip. "I never meant to…"

"Just go," Jane snapped.

"And the sooner the better," Cherry added.

"Don't you talk to me that way! I'm your mother!" Marie reminded her hotly.

"I'm ashamed of that," Cherry said harshly. "I've never been so ashamed of it in all my life!"

Marie's indrawn breath was audible. Her pale eyes filled with sudden tears. "I only wanted…" she began plaintively.

Cherry turned her back. Marie hesitated only for a moment before she scooped up her purse and went quickly to the front door. The tears were raining down her cheeks by the time she reached the Mercedes.

Inside the house, Jane was still trying to subdue her rage. She sat down again, aware of Cherry's worried gaze.

"Is what she said true? That your father owns a computer company, that he has a Ferrari and a Rolls and he's spending his vacation getting my ranch out of debt because he feels sorry for me?" Jane asked the girl.

Cherry groaned. "Oh, it's true, but it's not like that! Mother's just jealous because I talk about you so much. I guess I upset her when I made her realize how little we had in common. It's all my fault. Oh, Jane…!"

Jane took another steadying breath and folded her hands in her lap. "I wondered," she said absently. "I mean, with a brain like that, why would he still be working for somebody else, at his age. I've been a fool! He played me like a radio!"

"He didn't do it to hurt you," Cherry argued. "Jane, he just wanted to help. And then, after we'd been here for a while, he didn't know how to tell you. I'm sure that's why he hasn't said anything. He cares for you."

Cares. He'd said that he loved her. *But you don't keep secrets from people you love,* she was thinking. He'd lied by omission. He'd let her fall in love with him, and he had to know that there was no future for them. If he'd been a simple accountant, perhaps it would have worked out. But he was a multimillionaire, a powerful businessman. What would he want with a little country girl from south Texas who only had a high school education and no social skills? She wouldn't know what to do with herself at a society party. She wouldn't even know what utensils to use. And she was a rancher. Her eyes closed as the reality closed in on her.

"Talk to me," Cherry pleaded.

Jane couldn't. She gripped her legs hard as she fought with her demons. Todd was coming back today. She'd have to face him. How would she be able to face him, with what she knew?

Then the solution occurred to her. *Copper.* She could invite Copper over for supper, and play up to him—if she warned Copper first that she was going to—and she could put on a good act. It had all been a mistake, she hadn't meant what she said about loving him, she was lying...

"I don't want your father to know that your mother told me the truth," Jane said after a minute. Her blue eyes met Cherry's gray ones evenly. "I'll talk to him later."

"Mother's not vindictive, really," Cherry said in her mother's defense. "She's just shallow, and jealous. It's funny, really, because she doesn't even know how to talk to me. Not like you do. Please don't hate me because of this, Jane."

"Cherry!" Jane was genuinely shocked. "As if I could hate you!"

The young face softened. Cherry smiled. "We're still friends?"

"Certainly we are. None of this has anything to do with you and me."

"Oh, thank goodness," she said heavily.

"It's just as well, really," Jane continued without looking directly at Cherry, "because I'd decided that things wouldn't work out with your father and me, anyway. He isn't really the rancher type."

Cherry frowned. "But he comes from ranching people in Wyoming. He grew up around horses and cattle."

"Still, he doesn't spend much time with them now," Jane insisted. "If he's the president of a company, then he lives in the fast lane. I don't. I can't."

Cherry saw all her dreams coming apart. "You could get to know him better before you decide that you can't."

Jane smiled and shook her head. "No. You see, Dr. Coltrain and I were talking the other day. Copper's like me, he's from Jacobsville and his family has lived here as long as mine has. We're suited to each other. In fact," she lied, "I've invited him for supper tonight."

"You didn't tell me," Cherry protested.

"I didn't know you'd be here, did I?" she asked, and sounded so reasonable that Cherry was totally fooled. "For all I knew, your father was going to drive up to Victoria to get you tomorrow."

"Yes, that's so," Cherry admitted.

"You're welcome to have your supper with us," Jane offered, hoping against hope that Cherry would refuse and trying not to look too relieved when she did. She was also hoping that Copper would come to supper when she invited him, or she was going to get caught lying to save face.

"I expect Dad and I will go out and get something, when he gets home, like we do most nights," Cherry said uncomfortably.

"That will be nice."

"Jane, don't you care about him at all?" Cherry asked plaintively.

"I like him very much," Jane said at once. "He's a very nice man, and I owe him a lot."

Cherry felt sick. She managed a wan smile and made an excuse to go over to the small house where she and her father were staying.

When she was gone, Jane let go of the tears she'd been holding back and was just mopping herself up when Meg walked in with a tray of cookies and cake and tea, smiling.

The smile faded at once when she saw Jane's ravaged face. "Is she gone already? What in the world happened?"

Jane wiped savagely at the traces of tears. "Everything!" she raged. "That pirate! That cold-blooded, blond-headed snake!"

"Todd? Why are you mad at our accountant?"

"He's no accountant," Jane said viciously. "He's the head of a computer company and he's worth millions!"

Meg started, and then burst out laughing. "Oh, for heaven's sake, pull the other one!"

"It's true! He's got a Rolls at home!"

Meg set the tray down. "There, there, they were putting you on. Why, Todd's no millionaire!"

"He is," Jane insisted. "Cherry didn't want to agree with what her mother told me, but she did. Her mother might lie to me. Cherry never would."

Meg was less certain now. She frowned. "If he's a millionaire, why's he down here keeping your books?"

"Because I'm a poor cripple," Jane said huskily. "And he felt sorry for me. He's spending his vacation getting me out of the hole." She put her face in her hands and shook her head. "Now I don't have to wonder why the bank let me have the loan, either. I'm sure he stood good for it. I'll owe him my soul!"

Meg wiped her hands on her apron, hovering nervously. "Jane, you mustn't get upset like this. Wait until Todd gets back and talk to him about it."

"What will I tell him?"

"That you didn't know…"

"And now that I do?" she asked openly. "I'll tell him I know he's rich, and then he'll never be sure if I care for him or his wallet, will he? He might think I knew all along. His ex-wife said that he's been featured in all the business magazines. I don't read them, but he doesn't know that."

"I see what you mean."

Jane got up from the sofa. "Well, I'm going to set his mind at ease, with a little help."

"From whom?"

"Copper, of course," Jane said. "He's already said that Copper and I seemed to be an item. Why shouldn't we be? Copper said he'd marry me in a minute if I was willing."

"That's no reason to get married! Copper deserves better!"

Jane stared at her housekeeper. "Of course he does, and it won't be for real. I'm going to ask an old friend for a favor, that's all."

Meg relaxed. "As long as he doesn't get hurt."

"He won't." She didn't add that she would. She'd already been hurt. But Todd wasn't going to know. She was going to turn the tables on him and save her pride. It was the only thing she had left to protect herself with now.

* * *

As she'd guessed, Copper was willing to help her out by coming over to supper. He was on call, though, so he brought his beeper with him. They sat down to an early supper of fried chicken and vegetables. Jane was wearing a white dress and her hair was immaculately brushed back and secured with white combs. She looked elegant and very beautiful, except for the hollow expression in her eyes.

"Does it matter so much that he's got money?" Copper asked her over coffee.

"It would to him, if he thought it was the reason I was attracted to him," she said.

"He'll know better."

"How?"

"He loves you, you idiot," Copper said curtly. "He'll be furious, and not at you. I don't doubt he'll have some choice words for his ex-wife."

"Maybe he'll thank her," she returned lightly. "After all, he was in a bit of a muddle here. He'd backed himself into a corner playing the part of a working man with no prospects."

"It probably meant more to him that you loved him in his disguise."

"How would he know that I hadn't been in on the secret all along?"

Copper nodded; it was a logical question. But he was smiling when he put down his napkin. "Because Cherry will tell him how shocked you were."

"Maybe I'm a good actress. Cherry's mother said that plenty of women had wanted him for his bank account."

"And don't you think he'd know the difference between a woman who wanted money and a woman who wanted him?"

"I don't know," Jane said honestly.

"Listen…"

The front door opened without even a knock and Todd stalked into the dining room. He was wearing a gray business suit with a spotless white shirt and a silk tie. His boots were hand-tooled leather. He was wearing a Rolex watch on his left wrist and a signet ring with a diamond that would have blinded a horse. For the first time, Jane saw him as he really was: an authority figure bristling with money and power.

He didn't smile as he stared at her, and his gaze didn't waver. "When Miss Emory finally got to me with Marie's message, I canceled a meeting. I was waiting for Marie when she got back home. I've had her version of what she said. Let's have yours."

Copper cleared his throat, to make sure that Todd knew he was sitting there.

Todd glanced at him with cold gray eyes. "I haven't missed the cozy supper scenario," he told the doctor. "But I know why it's being played out. Do you?"

"Oh, I have a dandy idea," Copper replied. "Wouldn't it have been easier all around to just tell the truth in the first place? Or were you having fun at Jane's expense?"

Todd laughed without mirth. He stuck his hands into his slacks pockets and stared at Jane from his superior, elegant height. "Fun. I've got merger negotiations stacked one on another, international contracts waiting for consideration, stockholders telephoning twice a day… No, I haven't been having fun. I've put my life on hold trying to get this horse ranch out of bankruptcy so that Jane would at least have a roof over her head. It was an impulse. Once I started the charade, I couldn't find a way to stop it."

"You could have told me the truth," Jane said stiffly.

"What truth?" he asked pleasantly. "That I felt sorry for you, because you were hurt and such a fighter despite your injuries? And that you stood to lose everything you owned just for lack of an accountant? I couldn't walk away."

"Well, thanks for all you did," Jane replied, averting her eyes. "But now that you've got me on my feet, I can stay there all by myself."

"Sure you can," he agreed. "You've got a licensing contract and some decent stock to breed. You'll make it. You would have anyway, if Tim had been a little sharper in the math department. This is a first-class operation. All I did was pull the loose ends together. You're a born rancher. You've got what it takes to make this place pay, with a little help from Tim and Meg."

The praise unsettled her, even as it thrilled her. At least he didn't think she was an idiot. That was something. But the distance between them was more apparent than ever now that she knew the truth about him.

She clasped her hands tightly out of sight in her lap. "And you?"

"I've got a business of my own to run," he said. "Cherry will start back to school soon. We'd have had to leave anyway, a little later than this, perhaps. Cherry owes you a lot for what you've taught her. She has a chance in rodeo now."

"Cherry is my friend. I hope she always will be."

"Cherry. But not me?"

She looked up into his eyes. "I'm grateful for what you did. But you must surely see that we live in different worlds." She sighed wearily. "I'm not cut out for yours, any more than you're cut out for mine. It's just as well that it worked out this way."

"You haven't tried," he said angrily.

"I'm not going to," was the quiet reply. "I like my life as it is. Exactly as it is. I'm very grateful for the help you gave me. I'll repay the loan."

His face hardened. "I never doubted that you would. I backed it. I didn't fund it."

She nodded. "Thank you."

His chest rose and fell heavily. He glared at Copper, because he could say none of what he wanted to say with the unwanted audience.

"Shall I leave?" Copper offered.

"Not on your life," Jane said shortly.

"Afraid of me?" Todd murmured with a mocking smile.

"There's nothing more to say," she replied. "Except goodbye."

"Cherry will be devastated," he said.

She drew in a breath. "Yes, I know. I'm sorry. I don't want to hurt her. But, it's the only thing to do."

He looked unapproachable. "Perhaps we see different things. If you'll have Tim phone me Monday morning, I'll explain to him what I've done. You need a business manager, unless you want to end up in the same financial tangle you started in."

"I know that. I'll take care of it."

"Then I'll say good night."

"I'm grateful for everything," Jane added stiffly.

He looked at her for a long moment. "Everything?" he said in a sensuous tone.

She colored. It seemed to be the reaction he'd wanted, because he laughed coldly, nodded to Coltrain and stalked out, closing the door behind him.

Copper stared at her. "You fool. Is pride worth more than he is to you?"

"At the moment, yes," she said icily. She was fighting tears and trying not to show it. "He's a pompous, hateful…"

"You shouldn't have forced this discussion on him before you had a couple of days to think about what you wanted to do," he said gently. "Impulses are very often regretted."

"Is that a professional opinion?" she asked angrily.

"Personal, professional, there isn't much difference," he replied. "You're going to be sorry that you didn't give him a chance to talk."

"I did," she said with wide, innocent eyes. "And he did."

"He defended himself. That's all he had time to do. With me sitting here, he hardly had the opportunity to do any real discussing."

"It's all for the best," she told him quietly.

"If you want to spend the rest of your life alone, maybe it is. But money isn't everything."

"When you don't have any, it is."

He glowered at her. "Listen to me, this might be the last chance you get. He's proud, too, you know. He won't come crawling back, any more than I would in his place. He's not the sort."

She knew that, too. She put her napkin on the table and stood up. "Thanks for coming over tonight. I don't think I'd have had the nerve to face him if you hadn't been here."

"What are friends for?" he asked. He stood up, too, and took her gently by the shoulders. "There's still time to stop him. You could go over to the cabin and have it out."

"We had it out," she argued.

"No, you didn't. You sat there like a polite hostess, but you sure as hell didn't do any discussing."

"I can take care of my own life, thank you."

"If that's true, what am I doing here?"

She searched his eyes. "Moral support."

He smiled. "I asked for that."

"I'm sorry. I really do appreciate your coming over so quickly when I asked."

"You're welcome. I hope you'll do the same for me if I'm ever in a comparable situation. But all you did was postpone the problem, you know. You didn't solve anything."

"I saved face," she replied. "He'll go back to Victoria and run his company, and I'll stay down here and breed horses and make money selling clothes."

"You'll be lonely."

She looked up. "That's nothing new. I was lonely before he came here. But people learn every day how to live with being lonely. I have a roof over my head, my books are in great shape, my body's healing nicely and I'm going to get this ranch back on its feet. It's what Dad would have wanted."

"Your dad would have wanted to see you happy."

She smiled. "Yes, but he was a realist. Todd wouldn't have married me," she said quietly. "You know it, too. I'm not the sort of woman rich men marry. I've got rustic manners and I don't know how to dress or use six forks for one meal."

"You could learn those things. You're beautiful, and elegant, and you have charm and grace. No woman born with a silver spoon could do better."

She grinned through her heartbreak. "You're a prince."

He sighed and checked his watch. "I'm done talking. I have to make rounds at the hospital. Call if you need me. But I wish you'd reconsider. You're not perfect. Why expect it of other people?"

"I never lied to him," she said pointedly. "In fact, I don't think I've ever really lied at all."

"You let him think we were romantically involved. That's lying."

"Implying," she corrected. "The rules don't say you can't imply things."

"I'll keep that in mind. I'll be in touch." He bent and kissed her cheek gently. "Try not to brood too much."

"I will."

She watched him go. The house was suddenly emptier than ever, and when she heard a car door slam minutes later, the whole world seemed that way. She peered through the curtains just in time to watch Todd and Cherry go down the driveway for the last time. The house they'd occupied was closed up and dark, like the cold space under her own heart.

Chapter Ten

Life became boring and tedious without Todd and Cherry, but the ranch prospered. Jane was a natural organizer. She discovered talents she hadn't ever realized she possessed, because her father had always taken care of the business end of the ranch. Now, she called breeders, made contacts, put ads in horse magazines and newspapers, faxed messages back and forth on sales and hired people to create sales catalogs for her. It was becoming second nature to handle things. Even Tim stood in awe of her.

The clothes licensing was also moving right along. The first of the television commercials had aired, and she was told that sales had shot up overnight. The commercials helped get her name in front of a larger segment of the public and helped in the stud operation. She was suddenly a household word. Despite the fact that she didn't like looking at herself on television and in print media ads, she had to admit that it was getting business.

But it was a lonely sort of life. She couldn't ride, although she'd tried once and ended up in bed for several days with a stiff and painful back. She could keep books, though, by using Todd's figures and backtracking to see how he'd arrived at them. While she was by no means his equal, she had a good head for figures and she picked up what was necessary very quickly. Life was good, but it was a lonely life. She wondered if Todd was glad to be gone out of her life.

In fact, some of Todd's employees wished that he would go out of their lives! Since his return to Victoria, nothing had been done right in any department he visited. The desks in the secretarial pool were sloppy. The new products division wasn't designing anything he liked. Furthermore, people weren't taking proper care of their floppy disks—he found one lying next to a cup of coffee on a desk. The marketing department wasn't out in the field enough selling new programs. And even Todd's secretary, the highly prized Miss Emory, was admonished about the state of her filing system when he went looking for a file and couldn't find it where he thought it should be.

It was no better at home. Cherry came in for criticism about the clothes she chose to wear to begin the next school year, her lack of attention to educational programming, and the certainty that she would end up in prison because she watched episodes of a popular adult cartoon on a music network. In fact, the first time he saw an episode of the cartoon, he called the cable company and had the channel that carried it taken out of his cable package.

Cherry was willing to go along with the understandable reaction—after all there was a generation gap. But when he canceled Cherry's horsemanship magazine after it featured an article on Jane, she felt that he was carrying things a bit too far.

"Dad," she ventured the week of the Victoria rodeo

in which she was to compete, "don't you think you're getting just a little loopy lately?"

He glared at her over the top of his *Wall Street Journal*. "Loopy?"

"Overreacting. You know—canceling stuff." She cleared her throat at the unblinking glower she received. "Honestly, Dad, Miss Emory used a word I'll bet she never even thought until this week, after you grumbled about a letter she typed. And that's nothing to what Chris said when you threw his new computer program at him."

He put down the newspaper. "Is it my fault that people around me have suddenly forgotten how to do anything?" he asked curtly. "I have every right to expect good work from my employees. And you know why I canceled that garbage on television, not to mention that magazine..."

"Jane was in the magazine in two places," she said. "In a feature article, with color photos, and in a full-page ad. Didn't she look great?"

He averted his eyes. "I didn't notice."

"Really?" she asked. "Then why did you have the magazine open on your desk, where the photo was?"

He flapped the pages of his financial paper noisily. "Don't you have homework to do?"

"Dad, school hasn't started back yet."

He frowned. "Hasn't it?"

She got up out of her chair. "You could call her, you know."

"Call her!" He threw the paper down. His gray eyes flashed fire. "Call her, hell! She wouldn't even listen! She gave me all this *toro excretio* about different worlds and how...what are you laughing at?"

"Toro excretio?" she emphasized, giggling as she realized what the slang meant.

"I heard it from the wife of a concrete magnate," he said. "We sat on a committee together. Best description I ever heard. Anyway, don't change the subject."

"You could have tried to change Jane's mind."

"What would be the point?" he muttered. "She wanted to get married, until she found out who I was."

Cherry smiled. "That sounds nice. She'd certainly look lovely in high fashion, and I can't think of anyone who'd make a better stepmother."

"You've got a mother," he said harshly.

"We don't speak, haven't you noticed?" she asked coldly. "She hurt Jane."

He avoided her gaze. "Yes. Don't think I didn't give her my two cents' worth as well about that, but she's pregnant, I understand. She was emotional when she carried you."

"Maybe a new baby will make her happier."

"Ha!"

"Well, it will keep her occupied," Cherry continued. "What about Jane?"

"She's going to marry the cowboy doctor from hell and have little doctors, I guess," he muttered.

Cherry grinned. "Fat chance, when she's crazy about you. You're crazy about her, too. You just won't admit it. You'd rather roar around up here and drive everybody who works for you to using strong language or getting drunk on weekends."

"They don't do that!"

"Chris did, after you threw his program at him," Cherry informed him. "And he said that he was going to move out to California and help develop a virtual reality program for disgruntled employees so that they could turn their bosses into mud puddles and drop rocks in them."

"Vicious boy." He sighed. "I guess I'll have to give him a raise. God knows, he'd set virtual reality back twenty years."

She laughed. "And what about Jane?"

"Stop asking me that!"

"I'll bet she cries herself to sleep every night, thinking she's not good enough for you."

His face went very still. "What?"

"Well, that's what she thought. When Mom told her you were the head of a company and filthy rich, she went as white as a sheet. Mom made her feel bad about being a rancher and not reading intellectual magazines and not being upper crust."

"How dare she!" Todd said icily. "Jane's every bit as upper crust as your mother is!"

"Nobody told Jane that. She has a very low self-image."

"Stop talking like a psychologist."

"Merry's going to be one. She says I have a very good self-image."

"Nice of her."

"Anyway, Jane only has a high school education…"

"So do I, for God's sake!"

"…and she doesn't feel comfortable around high society people…"

"You know how I hate parties," he muttered.

"…and she thought you'd probably not want to have somebody like her in your life in a serious way."

"Of all the harebrained, idiotic, half-baked ideas! She's beautiful, doesn't she know that? Beautiful and kind and warm and loving." His voice grew husky with memory, and his body tingled with sweet memories. "She's everything a woman should be."

"The doctor sure thinks so," Cherry said with a calculating glance. "In fact, it wouldn't surprise me one bit if she didn't marry him on the rebound. He'd be over the moon. He's crazy about her."

His eyes narrowed. "She doesn't love him."

"Lots of people get married when they don't love each other. He's a good doctor. He can give her everything she wants, and they've always been good friends. I'll bet they'd make a wonderful marriage."

"Cherry…!"

"Well, Dad, that shouldn't bother you," she said pointedly. "After all, you don't want to marry her."

"The hell I don't!"

Cherry's eyebrows shot up. "You do?"

He hesitated, started to deny the impulsive outburst, and then settled into the chair with a heavy sigh. "Of course I do," he said harshly. "But it's too late. I wasn't honest with her at the beginning. I've made so many mistakes that I doubt she'd even talk to me now."

"If she loves you, she would."

"Sure," he scoffed. "The minute I call her up, she'll hang up. If she knows I'm coming to the ranch, she'll leave. I didn't spend several weeks there without learning something about her reactions."

Cherry puzzled over that. He was right. Jane would be like a whipped pup, eager to avoid any more blows.

Then she had a thought. "The rodeo," she said. "I'm going to compete in the rodeo, and Jane knows about it. Do you really think she'd miss watching me through my paces after all the time she put in on me?"

He pursed his lips, deep in thought. "No. But she'll disguise herself."

"Probably."

"And she'll sit as far away as possible."

"That, too." She grinned. "You could ask Chris to sit in the audience up on the top of the stands and watch out for her."

"Chris would sell me down the river..."

"Not if you give him that raise."

He groaned. "The things I don't do for you!"

"We'll all live happily ever after," Cherry said smugly. "After you grovel enough to Jane and convince her that you can make her happy."

"I'm not groveling."

She grinned. "Have it your way."

"I'm not!"

She left him protesting and went over to Merry's house to watch television.

Tim and Meg had a light supper with Jane the afternoon of the Victoria rodeo. She sat there deep in thought, picking at her food, as usual, and not talking, also as usual.

"Are you going up to Victoria to watch Cherry compete?" Tim asked her.

She glowered at him. "No. *He'll* be there."

"Of course he will, he's her father."

She stabbed a piece of carrot. "I'd like to watch her. But I don't want to run into him."

"You could wear a scarf and dark glasses," Meg advised. "And a dress. You never wear dresses. He wouldn't recognize you. Especially if you sat way up in the stands. He'll be right down front where Cherry is."

Jane thought about that. Meg was right. That's exactly where he'd be. She dropped the piece of carrot into her mouth and chewed it. "I guess I could do that. There'll be a huge crowd. Anyway, I doubt if he'll even look for me."

"Well, of course he would…" Tim argued.

Meg kicked him under the table and he winced.

"I mean, of course he wouldn't," Tim amended.

Jane glanced at him and then at Meg. "Are you two up to something?"

"My goodness, no," Meg said easily and smiled. "But it would be nice to know how Cherry did in the competition. We watched her practice, day after day."

That would explain their interest. "I guess I might go up for the barrel racing, if Tim can drive me," Jane said.

"Sure I can. Meg can come, too."

"I'd love to," Meg agreed. Jane missed the relief on Meg's features that was quickly erased.

"We'd better get a move on, then," Jane said after a glance at her watch. "It will take us a little while to get there, and there's sure to be a crowd."

She pulled on a simple green-and-white cotton sundress, with sandals and a white cardigan. She put up her long blond hair and tied a scarf over it and then secured a pair of dark glasses over her eyes.

Meg walked past the door and looked in.

"Will it do?" Jane asked, turning toward her.

"It's perfect," Meg assured her, and went on down the hall.

Jane nodded at her reflection. Nobody would recognize her in this getup, she concluded.

She might not have been so confident if she'd heard Meg on the telephone in her quarters a couple of minutes later, telling Cherry every detail of Jane's disguise, as they'd already conspired.

"I feel guilty," Meg said.

"Never you mind," Cherry replied. "It's all for a good cause. Think how miserable Jane and Dad are going to be if we don't do something!"

"Jane's lost weight."

"Dad's lost weight *and* employees," Cherry murmured dryly. "If he keeps on like this, some of the people in his software development department are going to stuff him into a computer and ship him overseas. This has just got to work. I'll see you both tonight."

"Good luck, honey," Meg said with genuine affection. "We'll all be rooting for you."

"Thanks. I think I'm going to need all the help I can get. But knowing that Jane is in the stands will do me more good than anything."

"She'll be there. Don't you worry."

Meg hung up and went to meet Jane in the hall. "Goodness, you certainly do look different!" she said.

"I feel different. Now all I have to do is sit far enough away so that nobody recognizes me."

"Your own dad, God rest his soul, wouldn't recognize you like that," Meg said dryly.

"Well, hopefully Todd won't," Jane murmured, adjusting the scarf. "I have no wish whatsoever to get into any more arguments with him. But I can't miss seeing Cherry ride. I hope she wins."

"So do we," Tim agreed.

They drove up to Victoria in the truck. Riding was much easier for Jane since the pain in her back had eased. The damage was repairing itself and the pain only came now when she did stupid things—like trying to gallop on horseback.

It had been a bitter blow to realize that her rodeo days were over, but she was dealing with that. If only she could deal half as well with the sorrow that losing Todd had caused her. Not a day went by when she didn't long for him.

He wouldn't feel that way about her, she was certain. A man with so much wealth and status wouldn't want an ordinary rancher from south Texas. Not when he could have movie actresses or top models or high-powered business executives. Having seen Marie, so poised and capable and able to run her own business, she had some idea of the sort of woman who appealed to Todd. And Jane was not that type.

It was more than likely that Marie had told the truth: Todd had only taken the job on an impulse because he felt sorry for Jane. He'd been kind, in his way, but she didn't need his pity. The best thing she could do now was to stay out of his way and not spoil Cherry's big night.

Cherry would be the one to suffer, if they had another argument, and Jane thought the girl had been hurt enough already.

Cherry wrote to her, though, and she wrote back. It wasn't as if they'd parted in anger. But Todd complicated that tenuous friendship. Jane was fairly certain that he didn't approve of his daughter's friendship with Jane, and it was a fair bet that Marie didn't.

When they arrived at the arena the parking lot was almost full. The floodlights were silhouetted against the dark sky and the opening ceremonies had already begun.

They got their tickets and then Jane made her way very carefully to the top rung of the spectator section, leaving Meg and Tim down front. She sat apart from the other few people, but she noticed a young man giving her covert looks. If he was a masher, she mused, he had a long way to fall. He'd better keep his distance.

She settled into her seat. The light cardigan felt good, because there was a slight nip in the summer night air. She sighed and worked to keep her mind on the people in the arena. But all it really wanted to do was think about Todd. Her heart raced at the thought that he was here, somewhere, in this very place. She was close to him again, even if he didn't know it. How wonderful it felt to know that.

There was competition after competition. She sat through bareback bronc riding, steer riding, steer wrestling and calf roping. The competitors were narrowed down as man after man failed to meet the time limit. Prizes were awarded. And then, finally, the barrel-racing competition was announced and the first rider was out of the gate.

Cherry was fourth. An excited Jane sat on the edge of her seat. Part of her mourned because she would never compete again. But her heart raced, her blood surged as she watched Cherry go through her paces, watched the girl match the best time Jane had ever done. There were cheers when Cherry rode out of the arena. Jane felt the sting of tears in her eyes as she knew, deep inside, that nobody was going to beat Cherry tonight. All the hard work and practice and patience had paid off. She felt as if she were in the saddle with her protégé. It was a wonderful feeling—the sort a parent might have, pride in a child.

It was no surprise at all when the winner was announced, and it was Cherry. Jane watched her accept her trophy as flashbulbs went off, and her proud father gave her a warm hug from the sidelines.

Todd! Jane watched him with an ache that went all the way to her toes. She'd been in his arms, too. She knew how it felt, but in a different way than a daughter would. She was empty inside, an outsider looking into a warm family circle that she could never share.

It was time to go. She got up from her seat and carefully made her way down to the seats where she'd left Tim and Meg, but they were nowhere in sight. Perhaps they'd gone to congratulate Cherry, something Jane would love to have done, but she didn't dare. Not with Todd so close.

With a sigh of pure longing, she went toward the place where they'd left the truck, but she must have forgotten its exact position. She couldn't seem to find it.

While she was standing among the dark vehicles, searching, there was a sound nearby and she was suddenly picked up in hard, warm arms that felt all too familiar.

Her eyes met gray ones in a set face as she was carried toward a waiting black Ferrari.

"Take off those damn glasses," Todd said curtly.

She fumbled them away from her wide, shocked blue eyes. "How did you…?"

"Cherry conspired with Tim and Meg," he replied, turning toward his car.

"Where are they?"

"At the house, waiting for us." He met her eyes as he reached the car. "They're going to have a long wait," he added sensuously. "We have some lost time to make up."

"Now, you just wait a minute," she began.

"I've waited too damn long already," he breathed as

his mouth lowered onto hers and stilled every word in her mouth and every thought in her whirling brain.

She faltered, trying to decide how to save her pride.

"Give up," he whispered. "Kiss me."

"I can't… We don't… It wouldn't—" she murmured dizzily.

"You can, we do, and it *will* work," he said on a husky laugh. "We're going to get married and raise several more cowgirls and maybe even a cowboy or two."

"You don't want to marry someone like me," she said sadly.

"Yes," he told her, his loving eyes on her face. "I want to marry someone exactly like you, a woman who has a heart as beautiful as her face and body, a woman who loves me and my daughter fiercely. I want you, Jane. Now and forever."

She couldn't believe it was really happening. She looked into his eyes and sailed among the stars.

"I see dreams in your eyes," he said softly. "Marry me, and I'll make them all come true, every one."

"I'm not educated…"

"Neither am I." He kissed her hungrily before he opened the door.

"I'm not sophisticated," she persisted.

"Neither am I." He put her into the passenger seat and carefully belted her in.

"I can't stand high society parties…"

"Neither can I." He closed her door and got in beside her.

"Todd…"

He cranked the powerful engine, reversed the car, eased it out of the parking lot and headed for open country. His hand found hers after he'd shifted into the final gear, and he held on tight.

"I've been lonely. Have you?" he asked.

"Lonelier than I ever knew I could be," she said, capitulating.

"I wanted to telephone you, or come to see you, but I knew you wouldn't listen. You're as proud as I am."

"Sadly, yes."

"But we'll manage to get along, most of the time. And after we argue, we'll make up."

She smiled, leaning her head on his shoulder. "Oh, yes."

"And Cherry will be the happiest girl in her class when school starts in Jacobsville."

"Are we going to live in Jacobsville?" she asked with a start.

"Of course. I haven't finished saving the ranch yet," he said dryly.

"Oh, I see. So that's it. You want my ranch, you blackhearted villain," she accused and ruined it with a giggle.

"Yes, I do," he said fervently. "Because without me, you'll end up right back in the red again. You'll forget to use purchasing orders for supplies, you'll get the figures in the wrong columns, you'll forget to keep proper receipts for taxes…"

"Actually," she said sheepishly, "I've already done all those things."

"God help me!"

"Now, now. I'm sure you'll get us in the black again in no time," she said, making a mental note to mess up her accounts before he took a look at them. "After all, you did start a computer company all by yourself."

He glowered at her. "It was easier than trying to run a ranch, all things considered. At my business, people do what I tell them to."

"I'll do what you tell me to. Some of the time," she replied.

"That's what I was afraid of."

She closed her eyes. "I'll make you like it."

He chuckled and drew her close. "Of course you will."

Halfway home, he found a small dirt track and pulled the car onto it, under some trees. He turned off the engine and turned to Jane. He held his arms out and she went into them.

Turbulent minutes later, he lifted his head. Her eyes in the dim light were sparkling with emotion like blue sapphires and she was clinging to him, trembling faintly as his lean hand smoothed softly over her bare breasts.

"We have to go home," he whispered reluctantly.

"Are you sure?" She reached up and kissed him hungrily.

He groaned, but he pulled back just a fraction of an inch. "Not really. But this isn't wise."

"Why not?"

He glanced in the rearview mirror with a rueful smile and quickly rearranged her disheveled clothing. "Because the local sheriff's department has deputies with no romance in their souls."

"How do you..." The flashing lights behind them caught her eye, and she made a shocked sound as a tall man came up to the driver's side of the car and knocked.

A resigned Todd let the window down and grinned at the unsmiling uniformed man. "I know, this is the wrong place for what we were doing. But our daughter and several other people are congregated in our living room at home, and there's no privacy anywhere!"

The uniformed man looked from Jane to Todd and made an amused sound deep in his throat. "I know what you mean. My wife and I have four kids and they never leave the house. Lot of garbage, that talk about teenagers always being on the go. All mine want to do is play video games and eat pizza."

"I know just what you mean."

"All the same," the deputy said wryly, "this really isn't..."

"The best place. I get the idea." Todd grinned again. "Okay. We'll go home."

"Rent them a movie," he suggested. "Works for my brood. You put on one of those new thrillers and they won't even know if you're still in the house."

"That's the best idea yet. Thanks!"

He smiled. "My wife and I have been married twenty-six years," he said with a chuckle. "You wouldn't believe some of the diversions we've come up with to keep them busy. Have a nice evening." He touched the brim of his hat and went back to his car.

"You let him think we were married," she accused gently.

"Why not, when we will be by the end of the week," he said warmly. "I can't wait."

She slid her hand into his when he cranked the car and started to reverse it. "Neither can I."

They were married a few days later, with Tim and Meg as witnesses and Cherry as maid of honor. It was a quiet ceremony in Jacobsville, with no one except the four of them. Afterward, they all went out to eat at Ja-

cobsville's best restaurant and then Todd and Jane flew
down to Jamaica for a very brief honeymoon before
school started.

Despite their need for each other, they'd been very
circumspect until the vows were spoken. But no sooner
were they installed in their room overlooking the bay
in their luxurious Montego Bay hotel suite when Todd
picked her up and tossed her onto the king-size bed, following her down before she had time to get her breath.

"Oh, but we really should…go and look…at the
ocean," she teased as he brushed lazy, sensuous kisses on
her parted lips.

"Indeed we should." His lean hand smoothed down
her body, kindling sharp desires, awakening nerves. She
gasped and shivered when he trespassed under the thin
elastic of her briefs. "Do you want to go now?" he whispered into her mouth as his hand moved exploringly.

She moaned.

He laughed softly, moving his mouth to the soft
curve of her breasts under the scoop-neck knit top.
"That's what I thought."

In no time at all, they were both nude, twisting
against each other in a fever of deprived need. He ur-
gently drew her into the taut curve of his body, but even
then he was tender, fitting her to him in a silence punctuated with the soft gasps of pleasure that he drew from
her mouth with each glorious lunge of his body as it
worked its way hungrily into hers.

He nibbled at her mouth while his hand, curved
over her upper thigh, drew her insistently to meet the
rhythm of his powerful body.

He lifted his head to watch her reactions from time
to time, and despite the glitter of his eyes and the sharp

drag of his breathing, he seemed totally in control. On the other hand, she was sobbing and shivering, clinging desperately to him as the sensations, which were still so new to her, flung her body to and fro against his in waves of hot pleasure.

She arched into him violently, and his hand contracted. "Gently," he whispered. "We have to be careful of your back."

"Gen…tly?" she groaned. "Oh, Todd…I'm…dying!" She pushed against him again, following the trail of the pleasure that had grasped her so viciously just seconds before.

"Here, then." He guided her, watching until he saw her response quicken. He smiled through his own tension as he gave her the ecstasy she pleaded for. Her eyes widened and went black with shock as she stiffened and then convulsed under his delighted gaze.

She felt the tears slide from her eyes as oblivion carried her to heights she'd never dreamed of scaling. And then, just when she was returning to her body, she saw him laugh and then groan as he pushed against her and shuddered with his own satisfaction.

He fell heavily against her, his heartbeat shaking him, and rolled to his side with her clasped against him. One long leg wrapped around her, drawing her even closer while he worked to breathe.

"If it keeps getting better," she whispered into his throat, "I think it may kill me."

He chuckled. "Both of us."

"You laughed," she accused softly.

He lifted his damp head and looked into her eyes, smiling. "Oh, yes." He traced her mouth. "With shock and pleasure and the glory of loving and being loved while I made love. I've never felt so complete before."

She smiled shyly. "Neither have I. Even though it was good the first time."

He kissed her softly. "We'll have years and years of this, and children, and challenges to keep us fit. And I'll love you until I die," he added fervently.

She pressed closer. "I'll love you just as long!" She closed her eyes. "Even longer."

He made a contented sound and bent to kiss her soft mouth. But very quickly the tenderness grew stormy and hungry, and she rolled into his arms again, as hungry as he.

Later, lying in Todd's arms as the morning sun silvered the bed, she thought that she'd never been happier or more fulfilled in her whole life. Or more weary.

"Exhausted already?" he exclaimed when she shifted in his arms and groaned as her sore muscles protested. "I'll have to feed you more oysters!"

"I'll feed you to the oysters if you don't let me sleep," she teased, nuzzling closer. "I know we agreed that it would be nice to start our family right away, but I'll die of fatigue before we get to the first one at this rate!"

He chuckled and kissed her forehead softly. "We'll sleep a bit longer, then. Happy?" he murmured drowsily.

"Happier than I ever dreamed I could be."

"And your back...is it all right?"

"It's fine. Actually, I think this is therapeutic for it."

"All the more reason to exercise it twice a day."

She kissed his bare shoulder. "Later. I've had no sleep in two days. I kept thinking that your ex-wife would find some way to sabotage the ceremony."

"That wasn't likely," he said with a weary grin. "Cherry had made several threats. I think she's going to be a very formidable surgeon when she gets out of medical school. Anyone who can buffalo Marie shouldn't have any trouble with hospital staff."

Jane smiled. "She and her mother do get along better now, at least."

"Oh, Marie learned her lesson the hard way. If she isn't nice to you, she'll lose her daughter. That's the one thing that made her apologize to you, and it's kept her pleasant." He stretched lazily. "She even offered to redecorate the ranch house for you free after she has the baby."

"I'll think about that."

"I had a feeling that's what you'd say. She means well."

"I know. I love you."

He smiled. "I love you."

He drew her close and pulled the sheet up over them. In the distance, the crash of the surf was like a watery serenade. Jane closed her eyes and turned her face into Todd's chest. And her dreams were sweet.

* * * * *

COLTRAIN'S PROPOSAL

Chapter One

The little boy's leg was bleeding profusely. Dr. Louise Blakely knew exactly what to do, but it was difficult to get the right pressure on the cut so that the nicked artery would stop emptying onto the brown, dead December grass.

"It hurts!" the little boy, Matt, cried. "Ow!"

"We have to stop the bleeding," she said reasonably. She smiled at him, her dark eyes twinkling in a face framed by thick, medium blond hair. "Maybe your mom could get you an ice cream after we've patched you up." She glanced at the white-faced lady beside them, who nodded enthusiastically. "Okay?"

"Well…" He grimaced, holding his leg above where Lou was putting pressure to bear.

"Only a minute more," she promised, looking around for the ambulance she'd asked a bystander to call. It was on the way. She could hear the siren. Even in a small town like Jacobsville, there was an efficient ambulance service. "You're going to get to ride in a real ambulance," she told the child. "You can tell your friends all about it on Monday at school!"

"Will I have to go back?" he asked, enthusiastic

now. "Maybe I could stay in the hospital for a whole week?"

"I really think the emergency room is as far as you're going to get this time." Lou chuckled. "Now pay attention while they're loading you up, so that you can remember everything!"

"I sure will!" he said.

She stood up as the ambulance pulled alongside the police car and two attendants jumped out. They started loading the boy onto a stretcher. Lou had a brief word with the female EMT and described the boy's injuries and gave instructions. She was on staff at the local hospital where he would be taken, and she planned to follow the ambulance in her own car.

The police officer who'd been citing the reckless driver for hitting the small boy on the bicycle came over to talk to Lou. "Good thing you were having lunch in the café," he remarked with a grin. "That was a bad cut."

"He'll be okay," Lou said as she closed her medical bag. She always had it in the car when she left the office, and this time it had paid off.

"You're Dr. Coltrain's partner, aren't you?" he asked suddenly.

"Yes." She didn't add anything to that. The expression on the officer's face said enough. Most people around Jacobsville knew that Dr. Coltrain had as little use for his partner as he had for alcohol. He'd made it all too evident in the months she'd been sharing his practice.

"He's a good man," the officer added. "Saved my

wife when her lung collapsed." He smiled at the memory. "Nothing shakes him up. Nor you, either, judging by what I just saw. You're a good hand in an emergency."

"Thanks." She gave him a brief smile and went to her small gray Ford to follow the ambulance to the hospital.

The emergency room was full, as usual. It was Saturday and accidents always doubled on weekends. She nodded to a couple of her patients that she recognized, and she kept walking, right behind the trolley that was taking young Matt to a treatment room.

Dr. Coltrain was on his way back from surgery. They met in the hall. The green surgical uniform looked sloppy on some of the surgeons, but not on Coltrain. Despite the cap that hid most of his thick red hair, he looked elegant and formidable.

"Why are you here on Saturday? I'm supposed to be doing rounds today for both of us," he asked sharply.

Here he goes again, practicing Coltrain's First Law... jump to conclusions, she thought. She didn't grin, but she felt like it.

"I wound up at a car accident scene," she began.

"The hospital pays EMTs to work wrecks," he continued, glaring at her while hospital personnel came and went around them.

"I did not go out to—" she began hotly.

"Don't let this happen again, or I'll have a word with Wright, and you'll be taken off staff here. Is that clear?" he added coldly. Wright was the hospital administrator and Coltrain was medical chief of staff. He had the authority to carry out the threat.

"Will you listen?" she asked irritably. "I didn't go out with the ambulance…!"

"Doctor, are you coming?" one of the EMTs called to her.

Coltrain glanced toward the EMT and then back at Louise, irritably jerking off his cap and mask. His pale blue eyes were as intimidating as his stance. "If your social life is this stale, Doctor, perhaps you need to consider a move," he added with biting sarcasm.

She opened her mouth to reply, but he was already walking away. She threw up her hands furiously. She couldn't ever get a word in, because he kept talking, or interrupted her, and then stormed off without giving her a chance to reply. It was useless to argue with him, anyway. No matter what she said or did, she was always in the wrong.

"One day you'll break something," she told his retreating back. "And I'll put you in a body cast, so help me God!"

A passing nurse patted her on the shoulder. "There, there, Doctor, you're doing it again."

She ground her teeth together. It was a standing joke in the hospital staff that Louise Blakely ended up talking to herself every time she argued with Dr. Coltrain. That meant that she talked to herself almost constantly. Presumably he heard her from time to time, but he never gave a single indication that he had.

With a furious groan deep in her throat, she turned down the hall to join the EMT.

* * *

It took an hour to see to the boy, who had more than one cut that needed stitches. His mother was going to have to buy him a lot of ice cream to make up for the pain, Lou thought, and she'd been wrong about another thing, too—he did have to stay overnight in the hospital. But that would only give him status among his peers, she thought, and left him smiling with a cautionary word about the proper way to ride a bicycle in town.

"No need to worry about that," his mother said firmly. "He won't be riding his bike across city streets anymore!"

She nodded and left the emergency room, her bag in hand. She looked more like a teenager on holiday than a doctor, she mused, in her blue jeans and T-shirt and sneakers. She'd pulled her long blond hair up into its habitual bun and she wore no makeup to enhance her full mouth or her deep brown eyes. She had no man to impress, except the one she loved, and he wouldn't notice if she wore tar and feathers to the office they shared. "Copper" Coltrain had no interest in Lou Blakely, except as an efficient co-worker. Not that he ever acknowledged her efficiency; instead he found fault with her constantly. She wondered often why he ever agreed to work with her in the first place, when he couldn't seem to stand the sight of her. She wondered, too, why she kept hanging on where she wasn't wanted. The hunger her poor heart felt for him was her only excuse. And one day, even that wouldn't be enough.

Dr. Drew Morris, the only friend she had on staff, came down the hall toward her. Like Coltrain, he'd been operating, because he was wearing the same familiar green surgical clothing. But where Coltrain did chest surgery, Drew's talents were limited to tonsils, adenoids, appendices and other minor surgeries. His speciality was pediatrics. Coltrain's was chest and lungs, and many of his patients were elderly.

"What are you doing here? It's too early or too late for rounds, depending on your schedule," he added with a grin. "Besides, I thought Copper was doing them today."

Copper, indeed. Only a handful of people were privileged to call Dr. Coltrain by that nickname, and she wasn't numbered among them.

She grimaced at him. He was about her height, although she was tall, and he had dark hair and eyes and was a little overweight. He was the one who'd phoned her at the Austin hospital where she was working just after her parents' deaths, and he'd told her about the interviews Coltrain was holding for a partner. She'd jumped at the chance for a new start, in the hometown where her mother and father had both been born. And amazingly, in light of his ongoing animosity toward her, Coltrain had asked her to join him after a ten-minute interview.

"There was an accident in front of the café," she said. "I was having lunch there. I haven't been to the grocery store yet," she added with a grimace. "I hate shopping."

"Who doesn't?" He smiled. "Doing okay?"

She shrugged. "As usual."

He stuck his hands on his hips and shook his head. "It's my fault. I thought it would get better, but it hasn't, has it? It's been almost a year, and he still suffers you."

She winced. She didn't quite avert her face fast enough to hide it.

"You poor kid," he said gently. "I'm sorry. I suppose I was too enthusiastic about getting you here. I thought you needed a change, after…well, after your parents' deaths. This looked like a good opportunity. Copper's one of the best surgeons I've ever known, and you're a skilled family practitioner. It seemed a good match of talent, and you've taken a load off him in his regular practice so that he could specialize in the surgery he's so skilled at." He sighed. "How wrong can a man be?"

"I signed a contract for one year," she reminded him. "It's almost up."

"Then what?"

"Then I'll go back to Austin."

"You could work the ER," he teased. It was a standing joke between them. The hospital had to contract out the emergency room staff, because none of the local doctors wanted to do it. The job was so demanding that one young resident had walked out in the middle of the unnecessary examination of a known hypochondriac at two in the morning and never came back.

Lou smiled, remembering that. "No, thanks. I like private practice, but I can't afford to set up and equip an office of my own just yet. I'll go back to the drawing board. There's bound to be a practice somewhere in Texas."

"You're fit for this one," he said shortly.

"Not to hear my partner tell it," she said curtly. "I'm never right, didn't you know?" She let out a long breath. "Anyway, I'm in a rut, Drew. I need a change."

"Maybe you do, at that." He pursed his lips and smiled. "What you really need is a good social life. I'll be in touch."

She watched him walk away with grave misgivings. She hoped that he didn't mean what it sounded like he meant. She wanted nothing to do with Drew in a romantic way, although she did like him. He was a kind man, a widower who'd been in love with his wife and was still, after five years, getting over her. Drew was a native of Jacobsville, and knew Lou's parents. He'd been very fond of her late mother. He'd met up with them again in Austin—that's where Lou had met him.

Lou decided not to take Drew's teasing seriously because she knew about his devotion to his wife's memory. But he'd looked very solemn when he'd remarked that her social life needed uplifting.

She was probably imagining things, she told herself. She started out to the parking lot and met Dr. Coltrain, dressed in an expensive gray vested suit, bent on the same destination. She ground her teeth together and slowed her pace, but she still reached the doors at the same time he did.

He spared her a cold glance. "You look unprofessional," he said curtly. "At least have the grace to dress decently if you're going to cruise around with the ambulance service."

She stopped and looked up at him without expression. "I wasn't cruising anywhere. I don't have a boat, so how could I cruise?"

He just looked at her. "They don't need any new EMTs..."

"You shut up!" she snapped, surprising him speechless. "Now you listen to me for a change, and don't interrupt!" she added, holding up her hand when his thin lips parted. "There was an accident in town. I was in the café, so I gave assistance. I don't need to hang out with the ambulance crew for kicks, Doctor! And how I dress on my days off is none of your—" she almost turned blue biting back the curse "—*business*, Doctor!"

He was over his shock. His hand shot out and caught the wrist of her free hand, the one that wasn't holding her black medical bag, and jerked. She caught her breath at the shock of his touch and squirmed, wrestling out of his grip. The muted violence of it brought back protective instincts that she'd almost forgotten. She stood very still, holding her breath, her eyes the size of saucers as she looked at him and waited for that hand to tighten and twist...

But it didn't. He, unlike her late father, never seemed to lose control. He released her abruptly. His blue eyes narrowed. "Cold as ice, aren't you?" he drawled mockingly. "You'd freeze any normal man to death. Is that why you never married, Doctor?"

It was the most personal thing he'd ever said to her, and one of the most insulting.

"You just think what you like," she said.

"You might be surprised at what I think," he replied.

He looked at the hand he'd touched her with and laughed deep in his throat. "Frostbitten," he pronounced. "No wonder Drew Morris doesn't take you out. He'd need a blowtorch, wouldn't he?" he added with a meaningful, unblinking blue stare.

"Maybe so, but you'd need a grenade launcher," she retorted without thinking.

He lifted an eyebrow and gave her a look that held mingled contempt and distaste. "You'd be lucky."

The remark was painful, but she didn't let him see that. Her own eyebrows lifted. "Really?" She laughed and walked off to her car, happy to have seen him stiffen. She walked past his Mercedes without even a glance. Take that, she thought furiously. She didn't care what he thought about her, she told herself. She spent most of her free time telling herself that. But she did care about him, far too much. That was the whole problem.

He thought she was cold, but she wasn't. It was quite the reverse where he was concerned. She always jerked away when he came too close, when he touched her infrequently. It wasn't because she found him repulsive but because his touch excited her so much. She trembled when he was too close, her breathing changed. She couldn't control her shaky legs or her shaky voice. The only solution had been to distance herself physically from him, and that was what she'd done.

There were other reasons, too, why she avoided physical involvement. They were none of his business, or anyone else's. She did her job and avoided trouble as much as possible. But just lately, her job was becoming an ordeal.

She drove home to the small dilapidated white house on the outskirts of town. It was in a quiet neighborhood that was just beginning to go downhill. The rent was cheap. She'd spent weekends painting the walls and adding bits and pieces to the house's drab interior. She had it all but furnished now, and it reflected her own quiet personality. But there were other dimensions to the room, like the crazy cat sculpture on the mantel and the colorful serapes on the chairs, and the Indian pottery and exotic musical instruments on the bookshelf. The paintings were her own, disturbingly violent ones with reds and blacks and whites in dramatic chaos. A visitor would have found the combinations of flowers amid those paintings confusing. But, then, she'd never had a visitor. She kept to herself.

Coltrain did, too, as a rule. He had visitors to his ranch from time to time, but his invitations even when they included the medical staff invariably excluded Louise. The omission had caused gossip, which no one had been brave enough to question to his face. Louise didn't care if he never invited her to his home. After all, she never invited him to hers.

Secretly she suspected that he was grieving for Jane Parker, his old flame who'd just recently married Todd Burke. Jane was blond and blue-eyed and beautiful, a former rodeo star with a warm heart and a gentle personality.

Lou often wondered why he'd ever agreed to work

with someone he disliked so much, and on such short acquaintance. He and Dr. Drew Morris were friends, and she'd tried to question Drew about her sudden acceptance, but Drew was a clam. He always changed the subject.

Drew had known her parents in Jacobsville and he had been a student of her father's at the Austin teaching hospital where he'd interned. He'd become an ally of her mother during some really tough times, but he didn't like Lou's father. He knew too much about his home life, and how Lou and her mother were treated.

There had been one whisper of gossip at the Jacobsville hospital when she'd first gone there on cases. She'd heard one of the senior nurses remark that it must disturb "him" to have Dr. Blakely's daughter practicing at this hospital and thank God she didn't do surgery. Lou had wanted to question the nurse, but she'd made herself scarce after that and eventually had retired.

Louise had never found out who "he" was or what was disturbing about having another Blakely practice at the Jacobsville hospital. But she did begin to realize that her father had a past here.

"What did my father do at this hospital, Drew?" she'd asked him one day suddenly, while they were doing rounds at the hospital.

He'd seemed taken aback. "He was a surgeon on staff, just as I am," he said after a hesitation.

"He left here under a cloud, didn't he?" she persisted.

He shook his head. "There was no scandal, no cloud

on his reputation. He was a good surgeon and well respected, right until the end. You know that. Even if he was less than admirable as a husband and father, he was an exceptional surgeon."

"Then why the whispers about him when I first came here?"

"It was nothing to do with his skill as a surgeon," he replied quietly. "It's nothing that really even concerns you, except in a roundabout way."

"But what…?"

They'd been interrupted and he'd looked relieved. She hadn't asked again. But she wondered more and more. Perhaps it had affected Dr. Coltrain in some way and that was why he disliked Lou. But wouldn't he have mentioned it in a whole year?

She didn't ever expect to understand the so-controlled Dr. Coltrain or his venomous attitude toward her. He'd been much more cordial when she first became his partner. But about the time she realized that she was in love with him, he became icy cold and antagonistic. He'd been that way ever since, raising eyebrows everywhere.

The remark he'd made this morning about her coldness was an old one. She'd jerked back from him at a Christmas party, soon after she'd come to work in his office in Jacobsville, to avoid a kiss under the mistletoe. She could hardly have admitted that even then the thought of his hard, thin mouth on hers made her knees threaten to buckle. Her attraction to him had been explosive and immediate, a frightening experience to a woman whose whole life had been wrapped around academic excellence and night upon night of exhaustive studying. She had no social life at all—even in high school. It had been the one thing that kept her father's vicious sarcasm and brutality at bay, as long as she made good grades and stayed on the dean's list.

Outside achievements had been the magic key that kept the balance in her dysfunctional family. She studied and won awards and scholarships and praise, and her father basked in it. She thought that he'd never felt much for her, except pride in her ability to excel. He was a cruel man and grew crueler as his addiction climbed year after year to new heights. Drugs had caused the plane crash. Her mother had died with him. God knew, that was fitting, because she'd loved him to the point of blindness, overlooking his brutality, his addiction, his cruelty in the name of fidelity.

Lou wrapped her arms around herself, feeling the chill of fear. She'd never marry. Any woman could wake up in a relationship that damaging. All she had to do was fall in love, lose control, give in to a man's dominance. Even the best man could become a predator if he sensed vulnerability in a woman. So she would never be vulnerable, she assured herself. She would never be at a man's mercy as her mother had been.

But Copper Coltrain made her vulnerable, and that was why she avoided any physical contact with him. She couldn't give in to the feelings he roused in her, for fear of becoming a victim. Loneliness might be a disease, but it was certainly a more manageable one than love.

The ringing of the telephone caught her attention.

"Dr. Blakely?" Brenda, her office nurse, queried. "Sorry to bother you at home, but Dr. Coltrain said there's been a wreck on the north end of town and they'll be bringing the victims to the emergency room. Since he's on call, you'll have to cover the two-hour Saturday clinic at the office."

"I'll be right over," she promised, wasting no more time in conversation.

The clinic was almost deserted. There was a football game at the local high school that night, and it was sunny and unseasonably warm outside for early December. It didn't really surprise Lou that she only needed to see a handful of patients.

"Poor Dr. Coltrain," Brenda said with a sigh as they finished the last case and closed up the office. "I'll bet he won't be in until midnight."

"It's a good thing he isn't married," Lou remarked. "He'd have no home life at all, as hard as he works."

Brenda glanced at her, but with a kind smile. "That is true. But he should be thinking about it. He's in his thirties now, and time is passing him by." She turned the key in the lock. "Pity about Miss Parker marrying that Burke man, isn't it? Dr. Coltrain was sweet on her for so many years. I always thought—I guess most people here did—that they were made for each other. But she was never more than friendly. If you saw them together, it was obvious that she didn't feel what he did."

In other words, Dr. Coltrain had felt a long and unrequited love for the lovely blond former rodeo cowgirl, Jane Parker. That much, Lou had learned from gossip. It must have hurt him very badly when she married someone else.

"What a pity that we can't love to order," Lou remarked quietly, thinking how much she'd give to be unscarred and find Dr. Coltrain as helplessly drawn to her as she was to him. That was the stuff of fantasy, however.

"Wasn't it surprising about Ted Regan and Coreen Tarleton, though?" Brenda added with a chuckle.

"Indeed it was," Lou agreed, smiling as she remembered having Ted for a patient. "She was shaking all over when she got him to me with that gored arm. He was cool. Nothing shakes Ted. But Coreen was as white as milk."

"I thought they were already married," Brenda groaned. "Well, I was new to the area and I didn't know them. I do now," she added, laughing. "I pass them at least once a week on their way to the obstetrician's office. She's due any day."

"She'll be a good mother, and Ted will certainly be a good father. Their children will have a happy life."

Brenda caught the faint bitterness in the words and glanced at Lou, but the other woman was already calling her goodbyes and walking away.

She went home and spent the rest of the weekend buried in medical journals and the latest research on the new strain of bacteria that had, researchers surmised, mutated from a deadly scarlet fever bacterium that had caused many deaths at the turn of the century.

Chapter Two

Monday morning brought a variety of new cases, and Louise found herself stuck with the most routine of them, as usual. She and Coltrain were supposed to be partners, but when he wasn't operating, he got the interesting, challenging illnesses. Louise got fractured ribs and colds.

He'd been stiff with her this morning, probably because he was still fuming over the argument they'd had about his mistaken idea of her weekend activities. Accusing her of lollygagging with the EMTs for excitement; really!

She watched his white-coated back disappear into an examination room down the hall in their small building and sighed half-angrily as she went back to check an X ray in the files. The very worst thing about unrequited love, she thought miserably, was that it fed on itself. The more her partner in the medical practice ignored and antagonized her, the harder she had to fight her dreams about him. She didn't want to get married; she didn't even want to get involved. But he made her hungry.

He'd spent a lot of time with Jane Parker until she

married that Burke man, and Lou had long ago given up hope that he would ever notice her in the same way he always noticed Jane. The two of them had grown up together, though, whereas Lou' had only been in partnership with him for a year. She was a native of Austin, not Jacobsville. Small towns were like extended families. Everybody knew each other, and some families had been friends for more than one generation. Lou was a true outsider here, even though she *was* a native Texan. Perhaps that was one of many reasons that Dr. Coltrain found her so forgettable.

She wasn't bad looking. She had long, thick blond hair and big brown eyes and a creamy, blemish-free complexion. She was tall and willowy, but still shorter than her colleague. She lacked his fiery temper and his authoritarian demeanor. He was tall and whipcord lean, with flaming red hair and blue eyes and a dark tan from working on his small ranch when he wasn't treating patients. That tan was odd in a redhead, although he did have a smattering of freckles over his nose and the backs of his big hands. She'd often wondered if the freckles went any farther, but she had yet to see him without his professional white coat over his very formal suit. He wasn't much on casual dressing at work. At home, she was sure that he dressed less formally.

That was something Lou would probably never know. She'd never been invited to his home, despite the fact that most of the medical staff at the local hospital had. Lou was automatically excluded from any social gathering that he coordinated.

Other people had commented on his less than

friendly behavior toward her. It puzzled them, and it puzzled her, because she hadn't become his partner in any underhanded way. He had known from the day of her application that she was female, so it couldn't be that. Perhaps, she thought wistfully, he was one of those old-line dominating sort of men who thought women had no place in medicine. But he'd been instrumental in getting women into positions of authority at the hospital, so that theory wasn't applicable, either. The bottom line was that he simply did not like Louise Blakely, medical degree or no medical degree, and she'd never known why.

She really should ask Drew Morris why, she told herself with determination. It had been Drew, a surgeon and friend of her family, who'd sent word about the opening in Coltrain's practice. He'd wanted to help Lou get a job near him, so that he could give her some moral support in the terrible days following the deaths of her parents. She, in turn, had liked the idea of being in practice in a small town, one where she knew at least one doctor on the staff of the hospital. Despite growing up in Austin, it was still a big city and she was lonely. She was twenty-eight, a loner whose whole life had been medicine. She'd made sure that her infrequent dates never touched her heart, and she was innocent in an age when innocence was automatically looked on with disdain or suspicion.

Her nurse stuck her head in the doorway. "There's a call for you. Dr. Morris is on line two."

"Thanks, Brenda."

She picked up the receiver absently, her finger poised

over the designated line. But when she pressed it, before she could say a word, the sentence she'd intercepted accidentally blared in her ear in a familiar deep voice.

"...told you I wouldn't have hired her in the first place, if I had known who she was related to. I did you a favor, never realizing she was Blakely's daughter. You can't imagine that I'll ever forgive her father for what he did to the girl I loved, do you? She's been a constant reminder, a constant torment!"

"That's harsh, Copper," Drew began.

"It's how I feel. She's nothing but a burden here. But to answer your question, hell no, you're not stepping on my toes if you ask her out on a date! I find Louise Blakely repulsive and repugnant, and an automaton with no attractions whatsoever. Take her with my blessing. I'd give real money if she'd get out of my practice and out of my life, and the sooner the better!" There was a click and the line, obviously open, was waiting for her.

She clicked the receiver to announce her presence and said, as calmly as she could, "Dr. Lou Blakely."

"Lou! It's Drew Morris," came the reply. "I hope I'm not catching you at a bad moment?"

"No." She cleared her throat and fought to control her scattered emotions. "No, not at all. What can I do for you?"

"There's a dinner at the Rotary Club Thursday. How about going with me?"

She and Drew occasionally went out together, in a friendly but not romantic way. She would have refused, but what Coltrain had said made her mad. "Yes, I would like to, thanks," she said.

Drew laughed softly. "Great! I'll pick you up at six on Thursday, then."

"See you then."

She hung up, checked the X ray again meticulously, and put it away in its file. Brenda ordinarily pulled the X rays for her, but it was Monday and, as usual, they were overflowing with patients who'd saved their weekend complaints for office hours.

She went back to her patient, her color a little high, but no disturbance visible in her expression.

She finished her quota of patients and then went into her small office. Mechanically she picked up a sheet of letterhead paper, with Dr. Coltrain's name on one side and hers on the other. Irrelevantly, she thought that the stationery would have to be replaced now.

She typed out a neat resignation letter, put it in an envelope and went to place it on Dr. Coltrain's desk. It was lunchtime and he'd already left the building. He made sure he always did, probably to insure that he didn't risk having Lou invite herself to eat with him.

Brenda scowled as her boss started absently toward the back door. "Shouldn't you take off your coat first?" she asked hesitantly.

Lou did, without a word, replaced it in her office, whipped her leather fanny pack around her waist and left the building.

It would have been nice if she'd had someone to talk to, she thought wistfully, about this latest crisis. She sat alone in the local café, drinking black coffee and picking at a small salad. She didn't mingle well with people. When she wasn't working, she was quiet and shy, and she kept to herself. It was difficult for strangers to approach her, but she didn't realize that. She stared into her coffee and remembered every word Coltrain had said to Drew Morris about her. He hated her. He couldn't possibly have made it clearer. She was repugnant, he'd said.

Well, perhaps she was. Her father had told her so, often enough, when he was alive. He and her mother were from Jacobsville but hadn't lived in the area for years. He had never spoken of his past. Not that he spoke to Lou often, anyway, except to berate her grades and tell her that she'd never measure up.

"Excuse me?"

She looked up. The waitress was staring at her. "Yes?" she asked coolly.

"I don't mean to pry, but are you all right?"

The question surprised Lou, and touched her. She managed a faint smile through her misery. "Yes. It's been a…long morning. I'm not really hungry."

"Okay." The waitress smiled again, reassuringly, and went away.

Just as Lou was finishing her coffee, Coltrain came in the front door. He was wearing the elegant gray suit that looked so good on him, and carrying a silver belly Stetson by the brim. He looked furiously angry as his pale eyes scanned the room and finally spotted Lou, sitting all alone.

He never hesitated, she thought, watching him walk

purposefully toward her. There must be an emergency…

He slammed the opened envelope down on the table in front of her. "What the hell do you mean by that?" he demanded in a dangerously quiet tone.

She raised her dark, cold eyes to his. "I'm leaving," she explained and averted her gaze.

"I know that! I want to know why!"

She looked around. The café was almost empty, but the waitress and a local cowboy at the counter were glancing at them curiously.

Her chin came up. "I'd rather not discuss my private business in public, if you don't mind," she said stiffly.

His jaw clenched, and his eyes grew glittery. He stood back to allow her to get up. He waited while she paid for her salad and coffee and then followed her out to where her small gray Ford was parked.

Her heart raced when he caught her by the arm before she could get her key out of her jeans pocket. He jerked her around, not roughly, and walked her over to Jacobsville's small town square, to a secluded bench in a grove of live oak and willow trees. Because it was barely December, there were no leaves on the trees and it was cool, despite her nervous perspiration. She tried to throw off his hand, to no avail.

He only loosened his grip on her when she sat down on a park bench. He remained standing, propping his boot on the bench beside her, leaning one long arm over his knee to study her. "This is private enough," he said shortly. "Why are you leaving?"

"I signed a contract to work with you for one year.

It's almost up, anyway," she said icily. "I want out. I want to go home."

"You don't have anyone left in Austin," he said, surprising her.

"I have friends," she began.

"You don't have those, either. You don't have friends at all, unless you count Drew Morris," he said flatly.

Her fingers clenched around her car keys. She looked at them, biting into the flesh even though not a speck of emotion showed on her placid features.

His eyes followed hers to her lap and something moved in his face. There was an expression there that puzzled her. He reached down and opened her rigid hand, frowning when he saw the red marks the keys had made in her palm.

She jerked her fingers away from him.

He seemed disconcerted for a few seconds. He stared at her without speaking and she felt her heart beating wildly against her ribs. She hated being helpless.

He moved back, watching her relax. He took another step and saw her release the breath she'd been holding. Every trace of anger left him.

"It takes time for a partnership to work," he said abruptly. "You've only given this one a year."

"That's right," she said tonelessly. "*I've* given it a year."

The emphasis she placed on the first word caught his attention. His blue eyes narrowed. "You sound as if you don't think I've given it any time at all."

She nodded. Her eyes met his. "You didn't want me in the practice. I suspected it from the beginning, but it wasn't until I heard what you told Drew on the phone this morning that—"

His eyes flashed oddly. "You heard what I said?" he asked huskily. "You heard…all of it!" he exclaimed.

Her lips trembled just faintly. "Yes," she said.

He was remembering what he'd told Drew Morris in a characteristic outburst of bad temper. He often said things in heat that he regretted later, but this he regretted most of all. He'd never credited his cool, unflappable partner with any emotions at all. She'd backed away from him figuratively and physically since the first day she'd worked at the clinic. Her physical withdrawal had maddened him, although he'd always assumed she was frigid.

But in the past five minutes, he'd learned disturbing things about her without a word being spoken. He'd hurt her. He didn't realize she'd cared that much about his opinion. Hell, he'd been furious because he'd just had to diagnose leukemia in a sweet little boy of four. It had hurt him to do that, and he'd lashed out at Morris over Lou in frustration at his own helplessness. But he'd had no idea that she'd overheard his vicious remarks. She was going to leave and it was no less than he deserved. He was genuinely sorry. She wasn't going to believe that, though. He could tell by her mutinous expression, in her clenched hands, in the tight set of her mouth.

"You did Drew a favor and asked me to join you, probably over some other doctor you really wanted," she said with a forced smile. "Well, no harm done. Perhaps you can get him back when I leave."

"Wait a minute," he began shortly.

She held up a hand. "Let's not argue about it," she said, sick at knowing his opinion of her, his real opinion. "I'm tired of fighting you to practice medicine here. I haven't done the first thing right, according to you. I'm a burden. Well, I just want out. I'll go on working until you can replace me." She stood up.

His hand tightened on the brim of his hat. He was losing this battle. He didn't know how to pull his irons out of the fire.

"I had to tell the Dawes that their son has leukemia," he said, hating the need to explain his bad temper. "I say things I don't mean sometimes."

"We both know that you meant what you said about me," she said flatly. Her eyes met his levelly. "You've hated me from almost the first day we worked together. Most of the time, you can't even be bothered to be civil to me. I didn't know that you had a grudge against me from the outset…"

She hadn't thought about that until she said it, but there was a subtle change in his expression, a faint distaste that her mind locked on.

"So you heard that, too." His jaw clenched on words he didn't want to say. But maybe it was as well to say them. He'd lived a lie for the past year.

"Yes." She gripped the wrought-iron frame of the park bench hard. "What happened? Did my father cause someone to die?"

His jaw tautened. He didn't like saying this. "The girl I wanted to marry got pregnant by him. He performed a secret abortion and she was going to marry me anyway." He laughed icily. "A fling, he called it. But the medical authority had other ideas, and they invited him to resign."

Lou's fingers went white on the cold wrought iron. Had her mother known? What had happened to the girl afterward?

"Only a handful of people knew," Coltrain said, as if he'd read her thoughts. "I doubt that your mother did. She seemed very nice—hardly a fit match for a man like that."

"And the girl?" she asked levelly.

"She left town. Eventually she married." He rammed his hands into his pockets and glared at her. "If you want the whole truth, Drew felt sorry for you when your parents died so tragically. He knew I was looking for a partner, and he recommended you so highly that I asked you. I didn't connect the name at first," he added on a mocking note. "Ironic, isn't it, that I'd choose as a partner the daughter of a man I hated until the day he died."

"Why didn't you tell me?" she asked irritably. "I would have resigned!"

"You were in no fit state to be told anything," he replied with reluctant memories of her tragic face when she'd arrived. His hands clenched in his pockets. "Besides, you'd signed a one-year contract. The only way out was if you resigned."

It all made sense immediately. She was too intelligent not to understand why he'd been so antagonistic. "I see," she breathed. "But I didn't resign."

"You were made of stronger stuff than I imagined,"

he agreed. "You wouldn't back down an inch. No matter how rough it got, you threw my own bad temper back at me." He rubbed his fingers absently over the car keys in his pocket while he studied her. "It's been a long time since anyone around here stood up to me like that," he added reluctantly.

She knew that without being told. He was a holy terror. Even grown men around Jacobsville gave him a wide berth when he lost his legendary temper. But Lou never had. She stood right up to him. She wasn't fiery by nature, but her father had been viciously cruel to her. She'd learned early not to show fear or back down, because it only made him worse. The same rule seemed to apply to Coltrain. A weaker personality wouldn't have lasted in his office one week, much less one year, male or female.

She knew now that Drew Morris had been doing what he thought was a good deed. Perhaps he'd thought it wouldn't matter to Coltrain after such a long time to have a Blakely working for him. But he'd obviously underestimated the man. Lou would have realized at once, on the shortest acquaintance, that Coltrain didn't forgive people.

He stared at her unblinkingly. "A year. A whole year, being reminded every day I took a breath what your father cost me. There were times when I'd have done anything to make you leave. Just the sight of you was painful." He smiled wearily. "I think I hated you, at first."

That was the last straw. She'd loved him, against her will and all her judgment, and he was telling her that all he saw when he looked at her was an ice woman whose father had betrayed him with the woman he loved. He hated her.

It was too much all at once. Lou had always had impeccable control over her emotions. It had been dangerous to let her father know that he was hurting her, because he enjoyed hurting her. And now here was the one man she'd ever loved telling her that he hated her because of her father.

What a surprise it would be for him to learn that her father, at the last, had been little more than a high-class drug addict, stealing narcotics from the hospital where he worked in Austin to support his growing habit. He'd been as high as a kite on narcotics, in fact, when the plane he was piloting went down, killing himself and his wife.

Tears swelled her eyelids. Not a sound passed her lips as they overflowed in two hot streaks down her pale cheeks.

He caught his breath. He'd seen her tired, impassive, worn-out, fighting mad, and even frustrated. But he'd never seen her cry. His lean hand shot out and touched the track of tears down one cheek, as if he had to touch them to make sure they were real.

She jerked back from him, laughing tearfully. "So that was why you were so horrible to me." She choked out the words. "Drew never said a word…no wonder you suffered me! And I was silly enough to dream…!" The laughter was harsher now as she dashed away the tears, staring at him with eyes full of pain and loss. "What a fool I've been," she whispered poignantly. "What a silly fool!"

She turned and walked away from him, gripping the car keys in her hand. The sight of her back was as eloquently telling as the words that haunted him. She'd dreamed…what?

For the next few days, Lou was polite and remote and as courteous as any stranger toward her partner. But something had altered in their relationship. He was aware of a subtle difference in her attitude toward him, in a distancing of herself that was new. Her eyes had always followed him, and he'd been aware of it at some subconscious level. Perhaps he'd been aware of more than covert glances, too. But Lou no longer watched him or went out of her way to seek him out. If she had questions, she wrote them down and left them for him on his desk. If there were messages to be passed on, she left them with Brenda.

The one time she did seek him out was Thursday afternoon as they closed up.

"Have you worked out an advertisement for someone to replace me?" she asked him politely.

He watched her calm dark eyes curiously. "Are you in such a hurry to leave?" he asked.

"Yes," she said bluntly. "I'd like to leave after the Christmas holidays." She turned and would have gone out the door, but his hand caught the sleeve of her white jacket. She slung it off and backed away. "At the first of the year."

He glared at her, hating the instinctive withdrawal that came whenever he touched her. "You're a good doctor," he said flatly. "You've earned your place here."

High praise for a man with his grudges. She looked over her shoulder at him, her eyes wounded. "But you hate me, don't you? I heard what you said to Drew, that every time you looked at me you remembered what my father had done and hated me all over again."

He let go of her sleeve, frowning. He couldn't find an answer.

"Well, don't sweat it, Doctor," she told him. "I'll be gone in a month and you can find someone you like to work with you."

She laughed curtly and walked out of the office.

She dressed sedately that evening for the Rotary Club dinner, in a neat off-white suit with a pink blouse. But she left her blond hair long around her shoulders for once, and used a light dusting of makeup. She didn't spend much time looking in the mirror. Her appearance had long ago ceased to matter to her.

Drew was surprised by it, though, and curious. She looked strangely vulnerable. But when he tried to hold her hand, she drew away from him. He'd wanted to ask her for a long time if there were things in her past that she might like to share with someone. But Louise was an unknown quantity, and she could easily shy away. He couldn't risk losing her altogether.

Drew held her arm as they entered the hall, and Lou was disconcerted to find Dr. Coltrain there. He almost never attended social functions unless Jane Parker was in attendance. But a quick glance around the room ascertained that Jane wasn't around. She wondered if the doctor had brought a date. It didn't take long to have that question answered, as a pretty young brunette came up beside him and clung to his arm as if it was the ticket to heaven.

Coltrain wasn't looking at her, though. His pale, narrow eyes had lanced over Lou and he was watching her closely. He hadn't seen her hair down in the year they'd worked together. She seemed more approachable tonight than he'd ever noticed, but she was Drew's date. Probably Drew's woman, too, he thought bitterly, despite her protests and reserve.

But trying to picture Lou in Drew's bed was more difficult than he'd thought. It wasn't at all in character. She was rigid in her views, just as she was in her mode of dress and her hairstyle. Just because she'd loosened that glorious hair tonight didn't mean that she'd suddenly become uninhibited. Nonetheless, the change disturbed him, because it was unexpected.

"Copper's got a new girl, I see," Drew said with a grin. "That's Nickie Bolton," he added. "She works as a nurse's aide at the hospital."

"I didn't recognize her out of uniform," Lou murmured.

"I did," he said. "She's lovely, isn't she?"

She nodded amiably. "Very young, too," she added with an indulgent smile.

He took her hand gently and smiled down at her. "You aren't exactly over the hill yourself," he teased.

She smiled up at him with warm eyes. "You're a nice man, Drew."

Across the room, a redheaded man's grip tightened ominously on a glass of punch. For over a year, Louise had avoided even his lightest touch. A few days ago, she'd thrown off his hand violently. But there she stood not only allowing Drew to hold her hand, but actually smiling at him. She'd never smiled at Coltrain that way; she'd never smiled at him any way at all.

His companion tapped him on the shoulder.

"You're with me, remember?" she asked with a pert smile. "Stop staring daggers at your partner. You're off duty. You don't have to fight all the time, do you?"

He frowned slightly. "What do you mean?"

"Everyone knows you hate her," Nickie said pleasantly. "It's common gossip at the hospital. You rake her over the coals and she walks around the corridors, red in the face and talking to herself. Well, most of the time, anyway. Once, Dr. Simpson found her crying in the nursery. But she doesn't usually cry, no matter how bad she hurts. She's pretty tough, in her way. I guess she's had to be, huh? Even if there are more women in medical school these days, you don't see that many women doctors yet. I'll bet she had to fight a lot of prejudice when she was in medical school."

That came as a shock. He'd never seen Lou cry until today, and he couldn't imagine her being upset at any temperamental display of his. Or was it, he pondered uneasily, just that she'd learned how not to show her wounds to him?

Chapter Three

At dinner, Lou sat with Drew, as far away from Coltrain and his date as she could get. She listened attentively to the speakers and whispered to Drew in the spaces between speakers. But it was torture to watch Nickie's small hand smooth over Coltrain's, to see her flirt with him. Lou didn't know how to flirt. There were a lot of things she didn't know. But she'd learned to keep a poker face, and she did it very well this evening. The one time Coltrain glanced down the table toward her, he saw nothing on her face or in her eyes that could tell him anything. She was unreadable.

After the meeting, she let Drew hold her hand as they walked out of the restaurant. Behind them, Coltrain was glaring at her with subdued fury.

When they made it to the parking lot, she found that the other couple had caught up with them.

"Nice bit of surgery this morning, Copper," Drew remarked. "You do memorable stitches. I doubt if Mrs. Blake will even have a scar to show around."

He managed a smile and held Nickie's hand all the tighter. "She was adamant about that," he remarked. "It seems that her husband likes perfection."

"He'll have a good time searching for it in this imperfect world," Drew replied. "I'll see you in the morning. And I'd like your opinion on my little strep-throat patient. His mother wants the whole works taken out, tonsils and adenoids, but he doesn't have strep often and I don't like unnecessary surgery. Perhaps she'd listen to you."

"Don't count on it," Copper said dryly. "I'll have a look if you like, though."

"Thanks."

"My pleasure." He glanced toward Lou, who hadn't said a word. "You were ten minutes late this morning," he added coldly.

"Oh, I overslept," she replied pleasantly. "It wears me out to follow the EMTs around looking for work."

She gave him a cool smile and got into the car before he realized that she'd made a joke, and at his expense.

"Be on time in the morning," he admonished before he walked away with Nickie on his arm.

"On time," Lou muttered beside Drew in the comfortable Ford he drove. Her hands crushed her purse. "I'll give him on time! I'll be sitting in *his* parking spot at eight-thirty on the dot!"

"He does it on purpose," he told her as he started the car. "I think he likes to make you spark at him."

"He's overjoyed that I'm leaving," she muttered. "And so am I!"

He gave her a quick glance and hid his smile. "If you say so."

She twisted her small purse in her lap, fuming, all the way back to her small house.

"I haven't been good company, Drew," she said as he walked her to the door. "I'm sorry."

He patted her shoulder absently. "Nothing wrong with the company," he said, correcting her. He smiled down at her. "But you really do rub Copper the wrong way, don't you?" he added thoughtfully. "I've noticed that antagonism from a distance, but tonight is the first time I've seen it at close range. Is he always like that?"

She nodded. "Always, from the beginning. Well, not quite," she confessed, remembering. "From last Christmas."

"What happened last Christmas?"

She studied him warily.

"I won't tell him," he promised. "What happened?"

"He tried to kiss me under the mistletoe and I, well, I sort of ducked and pulled away." She flushed. "He rattled me. He does, mostly. I get shaky when he comes too close. He's so forceful, and so physical. Even when he wants to talk to me, he's forever trying to grab me by the wrist or a sleeve. It's as if he knows how much it disturbs me, so he does it on purpose, just to make me uncomfortable."

He reached down and caught her wrist very gently, watching her face distort and feeling the instinctive, helpless jerk of her hand.

He let go at once. "Tell me about it, Lou."

With a wan smile, she rubbed her wrist. "No. It's history."

"It isn't, you know. Not if it makes you shaky to have people touch you…"

"Not everyone, just him," she muttered absently.

His eyebrows lifted, but she didn't seem to be aware of what she'd just confessed.

She sighed heavily. "I'm so tired," she said, rubbing the back of her neck. "I don't usually get so tired from even the longest days."

He touched her forehead professionally and frowned. "You're a bit warm. How do you feel?"

"Achy. Listless." She grimaced. "It's probably that virus that's going around. I usually get at least one every winter."

"Go to bed and if you aren't better tomorrow, don't go in," he advised. "Want me to prescribe something?"

She shook her head. "I'll be okay. Nothing does any good for a virus, you know that."

He chuckled. "Not even a sugarcoated pill?"

"I can do without a placebo. I'll get some rest. Thanks for tonight. I enjoyed it."

"So did I. I haven't done much socializing since Eve died. It's been five long years and I still miss her. I don't think I'll ever get over her enough to start a new relationship with anyone. I only wish we'd had a child. It might have made it easier."

She was studying him, puzzled. "It's said that many people marry within months of losing a mate," she began.

"I don't fit that pattern," he said quietly. "I only loved once. I'd rather have my memories of those twelve years with Eve than a hundred years with someone else. I suppose that sounds old-fashioned."

She shook her head. "It sounds beautiful," she said softly. "Lucky Eve, to have been loved so much."

He actually flushed. "It was mutual."

"I'm sure it was, Drew. I'm glad to have a friend like you."

"That works both ways." He smiled ruefully. "I'd like to take you out occasionally, so that people will stop thinking of me as a mental case. The gossip is beginning to get bad."

"I'd love to go out with you," she replied. She smiled. "I'm not very worldly, you know. It was books and exams and medicine for eight long years, and then internship. I was an honor student. I never had much time for men." Her eyes darkened. "I never wanted to have much time for them. My parents' marriage soured me. I never knew it could be happy or that people could love each other enough to be faithful—" She stopped, embarrassed.

"I knew about your father," he said. "Most of the hospital staff did. He liked young girls."

"Dr. Coltrain told me," she said miserably.

"He what?"

She drew in a long breath. "I overheard what he said to you on the telephone the other day. I'm leaving. My year is up after New Year's, anyway," she reminded him. "He told me what my father had done. No wonder he didn't want me here. You shouldn't have done it, Drew. You shouldn't have forced him to take me on."

"I know. But it's too late, isn't it? I thought I was helping, if that's any excuse." He searched her face. "Maybe I hoped it would help Copper, too. He was infatuated with Jane Parker. She's a lovely, sweet woman, and she has a temper, but she was never a match for

Copper. He's the sort who'd cow a woman who couldn't stand up to him."

"Just like my father," she said shortly.

"I've never mentioned it, but one of your wrists looks as if it's suffered a break."

She flushed scarlet and drew back. "I have to go in now. Thanks again, Drew."

"If you can't talk to me, you need to talk to someone," he said. "Did you really think you could go through life without having the past affect the future?"

She smiled sweetly. "Drive carefully going home."

He shrugged. "Okay. I'll drop it."

"Good night."

"Good night."

She watched him drive away, absently rubbing the wrist he'd mentioned. She wouldn't think about it, she told herself. She'd go to bed and put it out of her mind.

Only it didn't work that way. She woke up in the middle of the night in tears, frightened until she remembered where she was. She was safe. It was over. But she felt sick and her throat was dry. She got up and found a pitcher, filling it with ice and water. She took a glass along with her and went back to bed. Except for frequent trips to the bathroom, she finally slept soundly.

There was a loud, furious knock at the front door. It kept on and on, followed by an equally loud voice. What a blessing that she didn't have close neighbors, she thought drowsily, or the police would be screaming up the driveway.

She tried to get up, but surprisingly, her feet wouldn't support her. She was dizzy and weak and sick at her stomach. Her head throbbed. She lay back down with a soft groan.

A minute later, the front door opened and a furious redheaded man in a lab coat came in the bedroom door.

"So this is where you are," he muttered, taking in her condition with a glance. "You couldn't have called?"

She barely focused on him. "I was up most of the night…"

"With Drew?"

She couldn't even manage a glare. "Being sick," she corrected. "Have you got anything on you to calm my stomach? I can't keep down anything to stop the nausea."

"I'll get something."

He went back out, grateful that she kept a key under the welcome mat. He didn't relish having to break down doors, although he had in the past to get to a patient.

He got his medical bag and went back into the bedroom. She was pale and she had a fever. He turned off the electronic thermometer and checked her lungs. Clear, thank God.

Her pulse was a little fast, but she seemed healthy enough. "A virus," he pronounced.

"No!" she exclaimed with weak sarcasm.

"You'll live."

"Give me the medicine, please," she asked, holding out a hand.

"Can you manage?"

"If you'll get me to the bathroom, sure."

He helped her up, noticing the frailty of her body. She didn't seem that thin in her clothing, but she was wearing silky pajamas that didn't conceal the slender lines of her body. He supported her to the door, and watched the door close behind her.

Minutes later, she opened the door again and let him help her back into bed.

He watched her for a minute and then, with resolution, he picked up the telephone. He punched in a number. "This is Dr. Coltrain. Send an ambulance out to Dr. Blakely's home, 23 Brazos Lane. That's right. Yes. Thank you."

She glared at him. "I will not…!"

"Hell, yes, you will," he said shortly. "I'm not leaving you out here alone to dehydrate. At the rate you're losing fluids, you'll die in three days."

"What do you care if I die?" she asked furiously.

He reached down to take her pulse again. This time, he caught the left wrist firmly, but she jerked it back. His blue eyes narrowed as he watched her color. Drew had been holding her right hand. At the table, it was her right hand he'd touched. But most of the time, Copper automatically reached for the left one…

He glanced down to where it lay on the coverlet and he noticed what Drew had; there was a definite break there, one which had been set but was visible.

She clenched her fist. "I don't want to go to the hospital."

"But you'll go, if I have to carry you."

She glared at him. It did no good at all. He went into the kitchen to turn off all the appliances except the refrigerator. On his way back, he paused to look around the living room. There were some very disturbing paintings on her walls, side by side with beautiful pastel drawings of flowers. He wondered who'd done them.

The ambulance arrived shortly. He watched the paramedics load her up and he laid the small bag she'd asked him to pack on the foot of the gurney.

"Thank you so much," she said with her last lucid breath. The medicine was beginning to take effect, and it had a narcotic in it to make her sleep.

"My pleasure, Dr. Blakely," he said. He smiled, but it didn't reach his eyes. They were watchful and thoughtful. "Do you paint?" he asked suddenly.

Her dark eyes blinked. "How did you know?" she murmured as she drifted off.

She awoke hours later in a private room, with a nurse checking her vital signs. "You're awake!" the nurse said with a smile. "Feeling any better?"

"A little." She touched her stomach. "I think I've lost weight."

"No wonder, with so much nausea. You'll be all right now. We'll take very good care of you. How about some soup and Jell-O and tea?"

"Coffee?" she asked hopefully.

The nurse chuckled. "Weak coffee, perhaps. We'll see." She charted her observations and went to see about supper.

It was modest fare, but delicious to a stomach that

had hardly been able to hold anything. Imagine being sent to the hospital with a twenty-four-hour virus, Lou thought irritably, and wanted to find Dr. Coltrain and hit him.

Drew poked his head in the door while he was doing rounds. "I told you you felt feverish, didn't I?" he teased, smiling. "Better?"

She nodded. "But I would have been just fine at home."

"Not to hear your partner tell it. I expected to find your ribs sticking through your skin," he told her, chuckling. "I'll check on you later. Stay put."

She groaned and lay back. Patients were stacking up and she knew that Brenda had probably had to deal with angry ones all day, since Dr. Coltrain would have been operating in the morning. Everyone would be sitting in the waiting room until long after dark, muttering angrily.

It was after nine before he made rounds. He looked worn, and she felt guilty even if it couldn't be helped.

"I'm sorry," she said irritably when he came to the bedside.

He cocked an eyebrow. "For what?" He reached down and took her wrist—the right one—noticing that she didn't react while he felt her pulse.

"Leaving you to cope with my patients as well as your own," she said. The feel of his long fingers was disturbing. She began to fidget.

He leaned closer, to look into her eyes, and his hand remained curled around her wrist. He felt her pulse jump as his face neared hers and suddenly a new thought leapt into his shocked mind and refused to be banished.

She averted her gaze. "I'm all right," she said. She sounded breathless. Her pulse had gone wild under his searching fingers.

He stood up, letting go of her wrist. But he noticed the quick rise and fall of her chest with new interest. What an odd reaction for a woman who felt such antagonism toward him.

He picked up her chart, still frowning, and read what was written there. "You've improved. If you're doing this well in the morning, you can go home. Not to work," he added firmly. "Drew's going to come in and help me deal with the backlog in the morning while he has some free time."

"That's very kind of him."

"He's a kind man."

"Yes. *He* is."

He chuckled softly. "You don't like me, do you?" he asked through pursed lips. "I've never given you any reason to. I've been alternately hostile and sarcastic since the day you came here."

"Your normal self, Doctor," she replied.

His lips tugged up. "Not really. You don't know me."

"Lucky me."

His blue eyes narrowed thoughtfully. She'd reacted to him from the first as if he'd been contagious. Every approach he'd made had been met with instant withdrawal. He wondered why he'd never questioned her reactions. It wasn't revulsion. Oh, no. It was something much more disturbing on her part. She was vulnerable, and he'd only just realized it, when it was too late. She would leave before he had the opportunity to explore his own feelings.

He stuck his hands into his pockets and his eyes searched her pale, worn face. She wasn't wearing a trace of makeup. Her eyes held lingering traces of fever and her hair was dull, lackluster, disheveled by sleep. But even in that condition, she had a strange beauty.

"I know how I look, thanks," she muttered as she saw how he was looking at her. "You don't need to rub it in."

"Was I?" He studied her hostile eyes.

She dropped her gaze to her slender hands on the sheets. "You always do." Her eyes closed. "I don't need you to point out my lack of good looks, Doctor. My father never missed an opportunity to tell me what I was missing."

Her father. His expression hardened as the memories poured out. But even as they nagged at his mind, he began to remember bits and pieces of gossip he'd heard about the way Dr. Fielding Blakely treated his poor wife. He'd dismissed it at the time, but now he realized that Mrs. Blakely had to be aware of her husband's affairs. Had she not minded? Or was she afraid to mind...

He had more questions about Lou's family life than he had answers, and he was curious. Her reticence with him, her broken wrist, her lack of self-esteem—they began to add up.

His eyes narrowed. "Did your mother know that your father was unfaithful to her?" he asked.

She stared at him as if she didn't believe what she'd heard. "What?"

"You heard me. Did she know?"

She drew the sheet closer to her collarbone. "Yes." She bit off the word.

"Why didn't she leave him?"

She laughed bitterly. "You can't imagine."

"Maybe I can." He moved closer to the bed. "Maybe I can imagine a lot of things that never occurred to me before. I've looked at you for almost a year and I've never seen you until now."

She fidgeted under the cover. "Don't strain your imagination, Doctor," she said icily. "I haven't asked for your attention. I don't want it."

"Mine, or any other man's, right?" he asked gently.

She felt like an insect on a pin. "Will you stop?" she groaned. "I'm sick. I don't want to be interrogated."

"Is that what I'm doing? I thought I was showing a belated interest in my partner," he said lazily.

"I won't be your partner after Christmas."

"Why?"

"I've resigned. Have you forgotten? I even wrote it down and gave it to you."

"Oh. That. I tore it up."

Her eyes popped. "You what?"

"Tore it up," he said with a shrug. "I can't do without you. You have too many patients who won't come back if they have to see me."

"You had a fine practice…"

"Too fine. I never slept or took vacations. You've eased the load. You've made yourself indispensable. You have to stay."

"I do not." She shot her reply back instantly. "I hate you!"

He studied her, nodding slowly. "That's healthy. Much healthier than withdrawing like a frightened clam into a shell every time I come too close."

She all but gasped at such a blunt statement. "I do not...!"

"You do." He looked pointedly at her left wrist. "You've kept secrets. I'm going to worry you to death until you tell me every last one of them, beginning with why you can't bear to have anyone hold you by the wrist."

She couldn't get her breath. She felt her cheeks becoming hot as he stared down at her intently. "I'm not telling you any secrets," she assured him.

"Why not?" he replied. "I don't ever tell what I know."

She knew that. If a patient told him anything in confidence, he wouldn't share it.

She rubbed the wrist absently, wincing as she remembered how it had felt when it was broken, and how.

Coltrain, watching her, wondered how he could ever have thought her cold. She had a temper that was easily the equal of his own, and she never backed away from a fight. She'd avoided his touch, but he realized now that it was the past that made her afraid, not the present.

"You're mysterious, Lou," he said quietly. "You hold things in, keep things back. I've worked with you for a year, but I know nothing about you."

"That was your choice," she reminded him coolly. "You've treated me like a leper in your life."

He started to speak, took a breath and finally, nodded. "Yes. Through no fault of your own, I might add. I've held grudges."

She glanced at his hard, lean face. "You were entitled," she admitted. "I didn't know about my father's past. I probably should have realized there was a reason he never went back to Jacobsville, even to visit, while his brother was still alive here. Afterward, there wasn't even a cousin to write to. We all lost touch. My mother never seemed to mind that we didn't come back." She looked up at him. "She probably knew…" She flushed and dropped her eyes.

"But she stayed with him," he began.

"She had to!" The words burst out. "If she'd tried to leave, he'd have…" She swallowed and made a futile gesture with her hand.

"He'd have what? Killed her?"

She wouldn't look at him. She couldn't. The memories came flooding back, of his violence when he used narcotics, of the threats, her mother's fear, her own. The weeping, the cries of pain…

She sucked in a quick breath, and all the suffering was in the eyes she lifted to his when he took her hand.

His fingers curled hard around hers and held them, as if he could see the memories and was offering comfort.

"You'll tell me, one day," he said abruptly, his eyes steady on her own. "You'll tell me every bit of it."

She couldn't understand his interest. She searched his eyes curiously and suddenly felt a wave of feeling encompass her like a killing tide, knocking her breathless. Heat surged through her slender body, impaling her, and in his hard face she saw everything she knew of love, would ever know of it.

But he didn't want her that way. He never would. She was useful to the practice, but on a personal level, he was still clutching hard at the past; at the girl her father had taken from him, at Jane Parker. He was sorry for her, as he would be for anyone in pain, but it wasn't a personal concern.

She drew her hand away from his slowly and with a faint smile. "Thanks," she said huskily. "I...I think too hard sometimes. The past is long dead."

"I used to think so," he said, watching her. "Now, I'm not so sure."

She didn't understand what he was saying. It was just as well. The nurse came in to do her round and any personal conversation was banished at once.

Chapter Four

The next day, Lou was allowed to go home. Drew had eaten breakfast with her and made sure that she was well enough to leave before he agreed with Copper that she was fit. But when he offered to drive her home, Coltrain intervened. His partner, he said, was his responsibility. Drew didn't argue. In fact, when they weren't looking, he grinned.

Copper carried her bag into the house and helped her get settled on the couch. It was lunchtime and he hesitated, as if he felt guilty about not offering to take her out for a meal.

"I'm going to have some soup later," she murmured without looking at him. "I'm not hungry just yet. I expect you are."

"I could eat." He hesitated again, watching her with vague irritation. "Will you be all right?"

"It was only a virus," she said, making light of it. "I'm fine. Thank you for your concern."

"You might as well enjoy it, for novelty value if nothing else," he said without smiling. "It's been a long time since I've given a damn about a woman's comfort."

"I'm just a colleague," she replied, determined to

show him that she realized there was nothing personal in their relationship. "It isn't the same thing."

"No, it isn't," he agreed. "I've been very careful to keep our association professional. I've never even asked you to my home, have I?"

He was making her uneasy with that unblinking stare. "So what? I've never asked you to mine," she replied. "I wouldn't presume to put you in such an embarrassing situation."

"Embarrassing? Why?"

"Well, because you'd have to find some logical excuse to refuse," she said.

He searched her quiet face and his eyes narrowed thoughtfully. "I don't know that I'd refuse. If you asked me."

Her heart leapt and she quickly averted her eyes. She wanted him to go, now, before she gave herself away. "Forgive me, but I'm very tired," she said.

She'd fended him off nicely, without giving offense. He wondered how many times over the years she'd done exactly that to other men.

He moved closer to her, noticing the way she tensed, the telltale quickening of her breath, the parting of her soft lips. She was affected by his nearness and trying valiantly to hide it. It touched him deeply that she was so vulnerable to him. He could have cursed himself for the way he'd treated her, for the antagonism that made her wary of any approach now.

He stopped when there was barely a foot of space between them, with his hands in his pockets so that he wouldn't make her any more nervous.

He looked down at her flushed oval face with curious pleasure. "Don't try to come in tomorrow if you don't feel like it. I'll cope."

"All right," she said in a hushed tone.

"Lou."

He hadn't called her by her first name before. It surprised her into lifting her eyes to his face.

"You aren't responsible for anything your father did," he said. "I'm sorry that I've made things hard for you. I hope you'll reconsider leaving."

She shifted uncomfortably. "Thank you. But I think I'd better go," she said softly. "You'll be happier with someone else."

"Do you think so? I don't agree." His hand lowered slowly to her face, touching her soft cheek, tracing it down to the corner of her mouth. It was the first intimate contact she'd ever had with him, and she actually trembled.

Her reaction had an explosive echo in his own body. His breath jerked into his throat and his teeth clenched as he looked at her mouth and thought he might die if he couldn't have it. But it was too soon. He couldn't...!

He drew back his hand as if she'd burned it. "I have to go," he said tersely, turning on his heel. Her headlong response had prompted a reaction in him that he could barely contain at all. He had to distance himself before he reached for her and ruined everything.

Lou didn't realize why he was in such a hurry to leave. She assumed that he immediately regretted that unexpected caress and wanted to make sure that she didn't read anything into it.

"Thank you for bringing me home," she said formally.

He paused at the door and looked back at her, his eyes fiercely intent on her slender body in jeans and sweatshirt, on her loosened blond hair and exquisite complexion and dark eyes. "Thank your lucky stars that I'm leaving in time." He bit off the words.

He closed the door on her puzzled expression. He was acting very much out of character lately. She didn't know why, unless he was sorry he'd tried to talk her out of leaving the practice. Oh, well, she told herself, it was no longer her concern. She had to get used to the idea of being out of his life. He had nothing to offer her, and he had good reason to hate her, considering the part her father had played in his unhappy past.

She went into the kitchen and opened a can of tomato soup. She'd need to replenish her body before she could get back to work.

The can slipped in her left hand and she grimaced. Her dreams of becoming a surgeon had been lost overnight in one tragic act. A pity, her instructor had said, because she had a touch that few surgeons ever achieved, almost an instinctive knowledge of the best and most efficient way to sever tissue with minimum loss of blood. She would have been famous. But alas, the tendon had been severed with the compound fracture. And the best efforts of the best orthopedic surgeon hadn't been able to repair the damage. Her father hadn't even been sorry....

She shook her head to clear away the memories and went back to her soup. Some things were better forgotten.

* * *

She was back at work the day after her return home, a bit shaky, but game. She went through her patients efficiently, smiling at the grievance of one small boy whose stitches she'd just removed.

"Dr. Coltrain doesn't like little kids, does he?" he muttered. "I showed him my bad place and he said he'd seen worse!"

"He has," she told the small boy. She smiled at him. "But you've been very brave, Patrick my boy, and I'm giving you the award of honor." She handed him a stick of sugarless chewing gum and watched him grin. "Off with you, now, and mind you don't fall down banks into any more creeks!"

"Yes, ma'am!"

She handed his mother the charge sheet and was showing them out the door of the treatment cubicle just as Coltrain started to come into it. The boy glowered at him, smiled at Lou and went back to his waiting mother.

"Cheeky brat," he murmured, watching him turn the corner.

"He doesn't like you," she told him smugly. "You didn't sympathize with his bad place."

"Bad place." He harrumphed. "Two stitches. My God, what a fuss he made."

"It hurt," she informed him.

"He wouldn't let me take the damn stitches out, either. He said that I didn't know how to do it, but you did."

She grinned to herself at that retort while she dealt with the mess she'd made while working with Patrick.

"You don't like children, do you?" she asked.

He shrugged. "I don't know much about them, except what I see in the practice," he replied. "I deal mostly with adults since you came."

He leaned against the doorjamb and studied her with his hands in the pockets of his lab coat, a stethoscope draped around his neck. His eyes narrowed as he watched her work.

She became aware of the scrutiny and turned, her eyes meeting his and being captured there. She felt her heart race at the way he looked at her. Her hands stilled on her preparations for the next patient as she stood helplessly in thrall.

His lips compressed. He looked at her mouth and traced the full lower lip, the soft bow of the upper, with her teeth just visible where her lips parted. The look was intimate. He was wondering how it would feel to kiss her, and she knew it.

Muffled footsteps caught them unawares, and Brenda jerked open the sliding door of the cubicle. "Lou, I've got the wrong... Oh!" She bumped into Coltrain, whom she hadn't seen standing there.

"Sorry," he muttered. "I wanted to ask Lou if she'd seen the file on Henry Brady. It isn't where I left it."

Brenda grimaced as she handed it to him. "I picked it up mistakenly. I'm sorry."

"No harm done." He glanced back at Lou and went out without another word.

"Not another argument," Brenda groaned. "Honestly, partners should get along better than this."

Lou didn't bother to correct that assumption. It was

much less embarrassing than what had really happened. Coltrain had never looked at her in that particular way before. She was glad that she'd resigned; she wasn't sure that she could survive any physical teasing from him. If he started making passes, she'd be a lot safer in Austin than she would be here.

After all he was a confirmed bachelor and there was no shortage of women on his arm at parties. Nickie was the latest in a string of them. And according to rumor, before Nickie, apparently he'd been infatuated with Jane Parker. He might be nursing a broken heart as well, since Jane's marriage.

Lou didn't want to be anybody's second-best girl. Besides, she never wanted to marry. It had been better when Coltrain treated her like the enemy. She wished he'd go back to his former behavior and stop looking at her mouth that way. She still tingled remembering the heat in his blue eyes. A man like that would be just plain hell to be loved by. He would be addictive. She had no taste for addictions and she knew already that Coltrain would break her heart if she let him. No, it was better that she leave. Then she wouldn't have the anguish of a hopeless relationship.

The annual hospital Christmas party was scheduled for Friday night, two weeks before Christmas so that the staff wouldn't be too involved with family celebrations to attend.

Lou hadn't planned to go, but Coltrain cornered her in his office as they prepared to leave that afternoon for the weekend.

"The Christmas party is tonight," he reminded her.

"I know. I'm not going."

"I'll pick you up in an hour," he said, refusing to listen when she tried to protest. "I know you still tire easily after the virus. We won't stay long."

"What about Nickie?" she asked irritably. "Won't she mind if you take your partner to a social event?"

Her antagonism surprised him. He lifted an indignant eyebrow. "Why should she?" he asked stiffly.

"You've been dating her."

"I escorted her to the Rotary Club meeting. I haven't proposed to her. And whatever you've heard to the contrary, she and I are not an item."

"You needn't bite my head off!" She shot the words at him.

His eyes dropped to her mouth and lingered there. "I know something I'd like to bite," he said deep in his throat.

She actually gasped, so stunned by the remark that she couldn't even think of a reply.

His eyes flashed back up to catch hers. He was a bulldozer, she thought, and if she didn't stand up to him, he'd run right over her.

She stiffened her back. "I'm not going to any hospital dance with you," she said shortly. "You've given me hell for the past year. Do you think you can just walk in here and wipe all that out with an invitation? Not even an invitation, at that—a command!"

"Yes, I do," he returned curtly. "We both belong to the hospital staff, and nothing will start gossip quicker than having one of us stay away from an annual event.

I do not plan to have any gossip going around here at my expense. I had enough of that in the past, thanks to your philandering father!"

She gripped her coat, furious at him. "You just got through saying that you didn't blame me for what he did."

"And I don't!" he said angrily. "But you're being blind and stupid."

"Thank you. Coming from you, those are compliments!"

He was all but vibrating with anger. He stared at her, glared at her, until her unsteady movement made him realize that she'd been ill.

He became less rigid. "Ben Maddox is going to be there tonight. He's a former colleague of ours from Canada. He's just installed a massive computer system with linkups to medical networks around the world. I think it's too expensive for our purposes, but I agreed to hear him out about it. You're the high-tech expert," he added with faint sarcasm. "I'd like your opinion."

"My opinion? I'm honored. You've never asked for it before."

"I've never given a damn about it before," he retorted evenly. "But maybe there's something to this electronic revolution in medicine." He lifted his chin in a challenge. "Or so you keep telling me. Put your money where your mouth is, Doctor. Convince me."

She glared at him. "I'll drive my own car and see you there."

It was a concession, of sorts. He frowned slightly.

"Why don't you want to ride with me? What are you afraid of?" he taunted softly.

She couldn't admit what frightened her. "It wouldn't look good to have us arrive together," she said. "It would give people something to talk about."

He was oddly disappointed, although he didn't quite know why. "All right, then."

She nodded, feeling that she'd won something. He nodded, too, and quietly left her. It felt like a sort of truce. God knew, they could use one.

Ben Maddox was tall, blond and drop-dead gorgeous. He was also married and the father of three. He had photographs, which he enjoyed showing to any of his old colleagues who were willing to look at them. But in addition to those photographs, he had information on a networking computer system that he used extensively in his own practice. It was an expensive piece of equipment, but it permitted the user instant access to medical experts in every field. As a diagnostic tool and a means of getting second opinions from recognized authorities, it was breathtaking. But so was the price.

Lou had worn a black silk dress with a lace overlay, a demure rounded neckline and see-through sleeves. Her hairstyle, a topknot with little tendrils of blond hair slipping down to her shoulders, looked sexy. So did her long, elegant legs in high heels, under the midknee fitted skirt. She wore no jewelry at all, except for a strand of pearls with matching earrings.

Watching her move, Coltrain was aware of old, unwanted sensations. At the party a year ago, she'd worn something a little more revealing, and he'd deliberately maneuvered her under the mistletoe out of mingled curiosity and desire. But she'd evaded him as if he had the plague, then and since. His ego had suffered a sharp blow. He hadn't felt confident enough to try again, so antagonism and anger had kept her at bay. Not that his memories of her father's betrayal hadn't added to his enmity.

She was animated tonight, talking to Ben about the computer setup as if she knew everything there was to know about the machines.

"Copper, you've got a savvy partner here," Ben remarked when he joined them. "She's computer literate!"

"She's the resident high-tech expert," Copper replied. "I like old-fashioned, hands-on medicine. She'd rather reach for a machine to make diagnoses."

"High tech is the way of the future," Ben said coaxingly.

"It's also the reason medical costs have gone through the roof," came the predictable reply. "The money we spend on these outrageously expensive machines has to be passed on to the patients. That raises our fees, the hospital's fees, the insurance companies' fees…"

"Pessimist!" Ben accused.

"I'm being realistic," Copper told him, lifting his highball glass in a mock toast. He drained it, feeling the liquor.

Ben frowned as his old colleague made his way past the dancers back to the buffet table. "That's odd," he remarked. "I don't remember ever seeing Copper take more than one drink."

Neither did Lou. She watched her colleague pour himself another drink and she frowned.

Ben produced a card from the computer company for her, and while he was explaining the setup procedure, she noticed Nickie going up to Coltrain. She was wearing an electric blue dress that could have started a riot. The woman was pretty anyway, but that dress certainly revealed most of her charms.

Nickie laughed and dragged Coltrain under the mistletoe, looking up to indicate it there, to the amusement of the others standing by. Coltrain laughed softly, whipped a lean arm around Nickie's trim waist and pulled her against his tall body. He bent his head, and the way he kissed her made Lou go hot all over. She'd never been in his arms, but she'd dreamed about it. The fever in that thin mouth, the way he twisted Nickie even closer, made her breath catch. She averted her eyes and flushed at the train of her own thoughts.

"Leave it to Coltrain to draw the prettiest girls." Ben chuckled. "The gossip mill will grind on that kiss for a month. He's not usually so uninhibited. He must be over his limit!"

She could have agreed. Her hand clenched around the piña colada she was nursing. "This computer system, is it reliable?" she asked through tight lips, forcing a smile.

"Yes, except in thunderstorms. Always unplug it, regardless of what they tell you about protective spikes. One good hit, and you could be down for days."

"I'll remember, if we get it."

"The system I have is expensive," Ben agreed, "but there are others available that would be just right for a small practice like yours and Copper's. In fact…"

His voice droned on and Lou tried valiantly to pay attention. She was aware at some level that Coltrain and Nickie were dancing and making the rounds of guests together. It was much later, and well into her second piña colada, when the lavish mistletoe began to get serious workouts.

Lou wasn't in the mood to dance. She refused Ben's offer, and several others. A couple of hours had passed and it felt safe to leave now, before her spirit was totally crushed by being consistently ignored by Coltrain. She put down her half-full glass. "I really do have to go," she told Ben. "I've been ill and I'm not quite back up to par yet." She shook his hand. "It was very nice to have met you."

"Same here. I wonder why Drew Morris didn't show up? I had hoped to see him again while I was here."

"I don't know," she said, realizing that she hadn't heard from Drew since she was released from the hospital. She had no idea where he was, and she hadn't asked.

"I'll check with Copper. He's certainly been elusive this evening. Not that I can blame him, considering his pretty companion over there." He raised his hand to catch the other man's eyes, to Lou's dismay.

Coltrain joined them with Nickie hanging on his arm. "Still here?" he asked Lou with a mocking smile. "I thought you'd be out the door and gone by now."

"I'm just about to leave. Do you know where Drew is?"

"He's in Florida at that pediatric seminar. Didn't Brenda tell you?"

"She was so busy she probably forgot," she said.

"So that's where the old devil has gone," Ben said ruefully. "I'm sorry I missed him."

"I'm sure he will be, too," Lou said. The sight of Nickie and Coltrain together was hurting her. "I'd better be off—"

"Oh, not yet," Copper said with glittery blue eyes. "Not before you've been kissed under the mistletoe, Doctor."

She flushed and laughed nervously. "I'll forgo that little ritual, I think."

"No, you won't." He sounded pleasant enough, but the expression on his face was dangerous. He moved away from Nickie and his lean arm shot around Lou's waist, maneuvering her under a low-hanging sprig of mistletoe tied with a red velvet bow. "You're not getting away this time," he said huskily.

Before she could think, react, protest, his head bent and his thin, cruel mouth fastened on hers with fierce intent. He didn't close his eyes when he kissed, she thought a bit wildly, he watched her all through it. His arm pressed her closer to the length of his muscular body, and his free hand came up so that his thumb could rub sensuously over her mouth while he kissed it, parting her lips, playing havoc with her nerves.

She gasped at the rough pleasure, and inadvertently gave him exactly what he wanted. His open mouth ground into hers, pressing her lips apart. She tasted him in an intimacy that she'd never shared with a man, in front of the amused hospital staff, while his cold eyes stared straight into hers.

She made a faint sound and he lifted his head, looking down at her swollen lips. His thumb traced over them with much greater tenderness than his mouth had given her, and he held her shocked eyes for a long moment before he reluctantly let her go.

"Merry Christmas, Dr. Blakely," he said in a mocking tone, although his voice was husky.

"And you, Dr. Coltrain," she said shakily, not quite meeting his eyes. "Good night, Ben…Nickie."

She slid away from them toward the door, on shaky legs, with a mouth that burned from his cold, fierce kiss. She barely remembered getting her coat and saying goodbye to the people she recognized on her way to the car park.

Coltrain watched her go with feelings he'd never encountered in his life. He was burning up with desire, and he'd had enough whiskey to threaten his control.

Nickie tugged on his sleeve. "You didn't kiss me like that," she protested, pouting prettily. "Why don't you take me home and we can…"

"I'll be back in a minute," he said, shaking her off.

She glared at him, coloring with embarrassment when she realized that two of the staff had overheard her. Rejection in private was one thing, but it hurt to have him make it so public. He hadn't called her since the night of the Rotary Club meeting. He'd just kissed her very nicely, but it looked different when he'd done it with his partner. She frowned. Something was going on. She followed at a distance. She was going to find out what.

Coltrain, unaware of her pursuit, headed after Lou with no real understanding of his own actions. He couldn't get the taste of her out of his head. He was pretty sure that she felt the same way. He couldn't let her leave until he knew…

Lou kept walking, but she heard footsteps behind her as she neared her car. She knew them, because she heard them every day on the slick tile of the office floor. She walked faster, but it did no good. Coltrain reached her car at the same time she reached it.

His hand came around her, grasping her car key and her fingers, pulling, turning her. She was pressed completely against the car by the warm weight of his body, and she looked up into a set, shadowy face while his mouth hovered just above her own in the starlit darkness.

"It wasn't enough," he said roughly. "Not nearly enough."

He bent and his mouth found hers expertly. His hands smoothed into hers and linked with her fingers. His hips slid sensuously over hers, seductive, refusing to entertain barriers or limits. His mouth began to open, brushing in soft strokes over her lips until they began to part, but she stiffened.

"Don't you know how to kiss?" he whispered, surprised. "Open your mouth, little one. Open it and fit it to mine… Yes, that's it."

She felt his tongue dance at the opening he'd made,

felt it slowly ease into her mouth and penetrate, teasing, probing, tasting. Her fingers clutched helplessly at his and she shivered. It was so intimate, so…familiar! She moaned sharply as his hips began to caress hers. She felt him become aroused and her whole body vibrated.

His mouth grew more insistent then. He released one of her hands and his fingers played with her mouth, as they had inside, but now there was the heat and the magic they were generating, and it was no cold, clinical experiment. He groaned against her mouth and she felt his body go rigid all at once.

He bit her lower lip, hard, when her teeth clenched at the soft probing of his tongue. Suddenly she came to her senses and realized what was happening. He tasted blatantly of whiskey. He'd had too much to drink and he'd forgotten which woman he was with. Did he think she was Nickie? she wondered dizzily. Was that why he was making love to her? And that was what it was, she realized with a shock. Only a lover would take such intimacy for granted, be so blind to surroundings and restraint.

Chapter Five

Despite the pleasure she felt, the whiskey on his breath brought back unbearable memories of another man who drank; memories not of kisses, but of pain and fear. Her hands pressed against his warm shirtfront under the open dinner jacket and she pushed, only vaguely aware of thick hair under the silkiness of the fabric.

"No," she whispered into his insistent mouth.

He didn't seem to hear her. His mouth hardened and a sound rumbled out of the back of his throat. "For God's sake, stop fighting me," he whispered fiercely. "Open your mouth!"

The intimacy he was asking for frightened her. She twisted her face, breathing like a runner. "Jebediah…no!" she whispered frantically.

The fear in her voice got through the intoxication. His mouth stilled against her cheek, but his body didn't withdraw. She could feel it against every inch of her like a warm, steely brand. His breathing wasn't steady, and over her breasts, his heart was beating like a frenzied bass drum.

It suddenly dawned on him what he was doing, and with whom.

"My God!" he whispered fiercely. His hands tightened for an instant before they fell away from her. A faint shudder went through his powerful body as he slowly, so slowly, pushed himself away from her, balancing his weight on his hands against the car doorframe.

She felt his breath on her swollen mouth as he fought for control. He was still too close.

"You haven't used my given name before," he said as he levered farther away from her. "I didn't know you knew it."

"It's…on our contract," she said jerkily.

He removed his hands from the car and stood upright, dragging in air. "I've had two highballs," he said on an apologetic laugh. "I don't drink. It hit me harder than I realized."

He was apologizing, she thought dazedly. That was unexpected. He wasn't that kind of man. Or was he? She hadn't thought he was the type to get drunk and kiss women in that intimate, fierce way, either. Especially her.

She tried to catch her own breath. Her mouth hurt from the muted violence of his kisses and her legs felt weak. She leaned back against the car, only now noticing its coldness. She hadn't felt it while he was kissing her. She touched her tongue to her lips and she tasted him on them.

She eased away from the car a little, shy now that he was standing back from her.

She was so shaky that she wondered how she was going to drive home. Then she wondered, with even more concern, how *he* was going to drive home.

"You shouldn't drive," she began hesitantly.

In the faint light from the hospital, she saw him smile sardonically. "Worried about me?" he chided.

She shouldn't have slipped like that. "I'd worry about anyone who'd had too much to drink," she began.

"All right, I won't embarrass you. Nickie can drive. She doesn't drink at all."

Nickie. Nickie would take him home and she'd probably stay to nurse him, too, in his condition. God only knew what might happen, but she couldn't afford to interfere. He'd had too much to drink and he'd kissed her, and she'd let him. Now she was ashamed and embarrassed.

"I have to go," she said stiffly.

"Drive carefully," he replied.

"Sure."

She found her keys where they'd fallen to the ground when he kissed her and unlocked the car door. She closed it once she was inside and started it after a bad fumble. He stood back from it, his hands in his pockets, looking dazed and not quite sober.

She hesitated, but Nickie came out the door, calling him. When he turned and raised a hand in Nickie's direction and answered her, laughing, Lou came to her senses. She lifted a hand toward both of them and drove away as quickly as she could. When she glanced back in the rearview mirror, it was to see Nickie holding Coltrain's hand as they went toward the building again.

So much for the interlude, she thought miserably. He'd probably only just realized who he'd kissed and was in shock.

That was close to the truth. Coltrain's head was spinning. He'd never dreamed that a kiss could be so explosive or addictive. There was something about Lou Blakely that made his knees buckle. He had no idea why he'd reacted so violently to her that he couldn't even let her leave. God knew what would have happened if she hadn't pushed him away when she did.

Nickie held on to him as they went back inside. "You've got her lipstick all over you," she accused.

He paused, shaken out of his brooding. Nickie was pretty, he thought, and uncomplicated. She already knew that he wasn't going to get serious however long they dated, because he'd told her so. It made him relax. He smiled down at her. "Wipe it off."

She pulled his handkerchief out of his pocket and did as he asked, smiling pertly. "Want to sample mine again?"

He tapped her on the nose. "Not tonight," he said. "We'd better leave. It's getting late."

"I'm driving," she told him.

"Yes, you are," he agreed.

She felt better. At least she was the one going home with him, not Lou. She wasn't going to give him up without a struggle, not when he was the best thing that had ever happened to her. Wealthy bachelor surgeons didn't come along every day of the week.

Lou drove home in a similar daze, overcome by the fervor of Coltrain's hard kisses. She couldn't understand why a man who'd always seemed to hate her had suddenly become addicted to her mouth; so addicted, in fact, that he'd followed her to her car. It had been the sweetest night of her life, but she had to keep her head and realize that it was an isolated incident. If Coltrain hadn't been drinking, it would never have happened. Maybe by Monday, she thought, he'd have convinced himself that it hadn't. She wished she could. She was more in love with him than ever, and he was as far out of her reach as he had ever been. Except that now he'd probably go even farther out of reach, because he'd lost his head and he wouldn't like remembering it.

She did her usual housework and answered emergency calls. She got more than her share because Dr. Coltrain had left word with their answering service that he was going to be out of town until Monday and Dr. Blakely would be covering for him.

Nice of him to ask her first, she thought bitterly, and tell her that he was going to be out of town. But perhaps he'd been reluctant to talk to her after what had happened. If the truth were known, he was more than likely as embarrassed as she was and just wanted to forget the whole thing.

She did his rounds and hers at the hospital, noticing absently that she was getting more attention than usual. Probably, she reasoned, because people were remembering the way Coltrain had kissed her. Maybe they thought something was going on between them.

"How's it going?" Drew asked on Sunday afternoon,

grinning at her. "I hear I missed a humdinger of a kiss at the Christmas party," he added wickedly.

She blushed to her hairline. "Lots of people got kissed."

"Not like you did. Not so that he followed you out to the parking lot and damn near made love to you on the hood of your car." He chuckled.

"Who…?"

"Nickie," he said, confirming her worst nightmare. "She was watching, apparently, and she's sweet on Copper. I guess she thought it might turn him off you if there was a lot of gossip about what happened. Rumors fly, especially when they're about two doctors who seem to hate each other."

"He'll walk right into it when he comes back," she said uneasily. "What can I do?"

"Nothing, I'm afraid."

Her eyes narrowed. "That's what you think."

She turned on her heel and went in search of Nickie. She found her in a patient's room and waited calmly while the girl, nervous and very insecure once she saw Lou waiting for her, finished the chore she was performing.

She went out into the hall with Lou, and she looked apprehensive.

Lou clutched a clipboard to her lab jacket. She didn't smile. "I understand you've been feeding the rumor mill. I'll give you some good advice. Stop it while you can."

By now, Nickie's face had gone puce. "I never meant…I was kidding!" she burst out. "That's all, just kidding!"

Lou studied her without emotion. "I'm not laughing. Dr. Coltrain won't be laughing, either, when he hears about it. And I'll make sure he knows where it came from."

"That's spiteful!" Nickie cried. "I'm crazy about him!"

"No, you aren't," Lou said shortly. "You'd never subject him to the embarrassment you have with all this gossip if you really cared."

Nickie's hands locked together. "I'm sorry," she said on a long sigh. "I really am. I was just jealous," she confessed, avoiding Lou's eyes. "He wouldn't even kiss me good-night, but he'd kiss you that way, and he hates you."

"Try to remember that he'd had too much to drink," Lou said quietly. "Only a fool would read anything into a kiss under the mistletoe."

"I guess so," Nickie said, but she wasn't really convinced. "I'm sorry. You won't tell him it was me, will you?" she added worriedly. "He'll hate me. I care so much, Dr. Blakely!"

"I won't tell him," Lou said. "But no more gossip!"

"Yes, ma'am!" Nickie brightened, grinned and went off down the hall, irrepressibly young and optimistic. Watching her, Lou felt ancient.

The next morning was Monday, and Lou went into the office to come face-to-face with a furious partner, who blocked her doorway and glared at her with blue eyes like arctic ice.

"Now what have I done?" she asked before he could

speak, and slammed her bag down on her desk, ready to do battle.

"You don't know?" he taunted.

She folded her arms over her breasts and leaned back against the edge of the desk. "There's a terrible rumor going around the hospital," she guessed.

His eyebrow jerked, but the ice didn't leave his eyes. "Did you start it?"

"Of course," she agreed furiously. "I couldn't wait to tell everybody on staff that you bent me back over the hood of my car and ravished me in the parking lot!"

Brenda, who'd started in the door, stood there with her mouth open, intercepted a furious glare from two pairs of eyes, turned on her heel and got out.

"Could you keep your voice down?" Coltrain snapped.

"Gladly, when you stop making stupid accusations!"

He glared at her and she glared back.

"I was drinking!"

"That's it, announce it to everyone in the waiting room, why don't you, and see how many patients run for their cars!" she raged.

He closed her office door, hard, and leaned back against it. "Who started the rumor?" he asked.

"That's more like it," she replied. "Don't accuse until you ask. I didn't start it. I have no wish to become the subject of gossip."

"Not even to force me to do something about the rumors?" he asked. "Such as announce our engagement?"

Her eyes went saucer-wide. "Please! I've just eaten!"

His jaw went taut. "I beg your pardon?"

"And so you should!" she said enthusiastically. "Marry you? I'd rather chain myself to a tree in an alligator swamp!"

He didn't answer immediately. He stared at her instead while all sorts of impractical ideas sifted through his mind.

A buzzer sounded on her desk. She reached over and pressed a button. "Yes?"

"What about the patients?" Brenda prompted.

"He doesn't *have* any patience," Lou said without thinking.

"Excuse me?" Brenda stammered.

"Oh. That sort of patients. Send my first one in, will you, Brenda? Dr. Coltrain was just leaving."

"No, he wasn't," he returned when her finger left the intercom button. "We'll finish this discussion after office hours."

"After office hours?" she asked blankly.

"Yes. But, don't get your hopes up about a repeat of Friday evening," he said with a mocking smile. "After all, I'm not drunk today."

Her eyes flashed murderously and her lips compressed. But he was already out the door.

Lou was never sure afterward how she'd managed to get through her patients without revealing her state of mind. She was furiously angry at Coltrain for his accusations and equally upset with Brenda for hearing what she'd said in retaliation. Now it would be all over the office as well as all over the hospital that she and

Coltrain had something going. And they didn't! Despite Lou's helpless attraction to him, it didn't take much imagination to see that Coltrain didn't feel the same. Well, maybe physically he felt something for her, but emotionally he still hated her. A few kisses wouldn't change that!

She checked Mr. Bailey's firm, steady heartbeat, listened to his lungs and pronounced him over the pneumonia she'd been treating him for.

As she started to go, leaving Brenda to help him with his shirt, he called to her.

"What's this I hear about you and Doc Coltrain?" he teased. "Been kissing up a storm at the hospital Christmas party, they say. Any chance we'll be hearing wedding bells?"

He didn't understand, he told Brenda on his way out, why Dr. Blakely had suddenly screamed like that. Maybe she'd seen a mouse, Brenda replied helpfully.

When the office staff went home, Coltrain was waiting at the front entrance for Lou. He'd stationed himself there after checking with the hospital about a patient, and he hadn't moved, in case Lou decided to try to sneak out.

He was wearing the navy blue suit that looked so good on him, lounging against the front door with elegant carelessness, when she went out of her office. His red hair caught the reflection of the overhead light and seemed to burn like flames over his blue, blue eyes. They swept down over her neat gray pantsuit to her long legs encased in slacks with low-heeled shoes.

"That color looks good on you," he remarked.

"You don't need to flatter me. Just say what's on your mind, please, and let me go home."

"All right." His eyes fell to her soft mouth and lingered there. "Who started the rumors about us?"

She traced a pattern on her fanny pack. "I promised I wouldn't tell."

"Nickie," he guessed, nodding at her shocked expression.

"She's young and infatuated," she began.

"Not that young," he said with quiet insinuation.

Her eyes flashed before she could avert them. Her hand dug into the fanny pack for her car keys. "It's a nine-days wonder," she continued. "People will find something else to talk about."

"Nothing quite this spicy has happened since Ted Regan went chasing off to Victoria after Coreen Tarleton and she came home wearing his engagement ring."

"There's hardly any comparison," she said, "considering that everyone knows how we feel about each other!"

"How *do* we feel about each other, Lou?" he replied quietly, and watched her expression change.

"We're enemies," she returned instantly.

"Are we?" He searched her eyes in a silence that grew oppressive. His arms fell to his sides. "Come here, Lou."

She felt her breathing go wild. That could have been an invitation to bypass him and leave the building. But the look in his eyes told her it wasn't. Those eyes blazed like flames in his lean, tanned face, beckoning, promising pleasures beyond imagination.

He lifted a hand. "Come on, coward," he chided softly, and his lips curled at the edges. "I won't hurt you."

"You're sober," she reminded him.

"Cold sober," he agreed. "Let's see how it feels when I know what I'm doing."

Her heart stopped, started, raced. She hesitated, and he laughed softly and started toward her, with that slow, deliberate walk that spoke volumes about his intent.

"You mustn't," she spoke quickly, holding up a hand.

He caught the hand and jerked her against him, imprisoning her there with a steely arm. "I must." He corrected her, letting his eyes fall to her mouth. "I *have* to know." He bit off the words against her lips.

She never found out what he had to know, because the instant she felt his lips probing her mouth, she went under in a blaze of desire unlike anything she'd felt before. She gasped, opened her lips, yielded to his enveloping arms without a single protest. If anything, she pushed closer into his arms, against that steely body that was instantly aroused by the feel of her.

She tried to speak, to protest, but he pushed his tongue into her mouth with a harsh groan, and his arms lifted her so that she fit perfectly against him from breast to thigh. She fought, frightened by the intimacy and the sensations kindled in her untried body.

Her frantic protest registered at once. He remembered she'd had the same reaction the night of the Christmas party. His mouth lifted, and his searching eyes met hers.

"You couldn't be a virgin," he said, making it sound more like an accusation than a statement of fact.

She bit her lip and dropped her eyes, shamed and embarrassed. "Rub it in," she growled.

"My God." He eased her back onto her feet and held her by the upper arms so that she wouldn't fall. "My God! How old are you, thirty?"

"Twenty-eight," she said unsteadily, gasping for breath. Her whole body felt swollen. Her dark eyes glowered up at him as she pushed back her disheveled hair. "And you needn't look so shocked, you of all people should know that some people still have a few principles! You're a doctor, after all!"

"I thought virgins were a fairy tale," he said flatly. "Damn it!"

Her chin lifted. "What's wrong, Doctor, did you see me as a pleasant interlude between patients?"

His lips compressed. He rammed his hands into his trouser pockets, all too aware of a throbbing arousal that wouldn't go away. He turned to the door and jerked it open. All weekend he'd dreamed of taking Louise Blakely home with him after work and seducing her in his big king-size bed. She was leaving anyway, and the hunger he felt for her was one he had to satisfy or go mad. It had seemed so simple. She wanted him; he knew she did. People were already talking about them, so what would a little more gossip matter? She'd be gone at the first of the year, anyway.

But now he had a new complication, one he'd never dreamed of having. She was no young girl, but it didn't take an expert to know why she backed away from intimacy like a repressed adolescent. He'd been baiting her with that accusation of virginity, but she hadn't realized it. She'd taken it at face value and she'd given him a truth he didn't even want. She was innocent. How could he seduce her now? On the other hand, how was he going to get rid of this very inconvenient and noticeable desire for her?

Watching him, Lou was cursing her own headlong response. She hated having him know how much she wanted him.

"Any man could have made me react that way!" she flared defensively, red-faced. "Any experienced man!"

His head turned and he stared at her, seeing through the flustering words to the embarrassment.

"It's all right," he said gently. "We're both human. Don't beat your conscience to death over a kiss, Lou."

She went even redder and her hands clenched at her sides. "I'm still leaving!"

"I know."

"And I won't let you seduce me!"

He turned. "I won't try," he said solemnly. "I don't seduce virgins."

She bit her lip and tasted him on it. She winced.

"Why?" he asked quietly.

She glared at him.

"Why?" he persisted.

Her eyes fell under that piercing blue stare. "Because I don't want to end up like my mother," she said huskily.

Of all the answers he might have expected, that was the last. "Your mother? I don't understand."

She shook her head. "You don't need to. It's personal. You and I are business partners until the end of the month, and then nothing that happened to me will be any concern of yours."

He didn't move. She looked vulnerable, hurt. "Counseling might be of some benefit," he said gently.

"I don't need counseling."

"Tell me how your wrist got broken, Lou," he said matter-of-factly.

She stiffened.

"Oh, a layman wouldn't notice, it's healed nicely. But surgery is my business. I know a break when I see one. There are scars, too, despite the neat stitching job. How did it happen?"

She felt weak. She didn't want to talk to him, of all people, about her past. It would only reinforce what he already thought of her father, though God only knew why she should defend such a man.

She clasped her wrist defensively, as if to hide what had been done to it. "It's an old injury," she said finally.

"What sort of injury? How did it happen?"

She laughed nervously. "I'm not your patient."

He absently jingled the change in his pocket, watching her. It occurred to him that she was a stranger. Despite their heated arguments over the past year, they'd never come close to discussing personal matters. Away from the office, they were barely civil to each other. In it, they never discussed anything except business. But he was getting a new picture of her, and not a very reassuring one. This was a woman with a painful past, so painful that it had locked her up inside an antiseptic prison. He wondered if she'd ever had the incentive to fight her way out, or why it should matter to him that she hadn't.

"Can you talk to Drew about it?" he asked suddenly.

She hesitated and then shook her head. Her fingers tightened around her wrist. "It doesn't matter, I tell you."

His hand came out of his pocket and he caught the damaged wrist very gently in his long fingers, prepared for her instinctive jerk. He moved closer, drawing that hand to his chest. He pressed it gently into the thick fabric of his vest.

"There's nothing you can't tell me," he said solemnly. "I don't carry tales, or gossip. Anything you say to me will remain between the two of us. If you want to talk, ever, I'll listen."

She bit her bottom lip. She'd never been able to tell anyone. Her mother knew, but she defended her husband, trying desperately to pretend that Lou had imagined it, that it had never happened. She excused her husband's affairs, his drinking bouts, his drug addiction, his brutality, his sarcasm…everything, in the name of love, while her marriage disintegrated around her and her daughter turned away from her. Obsessive love, one of her friends had called it—blind, obsessive love that refused to acknowledge the least personality flaw in the loved one.

"My mother was emotionally crippled," she said, thinking aloud. "She was so blindly in love with him that he could do no wrong, no wrong at all…" She remembered where she was and looked up at him with the pain still in her eyes.

"Who broke your wrist, Lou?" he asked gently.

She remembered aloud. "He was drinking and I tried to take the bottle away from him, because he'd hit my mother. He hit my wrist with the bottle, and it broke," she added, wincing at the memory of the pain. "And all the while, when they operated to repair the damage, he kept saying that I'd fallen through a glass door, that I'd tripped. Everyone believed him, even my mother. I told her that he did it, and she said that I was lying."

"He? Who did it, Lou?"

She searched his curious eyes. "Why…my father," she said simply.

Chapter Six

Coltrain searched her dark eyes, although the confession didn't really surprise him. He knew too much about her father to be surprised.

"So that was why the whiskey on my breath bothered you Friday night," he remarked quietly.

She averted her head and nodded. "He was a drunkard at the last, and a drug addict. He had to stop operating because he almost killed a patient. They let him retire and act in an advisory capacity because he'd been such a good surgeon. He was, you know," she added. "He might have been a terrible father, but he was a wonderful surgeon. I wanted to be a surgeon, to be like him." She shivered. "I was in my first year of medical school when it happened. I lost a semester and afterward, I knew I'd never be able to operate. I decided to become a general practitioner."

"What a pity," he said. He understood the fire for surgical work because he had it. He loved what he did for a living.

She smiled sadly. "I'm still practicing medicine. It isn't so bad. Family practice has its place in the scheme of things, and I've enjoyed the time I've spent in Jacobsville."

"So have I," he admitted reluctantly. He smiled at her expression. "Surprised? You've been here long enough to know how a good many people react to me. I'm the original bad boy of the community. If it hadn't been for the scholarship one of my teachers helped me get, I'd probably be in jail by now. I had a hard childhood and I hated authority in any form. I was in constant trouble with the law."

"You?" she asked, aghast.

He nodded. "People aren't always what they seem, are they?" he continued. "I was a wild boy. But I loved medicine and I had an aptitude for it and there were people who were willing to help me. I'm the first of my family to escape poverty, did you know?"

She shook her head. "I don't know anything about your family," she said. "I wouldn't have presumed to ask anyone something so personal about you."

"I've noticed that," he returned. "You avoid sharing your feelings. You'll fight back, but you don't let people close, do you?"

"When people get too close, they can hurt you," she said.

"A lesson your father taught you, no doubt."

She wrapped her arms around her chest. "I'm cold," she said dully. "I want to go home."

He searched her face. "Come home with me."

She hesitated warily.

He made a face. "Shame on you for what you're thinking. You should know better. You're off the endangered list. I'll make chili and Mexican corn bread

and strong coffee and we can watch a Christmas special. Do you like opera?"

Her eyes brightened. "Oh, I love it."

His own eyes brightened. "Pavarotti?"

"And Domingo." She looked worried. "But people
will talk…"

"They're already talking. Who cares?" he asked.
"We're both single adults. What we do together is nobody's business."

"Yes, well, the general consensus of opinion is that
we're public property, or didn't you hear what Mr. Bailey said?"

"I heard you scream," he mused.

She cleared her throat. "Well, it was the last straw."

He caught her hand, the undamaged one, and
locked her fingers into his, tugging her out the door.

"Dr. Coltrain," she began.

He locked the office door. "You know my name."

She looked wary. "Yes."

He glanced at her. "My friends call me Copper," he
said softly, and smiled.

"We're not friends."

"I think we're going to be, though, a year too late."
He tugged her toward his car.

"I can drive mine," she protested.

"Mine's more comfortable. I'll drive you home, and
give you a lift to work in the morning. Is it locked?"

"Yes, but…"

"Don't argue, Lou. I'm tired. It's been a long day and
we've still got to make rounds at the hospital later."

We. He couldn't know the anguish of hearing him

link them together when she had less than two weeks left in Jacobsville. He'd said that he'd torn up her resignation, but she was levelheaded enough to know that she had to go. It would be pure torment to be around him all the time and have him treat her as a friend and nothing more. She couldn't have an affair with him, either, so what was left?

He glanced down at her worried face and his fingers contracted. "Stop brooding. I promised not to seduce you."

"I know that!"

"Unless you want me to," he chided, chuckling at her expression. "I'm a doctor," he added in a conspiratorial whisper. "I know how to protect you from any consequences."

"Damn you!"

She jerked away from him, furiously. He laughed at her fighting stance.

"That was wicked," he acknowledged. "But I do love to watch you lose that hot temper. Are you Irish, by any chance?"

"My grandfather was," she muttered. She dashed a strand of blond hair out of her eyes. "You stop saying things like that to me!"

He unlocked her door, still smiling. "All right. No more jokes."

She slid into the leather seat and inhaled the luxurious scent of the upholstery while he got in beside her and started the car. It was dark. She sat next to him in perfect peace and contentment as they drove out to his ranch, not breaking the silence as they passed by farms and ranches silhouetted against the flat horizon.

"You're very quiet," he remarked when he pulled up in front of the Spanish-style adobe house he called home.

"I'm happy," she said without thinking.

He was quiet, then. He helped her out and they walked a little apart on the flagstone walkway that led to the front porch. It was wide and spacious, with gliders and a porch swing.

"It must be heaven to sit out here in the spring," she remarked absently.

He glanced at her curiously. "I never pictured you as the sort to enjoy a porch swing."

"Or walks in the woods, or horseback riding, or baseball games?" she asked. "Because I like those things, too. Austin does have suburbs, and I had friends who owned ranches. I know how to ride and shoot, too."

He smiled. She'd seemed like such a city girl. He'd made sure that he never looked too closely at her, of course. Like father, like daughter, he'd always thought. But she was nothing like Fielding Blakely. She was unique.

He unlocked the door and opened it. The interior was full of Spanish pieces and dark furniture with creams and beiges and browns softened by off-white curtains. It had the look of professional decorating, which it probably was.

"I grew up sitting on orange crates and eating on cracked plates," he commented as she touched a bronze sculpture of a bronc rider. "This is much better."

She laughed. "I guess so. But orange crates and cracked plates wouldn't be so bad if the company was pleasant. I hate formal dining rooms and extravagant place settings."

Now he was getting suspicious. They really couldn't have that much in common! His eyebrow jerked. "Full of surprises, aren't you? Or did you just take a look at my curriculum vitae and tell me what I wanted to hear?" he added in a crisp, suspicious tone.

Her surprise was genuine, and he recognized it immediately. She searched his face. "This was a mistake," she said flatly. "I think I'd like to go…"

He caught her arm. "Lou, I'm constantly on the defensive with women," he said. "I never know, you see…" He hesitated.

"Yes, I understand," she replied. "You don't have to say it."

"All that, and you read minds, too," he said with cool sarcasm. "Well, well."

She drew away from him. She seemed to read his mind quite well, she thought, because she usually knew what he was going to say.

That occurred to him, too. "It used to make me mad as hell when you handed me files before I asked for them," he told her.

"It wasn't deliberate," she said without thinking.

"I know." His jaw firmed as he looked at her. "We know too much about each other, don't we, Lou? We know things we shouldn't, without ever saying them."

She looked up, feeling the bite of his inspection all the way to her toes. "We can't say them," she replied. "Not ever."

He only nodded. His eyes searched hers intently. "I don't believe in happily ever after," he said. "I did, once, until your father came along and shattered all my illusions. She wouldn't let me touch her, you see. But she slept with him. She got pregnant by him. The hell of it was that she was going to marry me without telling me anything." He sighed. "I lost my faith in women on the spot, and I hated your father enough to beat him to his knees. When you came here, and I found out who you were…" He shook his head. "I almost decked Drew for not telling me."

"I didn't know, either," she said.

"I realize that." He smiled. "You were an asset, after I got over the shock. You never complained about long hours or hard work, no matter how much I put on you. And I put a lot on you, at first. I thought I could make you quit. But the more I demanded, the more you gave. After a while, it occurred to me that I'd made a good bargain. Not that I liked you," he added sardonically.

"You made that perfectly clear."

"You fought back," he said. "Most people don't. They knuckle under and go home and fume about it, and think up things they wish they'd said. You just jump in with both feet and give it all you've got. You're a hell of an adversary, Lou. I couldn't beat you down."

"I always had to fight for things," she recalled. "My father was like you." Her face contorted and she turned away.

"I don't get drunk as a rule, and I've never hurt a woman!" he snapped.

"I didn't mean that," she said quickly. "It's just that

you're forceful. You demand, you push. You don't ever give up or give in. Neither did he. If he thought he was right, he'd fight the whole world to prove it. But he fought the same when he was wrong. And in his later years, he drank to excess. He wouldn't admit he had a problem. Neither would my mother. She was his slave," she added bitterly. "Even her daughter was dispensable if the great man said so."

"Didn't she love you?"

"Who knows? She loved him more. Enough to lie for him. Even to die for him. And she did." She turned, her face hard. "She got into a plane with him, knowing that he was in no condition to fly. Maybe she had a premonition that he would go down and she wanted to go with him. I'm almost sure that she still would have gone with him if she'd known he was going to crash the plane. She loved him that much."

"You sound as if you can't imagine being loved that much."

"I can't," she said flatly, lifting her eyes. "I don't want that kind of obsessive love. I don't want to give it or receive it."

"What do you want?" he persisted. "A lifetime of loneliness?"

"That's what you're settling for, isn't it?" she countered.

He shrugged. "Maybe I am," he said after a minute. His blue eyes slid over her face and then averted. "Can you cook?" he asked on the way into the kitchen. Like the rest of the house, it was spacious and contained every modern device known to man.

"Of course," she said.

He glanced at her with a grin. "How well do you do chili?" he persisted.

"Well…"

"I've won contests with mine," he said smugly. He slid out of his jacket and vest and tie, opened the top buttons of his shirt and turned to the stove. "You can make the coffee."

"Trusting soul, aren't you?" she murmured as he acquainted her with the coffeemaker and the location of filters, coffee and measuring spoons.

"I always give a fellow cook the benefit of the doubt once," he replied. "Besides, you drink coffee all the time, just like I do. That means you must know how to make it."

She laughed. "I like mine strong," she warned.

"So do I. Do your worst."

Minutes later, the food was on the small kitchen table, steaming and delicious. Lou couldn't remember when she'd enjoyed a meal more.

"That's good chili," she had to admit.

He grinned. "It's the two-time winner of the Jacobsville Chili Cookoff."

"I'm not surprised. The corn bread was wonderful, too."

"The secret to good corn bread is to cook it in an iron skillet," he confessed. "That's where the crispness comes from."

"I don't own a single piece of iron cookware. I'll have to get a pan."

He leaned back, balancing his coffee mug in one

hand as he studied her through narrow eyes. "It hasn't all been on my side," he remarked suddenly.

Her eyes lifted to his. "What hasn't?"

"All that antagonism," he said. "You've been as prickly as I have."

Her slender shoulders rose and fell. "It's instinctive to recoil from people when we know they don't like us. Isn't it?"

"Maybe so." He checked his watch and finished his coffee. "I'll get these things in the dishwasher, then we'd better get over to the hospital and do rounds before the Christmas concert comes on the educational channel."

"I don't have my car," she said worriedly.

"We'll go together."

"Oh, that will certainly keep gossip down," she said on a sigh.

He smiled at her. "Damn gossip."

"Was that an adjective or a verb?"

"A verb. I'll rinse, you stack."

They loaded the dishes and he started the dishwasher. He slid back into his jacket, buttoned his shirt and fixed his tie. "Come on. We'll get the chores out of the way."

The hospital was crowded, and plenty of people noticed that Drs. Coltrain and Blakely came in together to make rounds. Lou tried not to notice as she went from patient to patient, checking charts and making conversation.

But when she finished, Coltrain was nowhere in

sight. She glanced out the window into the parking lot. His car was still there in his designated space. She went to the doctors' lounge looking for him, and turned the corner just in time to see him with a devastating blond woman in a dress that Lou would love to have been able to afford.

Coltrain saw Lou and he looked grim. He turned toward her with his hands in his pockets, and Lou noticed that the woman was clutching one of his arms tightly in both hands.

"This is my partner," he said, without giving her name. "Lou, this is Dana Lester, an old...friend."

"His ex-fiancée." The woman corrected him in a sweet tone. "How nice to meet you! I've just accepted an appointment as nursing director here, so we'll be seeing a lot of each other!"

"You're a nurse?" Lou asked politely, while she caved in inside.

"A graduate nurse," she said, nodding. "I've been working in Houston, but this job came open and was advertised in a local paper. I applied for it, and here I am! How lovely it will be to come home. I was born here, you know."

"Oh, really?" Lou said.

"Darling," she told Copper, "you didn't tell me your partner's name."

"It's Blakely," he said evenly. "Dr. Louise Blakely."

"Blakely?" the woman queried, her blue eyes pensive. "Why does that name sound so familiar...." She suddenly went pale. "No," she said, shaking her head. "No, that would be too coincidental."

"My father," Lou said coolly, "was Dr. Fielding Blakely. I believe you…knew him?" she added pointedly.

Dana's face looked like rice paper. She drew away from Coltrain. "I…I must fly, darling," she said. "Things to do while I get settled! I'll have you over for supper one night soon!"

She didn't speak to Lou again, not that it was expected. Lou watched her go with cold, angry eyes.

"You didn't want to tell her my name," Lou accused softly.

His face gave away nothing. "The past is best left alone."

"Did you know about her job here?"

His jaw clenched. "I knew there was an opening. I didn't know she'd been hired. If Selby Wills hadn't just retired as hospital administrator, she wouldn't have gotten the job."

She probed into the pocket of her lab coat without really seeing it. "She's pretty."

"She's blond, too, isn't that what you're thinking?"

She raised her face. "So," she added, "is Jane Parker."

"Jane Burke, now." He corrected her darkly. "I like blondes."

His tone dared her to make another remark. She lifted a shoulder and turned. "Some men do. Just don't expect me to welcome her with open arms. I'm sure that my mother suffered because of her. At least my father was less careless with women in his later years."

"It was over a long time ago," Copper said quietly. "If I can overlook your father, you can overlook her."

"Do you think so?"

"What happened between them was nothing to do with you," he persisted.

"He betrayed my mother with her, and it's nothing to do with me?" she asked softly.

He rammed his hands into his pockets, his face set and cold. "Are you finished here?"

"Oh, yes, I'm finished here," she agreed fervently. "If you'll drop me off at my car, I'd like to go home now. We'll have to save the TV Special for another time."

He hesitated, but only for a minute. Her expression told him everything he needed to know, including the futility of having an argument with her right now.

"All right," he agreed, nodding toward the exit. "Let's go."

He stopped at her car in the office parking lot and let her out.

"Thanks for my supper," she said politely.

"You're welcome."

She closed the door and unlocked her own car. He didn't drive away until she was safely inside and heading out toward home.

Dana Lester's arrival in town was met with another spate of gossip, because there were people in Jacobsville who remembered the scandal very well. Lou tried to pay as little attention to it as possible as she weathered the first few days with the new nursing supervisor avoiding her and Coltrain barely speaking to her.

It was, she told herself, a very good thing that she was leaving after the first of January. The situation was strained and getting worse. She couldn't work out if Dana was afraid of her or jealous of her. Gossip about herself and Coltrain had been lost in the new rumors about his ex-fiancée's return, which did at least spare Lou somewhat. She couldn't help but see that Dana spent a fair amount of time following Coltrain around the hospital, and once or twice she phoned him at the office. Lou pretended not to notice and not to mind, but it was cutting her up inside.

The night she'd had supper with her taciturn partner had been something of a beginning. But Dana's arrival had nipped it all in the bud. He'd turned his back on Lou and now he only spoke to her when it was necessary and about business. If he'd withdrawn, so had she. Poor Brenda and the office receptionist worked in an armed camp, walking around like people on eggshells. Coltrain's temper strained at the bit, and every time he flared up, Lou flared right back.

"We hear that Nickie and Dana almost came to blows the other night about who got to take Dr. Coltrain a file," Brenda remarked a few days later.

"Too bad someone didn't have a hidden camera, isn't it?" Lou remarked. She sipped her coffee.

Brenda frowned. "I thought... Well, it did seem that you and the doctor were getting along better."

"A temporary truce, nothing more," she returned. "I'm still leaving after the first of the year, Brenda. Nothing's really changed except that Coltrain's old flame has returned."

"She was poison," Brenda said. "I heard all about her from some of the older nurses at the hospital. Did you know that at least two threatened to quit when they knew she was taking over as head nurse at the hospital? One of the nurses she worked with in Houston has family here. They said she was about to be fired when she grabbed this job. Her credentials look impressive, but she's not a good administrator, regardless of her college background, and she plays favorites. They'll learn that here, the hard way."

"It's not my problem."

"Isn't it?" Brenda muttered. "Well, they also say that her real purpose in applying for this job was to see if Copper was willing to take her back and try again. She's looking for a husband and he's number one on her list."

"Lucky him," she said blithely. "She's very pretty."

"She's a blond tarantula," she said hotly. "She'll suck him dry!"

"He's a big boy, Brenda," Lou returned imperturbably. "He can take care of himself."

"No man is immune to a beautiful face and figure and having a woman absolutely worship him. You take my word for it, there's going to be trouble."

"I won't be here to see it," Lou reminded her. And for the first time, she was glad. Nickie and Dana could fight over Coltrain and may the best woman win, she thought miserably. At least she wouldn't have to watch the struggle. She'd always known that Coltrain wasn't for her. She might as well accept defeat with good grace and get out while she could.

She went back to work, all too aware of Coltrain's deep voice in one of the cubicles she passed. She wondered how her life was going to feel when this was all a bad memory, and she wouldn't hear his voice again.

Drew invited her out to eat and she went, gratefully, glad for the diversion. But the restaurant he chose, Jacobsville's best, had two unwelcome diners: Coltrain and his ex-fiancée.

"I'm sorry," Drew said with a smile and a grimace of apology. "I didn't know they'd be here or I'd have chosen another place to take you for supper."

"Oh, I don't mind," she assured him. "I have to see them at the hospital every day, anyway."

"Yes, *see* them being the key word here," he added knowingly. "I understand that they both avoid you."

"God knows why," she agreed. "She's anywhere I'm not when I need to ask her a question, and he only talks to me about patients. I'm glad I'm leaving, Drew. And with all respect to you, I'm sorry I came."

He smiled ruefully. "I'm sorry I got you into this," he said. "Nothing went as I planned."

"What exactly did you plan?" she asked probingly.

He lifted his water glass and took a sip. "Well, I had hoped that Copper would see something in you that he hadn't found anywhere else. You're unique, Lou. So is he, in some respects. You seemed like a match."

She glared at him. "We're chalk and cheese," she said, ignoring the things she and the redheaded doctor did have in common. "And we can't get along for more than five minutes."

"So I see." He looked around and made a face. "Oh, God, more complications!"

She followed his gaze. A determined Nickie, in a

skintight dress cut almost to the navel, was dragging an embarrassed intern to a table right beside Coltrain and Dana's.

"That won't do," she remarked, watching Coltrain's blue eyes start to glitter. "He won't like that. And if she thinks he'll forgo a scene, she's very wrong. Any minute now he's going to get up and walk out."

When he did exactly that, leaving an astonished Dana at one table and a shocked Nickie at the other, Drew whistled through his teeth and gave Lou a pointed stare.

"You know him very well," was all he said, though.

"I know him," Lou said simply. "He says I read his mind. Maybe I do, on some level."

He frowned. "Do you realize how rare a rapport that is?"

She shrugged. "Not really. He seems to read my mind, too. I shouldn't feel sorry for him, but I do. Imagine shuffling two women in one restaurant."

He didn't add that it was really three, and that Copper had been watching Lou surreptitiously ever since she and Drew entered the restaurant. But of the three women, Lou was the only one who wasn't blatantly chasing him.

"He's paying the check," he remarked. "And, yes, there he goes, motioning to Dana. Good thing they'd finished dessert, wasn't it? Poor Nickie. She won't forget this in a while."

"I told her she was pushing too hard," Lou remarked. "Too bad. She's so young. I suppose she hasn't learned that you can chase a man too relentlessly and lose him."

"Some women never chase a man at all," he said.

She looked up and saw the teasing expression on his face. She laughed. "Drew, you are a dear," she said genuinely.

He chuckled. "My wife always said that I was," he agreed. "What are you going to do?"

"Me? What do you mean? What am I going to do about what?"

"About Copper."

"Nothing," she replied. "Right after the holidays, I leave for Austin."

He pursed his lips as he lifted his coffee cup. "You know," he said, "I have a feeling you'll never get out of town."

Chapter Seven

Saturday morning, Lou woke to the sound of someone hammering on her front door. Half-asleep, with a pale pink satin robe whipped around her slender body and her hair disheveled, she made her way to open it.

The sight that met her eyes was shocking. Coltrain was standing there, dressed in jeans and boots and a faded cotton shirt under a fleece-lined jacket, with a weather-beaten gray Stetson in one lean hand.

She blinked. "Are we filming a new series called 'Cowboy Doctor'?"

"Cute," he remarked, but he wasn't smiling. "I have to talk to you."

She opened the door, still drowsy. "Come on in. I'll make coffee," she said, stifling a yawn as she shuffled toward the kitchen. She could have gone immediately to change, but she was more than adequately covered and he was a doctor. Besides, she reminded herself, he had two women chasing him relentlessly anyway.

"I'll make the coffee. How about some toast to go with it?"

"Plain or cinnamon?"

"Suit yourself."

She got out butter and cinnamon and, just as the coffee finished brewing, she had the toast ready—piping hot from the oven.

He watched her moving about the kitchen. He was sitting leaning back in one of her kitchen chairs with one booted foot on the floor and the chair propped against the wall. He looked out of humor and wickedly handsome all at the same time.

In the position he was occupying, his jeans clung closely to every powerful line of his long legs. He was muscular without being exaggerated, and with his faded shirt unbuttoned at the throat and his red hair disheveled from the hat, he looked more relaxed than she'd ever seen him.

It occurred to her that this was the way he usually was, except when he was working. It was like a private look into his secret life, and she was unexpectedly pleased to have been given it before she left town for good.

"Here." She put the toast on the table, handed him a plate, put condiments on the spotless white tablecloth and then poured coffee into two cups.

"The Christmas concert was nice," he remarked.

"Was it?" she replied. "I went to bed."

"I had nothing to do with getting Dana down here," he said flatly. "In case you wondered."

"It's none of my business."

"Yes, I know," he said heavily. He sipped coffee and munched toast, but he was preoccupied. "Nickie and Dana are becoming an embarrassment."

"Leave it to you to be irritated when two lovely

women compete for your attention," she remarked dryly.

His eyes narrowed on her face. "Irritation doesn't quite cover it. I feel like the stud of the month," he said disgustedly.

She burst out laughing. "Oh, I'm sorry!" she said when he glared at her. "It was the way you said it."

He was ruffled, and looked it. He sipped more coffee. "I wasn't trying to make a joke."

"I know. It must be difficult, especially when you have to make rounds at the hospital, with both of them working there."

"I understand you're having some problems of your own in that regard."

"You might say that," she agreed. "I can't find Dana or Nickie when I need them. I seem to have the plague."

"You know that it can't continue?"

"Of course I do," she assured him. "And when I leave, things will settle down, I'm sure."

He scowled. "What do you mean, when you leave? How will that help? Anyway, we'd already agreed that you were staying."

"We agreed on nothing," she returned. "I gave you my resignation. If you tore it up, that's your problem. I consider it binding."

He stared down into his coffee cup, deep in thought. "I had no idea that you meant it."

"Amazing," she mused, watching him. "You have such a convenient memory, Dr. Coltrain. I can't forget a single word you said to Drew about me, and you can't remember?"

His face hardened. "I didn't know you were listening."

"That makes everything all right?" she asked with mock solemnity.

He ran a hand through his already disheveled hair. "Things came to a head," he replied. "I'd just had to diagnose leukemia in a child who should have had years of happiness to look forward to. I'd had a letter from my father asking for money…"

She shifted against the table. "I didn't know that your parents were still alive."

"My mother died ten years ago," he replied. "My father lives in Tucson. He wrangles horses, but he likes to gamble. When he gets in too deep, he always comes to me for a grubstake." He said it with utter contempt.

"Is that all you mean to him? Money?" she asked gently.

"It was all I ever meant to him." He lifted cold blue eyes to hers. He smiled unpleasantly. "Who do you think put me up to breaking and entering when I was a teenager? I was a juvenile, you know. Juveniles don't go to jail. Oh, we didn't do it here," he added. "Not where he lived. We always went to Houston. He cased the houses and sent me in to do the actual work."

Her gasp was audible. "He should have been arrested!"

"He was," he replied. "He served a year and got probation. We haven't spent any time together since I was placed with a foster family when I was thirteen, long before I started medical school. I put all that behind me. Apparently so did he. But now that I'm making a comfortable living, he doesn't really see any good reason not to ask me for help when he needs it."

What sort of family life had *he* grown up in? she wondered. It was, in some ways, like her own upbringing. "What a pity that we can't choose our parents," she remarked.

"Amen." His broad shoulders shifted against the wall. "I was in a temper already, and Drew's phone call was the last straw. It irritated the hell out of me that you liked him, but you jerked away from my slightest touch as if I might contaminate you."

She hadn't thought he'd noticed. He took her reaction as a sign of her distaste for him, when it was a fierce, painful attraction. It was ironic.

She lowered her eyes. "You said when I first came to work with you that we would have a business relationship."

"So I did. But that didn't mean you should treat me like a leper," he remarked. Oddly, he didn't seem to be concerned about it anymore. He smiled, in fact, his blue eyes sparkling. "But I wouldn't have had you overhear what I told Drew for all the world, Lou. It shamed me when you asked to end our partnership."

She toyed with a fingernail. "I thought it would make you happy."

Her choice of words delighted him. He knew exactly what she felt for him. He'd had suspicions for a while now, but he hadn't been certain until he kissed her. He couldn't let her leave until he was sure about what he felt for her. But how was he going to stop her? His blue eyes ran searchingly over her face and a crazy idea popped into his mind. "If you and I were engaged," he mused aloud, "Dana and Nickie would give up."

The words rambled around in her mind like marbles as she stared at him. The sun was out. It was a nice December day. Her Christmas decorations lined the windows and the tinsel on the Christmas tree in the living room caught the sun through the curtains and glittered.

"Did you hear me?" he asked when she didn't react.

Her cheeks burned. "I don't think that's very funny," she remarked, turning away.

He got to his feet with an audible thud and before she could move three feet, he had her by the waist from behind. Steely hands pulled her back against him and when she caught them, she felt their warm strength under her cool fingers. She felt his breath against her hair, felt it as his chest moved at her back.

"Shall we stop dancing around it?" he asked roughly. "You're in love with me. I've pretended not to see it, but we both know it's why you're leaving."

She gasped aloud. Frozen in his arms, she hadn't even a comeback, a face-saving reply. She felt his hands contract under hers, as if he thought she might pull away and run for it.

"Don't panic," he said quietly. "Dodging the issue won't solve it."

"I...didn't realize you could tell," she whispered, her pride in ashes at his feet.

His lean arms contracted, bringing her soft warmth closer to his taut body. "Take it easy. We'll deal with it."

"You don't have to deal with anything," she began huskily. "I'm going to…"

He turned her while she was speaking and his mouth was on hers before she could finish. She fought him for an instant, as he anticipated. But he was slow and very gentle, and she began to melt into him like ice against a flame.

He brought her closer, aware of her instant response when she felt his body harden. He made a rough sound against her mouth and deepened the kiss.

Her fingers caught in the cool flames of his hair, holding on for dear life as his ardor burned high and wild. He kissed her as he'd kissed Nickie at the party, not an inch of space between their bodies, no quarter in the thin lips devouring her open mouth. This time when his tongue penetrated, she didn't pull away. She accepted the intimate contact without a protest, shivering a little as it ignited new fires in her own taut body. The sensation was unlike anything she'd known. She held on tight, moaning, aware somewhere in the back of her mind that his hand was at the base of her spine, rubbing her against him, and that she should say something.

She was incapable of anything except blind response.

She didn't resist even when he eased her back onto her feet and, still kissing her hungrily, slid his hand under her robe against the soft, tight curve of her breast. He felt her heartbeat run away. With a groan, he fought his way under the gown, against the petal-soft warmth of her skin, and cupped her tenderly, dragging his thumb against the small hardness he found. She shivered again. Reeling, he traced the tight nub with his thumb and forefinger, testing its hardness. She sobbed against his mouth. Probably, he thought dizzily, she'd never had such a caress. And he could give her something more; another pleasure that she didn't know yet.

His mouth left hers and found its way down past her collarbone to the softness under his hand. It opened on her body, and he drank in the scented warmth of her while his tongue took the place of his thumb. She gasped and struggled, but he began to suckle her, his arms swallowing her, and she shuddered once and gave in. He felt her body go lax in his arms, so that if he hadn't supported her, she would have fallen. She caressed his nape with trembling hands, gasping a little as he increased the pressure, but clinging, not pushing.

When he thought he might explode from the pleasure it was giving him, he forced his mouth to release her and he stood erect, pulling her up abruptly.

His face was ruddy with high color, his eyes blazing as they met her half-open, dazed ones. She was oblivious to everything except the taste of him. Her lips were swollen. Even her tongue felt swollen. She couldn't say a word.

He searched over her face and then dropped his eyes to her bodice. He moved it out of the way and looked at the small, firm breast he'd been tasting. She looked like a rosebud there, the nipple red from his mouth.

He traced around it lazily and then looked back up at the shocked pleasure in her dark, dark eyes.

"I could have you on the kitchen table, right now,"

he said in a deep, quiet tone. "And you think you're leaving in two weeks?"

She blinked. It was all so unreal. He'd all but seduced her. His hand was still on her breast and he'd pulled the robe and gown aside. He was looking at her...!

She gasped, horrified, jerking back from him. Her hands grappled with the unruly fabric before she finally got her body covered. She backed away, blushing, glaring at him accusingly.

He didn't move, except to lean back against the kitchen counter and cross his long legs. That action drew her eyes to something she'd felt earlier, and she blushed scarlet before she managed to look away. What had she done? What had she let him do?

"You look outraged," he mused. "I think I like having you blush when I look at you."

"Would you leave, please?" she asked tightly.

"No, I don't think so," he said pleasantly. "Get dressed. Wear jeans and boots. I'm taking you riding."

"I don't want to go anywhere with you!"

"You want to go to bed with me," he corrected, smiling gently. "I can't think of anything I'd enjoy more, but I saddled the horses and left them in the stable before I came over here."

She huddled in her robe, wincing as it rubbed against her body.

"Breast sore?" he asked softly. "I'm sorry. I lost my head a little."

She flushed more and the robe tightened. "Dr. Coltrain..."

"Copper," he reminded her. "Or you can call me Jeb, if you like." He pursed his lips and his eyes were hot and possessive. "You'd really better get dressed, Lou," he murmured. "I'm still pretty hot, and aroused men are devious."

She moved back. "I have things to do…"

"Horseback riding or…?" He moved toward her.

She turned and ran for the bedroom. She couldn't believe what had just happened, and he'd said something about them becoming engaged. She must be losing her mind. Yes, that was it, she'd worried over leaving so much that she was imagining things. The whole thing had probably been a hallucination.

He'd cleared away the breakfast things by the time she washed, dressed, pulled her hair back into a pony-tail with a blue ribbon and came into the kitchen with a rawhide jacket on.

He smiled. "You look like a cowgirl."

She'd felt a bit uneasy about facing him after that torrid interlude, but apparently he wasn't embarrassed. She might as well follow his lead. She managed a smile in return. "Thanks. But I may not quite merit the title. I haven't ridden in a long time."

"You'll be all right. I'll look after you."

He opened the door and let her out, waiting for her to lock it. Then he helped her into the Jaguar and drove her to his ranch.

The woods were lovely, despite their lack of leaves. The slow, easy rhythm of the horses was relaxing, even if the company wasn't. She was all too aware of Coltrain beside her, tall and elegant even on horseback. With the Stetson pulled low over his eyes, he looked so handsome that he made her toes tingle.

"Enjoying yourself?" he asked companionably.

"Oh, yes," she admitted. "I haven't been riding in a long time."

"I do more of it than I like sometimes," he confessed. "This isn't a big ranch, but I run about fifty head of pedigree cattle. I have two married cowhands who help out."

"Why do you keep cattle?" she asked.

"I don't know. It was always a dream of mine, I guess, from the time I was a boy. My grandfather had one old milk cow and I'd try to ride her." He chuckled. "I fell off a lot."

She smiled. "And your grandmother?"

"Oh, she was a cook of excellent proportions," he replied. "She made cakes that were the talk of the county. When my dad went wrong, it broke her heart, and my grandfather's. I think they took it harder because he lured me into it with him." He shook his head. "When a kid goes bad, everyone blames it on the upbringing. But my grandparents were kind, good people. They were just poor. A lot of people were...still are."

She'd noticed that he had a soft spot for his needy patients. He made extra time for them, acting as counselor and even helping them get in touch with the proper government agencies when they needed help. At Christmas, he was the first to pledge a donation to local charities and contribute to parties for children who wouldn't otherwise have presents. He was a good man, and she adored him.

"Do you want children, eventually?" she asked.

"I'd like a family," he said noncommittally. He glanced at her. "How about you?"

She grimaced. "I don't know. It would be hard for me to juggle motherhood and medicine. I know plenty of people do, but it seems like begging from Peter to pay Paul, you know? Children need a lot of care. I think plenty of social problems are caused by parents who can't get enough time off from work to look after their children. And good day care is a terrible financial headache. Why isn't day care free?" she asked abruptly. "It should be. If women are going to have to work, companies should provide access to day care for them. I know of hospitals and some companies that do it for their employees. Why can't every big company?"

"Good question. It would certainly take a burden off working parents."

"All the same, if I had kids, I'd want to be with them while they were young. I don't know if I could give up practice for so long...."

He reined in his horse and caught her bridle, bringing her horse gently around so that they were facing each other at the side. "That's not the reason. Talk to me," he said quietly. "What is it?"

She huddled into her jacket. "I hated being a child," she muttered. "I hated my father and my mother and my life."

His eyebrows lifted. "Do you think a child would hate me?"

She laughed. "Are you kidding? Children love you. Except that you don't do stitches as nicely as I do," she added.

He smiled ruefully. "Thanks for small favors."

"The secret is the chewing gum I give them afterward."

"Ah, I see. Trade a few stitches for a few cavities."

"It's sugarless gum," she said smugly.

He searched her face with warm eyes. "Touché."

He wheeled his horse and led her off down a pasture path to where the big barn was situated several hundred yards away from the house. He explained the setup, and how he'd modernized his small operation.

"I'm not as up-to-date as a lot of ranchers are, and this is peanut scale," he added. "But I've put a lot of work and time into it, and I'm moderately proud of what I've accomplished. I have a herd sire who's mentioned in some of the bigger cattle magazines."

"I'm impressed. Do I get to see him?"

"Do you want to?"

"You sound surprised. I like animals. When I started out, it was a toss-up between being a doctor and being a vet."

"What swayed you?"

"I'm not really sure. But I've never regretted my choice."

He swung out of the saddle and waited for her to dismount. He tied the horses to the corral rail and led the way into the big barn.

It was surprisingly sanitary. The walkway was paved, the stalls were spacious with metal gates and fresh hay.

The cows were sleek and well fed, and the bull he'd mentioned was beautiful even by bovine standards.

"Why, he's gorgeous," she enthused as they stood at the gate and looked at him. He was red-coated, huge, streamlined and apparently docile, because he came up to let Coltrain pet his muzzle.

"How are you, old man?" he murmured affectionately. "Had enough corn, have you?"

"He's a Santa Gertrudis, isn't he?" she asked curiously.

His hand stilled on the bull's nose. "How did you know that?" he asked.

"Ted Regan is one of my patients. He had a breeder's edition of some magazine with him one day, and he left it behind. I got a good idea of coat colors, at least. We have a lot of cattlemen around here," she added. "It never hurts to know a little bit about a good bull."

"Why, Lou," he mused. "I'm impressed."

"That's a first."

He chuckled. His blue eyes twinkled down at her as he propped one big boot on the low rail of the gate. "No, it's not. You impressed me the first week you were here. You've grown on me."

"Good heavens, am I a wart?"

He caught a strand of her hair and wound it around his finger. "You're a wonder," he corrected, searching her eyes. "I didn't realize we had so much in common. Funny, isn't it? We've worked together for a year, but I've found out more about you in the past two weeks than I ever knew."

"That goes for me, too."

She dropped her eyes to his chest, where the faded shirt clung to the hard muscles. She loved the way he stood, the way he walked, the way he looked with that hat tilted rakishly over one eye. She remembered the feel of his warm arms around her and she felt suddenly cold.

Her expressions fascinated him. He watched them change, saw the hunger filter into her face.

She drew a wistful breath and looked up at him with a wan smile.

He frowned. Without understanding why, he held out a lean arm.

She accepted the invitation without question. Her body went against his, pressing close. Her arms went under his and around him, so that her hands could flatten on the muscles of his long back. She closed her eyes and laid her cheek against his chest, and listened to his heart beat.

He was surprised, yet he wasn't. It felt natural to have Lou in his arms. He drew her closer, in a purely nonsexual way, and absently stroked her hair while he watched his bull eat corn out of the trough in his pen.

"Next week is Christmas," he said above her head.

"Yes, I know. What do you do for Christmas? Do you go to friends, or invite people over?"

He laughed gently. "I used to have it with Jane, before she married," he recalled, feeling her stiffen without really thinking much about it. "But last year, since she married, I cooked a TV dinner and watched old movies all day."

She didn't answer for a minute. Despite what she'd

heard about Coltrain and Jane Parker in the past year, she hadn't thought that he and Jane had been quite so close. But it seemed that they were. It depressed her more than anything had in recent weeks.

He wasn't thinking about Christmases past. He was thinking about the upcoming one. His hand explored her hair strand by strand. "Where are we going to have Christmas dinner, and who's going to cook it?" he asked matter-of-factly.

That was encouraging, that he wanted to spend Christmas with her. She couldn't refuse, even out of hurt pride. "We could have it at my house," she offered.

"I'll help cook it."

She smiled. "It would be nice to have someone to eat it with," she confessed.

"I'll make sure we're on call Christmas Eve, not Christmas Day," he promised. His arm slid down her back and drew her closer. He was aware of a kind of contentment he'd never experienced before, a belonging that he hadn't known even with Jane. Funny, he thought, until Lou came along, it had never occurred to him that he and Jane couldn't have had a serious relationship even if Todd Burke hadn't married her.

It was a sobering thought. This woman in his arms had come to mean a lot to him, without his realizing it until he'd kissed her for the first time. He laid his cheek against her head with a long sigh. It was like coming home. He'd been searching all his life for something he'd never found. He was closer to it than he'd ever been right now.

Her arms tightened around his lean waist. She could feel the wall of his chest hard against her breasts, the buckle of his belt biting into her. But it still wasn't quite close enough. She moved just a little closer, so that her legs brushed his.

He moved to accommodate her, sliding one boot higher on the fence so that she could fit against him more comfortably. But the movement aroused him and he caught his breath sharply.

"Sorry," she murmured and started to step away.

But his hand stayed her hips. "I can't help that," he said at her temple, secretly delighted at his headlong physical response to her. "But it isn't a threat."

"I didn't want to make you uncomfortable."

He smiled lazily. "I wouldn't call it that." He brushed a kiss across her forehead. "Relax," he whispered. "It's pretty public here, and I'm sure you know as well as I do that making love in a hay barn is highly unsanitary."

She laughed at his humor. "Oh, but this barn is very clean."

"Not that clean," he murmured dryly. "Besides," he added, "it's been a long, dry spell. When I'm not in the market for a companion, I don't walk around prepared for sweet interludes."

She lifted her face and searched his mocking eyes demurely. "A long, dry spell? With Nickie prancing around half-naked to get your attention?"

He didn't laugh, as she expected him to. He traced her pert nose. "I don't have affairs," he said. "And I'm the soul of discretion in my private life. There was a widow in a city I won't name. She and I were good friends, and we supplied each other with something neither of us was comfortable spreading around. She married year before last. Since then, I've concentrated on my work and my cattle. Period."

She was curious. "Can you...well, do it...without love?"

"I was fond of her," he explained. "She was fond of me. We didn't have to be in love."

She moved restlessly.

"It would have to be love, for you, wouldn't it, Lou?" he asked. "Even desperate desire wouldn't be enough." He traced her soft lips with deliberation. "But you and I are an explosive combination. And you do love me."

She laid her forehead at his collarbone. "Yes," she admitted. "I love you. But not enough to be your mistress."

"I know that."

"Then it's hopeless."

He laughed mirthlessly. "Is it? I thought I mentioned that we could get engaged."

"Engaged isn't married," she began.

He put a finger over her lips, and he looked solemn. "I know that. Will you let me finish? We can be engaged until the first of the year, when I can afford to take a little time off for a honeymoon. We could have a New Year's wedding."

Chapter Eight

"You mean, get married? Us?" she echoed blankly.

He tilted up her chin and searched her dark, troubled eyes. "Sex doesn't trouble you half as much as marriage does, is that it? Marriage means commitment, and to you, that's like imprisonment."

She grimaced. "My parents' marriage was horrible. I don't want to become like my mother."

"So you said." He traced her cheek. "But I'm not like your father. I don't drink. Well," he murmured with a sheepish grin, "maybe just once, and I had justification for that. You were letting Drew hold your hand, when you always jerked back if I touched you at all."

She was surprised. She smiled. "Was *that* why?"

He chuckled. "Yes, that was why."

"Imagine that!"

"Take one day at a time, okay?" he asked. "Let's rock along for a couple of weeks, and spend Christmas together. Then we'll talk about this again."

"All right."

He bent and kissed her softly. She pressed up against him, but he stepped back.

"None of that," he said smartly. "We're going to get

to know each other before we let our glands get in the way."

"*Glands!*"

"Don't you remember glands, Doctor?" He moved toward her threateningly. "Let me explain them to you."

"I think I've got the picture," she said on a laugh. "Keep away, you lecher!"

He laughed, too. He caught her hand and tangled her fingers with his as they walked back to where the horses were tied. He'd never been quite this interested in marriage, even if he'd once had it in the back of his mind when he'd dated Jane. But when he'd had Lou close in his arms, in the barn, he'd wanted it with a maddening desire. It wasn't purely physical, although she certainly attracted him that way. But despite the way she felt about him, he had a feeling that she'd have to be carefully coaxed down the aisle. She was afraid of everything marriage stood for because of her upbringing. Their marriage wouldn't be anything like her parents', but he was going to have to convince her of that first.

They made rounds together the next morning at the hospital, and as usual, Dana was lying in wait for Coltrain.

But this time, he deliberately linked Lou's hand in his as he smiled at her.

"Good morning," he said politely.

Dana was faintly startled. "Good morning, doctors," she said hesitantly, her eyes on their linked hands.

"Lou and I became engaged yesterday," he said.

Dana's face paled. She drew a stiff breath and managed the semblance of a smile. "Oh, did you? Well, I suppose I should offer my congratulations!" She laughed. "And I had such high hopes that you and I might regain something of the past."

"The past is dead," he said firmly, his blue eyes steady on her face. "I have no inclination whatsoever to revive it."

Dana laughed uncomfortably. "So I see." She glanced at Lou's left hand. "Quite a sudden engagement, was it?" she added slyly. "No ring yet?"

Lou's hand jerked in his, but he steadied it. "When Lou makes up her mind what sort she wants, I'll buy her one," he said lazily. "I'd better get started. Wait for me in the lounge when you finish, sweet," he told Lou and squeezed her fingers before he let them go.

"I will," she promised. She smiled at Dana carelessly and went down the hall to begin her own rounds.

Dana followed her. "Well, I hope you fare better than I did," she muttered. "He's had the hots for Jane Parker for years. He asked me to marry him because he wanted me and I wouldn't give in, but even so, I couldn't compete with dear Jane," she said bitterly. "Your father was willing, so I indulged in a stupid affair, hoping I might make him jealous. That was the lunatic act of the century!"

"So I heard," Lou said stiffly, glaring at the other woman.

"I guess you did," the older woman said with a grimace. "He hated me for it. There's one man who doesn't move with the times, and he never forgets a wrong you do him." Her eyes softened as she looked at Lou's frozen face. "Your poor mother must have hated me. I know your father did. He was livid that I'd been so careless, and of course, I ruined his chances of staying here. But he didn't do so bad in Austin."

Lou had different memories of that. She couldn't lay it all at Dana's door, however. She paused at her first patient's door. "What do you mean about Jane Parker?" she asked solemnly.

"You must have heard by now that she was his first love, his only love, for years. I gave up on him after my fling with your father. I thought it was surely over between them until I came back here. She's married, you know, but she still sees Copper socially." Her eyes glittered. "They say he sits and stares at her like an oil painting when they're anywhere together. You'll find that out for yourself. I should be jealous, but I don't think I am. I feel sorry for you, because you'll always be his second choice, even if he marries you. He may want you, but he'll never stop loving Jane."

She walked away, leaving a depressed, worried Lou behind. Dana's former engagement to Coltrain sounded so much like her own "engagement" with him that it was scary. She knew that he wanted her, but he didn't show any signs of loving her. Did he still love Jane? If he did, she couldn't possibly marry him.

Nickie came up the hall when Lou had finished her rounds and was ready to join Coltrain in the lounge.

"Congratulations," she told Lou with a resigned smile. "I guess I knew I was out of the running when I saw him kiss you in the car park. Good luck. From what I hear, you'll need it." She kept walking.

Lou was dejected. It was in her whole look when she went into the doctors' lounge, where Coltrain had just finished filling out a form at the table near the window. He looked up, frowning.

"What is it?" he asked curtly. "Have Dana and Nickie been giving you a hard time?"

"Not at all," she said. "I'm just a little tired." She touched her back and winced, to convince him. "Horseback riding takes some getting used to, doesn't it?"

He smiled, glad that he'd mistaken soreness for depression. "Yes, it does. We'll have to do more of it." He picked up the folder. "Ready to go?"

"Yes."

He left the form at the nurses' station, absorbing more congratulations from the nurses, and led Lou out to his Jaguar.

"We'll take some time off this afternoon for lunch and shop for a ring," he said.

"But I don't need…"

"Of course you do," he said. "We can't let people think I'm too miserly to buy you an engagement ring!"

"But what if…?"

"Lou, it's my money," he declared.

She grimaced. Well, if he wanted to be stuck with a diamond ring when she left town, that was his business. The engagement, as far as she was concerned, was nothing more than an attempt to get his life back on an even keel and discourage Nickie and Dana from hounding him.

She couldn't forget what had been said about Jane Parker, Jane Burke now, and she was more worried than ever. She knew how entangled he'd been with Jane, all right, because she'd considered her a rival until the day Jane married Todd Burke. Coltrain's manner even when he spoke to the woman was tender, solicitous, almost reverent.

He'd proposed. But even though he knew Lou loved him, he'd never mentioned feeling anything similar for her. He was playing make-believe. But she wondered what would happen if Jane Burke suddenly became a free woman. It would be a nightmare to live with a man who was ever yearning for someone else, someone he'd loved most of his life. Jane was a habit he apparently couldn't break. She was married. But could that fact stop him from loving her?

"You're very quiet," he remarked.

"I was thinking about Mr. Bailey," she hedged. "He really needs to see a specialist about that asthma. What do you think of referring him to Dr. Jones up in Houston?"

He nodded, diverted. "A sound idea. I'll give you the number."

They worked in harmony until the lunch hour. Then, despite her arguments, they drove to a jewelry shop in downtown Jacobsville. As bad luck would have it, Jane Burke was in there, alone, making a purchase.

She was so beautiful, Lou thought miserably. Blond, blue-eyed, with a slender figure that any man would covet.

"Why hello!" Jane said enthusiastically, and hugged Copper as if he was family.

He held her close and kissed her cheek, his smile tender, his face animated. "You look terrific," he said huskily. "How's the back? Still doing those exercises?"

"Oh, yes," she agreed. She held him by the arms and searched his eyes. "You look terrific yourself." She seemed only then to notice that he wasn't alone. She glanced at Lou. "Dr. Blakely, isn't it?" she asked politely, and altered the smile a little. "Nice to see you again."

"What are you doing here?" Coltrain asked her.

"Buying a present for my stepdaughter for Christmas. I thought she might like a nice strand of pearls. Aren't these lovely?" she asked when the clerk had taken them out of the case to show them. "I'll take them," she added, handing him her credit card.

"Is she staying with you and Todd all the time now?"

She nodded. "Her mother and stepfather and the baby are off to Africa to research his next book," she said with a grin. "We're delighted to have her all to ourselves."

"How's Todd?"

Lou heard the strained note in his voice with miserable certainty that Dana had been telling the truth.

"He's as impossible as ever." Jane chuckled. "But we scratch along, me with my horses and my clothing line and he with his computer business. He's away so much these days that I feel deserted." She lifted her eyes to his and grinned. "I don't guess you'd like to come to supper tonight?"

"Sure I would," he said without thinking. Then he

made a sound. "I can't. There's a hospital board meeting."

"Oh, well," she muttered. "Another time, then." She glanced at Lou hesitantly. "Are you two out Christmas shopping—together?" she added as if she didn't think that was the case.

Coltrain stuck his hands deep into his pockets. "We're shopping for an engagement ring," he said tersely.

Her eyes widened. "For whom?"

Lou wanted to sink through the floor. She flushed to the roots of her hair and clung to her shoulder bag as if it were a life jacket.

"For Lou," Coltrain said. "We're engaged."

He spoke reluctantly, which only made Lou feel worse.

Jane's shocked expression unfroze Lou's tongue. "It's just for appearances," she said, forcing a smile. "Dana and Nickie have been hounding him."

"Oh, I see!" Jane's face relaxed, but then she frowned. "Isn't that a little dishonest?"

"It was the only way, and it's just until my contract is up, the first of the year," Lou forced herself to say. "I'll be leaving then."

Coltrain glared at her. He wasn't certain what he'd expected, but she made the proposal sound like a hoax. He hadn't asked her to marry him to ward off the other women; he'd truly wanted her to be his wife. Had she misunderstood totally?

Jane was as startled as Coltrain was. She knew that Copper wasn't the sort of man to give an engagement ring lightly, although Lou seemed to think he was. Since Dana's horrible betrayal, Copper had been impervious to women. But even Jane had heard about the hospital Christmas party and the infamous kiss. She'd hoped that Copper had finally found someone to love, although it was surprising that it would be the partner with whom he fought with so enthusiastically. Now, looking at them together, she was confused. Lou looked as if she were being tortured. Copper was taciturn and frozen. And they said it was a sham. Lou didn't love him. She couldn't, and be so lighthearted about it. Copper looked worn.

Jane glared at Lou and put a gentle hand on Coltrain's arm. "This is a stupid idea, Copper. You'll be the butt of every joke in town when Lou leaves, don't you realize it? It could even damage your reputation, hurt your practice," she told Copper intently.

His jaw tautened. "I appreciate your concern," he said gently, even as it surprised him that Jane should turn on Lou, who was more an innocent bystander than Coltrain's worst enemy.

That got through to Lou, too. She moved restlessly, averting her gaze from the diamond rings in the display case. "She's right. It *is* stupid. I can't do this," she said suddenly, her eyes full of torment. "Please, excuse me, I have to go!"

She made it out the door before the tears were visible, cutting down an alley and ducking into a department store. She went straight to the women's rest room and burst into tears, shocking a store clerk into leaving.

In the jewelry store, Coltrain stood like a statue, unspeakably shocked at Lou's rash departure and furious at having her back out just when he'd got it all arranged.

"For God's sake, did you have to do that?" Coltrain asked harshly. He rammed his hands into his pockets. "It's taken me days just to get her to agree on any pretext…!"

Jane realized, too late, what she'd done. She winced. "I didn't know," she said miserably. "It's my fault that she's bolted," Jane said quickly. "Copper, I'm sorry!"

"Not your fault," he said stiffly. "I used Dana and Nickie to accomplish this engagement, but she was reluctant from the beginning." He sighed heavily. "I guess she'll go, now, in spite of everything."

"I don't understand what's going on."

He moved a shoulder impatiently. "She's in love with me," he said roughly, and rammed his hands deeper into his pockets.

"Oh, dear." Jane didn't know what to say. She'd lashed out at the poor woman, and probably given Lou a false picture of her relationship with Copper to boot. They were good friends, almost like brother and sister, but there had been rumors around Jacobsville for years that they were secret lovers. Until she married Todd, that was. Now, she wondered how much Lou had heard and if she'd believed it. And Jane had brazenly invited him to supper, ignoring Lou altogether.

She grimaced. "I've done it now, haven't I? I would have included her in my invitation if I'd had any idea. I thought she was just tagging along with you on her lunch hour!"

"I'd better go after her," he said reluctantly.

"It might be best if you didn't," she replied. "She's hurt. She'll want to be alone for a while, I should think."

"I can't strand her in town." He felt worse than he could ever remember feeling. "Maybe you're both right, and this whole thing was a stupid idea."

"If you don't love her, it certainly was," she snapped at him. "What are you up to? Is it really just to protect you from a couple of lovesick women? I'm shocked. A few years ago, you'd have cussed them both to a fare-thee-well and been done with it."

He didn't reply. His face closed up and his blue eyes glittered at her. "My reasons are none of your business," he said, shutting her out.

Obviously Lou had to mean something to him. Jane felt even worse. She made a face. "We were very close once. I thought you could talk to me about anything."

"Anything except Lou," he said shortly.

"Oh." Her eyes were first stunned and then amused.

"You can stop speculating, too," he added irritably, turning away.

"She sounds determined to leave."

"We'll see about that."

Despite Jane's suggestion, he went off toward the department store where Lou had vanished and strode back to the women's rest room. He knew instinctively that she was there. He caught the eye of a female clerk.

"Could you ask Dr. Blakely to come out of there, please?"

"Dr. Blakely?"

"She's so high—" he indicated her height with his

hand up to his nose "—blond hair, dark eyes, wearing a beige suit."

"Oh, her! She's a doctor? Really? My goodness, I thought doctors never showed their emotions. She was crying as if her heart would break. Sure, I'll get her for you."

He felt like a dog. He'd made her cry. The thought of Lou, so brave and private a person, with tears in her eyes made him hurt inside. And it had been so unnecessary. If Jane had only kept her pretty mouth shut! She was like family, and she overstepped the bounds sometimes with her comments about how Coltrain should live his life. He'd been more than fond of her once, and he still had a soft spot for her, but it was Lou who was disrupting his whole life.

He leaned against the wall, his legs and arms crossed, and waited. The female clerk reappeared, smiled reassuringly, and went to wait on a customer.

A minute later, a subdued and dignified Lou came out of the small room, her chin up. Her eyes were slightly red, but she didn't look as if she needed anyone's pity.

"I'm ready to go if you are," she said politely.

He searched her face and decided that this wasn't the time for a row. They still had to get lunch and get back to the office.

He turned, leaving her to follow. "I'll stop by one of the hamburger joints and we can get a burger and fries."

"I'll eat mine at the office, if you don't mind," she said wearily. "I'm not in the mood for a crowd."

Neither was he. He didn't argue. He opened the car

door and let her in, then he went by the drive-in window of the beef place and they carried lunch back.

Lou went directly into her office and closed the door. She hardly tasted what she was eating. Her heart felt as if it had been burned alive. She knew what Dana meant now. Jane Parker was as much a part of Coltrain's life as his cattle, his practice. No woman, no matter how much she loved him, could ever compete with his love for the former rodeo star.

She'd been living in a fool's paradise, but fortunately there was no harm done. They could say that the so-called "engagement" had been a big joke. Surely Coltrain could get Nickie and Dana out of his hair by simply telling them the truth, that he wasn't interested. God knew, once he got started, he wasn't shy about expressing his feelings any other time, regardless of who was listening. Which brought to mind the question of why he'd asked her to marry him. He wasn't in love with her. He wanted her. Had that been the reason? Was he getting even with Jane because she'd married and deserted him? She worried the question until she finished eating. Then her patients kept her occupied for the rest of the day, so that she had no time to think.

Jane had wondered if she could help undo the damage she'd already done to Copper's life, and at last she came up with a solution. She decided to give a farewell party for Lou. She called Coltrain a few days later to tell him the news.

"Christmas is next week," he said shortly. "And I

doubt if she'd come. She only speaks to me when she has to. I can't get near her anymore."

That depressed Jane even more. "Suppose I phone her?" she asked.

"Oh, I know she won't talk to you." He laughed without humor. "We're both in her bad books."

Jane sighed. "Then who can we have talk to her?"

"Try Drew Morris," he said bitterly. "She likes him."

That note in his voice was disturbing. Surely he knew that Drew was still mourning his late wife. If he and Lou were friends, it was nothing more than that, despite any social outings together.

"You think she'd listen to Drew?" she asked.

"Why not?"

"I'll try, then."

"Don't send out any invitations until she gives you an answer," he added. "She's been hurt enough, one way or the other."

"Yes, I know," Jane said gently. "I had no idea, Copper. I really meant well."

"I know that. She doesn't."

"I guess she's heard all the old gossip, too."

He hadn't considered that. "What old gossip?"

"About us," she persisted. "That we had something going until I married Todd."

He smoothed his fingers absently over the receiver. "She might have, at that," he said slowly. "But she must know that—" He stopped dead. She'd have heard plenty from Dana, who had always considered Jane, not her affair with Fielding Blakely, the real reason for their broken engagement. Others in the hospital knew those old rumors, too, and Jane had given Lou the wrong impression of their relationship in the jewelry store.

"I'm right, aren't I?" Jane asked.

"You might be."

"What are you going to do?"

"What can I do?" he asked shortly. "She doesn't really want to marry anyone."

"You said she loves you," she reminded him.

"Yes, and she does. It's the only thing I'm sure of. But she doesn't want to marry me. She's so afraid that she'll become like her mother, blindly accepting faults and abuse without question, all in the name of love."

"Poor girl," she said genuinely. "What a life she must have had."

"I expect it was worse than we'll ever know," he agreed. "Well, call Drew and see if he can get through to her."

"If he can, will you come, too?"

"It would look pretty bad if I didn't, wouldn't it?" he asked dryly. "They'd say we were so antagonistic toward each other that we couldn't even get along for a farewell party. And coming on the heels of our 'engagement,' they'd really have food for thought."

"I'd be painted as the scarlet woman who broke it up, wouldn't I?" Jane groaned. "Todd would love that! He's still not used to small-town life."

"Maybe Drew can reach her. If he can't, you'll have to cancel it. We can't embarrass her."

"I wouldn't dream of it."

"I know that. Jane, thanks."

"For what?" she asked. "I'm the idiot who got you

into this mess in the first place. The least I owe is to try to make amends for what I said to her. I'll let you know what happens."

"Do that."

He went back to work, uncomfortably aware of Lou's calm demeanor. She didn't even look ruffled after all the turmoil. Of course, he remembered that she'd been crying like a lost child in the department store after Jane's faux pas. But that could have been so much more than a broken heart.

She hadn't denied loving him, but could love survive a year of indifference alternating with vicious antagonism, such as he'd given her? Perhaps loving him was a sort of habit that she'd finally been cured of. After all, he'd given her no reason to love him, even to like him. He'd missed most of his chances there. But if Drew could convince her to come to a farewell party, on neutral ground, Coltrain had one last chance to change her mind about him. That was his one hope; the only one he had.

Chapter Nine

Drew invited Lou to lunch the next day. It was Friday, the week before the office closed for Christmas holidays. Christmas Eve would be on a week from Saturday night, and Jane had changed her mind about dates. She wanted to give the farewell party the following Friday, the day before New Year's Eve. That would, if Lou didn't reconsider her decision, be Lou's last day as Coltrain's partner.

"I'm surprised," Lou told him as they ate quiche at a local restaurant. "You haven't invited me to lunch in a long time. What's on your mind?"

"It could be just on food."

She laughed. "Pull the other one."

"Okay. I'm a delegation of one."

She held her fork poised over the last morsel of quiche on her plate. "From whom?"

"Jane Burke."

She put the fork down, remembering. Her expression hardened. "I have nothing to say to her."

"She knows that. It's why she asked me to talk to you. She got the wrong end of the stick and she's sorry. I'm to make her apologies to you," he added. "But she also wants to do something to make up for what she said to you. She wants to give you a farewell party on the day before New Year's Eve."

She glared at Drew. "I don't want anything to do with any parties given by that woman. I won't go!"

His eyebrows lifted. "Well! You are miffed, aren't you?"

"Accusing me of trying to ruin Jebediah's reputation and destroy his privacy…how dare she! I'm not the one who's being gossiped about in connection with him! And she's married!"

He smiled wickedly. "Lou, you're as red as a beet."

"I'm mad," she said shortly. "That…woman! How dare she!"

"She and Copper are friends. Period. That's all they've ever been. Are you listening?"

"Sure, I'm listening. Now," she added, leaning forward, "tell me he wasn't ever in love with her. Tell me he isn't still in love with her."

He wanted to, but he had no idea of Coltrain's feelings for Jane. He knew that Coltrain had taken her marriage hard, and that he seemed sometimes to talk about her to the exclusion of everyone else. But things had changed in the past few weeks, since the hospital Christmas dance the first week of December.

"You see?" she muttered. "You can't deny it. He may have proposed to me, but it was…"

"Proposed?"

"Didn't you know?" She lifted her coffee cup to her lips and took a sip. "He wanted me to pretend to be engaged to him, just to get Nickie and Dana off his back.

Then he decided that we might as well get married for real. He caught me at a weak moment," she added, without details, "and we went to buy an engagement ring. But Jane was there. She was rude to me," she said miserably, "and Jebediah didn't say a word to stop her. In fact, he acted as if I wasn't even there."

"And that was what hurt most, wasn't it?" he queried gently.

"I guess it was. I have no illusions about him, you know," she added with a rueful smile. "He likes kissing me, but he's not in love with me."

"Does he know how you feel?"

She nodded. "I don't hide things well. It would be hard to miss."

He caught her hand and held it gently. "Lou, isn't he worth taking a chance on?" he asked. "You could let Jane throw this party for you, because she badly wants to make amends. Then you could talk to Copper and get him to tell you exactly why he wants to marry you. You might be surprised."

"No, I wouldn't. I know why he wants to marry me," she replied. "But I don't want to get married. I'm crazy about him, that's the truth, but I've seen marriage. I don't want it."

"You haven't seen a good marriage," he emphasized. "Lou, I had one. I had twelve years of almost ethereal happiness. Marriage is what you make of it."

"My mother excused every brutal thing my father did," she said shortly.

"That sort of love isn't love," he said quietly. "It's a form of domination. Don't you know the difference? If she'd loved your father, she'd have stood up to him and tried to help him stop drinking, stop using drugs."

She felt as if her eyes had suddenly been opened. She'd never seen her parents' relationship like that. "But he was terrible to her…"

"Codependence," he said to her. "You must have studied basic psychology in college. Don't you remember any of it?"

"Yes, but they were my parents!"

"Your parents, anybody, can be part of a dysfunctional family." He smiled at her surprise. "Didn't you know? You grew up in a dysfunctional family, not a normal one. That's why you have such a hard time accepting the idea of marriage." He smoothed her hand with his fingers and smiled. "Lou, I had a normal upbringing. I had a mother and father who doted on me, who supported me and encouraged me. I was loved. When I married, it was a good, solid, happy marriage. They are possible, if you love someone and have things in common, and are willing to compromise."

She studied the wedding ring on Drew's left hand. He still wore it even after being widowed.

"It's possible to be happily married?" she asked, entertaining that possibility for the first time.

"Of course."

"Coltrain doesn't love me," she said.

"Make him."

She laughed. "That's a joke. He hated me from the beginning. I never knew it was because of my father, until I overheard him talking to you. I was surprised later when he was so cool to Dana, because he'd been bitter about her betrayal. But when I found out how close he was to Jane Burke, I guess I gave up entirely. You can't fight a ghost, Drew." She looked up. "And you know it, because no woman will ever be able to come between you and your memories. How would you feel if you found out some woman was crazily in love with you right now?"

He was stunned by the question. "Well, I don't know. I guess I'd feel sorry for her," he admitted.

"Which is probably how Coltrain feels about me, and might even explain why he offered to be engaged to me," she added. "It makes sense, doesn't it?"

"Lou, you don't propose to people out of pity."

"Coltrain might. Or out of revenge, to get back at Jane for marrying someone else. Or to get even with Dana."

"Coltrain isn't that scatty."

"Men are unpredictable when they're in love, aren't they?" she mused. "I wish he loved me, Drew. I'd marry him, with all my doubts and misgivings, in a minute if I thought there was half a chance that he did. But he doesn't. I'd know if he did feel that way. Somehow, I'd know."

He dropped his gaze to their clasped hands. "I'm sorry."

"Me, too. I've been invited to join a practice in Houston. I'm going Monday to speak with them, but they've tentatively accepted me." She lifted her sad face. "I understand that Coltrain is meeting some prospects too. So I suppose he's finally taken me at my word that I want to leave."

"Don't you know?"

She shrugged. "We don't speak."

"I see." So it was that bad, he thought. Coltrain and Lou had both withdrawn, afraid to take that final step to commitment. She had good reasons, but what were Copper's? he wondered. Did he really feel pity for Lou and now he was sorry he'd proposed? Or was Lou right, and he was still carrying a torch for Jane?

"Jane is a nice woman," he said. "You don't know her, but she isn't the kind of person who enjoys hurting other people. She feels very unhappy about what she said. She wants to make it up to you. Let her. It will be a nice gesture on your part and on hers."

"Dr. Coltrain will come," she muttered.

"He'd better," he said, "or the gossips will say he's glad to be rid of you."

She shook her head. "You can't win for losing."

"That's what I've been trying to tell you. Let Jane give the party. Lou, you'd like her if you got to know her. She's had a hard time of it since the wreck that took her father's life. Just being able to walk again at all is a major milestone for her."

"I remember," she said. And she did, because Coltrain had been out at the ranch every waking minute looking after the woman.

"Will you do it?"

She took a long breath and let it out. "All right."

"Great! I'll call Jane the minute I get home and tell her. You won't regret it. Lou, I wish you'd hold off about that spot in Houston."

She shook her head. "No, I won't do that. I have to

get away. A fresh start is what I need most. I'm sure I won't be missed. After all, Dr. Coltrain didn't want me in the first place."

He grimaced, because they both knew her present circumstances were Drew's fault. Saying again that he meant well wouldn't do a bit of good.

"Thanks for lunch," she said, remembering her manners.

"That was my pleasure. You know I'll be going to Maryland to have Christmas with my in-laws, as usual. So Merry Christmas, if I don't see you before I leave."

"You, too, Drew," she said with genuine affection.

It wasn't until the next Thursday afternoon that the office closed early for Christmas holidays—if Friday and Monday, added to the weekend, qualified as holidays—that Coltrain came into Lou's office. Lou had been to Houston and formally applied for a position in the family practitioner group. She'd also been accepted, but she hadn't been able to tell Coltrain until today, because he'd been so tied up with preholiday surgeries and emergencies.

He looked worn-out, she thought. There were new lines in his lean face, and his eyes were bloodshot from lack of sleep. He looked every year of his age.

"You couldn't just tell me, you had to put it in writing?" he asked, holding up the letter she'd written him.

"It's legal this way," she said politely. "I'm very grateful for the start you gave me."

He didn't say anything. He looked at the letter from the Houston medical group. It was written on decal-edge bond, very expensive, and the lettering on the letterhead was embossed.

"I know this group," he said. "They're high-powered city physicians, and they practice supermarket medicine. Do you realize what that means? You'll be expected to spend five minutes or less with every patient. A buzzer will sound to alert you when that time is up. As the most junior partner, you'll get all the dirty jobs, all the odd jobs, and you'll be expected to stay on call on weekends and holidays for the first year. Or until they can get another partner, more junior than you are."

"I know. They told me that." They had. It had depressed her no end.

He folded his arms across his chest and leaned back against the wall, his stethoscope draped around his neck. "We haven't talked."

"There's nothing to say," she replied, and she smiled kindly. "I notice that Nickie and Dana have become very businesslike, even to me. I'd say you were over the hump."

"I asked you to marry me," he said. "I was under the impression that you'd agreed and that was why we were picking out a ring."

The memory of that afternoon hurt. She lowered her eyes to the clipboard she held against her breasts. "You said it was to get Nickie and Dana off your back."

"You didn't want to get married at all," he reminded her.

"I still don't."

He smiled coldly. "And you're not in love with me?"

She met his gaze levelly. This was no time to back down. "I was infatuated with you," she said bluntly. "Perhaps it was because you were out of reach."

"You wanted me. Explain that."

"I'm human," she told him, blushing a little. "You wanted me, too, so don't look so superior."

"I hear you're coming to Jane's party."

"Drew talked me into it." She smoothed her fingers over the cold clipboard. "You and Jane can't help it," she said. "I understand."

"Damn it! You sound just like her husband!"

She was shocked at the violent whip of his deep voice. He was furious, and it showed.

"Everyone knows you were in love with her," she faltered.

"Yes, I was," he admitted angrily, and for the first time. "But she's married now, Lou."

"I know. I'm sorry," she said gently. "I really am. It must be terrible for you...."

He threw up his hands. "My God!"

"It's not as if you could help it, either of you," she continued sadly.

He just shook his head. "I can't get through to you, can I?" he asked with a bite in his deep voice. "You won't listen."

"There's really nothing to say," she told him. "I hope you've found someone to replace me when I go."

"Yes, I have. He's a recent graduate of Johns Hopkins. He wanted to do some rural practice before he made up his mind where he wanted to settle." He gazed at her wan face. "He starts January 2."

She nodded. "That's when I start, in Houston." She tugged the clipboard closer.

"We could spend Christmas together," he suggested.

She shook her head. She didn't speak. She knew words would choke her.

His shoulders rose and fell. "As you wish," he said quietly. "Have a good Christmas, then."

"Thanks. You, too."

She knew that she sounded choked. She couldn't help herself. She'd burned her bridges. She hadn't meant to. Perhaps she had a death wish. She'd read and studied about people who were basically self-destructive, who destroyed relationships before they could begin, who found ways to sabotage their own success and turn it to failure. Perhaps she'd become such a person, due to her upbringing. Either way, it didn't matter now. She'd given up Coltrain and was leaving Jacobsville. Now all she had to do was survive Jane's little going-away party and get out of town.

Coltrain paused in the doorway, turning his head back toward her. His eyes were narrow, curious, assessing. She didn't look as if the decision she'd made had lifted her spirits any. And the expression on her face wasn't one of triumph or pleasure.

"If Jane hadn't turned up in the jewelry store, would you have gone through with it?" he asked abruptly.

Her hands tightened on the clipboard. "I'll never know."

He leaned against the doorjamb. "You don't want to hear this, but I'm going to say it. Jane and I were briefly more than friends. It was mostly on my side. She loves her husband and wants nothing to do with anyone else. Whatever I felt for her is in the past now."

"I'm glad, for your sake," she said politely.

"Not for yours?" he asked.

She bit her lower lip, worriedly.

He let his blue gaze fall to her mouth. It lingered there so long that her heart began to race, and she couldn't quite breathe properly. His gaze lifted then, to catch hers, and she couldn't break it. Her toes curled inside her sensible shoes, her heart ran wild. She had to fight the urge to go to him, to press close to his lean, fit body and beg him to kiss her blind.

"You think you're over me?" he drawled softly, so that his voice didn't carry. "In a pig's eye, Doctor!"

He pushed away from the door and went on his way, whistling to himself as he went down the corridor to his next patient.

Lou, having given herself away, muttered under her breath and went to read the file on her next patient. But she waited until her hands stopped shaking before she opened the examining room door and went in.

They closed up the office. Coltrain had been called away at the last minute to an emergency at the hospital, which made things easier for Lou. She'd be bound to run into him while she was making her rounds, but that was an occupational hazard, and there would be plenty of other people around. She wouldn't have to worry about being alone with him. Or so she thought.

When she finished her rounds late in the afternoon, she stopped by the nurses' station to make sure they'd been able to contact a new patient's husband, who had been out of town when she was admitted.

"Yes, we found him," the senior nurse said with a smile. "In fact, he's on his way over here right now."

"Thanks," she said.

"No need. It goes with the job," she was assured.

She started back down the hall to find Coltrain coming from the emergency room. He looked like a thundercloud, all bristling bad temper. His red hair flamed under the corridor lights, and his blue eyes were sparking.

He caught Lou's arm, turned and drew her along with him without saying a word. People along the corridor noticed and grinned amusedly.

"What in the world are you doing?" she asked breathlessly.

"I want you to tell a—" he bit off the word he wanted to say "—*gentleman* in the emergency room that I was in the office all morning."

She gaped at him, but he didn't stop or even slow down. He dragged her into a cubicle where a big, angry-looking blond man was sitting on the couch having his hand bandaged.

Coltrain let Lou go and nodded curtly toward the other man. "Well, tell him!" He shot the words at Lou.

She gave him a stunned glance, but after a minute, she turned back to the tall man and said, "Dr. Coltrain was in the office all morning. He couldn't have escaped if he'd wanted to, because we had twice our usual number of patients, anticipating that we'd be out of the office over the holidays."

The blond man relaxed a little, but he was still glaring at Coltrain when there was a small commotion in the corridor and Jane Burke came in the door, harassed and frightened.

"Todd! Cherry said that you'd had an accident and she had to call an ambulance…!" She grabbed the blond man's hand and fought tears. "I thought you were killed!"

"Not hardly," he murmured. He drew her head to his shoulder and held her gently. "Silly woman." He chuckled. "I'm all right. I slammed the car door on my hand. It isn't even broken, just cut and bruised."

Jane looked at Coltrain. "Is that true?"

He nodded, still irritated at Burke.

Jane looked from him to Lou and back to her husband. "Now what's wrong?" she asked heavily.

Todd just glowered. He didn't say anything.

"You and I had been meeting secretly this morning at your house, while he and Cherry were away," Coltrain informed her. "Because the mailman saw a gray Jaguar sitting in your driveway."

"Yes, he did," Jane said shortly. "It belongs to the new divisional manager of the company that makes my signature line of leisure wear. *She* has a gray Jaguar exactly like Copper's."

Burke's hard cheekbones flushed a little.

"That's why you slammed the door on your hand, right?" she muttered. "Because the mailman is our wrangler's sister and he couldn't wait to tell you what your wife was doing behind your back! He'll be lucky if I don't have him for lunch!"

The flush got worse. "Well, I didn't know!" Todd snapped.

Coltrain slammed his clipboard down hard on the examination couch at Burke's hip. "That does it, by God," he began hotly.

He looked threatening and Burke stood up, equally angry.

"Now, Copper," Jane interrupted. "This isn't the place."

Burke didn't agree, but he'd already made a fool of himself once. He wasn't going to try for twice. He glanced at Lou, who looked as miserable as he felt. "They broke up your engagement, I understand," he added. "Pity they didn't just marry each other to begin with!"

Lou studied his glittery eyes for a moment, oblivious to the other two occupants of the cubicle. It was amazing how quickly things fell into place in her mind, and at once. She leaned against the examination couch. "Dr. Coltrain is the most decent man I know," she told Todd Burke. "He isn't the sort to do things in an underhanded way, and he doesn't sneak around. If you trusted your wife, Mr. Burke, you wouldn't listen to old gossip or invented tales. Small towns are hotbeds of rumor, that's normal. But only an idiot believes everything he hears."

Coltrain's eyebrows had arched at the unexpected defense.

"Thanks, Lou," Jane said quietly. "That's more than I deserve from you, but thank you." She turned back to her husband. "She's absolutely right," Jane told her husband. She was mad, too, and it showed. "I married you because I loved you. I still love you, God knows why! You won't even listen when I tell you the truth. You'd rather cling to old gossip about Copper and me."

Lou blushed scarlet, because she could have been accused of the same thing.

She wouldn't look at Coltrain at all.

"Well, here's something to take your mind off your foul suspicions," Jane continued furiously. "I was going to wait to tell you, but you can hear it now. I'm pregnant! And, no, it isn't Copper's!"

Burke gasped. "Jane!" He exploded, his injured hand forgotten as he moved forward to pull her hungrily into his arms. "Jane, is it true?"

"Yes, it's true," she muttered. "Oh, you idiot! You idiot…!"

He was kissing her, so she had to stop talking. Lou, a little embarrassed, edged out of the cubicle and moved away, only to find Coltrain right beside her as she left the emergency room.

"Maybe that will satisfy him," he said impatiently. "Thank you for the fierce defense," he added. "Hell of a pity that you didn't believe a word you were saying!"

She stuck her hands into her slacks pockets. "I believe she loves her husband," she said quietly. "And I believe that there's nothing going on between the two of you."

"Thanks for nothing."

"Your private life is your own business, Dr. Coltrain, none of mine," she said carelessly. "I'm already a memory."

"By your own damn choice."

The sarcasm cut deep. They walked through the parking lot to the area reserved for physicians and surgeons, and she stopped beside her little Ford.

"Drew loved his wife very much," she said. "He never got over losing her. He still spends holidays with his in-laws because he feels close to her that way, even though she's dead. I asked him how he'd feel if he knew that a woman was in love with him. Know what he said? He said that he'd pity her."

"Do you have a point?" he asked.

"Yes." She turned and looked up at him. "You haven't really gotten over Jane Burke yet. You have nothing to offer anyone else until you do. That's why I wouldn't marry you."

His brows drew together while he searched her face. He didn't say a word. He couldn't.

"She's part of your life," she continued. "A big part of it. You can't let go of the past, even if she can. I understand. Maybe someday you'll come to terms with it. Until you do, it's no good trying to be serious about anyone else."

He jiggled the change in his pockets absently. His broad shoulders rose and fell. "She was just starting into rodeo when I came back here as an intern in the hospital. She fell and they brought her to me. We had an instant rapport. I started going to watch her ride, she went out with me when I was free. She was special. Her father and I became friends as well, and when I bought my ranch, he helped me learn the ropes and start my herd. Jane and I have known each other a long, long time."

"I know that." She studied a button on his dark jacket. "She's very pretty, and Drew says she has a kind nature."

"Yes."

Her shoulders rose and fell. "I have to go."

He put out a lean hand and caught her shoulder, preventing her from turning away. "I never told her about my father."

She was surprised. She didn't think he had any secrets from Jane. She lifted her eyes and found him staring at her intently, as if he were trying to work out a puzzle.

"Curious, isn't it?" he mused aloud. "There's another curious thing, but I'm not ready to share that just yet."

He moved closer and she wanted to move away, to stop him... No, she didn't. His head bent and his mouth closed on hers, brushing, lightly probing. She yielded without a protest, her arms sliding naturally around his waist, her mouth opening to the insistence of his lips. He kissed her, leaning his body heavily on hers, so that she could feel the metal of the car at her back and his instant, explosive response to her soft warmth.

She made a sound, and he smiled against her lips.

"What?" He bit off the words against her lips.

"It's...very...public," she breathed.

He lifted his head and looked around. The parking lot was dotted with curious onlookers. So was the emergency room ramp.

"Hell," he said irritably, drawing away from her.

"Come home with me," he suggested, still breathing roughly.

She shook her head before her willpower gave out. "I can't."

"Coward," he drawled.

She flushed. "All right, I want to," she said fiercely. "But I won't, so there. Damn you! It isn't fair to play on people's weaknesses!"

"Sure it is," he said, correcting her. He grinned at her maddeningly. "Come on, be daring. Take a chance! Risk everything on a draw of the cards. You live like a scientist, every move debated, planned. For once in your life, be reckless!"

"I'm not the reckless sort," she said as she fought to get her breath back. "And you shouldn't be, either." She glanced ruefully toward the emergency room exit, where a tall blond man and a pretty blond woman were standing, watching. "Was it for her benefit?" she added, nodding toward them.

He glanced over her shoulder. "I didn't know they were there," he said genuinely.

She laughed. "Sure." She pulled away from him, unlocked her car, got in and drove off. Her legs were wobbly, but they'd stop shaking eventually. Maybe the rest of her would, too. Coltrain was driving her crazy. She was very glad that she'd be leaving town soon.

Chapter Ten

It didn't help that the telephone rang a few minutes after Lou got home.

"Still shaky, are we?" Coltrain drawled.

She fumbled to keep from dropping the receiver. "What do you want?" she faltered.

"An invitation to Christmas dinner, of course," he said. "I don't want to sit in front of the TV all day eating TV dinners."

She was still angry at him for making a public spectacle of them for the second time. The hospital would buzz with the latest bit of gossip for weeks. At least she wouldn't have long to put up with it.

"TV dinners are good for you," she said pointedly.

"Home cooking is better. I'll make the dressing and a fruit salad if you'll do turkey and rolls."

She hesitated. She wanted badly to spend that day with him, but in the long run, it would make things harder.

"Come on," he coaxed in a silky tone. "You know you want to. If you're leaving town after the first, it will be one of the last times we spend together. What have you got to lose?"

My *self-respect*, *my honor*, *my virtue*, *my pride*, she thought. But aloud, she said, "I suppose it wouldn't hurt."

He chuckled. "No, it wouldn't. I'll see you at eleven on Christmas morning."

He hung up before she could change her mind. "I don't want to," she told the telephone. "This is a terrible mistake, and I'm sure that I'll regret it for the rest of my life."

After a minute, she realized that she was talking to a piece of equipment. She shook her head sadly. Coltrain was driving her out of her mind.

She went to the store early on Christmas Eve and bought a turkey. The girl at the check-out stand was one of her patients. She grinned as she totaled the price of the turkey, the bottle of wine and the other groceries Lou had bought to cook Christmas dinner.

"Expecting company, Doctor?" she teased.

Lou flushed, aware that the woman behind her was one of Coltrain's patients. "No. No. I'm going to cook the turkey and freeze what I don't eat."

"Oh." The girl sounded disappointed.

"Going to drink all that wine alone, too?" the woman behind her asked wickedly. "And you a doctor!"

Lou handed over the amount the cashier asked for. "I'm not on duty on Christmas Day," she said irritably. "Besides, I cook with wine!"

"You won't cook with that," the cashier noted. She held up the bottle and pointed to the bottom of the label. It stated, quite clearly, Nonalcoholic Wine.

Lou had grabbed the bottle from the wrong aisle. But it worked to her advantage. She grinned at the woman behind her, who looked embarrassed.

The clerk packaged up her purchases and Lou pushed them out to her car. At least she'd gotten around that ticky little episode.

Back home, she put the turkey on to bake and made rolls from scratch. Nonalcoholic wine wasn't necessarily a bad thing, she told herself. She could serve it at dinner without having to worry about losing her wits with Coltrain.

The weather was sunny and nice, and the same was predicted for the following day. A white Christmas was out of the question, of course, but she wondered what it would be like to have snow on the ground.

She turned on the television that night, when the cooking was done and everything was put into the refrigerator for the next day. Curled up in her favorite armchair in old jeans, a sweatshirt and in her sock feet, she was relaxing after her housecleaning and cooking when she heard a car drive up.

It was eight o'clock and she wasn't on call. She frowned as she went to the front door. A gray Jaguar was sitting in the driveway and as she looked, a tall, redheaded man in jeans and a sweatshirt and boots got out of the car carrying a big box.

"Open the door," he called as he mounted the steps.

"What's that?" she asked curiously.

"Food and presents."

She was surprised. She hadn't expected him tonight

and she fumbled and faltered as she let him in and closed the door again.

He unloaded the box in the kitchen. "Salad." He indicated a covered plastic bowl. "Dressing." He indicated a foil-covered pan. "And a chocolate pound cake. No, I didn't make it," he added when she opened her mouth. "I bought it. I can't bake a cake. Is there room in the fridge for this?"

"You could have called to ask before you brought it," she reminded him.

He grinned. "If I'd phoned, you'd have listened to the answering machine and when you knew it was me, you'd have pretended not to be home."

She flushed. He was right. It was disconcerting to have someone so perceptive second-guessing her every move. "Yes, there's room."

She opened the refrigerator door and helped him fit his food in.

He went back to the big box and pulled out two packages. "One for me to give you—" he held up one "—and one for you to give me."

She glared at him. "I got you a present," she muttered.

His eyebrows shot up. "You did?"

Her lower lip pulled down. "Just because I didn't plan to spend Christmas with you didn't mean I was low enough not to get you something."

"You didn't give it to me at the office party," he recalled.

She flushed. "You didn't give me anything at the office party, either."

He smiled. "I was saving it for tomorrow."

"So was I," she returned.

"Can I put these under the tree?"

She shrugged. "Sure."

Curious, she followed him into the living room. The tree was live and huge; it covered the whole corner and reached almost to the nine-foot ceiling. It was full of lights and decorations and under it a big metal electric train sat on its wide tracks waiting for power to move it.

"I didn't notice that when I was here before," he said, delighted by the train. He stooped to look at it more closely. "This is an American Flyer by Lionel!" he exclaimed. "You've had this for a while, haven't you?"

"It's an antique," she recalled. "My mother got it for me." She smiled. "I love trains. I have two more sets and about a mile of track in a box in the closet, but it seemed sort of pointless to set all those trains up with just me to run them."

He looked up at her with sparkling eyes. "Which closet are they in?" he asked in a conspiratorial tone.

"The hall closet." Her eyes brightened. "You like trains?"

"Do I like trains? I have HO scale, N scale, G scale and three sets of new Lionel O scale trains at home."

She gasped. "Oh, my goodness!"

"That's what I say. Come on!"

He led her to the hall closet, opened it, found the boxes and started handing them out to her.

Like two children, they sat on the floor putting

tracks together with switches and accessories for the next two hours. Lou made coffee and they had it on the floor while they made connections and set up the low wooden scale buildings that Lou had bought to go with the sets.

When they finished, she turned on the power. The wooden buildings were lit. So were the engines and the cabooses and several passenger cars.

"I love to sit and watch them run in the dark," she said breathlessly as he turned on the switch box and the trains began to move. "It's like watching over a small village with the people all snug in their houses."

"I know what you mean." He sprawled, chest down, on the floor beside her to watch the trains chug and whistle and run around the various tracks. "God, this is great! I had no idea you liked trains!"

"Same here," she said, chuckling. "I always felt guilty about having them, in a way. Somewhere out there, there must be dozens of little kids who would do anything for just one train and a small track to run it on. And here I've got all this and I never play with it."

"I know how it is. I don't even have a niece or nephew to share mine with."

"When did you get your first train?"

"When I was eight. My granddad bought it for me so he could play with it," he added with a grin. "He couldn't afford a big set, of course, but I didn't care. I never had so much fun." His face hardened at the memories. "When Dad took me to Houston, I missed the train almost as much as I missed my granddad and grandmother. It was a long time before I got back there." He shrugged. "The train still worked by then, though, and it was more fun when the threat of my father was gone."

She rolled onto her side, peering at him in the dim light from the tree and the small village. "You said that you never told Jane about your father."

"I didn't," he replied. "It was something I was deeply ashamed of for a long time."

"Children do what they're told, whether it's right or wrong," she reminded him. "You can't be held responsible for everything."

"I knew it was wrong," he agreed. "But my father was a brutal man, and when I was a young boy, I was afraid of him." His head turned. He smiled at her. "You'd understand that."

"Yes."

He rested his chin on his hands and watched the trains wistfully. "I took my medicine—juvenile hall and years of probation. But people helped me to change. I wanted to pass that on, to give back some of the care that had been given to me. That's why I went into medicine. I saw it as an opportunity to help people."

"And you have," she said. Her eyes traced the length of his fit, hard-muscled body lovingly. He was so different away from the office. She'd never known him like this, and so soon, it would all be over. She'd go away. She wouldn't see him again. Her sad eyes went back to the trains. The sound of them was like a lullaby, comforting, delightful to the ears.

"We need railroad caps and those wooden whistles that sound like old steam engines," he remarked.

She smiled. "And railroad gloves and crossing guards and flashing guard lights."

"If there was a hobby shop nearby, we could go and get them. But everything would be closed up on Christmas Eve, anyway."

"I guess so."

He pursed his lips, without looking at her. "If you stayed, after the New Year, we could pool our layouts and have one big one. We could custom-design our own buildings and bridges, and we could go in together and buy one of those big transformer outfits that runs dozens of accessories."

She was thinking more of spending that kind of time with Coltrain than running model engines, but it sounded delightful all the same. She sighed wistfully. "I would have enjoyed that," she murmured. "But I've signed a new contract. I have to go."

"Contracts can be broken," he said. "There's always an escape clause if you look hard enough."

Her hips shifted on the rug they were lying on. "Too many people are gossiping about us already," she said. "Even at the grocery store, the clerk noticed that I bought a turkey and wine and the lady behind me said I couldn't possibly be going to drink it alone."

"You bought wine?" he mused.

"Nonalcoholic wine," she said, correcting him.

He chuckled. "On purpose?"

"Not really. I picked up the wrong bottle. But it was just as well. The lady behind me was making snide comments about it." She sighed. "It rubbed me the wrong way. She wouldn't have known that my father was an alcoholic."

"How did he manage to keep his job?"

"He had willing young assistants who covered for him. And finally, the hospital board forced him into early retirement. He *had* been a brilliant surgeon," she reminded him. "It isn't easy to destroy a career like that."

"It would have been better than letting him risk other people's lives."

"But he didn't," she replied. "Someone was always there to bail him out."

"Lucky, wasn't he, not to have been hit with a multimillion-dollar malpractice suit."

He reached out and threw the automatic switches to change the trains to another set of tracks. "Nice," he commented.

"Yes, isn't it? I love trains. If I had more leisure time, I'd do this every day. I'm glad we're not on call this weekend. How did you manage it?"

"Threats and bribery," he drawled. "We both worked last Christmas holidays, remember?"

"I guess we did. At each other's throats," she recalled demurely.

"Oh, that was necessary," he returned, rolling lazily onto his side and propping on an elbow. "If I hadn't snapped at you constantly, I'd have been laying you down on examination couches every other day."

"Wh…what?" she stammered.

He reached out and brushed back a long strand of blond hair from her face. "You backed away every time

I came close to you," he said quietly. "It was all that saved you. I've wanted you for a long, long time, Dr. Blakely, and I've fought it like a madman."

"You were in love with Jane Parker," she said.

"Not for a long time," he said. He traced her cheek lightly. "The way I felt about her was a habit. It was one I broke when she married Todd Burke. Although, like you, he seems to think Jane and I were an item even after they married. He's taken a lot of convincing. So have you."

She moved uncomfortably. "Everyone talked about you and Jane, not just me."

"I know. Small communities have their good points and their bad points." His finger had reached her mouth. He was exploring it blatantly.

"Could you...not do that, please?" she asked unsteadily.

"Why? You like it. So do I." He moved closer, easing one long, hard-muscled leg over hers to stay her as he shifted so that she lay on her back, looking up at him in the dim light.

"I can feel your heart beating right through your rib cage," he remarked with his mouth poised just above hers. "I can hear your breath fluttering." His hand slid blatantly right down over her breast, pausing there to tease its tip into a hard rise. "Feel that?" he murmured, bending. "Your body likes me."

She opened her mouth, but no words escaped the sudden hard, warm pressure of his lips. She stiffened, but only for a few seconds. It was Christmas Eve and she loved him. There was no defense; none at all.

He seemed to know that, because he wasn't insistent or demanding. He lay, just kissing her, his lips tender as they moved against hers, his hand still gently caressing her body.

"We both know," he whispered, "why your body makes every response it does to the stimuli of my touch. But what no one really understands is why we both enjoy it so much."

"Cause...and effect?" she suggested, gasping when his hand found its way under the sweatshirt and the lacy bra she was wearing to her soft flesh.

He shook his head. "I don't think so. Reach behind you and unfasten this," he added gently, tugging on the elastic band.

She did as he asked, feeling brazen.

"That's better." He traced over her slowly, his eyes on her face while he explored every inch of her above the waist. "Can you give this up?" he asked seriously.

"Wh...what?"

"Can you give it up?" he replied. "You aren't responsive to other men, or you wouldn't still be in your present pristine state. You allow me liberties that I'm certain you've never permitted any other man." He cupped her blatantly and caressed her. She arched, shivering. "You see?" he asked quietly. "You love my touch. I can give you something that you've apparently never experienced. Do you think you can find it with someone else, Lou?"

She felt his mouth cover hers. She didn't have enough breath to answer him, although the answer was certainly in the negative. She couldn't bear the thought of letting someone else be this intimate with her. She looped her arms around his neck and only sighed jerkily when he moved, easing his length against her, his legs between both of hers, so that when his hips pressed down again, she could feel every hardening line of his body.

"Jebediah," she moaned, and she wasn't certain if she was protesting or pleading.

His mouth found her closed eyelids and tasted the helpless tears of pleasure that rained from them. His hips shifted and she jerked at the surge of pleasure.

He felt it, too, like a throbbing ache. "We're good together," he whispered. "Even like this. Can you imagine how it would feel to lie naked under me like this?"

She cried out, burying her face in his neck.

His lips traced her eyelashes, his tongue tasted them. But his body lay very still over hers, not moving, not insisting. Her nails dug into his shoulders as she felt her control slipping away.

But he still had his own control. He soothed her, every soft kiss undemanding and tender. But he didn't move away.

"A year," he whispered. "And we knew nothing about each other, nothing at all." He nibbled her lips, smiling when they trembled. "Trains and old movies, opera and cooking and horseback riding. We have more in common than I ever dreamed."

She had to force her body to lie still. She wanted to wrap her legs tight around him and kiss him until she stopped aching.

He seemed to know it, because his hips moved in a

sensual caress that made her hands clench at his shoulders. "No fear of the unknown?" he whispered wickedly. "No virginal terror?"

"I'm a doctor." She choked out the words.

"So am I."

"I mean, I know…what to expect."

He chuckled. "No, you don't. You only know the mechanics of it. You don't know that you're going to crave almost more than I can give you, or that at the last minute you're going to sob like a hurt child."

She was too far gone to be embarrassed. "I don't have anything," she said miserably.

"Anything…?" He probed gently.

"To use."

"Oh. That." He chuckled and kissed her again, so tenderly that she felt cherished. "You won't need it tonight. I don't think babies should be born out of wedlock. Do you?"

She wasn't thinking. "Well, no. What does that have to do…with this?"

"Lou!"

She felt her cheeks burn. "Oh! You mean…!"

He laughed outrageously. "You've really gone off the deep end, haven't you?" he teased. "When people make love, the woman might get pregnant," he explained in a whisper. "Didn't you listen to the biology lectures?"

She hit him. "Of course I did! I wasn't thinking…Jeb!"

He was closer than he'd ever been and she was shivering, lost, helpless as she felt him in a burning, aching intimacy that only made it all worse.

He pressed her close and then rolled away, while he

could. "God, we're explosive!" he said huskily, lying very still on his belly. "You're going to have to marry me soon, Lou. Very soon."

She was sitting up, holding her knees to her chest, trying to breathe. It had never been that bad. She said so, without realizing that she'd spoken aloud.

"It will get worse, too," he said heavily. "I want you. I've never wanted you so much."

"But, Jane…"

He was laughing, very softly. He wasn't angry anymore. He rolled over and sat up beside her. He turned her face up to his. "I broke it off with Jane," he said gently. "Do you want to know why, now?"

"You…you did?"

He nodded.

"You never said that you ended it."

"There was no reason to. You wouldn't let me close enough to find out if we had anything going for us, and it didn't seem to matter what I said, you wanted to believe that I was out of my mind over Jane."

"Everyone said you were," she muttered.

He lifted an eyebrow. "I'm not everyone."

"I know." She reached out hesitantly and touched him. It was earthshaking, that simple act. She touched his hair and his face and then his lean, hard mouth. A funny smile drew up her lips.

"Don't stop there," he murmured, drawing her free hand down to his sweatshirt.

Her heart jumped. She looked at him uncertainly.

"I won't let you seduce me," he mused. "Does that make you feel more confident?"

"It was pretty bad a few minutes ago," she said seriously. "I don't want… Well, to hurt you."

"This won't," he said. "Trust me."

"I suppose I must," she admitted. "Or I'd have left months ago for another job."

"That makes sense."

He guided her hand under the thick, white fabric and drew it up until her fingers settled in the thick, curling hair that covered his chest. But it wasn't enough. She wanted to look…

There was just enough light so that he could see what she wanted in her expression. With a faint smile, he pulled the sweatshirt off and tossed it to one side.

She stared. He was beautiful like that, she thought dizzily, with broad shoulders and muscular arms. His chest was covered by a thick, wide wedge of reddish-gold hair that ran down to the buckle of his belt.

He reached for her, lifting her over him so that they were sitting face-to-face, joined where their bodies forked. She shivered at the stark intimacy, because she could feel every muscle, almost every cell of him.

"It gets better," he said softly. He reached down and found the hem of her own sweatshirt. Seconds later, that and her bra joined his sweatshirt on the floor. He looked down at her, savoring the hard peaks that rose like rubies from the whiteness of her breasts. Then he drew her to him and enveloped her against him, so that they were skin against skin. And he shivered, too, this time.

Her hands smoothed over his back, savoring his warm muscles. She searched for his mouth and for the first time, she kissed him. But even though it was sensual, and she could feel him wanting her, there was tenderness between them, not lust.

He groaned as his body surged against her, and then he laughed at the sudden heat of it.

"Jeb?" she whispered at his lips.

"It's all right," he said. "We won't go all the way. Kiss me again."

She did, clinging, and the world rocked around them.

"I love you," she murmured brokenly. "So much!"

His mouth bit into hers hungrily, his arms contracted. For a few seconds, it was as if electricity fused them together. Finally he was able to lift his lips, and his hands caught her hips to keep them still.

"Sorry," she said demurely.

"Oh, I like it," he replied ruefully. "But we're getting in a bit over our heads."

He lifted her away and stood up, pulling her with him. They looked at each other for a long moment before he handed her things to her and pulled his sweatshirt back on.

He watched the trains go around while she replaced her disheveled clothing. Then, with his hands in his pockets, he glanced down at her.

"That's why I broke up with Jane," he said matter-of-factly.

She was jealous, angry. "Because she wouldn't go all the way with you?"

He chuckled. "No. Because I didn't want her sexually."

She watched the trains and counted the times they crossed the joined tracks. Her mind must not be working. "What did you say?" she asked politely, turning to him.

"I said I was never able to want Jane sexually," he said simply. "To put it simply, she couldn't arouse me."

Chapter Eleven

"A woman can arouse any man if she tries hard enough," she said pointedly.

"Maybe so," he said, smiling, "but Jane just never interested me like that. It was too big a part of marriage to take a chance on, so I gradually stopped seeing her. Burke came along, and before any of us knew it, she was married. But I was her security blanket after the accident, and it was hard for her to let go. You remember how she depended on me."

She nodded. Even at the time, it had hurt.

"But apparently she and her husband have more than a platonic relationship, if their forthcoming happy event is any indication," he said, chuckling. "And I'm delighted for them."

"I never dreamed that it was like that for you, with her," she said, dazed. "I mean, you and I…!"

"Yes, indeed, you and I," he agreed, nodding. "I touch you and it's like a shot of lightning in my veins. I get drunk on you."

"So do I, on you," she confessed. "But there's a difference, isn't there? I mean, you just want me."

"Do I?" he asked gently. "Do I really just want you?

Could lust be as tender as this? Could simple desire explain the way we are together?"

"I love you," she said slowly.

"Yes," he said, his eyes glittering at her. "And I love you, Lou," he added quietly.

Dreams came true. She hadn't known. Her eyes were full of wonder as she looked at him and saw them in his own eyes. It was Christmas, a time of miracles, and here was one.

He didn't speak. He just looked at her. After a minute, he picked up the two parcels he'd put under the tree and handed them to her.

"But it's not Christmas," she protested.

"Yes, it is. Open them."

She only hesitated for a minute, because the curiosity was too great. She opened the smallest one and inside was a gray jeweler's box. With a quick glance at him, she opened it, to find half a key chain inside. She felt her heart race like a watch. It was half of a heart, in pure gold.

"Now the other one," he said, taking the key chain while she fumbled the paper off the second present.

Inside that box was the other half of the heart.

"Now put them together," he instructed.

She did, her eyes magnetized to the inscription. It was in French: *plus que hier, moins que demain*.

"Can you read it?" he asked softly.

"It says—" she had to stop and clear her throat "—more than yesterday, less than tomorrow."

"Which is how much I love you," he said. "I meant to ask you again tomorrow morning to marry me," he said. "But this is as good a time as any for you to say yes. I know you're afraid of marriage. But I love you and you love me. We've got enough in common to keep us together even after all the passion burns out, if it ever does. We'll work out something about your job and children. I'm not your father and you're not your mother. Take a chance, Lou. Believe me, there's very little risk that we won't make it together."

She hadn't spoken. She had both halves of the key chain in her hands and she was looking at them, amazed that he would have picked something so sentimental and romantic for a Christmas gift. He hadn't known if he could get her to stay or not, but he would have shown her his heart all the same. It touched her as a more expensive present wouldn't have.

"When did you get them?" she asked through a dry throat.

"After you left the jeweler's," he said surprisingly. "I believe in miracles," he added gently. "I see incredible things every day. I'm hoping for another one, right now."

She raised her eyes. Even in the dim light, he could see the sparkle of tears, the hope, the pleasure, the disbelief in her face.

"Yes?" he asked softly.

She couldn't manage the word. She nodded, and the next instant, she was in his arms, against him, close and safe and warm while his mouth ravished her lips.

It was a long time before he had enough to satisfy him, even momentarily. He wrapped her up tightly and rocked her in his arms, barely aware of the train chugging along at their feet. His arms were faintly unsteady and his voice, when he laughed, was husky and deep.

"My God, I thought I was going to lose you." He ground out the words. "I didn't know what to do, what to say, to keep you here."

"All you ever had to say was that you loved me," she whispered. "I would have taken any risk for it."

His arms tightened. "Didn't you know, you blind bat?"

"No, I didn't! I don't read minds, and you never said—!"

His mouth covered hers again, stopping the words. He laughed against her breath, anticipating arguments over the years that would be dealt with in exactly this way, as she gave in to him generously, headlong in her response, clinging as if she might die without his mouth on hers.

"No long engagement," he groaned against her mouth. "I can't stand it!"

"Neither can I," she admitted. "Next week?"

"Next week!" He kissed her again. "And I'm not going home tonight."

She laid her cheek against his chest, worried.

He smoothed her hair. "We won't make love," he assured her. "But you'll sleep in my arms. I can't bear to be parted from you again."

"Oh, Jeb," she whispered huskily. "That's the sweetest thing to say!"

"Don't you feel it, too?" he asked knowingly.

"Yes. I don't want to leave you, either."

He chuckled with the newness of belonging to someone. It was going to be, he decided, the best marriage of all time. He looked down into her eyes and saw years and years of happiness ahead of them. He said so. She didn't answer him. She reached up, and her lips said it for her.

The going-away party that Jane Burke threw for Lou became a congratulatory party, because it fell on the day after Coltrain and Lou were married.

They almost stayed at home, so wrapped up in the ecstasy of their first lovemaking that they wouldn't even get out of bed the next morning.

That morning, he lay looking at his new bride with wonder and unbounded delight. There were tears in her eyes, because it had been painful for her at first. But the love in them made him smile.

"It won't be like that again," he assured her.

"I know." She looked at him blatantly, with pride in his fit, muscular body, in his manhood. She lifted her eyes back up. "I was afraid…"

He traced her mouth, his eyes solemn. "It will be easier the next time," he said tenderly. "It will get better every time we love each other."

"I know. I'm not afraid anymore." She touched his hard mouth and smiled. "You were apprehensive, too, weren't you?"

"At first," he had to admit.

"I thought you were never going to start," she said on a sigh. "I know why you took so long, so that I'd be ready when it happened, but I wondered if you were planning on a night of torture."

He chuckled. "You weren't the only one who suffered." He kissed her tenderly. "It hurt me, to have to hurt you, did you know? I wanted to stop, but it was too late. I was in over my head before I knew it. I couldn't even slow down."

"Oh, I never noticed," she told him, delighted. "You made me crazy."

"That goes double for me."

"I thought I knew everything," she mused. "I'm a doctor, after all. But theory and practice are very different."

"Yes. Later, when you're in fine form again, I'll show you some more ways to put theory into practice," he drawled.

She laughed and pummeled him.

They were early for Jane's get-together, and the way they clung to each other would have been more than enough to prove that they were in love, without the matching Victorian wedding bands they'd chosen.

"You look like two halves of a whole," Jane said, looking from Lou's radiant face to Copper's.

"We know," he said ruefully. "They rode us high at the hospital when we made rounds earlier."

"Rounds!" Todd exclaimed. "On your honeymoon?"

"We're doctors," Lou reminded him, grinning. "It goes with the job description. I'll probably be trying to examine patients on the way into the delivery room eventually."

Jane clung to her husband's hand and sighed. "I can't wait for that to happen. Cherry's over the moon, too. She'll be such a good older sister. She works so hard at school. She's studying to be a surgeon, you know," she added.

"I wouldn't know," Copper muttered, "having already had four letters from her begging for an hour of my time to go over what she needs to study most during her last few years in school."

Jane chuckled. "That's my fault. I encouraged her to talk to you."

"It's all right," he said, cuddling Lou closer. "I'll make time for her."

"I see that everything finally worked out for you two," Todd said a little sheepishly. "Sorry about the last time we met."

"Oh, you weren't the only wild-eyed lunatic around, Mr. Burke," Lou said reminiscently. "I did my share of conclusion jumping and very nearly ruined my life because of it." She looked up at Coltrain adoringly. "I'm glad doctors are persistent."

"Yes." Coltrain chuckled. "So am I. There were times when I despaired. But Lionel saved us."

They frowned. "What?"

"Electric trains," Coltrain replied. "Don't you people know anything?"

"Not about trains. Those are kids' toys, for God's sake," Burke said.

"No, they are not," Lou said. "They're adult toys. People buy them for their children so they'll have an excuse to play with them. Not having children, we have no excuses."

"That's why we want to start a family right away," Coltrain said with a wicked glance at Lou. "So that we have excuses. You should see her layout," he added admiringly. "My God, it's bigger than mine!"

Todd and Jane tried not to look at each other, failed and burst into outrageous laughter.

Coltrain glared at them. "Obviously," he told his new wife, "some people have no class, no breeding and no respect for the institution of marriage."

"What are you two laughing at?" Drew asked curiously, having returned to town just in time for the party, if not the wedding.

Jane bit her lower lip before she spoke. "Hers is bigger than his." She choked.

"Oh, for God's sake, come and dance!" Coltrain told Lou, shaking his head as he dragged her away. The others, behind them, were still howling.

Coltrain pulled Lou close and smiled against her hair as they moved to the slow beat of the music. There was a live band. Jane had pulled out all the stops, even if it wasn't going to be a goodbye party.

"Nice band," Dana remarked from beside them. "Congratulations, by the way," she added.

"Thanks," they echoed.

"Nickie didn't come," she added, tongue-in-cheek. "I believe she's just accepted a job in a Victoria hospital as a nurse trainee."

"Good for her," Coltrain said.

Dana chuckled. "Sure. See you."

She wandered away toward one of the hospital staff.

"She's a good loser, at least," Lou said drowsily.

"I wouldn't have been," he mused.

"You've got a new partner coming," she remembered suddenly, having overlooked it in the frantic pace of the past few days.

"Actually," he replied, "I don't know any doctors from Johns Hopkins who would want to come to Jacobsville to practice in a small partnership. The minute I do, of course, I'll hire him on the...oof!"

She'd stepped on his toe, hard.

"Well, I had to say something," he replied, wincing as he stood on his foot. "You were holding all the aces. A man has his pride."

"You could have said you loved me," she said pointedly.

"I did. I do." He smiled slowly. "In a few hours, I'll take you home and prove it and prove it and prove it."

She flushed and pressed closer into his arms. "What a delicious idea."

"I thought so, too. Dance. At least while we're dancing I can hold you in public."

"So you can!"

Drew waltzed by with a partner. "Why don't you two go home?" he asked.

They laughed. "Time enough for private celebrations."

"I hope you have enough champagne," Drew said dryly, and danced on.

As it happened, they had a magnum of champagne between them before Coltrain coaxed his wife back into bed and made up for her first time in ways that left her gasping and trembling in the aftermath.

"That," she gasped, "wasn't in any medical book I ever read!"

"Darlin', you've been reading the wrong books," he whispered, biting her lower lip softly. "And don't go to sleep. I haven't finished yet."

"*What?*"

He laughed at her expression. "Did you think that was *all?*"

Her eyes widened as he moved over her and slid between her long legs. "But, it hasn't been five minutes, you can't, you *can't…!*"

He not only could. He did.

Two months later, on Valentine Day, Copper Coltrain gave his bride of six weeks a ruby necklace in the shape of a heart. She gave him the results of the test she'd had the day before. He told her later that the "valentine" she'd given him was the best one he'd ever had.

Nine months later, Lou's little valentine was delivered in Jacobsville's hospital; and he was christened Joshua Jebediah Coltrain.

* * * * *

Turn the page for a preview
of New York Times Bestselling author
Diana Palmer's
newest hardcover for HQN books

BEFORE SUNRISE

Available this July at your favorite book outlet

Chapter One

Knoxville, Tennessee, May 1994

THE CROWD WAS DENSE, but he stood out. He was taller than most of the other spectators and looked elegant in his expensive, tailored gray-vested suit. He had a lean, dark face, faintly scarred, with large, almond-shaped black eyes and short eyelashes. His mouth was wide and thin-lipped, his chin stubbornly jutted. His thick, jet-black hair was gathered into a neat ponytail that fell almost to his waist in back. Several other men in the stands wore their hair that way. But they were white. Cortez was Comanche. He had the background to wear the unconventional hairstyle. On him, it looked sensual and wild and even a little dangerous.

Another ponytailed man, a redhead with a receding hairline and thick glasses, grinned and gave him the victory sign. Cortez shrugged, unimpressed, and turned his attention toward the graduation ceremonies. He was here against his will and the last thing he felt like was being friendly. If he'd followed his instincts, he'd still be in Washington going over a backlog of federal cases he was due to prosecute in court.

The dean of the university was announcing the names of the graduates. He'd reached the Ks, and on the program, Phoebe Margaret Keller was the second name under that heading.

It was a beautiful spring day at the University of Tennessee at Knoxville, so the commencement ceremony was being held outside. Phoebe was recognizable by the long platinum blond braid trailing the back of her dark gown as she accepted her diploma with one hand and shook hands with the dean with the other. She moved past the podium and switched her tassel to the other side of her cap. Cortez could see the grin from where he was standing.

He'd met Phoebe a year earlier, while he was investigating some environmental sabotage in Charleston, South Carolina. Phoebe, an anthropology major, had helped him track down a toxic waste site. He'd found her more than attractive, despite her tomboyish appearance, but time and work pressure had been against them. He'd promised to come and see her graduate, and here he was. But the age difference was still pretty formidable, because he was thirty-six and she was twenty-three. He did know Phoebe's aunt Derrie, from having worked with her during the Kane Lombard pollution case. If he needed a reason for showing up at the graduation, Phoebe was Derrie's late brother's child and he was almost a friend of the family.

The dean's voice droned on, and graduate after graduate accepted a diploma. In no time at all, the exercises were over and whoops of joy and congratulations rang in the clear Tennessee air.

No longer drawing attention as the exuberant crowd moved toward the graduates, Cortez hung back, watching. His black eyes narrowed as a thought occurred to him. Phoebe wasn't one for crowds. Like himself, she was a loner. If she was going to work her way around the people to find her aunt Derrie, she'd do it away from the crowd. So he started looking for alternate routes from the stadium to the parking lot. Minutes later, he found her, easing around the side of the building, almost losing her balance as she struggled with the too-long gown, muttering to herself about people who couldn't measure people properly for gowns.

"Still talking to yourself, I see," he mused, leaning against the wall with his arms folded across his chest.

She looked up and saw him. With no time to prepare, her delight swept over her even features with a radiance that took his breath. Her pale blue eyes sparkled and her mouth, devoid of lipstick, opened on a sharply indrawn breath.

"Cortez!" she exclaimed.

She looked as if she'd run straight into his arms with the least invitation, and he smiled indulgently as he gave it to her. He levered away from the wall and opened his arms.

She went into them without any hesitation whatsoever, nestling close as he enfolded her tightly.

"You came," she murmured happily into his shoulder.

"I said I would," he reminded her. He chuckled at her unbridled enthusiasm. One lean hand tilted up her chin so that he could search her eyes. "Four years of hard work paid off, I see."

"So it did. I'm a graduate," she said, grinning.

"Certifiable," he agreed. His gaze fell to her soft pink mouth and darkened. He wanted to bend those few inches and kiss her, but there were too many reasons why he shouldn't. His hand was on her upper arm and, because he was fighting his instincts so hard, his grip began to tighten.

She tugged against his hold. "You're crushing me," she protested gently.

"Sorry." He let her go with an apologetic smile. "That training at Quantico dies hard," he added on a light note, alluding to his service with the FBI.

"No kiss, huh?" she chided with a loud sigh, searching his dark eyes.

One eye narrowed amusedly. "You're an anthropology major. Tell me why I won't kiss you," he challenged.

"Native Americans," she began smugly, "especially Native American men, rarely show their feelings in public. Kissing me in a crowd would be as distasteful to you as undressing in front of it."

His eyes softened as they searched her face. "Whoever taught you anthropology did a very good job."

She sighed. "Too good. What am I going to use it for in Charleston? I'll end up teaching…"

"No, you won't," he corrected. "One of the reasons I came was to tell you about a job opportunity."

Her eyes widened, brightened. "A job?"

"In D.C.," he added. "Interested?"

"Am I ever!" A movement caught her eye. "Oh, there's Aunt Derrie!" she said, and called to her aunt. "Aunt Derrie! Look, I graduated, I have proof!" She held up her diploma as she ran to hug her aunt and then shake hands with U.S. Senator Clayton Seymour, who'd been her aunt's boss for years before they became engaged.

"We're both very happy for you," Derrie said warmly. "Hi, Cortez!" she beamed. "You know Clayton, don't you?"

"Not directly," Cortez said, but he shook hands anyway.

Clayton's firm lips tugged into a smile. "I've heard a lot about you from my brother-in-law, Kane Lombard. He and my sister Nikki wanted to come today, but their twins were sick. If you're going to be in town tonight, we'd love to have you join us for supper," he told Cortez. "We're taking Phoebe out for a graduation celebration."

"I wish I had time," he said quietly. "I have to go back tonight."

"Of course. Then we'll see you again sometime, in D.C.," Derrie said, puzzled by the strong vibes she sensed between her niece and Cortez.

"I've got something to discuss with Phoebe," he said, turning to Derrie and Clayton. "I need to borrow her for an hour or so."

"Go right ahead," Derrie said. "We'll go back to the hotel and have coffee and pie and rest until about six. Then we'll pick you up for supper, Phoebe."

"Thanks," she said. "Oh, my cap and gown...!" She stripped it off, along with her hat, and handed them to Derrie.

"Wait, Phoebe, weren't the honor graduates invited

to a luncheon at the dean's house?" Derrie protested suddenly.

Phoebe didn't hesitate. "They'll never miss me," she said, and waved as she joined Cortez.

"An honor graduate, too," he mused as they walked back through the crowd toward his rental car. "Why doesn't that surprise me?"

"Anthropology is my life," she said simply, pausing to exchange congratulations with one of her friends on the way. She was so happy that she was walking on air.

"Nice touch, Phoebe," the girl's companion murmured with a dry glance at Cortez as they moved along, "bringing your anthropology homework along to graduation."

"Bill!" the girl cried, hitting him.

Phoebe had to stifle a giggle. Cortez wasn't smiling. On the other hand, he didn't explode, either. He gave Phoebe a stern look.

"Sorry," she murmured. "It's sort of a squirrelly day."

He shrugged. "No need to apologize. I remember what it's like on graduation day."

"Your degree would be in law, right?"

He nodded.

"Did your family come to your graduation?" she asked curiously.

He didn't answer her. It was a deliberate snub, and it should have made her uncomfortable, but she never held back with him.

"Another case of instant foot-in-mouth disease," she said immediately. "And I thought I was cured!"

He chuckled reluctantly. "You're as incorrigible as I remember you."

"I'm amazed that you did remember me, or that you took the trouble to find out when and where I was graduating so that you could be here," she said. "I couldn't send you an invitation," she added sheepishly, "because I didn't have your address. I didn't really expect you, either. We only spent an hour or two together last year."

"They were memorable ones. I don't like women very much," he said as they reached the unobtrusive rental car, a gray American-made car of recent vintage. He turned and looked down at her solemnly. "In fact," he added evenly, "I don't like being in public display very much."

She lifted both eyebrows. "Then why are you here?"

He stuck his hands deep into his pockets. "Because I like you," he said. His dark eyes narrowed. "And I don't want to."

"Thanks a lot!" she said, exasperated.

He stared at her. "I like honesty in a relationship."

"Are we having one?" she asked innocently. "I didn't notice."

His mouth pulled down at one corner. "If we were, you'd know," he said softly. "But I came because I promised that I would. And the offer of the job opportunity is genuine. Although," he added, "it's rather an unorthodox one."

"I'm not being asked to take over the archives at the Smithsonian, then? What a disappointment!"

Laughter bubbled out of his throat. "Funny girl." He opened the passenger door with exaggerated patience and he smiled faintly. "You bubble, don't you?" he remarked. "I've never known anyone so animated."

"Yes, well, that's because you're suffering from sensory deprivation resulting from too much time spent with your long nose stuck in law books. Dull, dry, boring things."

"The law is not boring," he returned.

"It depends which side you're sitting on." She frowned. "This job you're telling me about wouldn't have to do with anything legal, would it? Because I only had one course in government and a few hours of history, but…"

"I don't need a law clerk," he returned.

"Then what do you need?"

"You wouldn't be working for me," he corrected. "I have ties to a group that fights for sovereignty for the Native American tribes. They have a staff of attorneys. I thought you might fit in very well, with your background in anthropology. I've pulled some strings to get you an interview."

She didn't speak for a minute. "I think you're forgetting something. My major is anthropology. Most of it is forensic anthropology. Bones."

He glanced at her. "You wouldn't be doing that for them."

"What would I be doing?"

"It's a desk job," he admitted. "But a good one."

"I appreciate your thinking of me," she said carefully. "But I can't give up fieldwork. That's why I've applied at the Smithsonian for a position with the anthropology section."

He was quiet for a long moment. "Do you know how indigenous people feel about archaeology? We don't like having people dig up our sacred sites and our relatives, however old they are."

"I just graduated," she reminded him. "Of course I do. But there's a lot more to archaeology than digging up skeletons!"

His eyes were cold. "And it doesn't stop you from wanting to get a job doing something that resembles grave-digging?"

She gasped. "It is not grave-digging! For heaven's sake…"

He held up a hand. "We can agree to disagree, Phoebe," he told her. "You won't change my mind any more than I'll change yours. I'm sorry about the job, though. You'd have been an asset to them."

She unbent a little. "Thanks for recommending me, but I don't want a desk job. Besides, I may go on to graduate school after I've had a few months to get over the past four years. They've been pretty hectic."

"Yes, I remember."

"Why did you recommend me for that job? There must be a line of people who'd love to have it—people better qualified than I am."

He turned his head and looked directly into her eyes. There was something that he wasn't telling her, something deep inside him.

"Maybe I'm lonely," he said shortly. "There aren't many people who aren't afraid to come close to me these days."

"Does that matter? You don't like people close," she said.

She searched his arrogant profile. There were new

lines in that lean face, lines she hadn't seen last year, despite the solemnity of the time they'd spent together. "Something's upset you," she said out of the blue. "Or you're worried about something."

Both dark eyebrows went up. "I beg your pardon?" he asked curtly.

The hauteur went right over her head. "Not something to do with work, either," she continued, reasoning aloud. "It's something very personal…"

"Stop right there," he said shortly. "I invited you out to talk about a job, not about my private life."

"Ah. A closed door. Intriguing." She stared at him. "Not a woman?"

"You're the only woman in my life."

She laughed unexpectedly. "That's a good one."

"I'm not kidding. I don't have affairs or relationships." He glanced at her as he merged into traffic again and turned at the next corner. "I might make an exception for you, but don't get your hopes up. A man has his reputation to consider."

She grinned. "I'll remember that you said that."

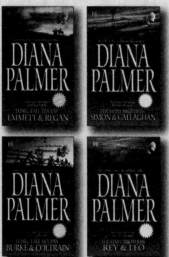

If you enjoyed what you just read,
then we've got an offer you can't resist!

Take 2 bestselling novels FREE!
Plus get a FREE surprise gift!